ALSO BY

VALERIO MASSIMO MANFREDI

The Ides of March

A WINTER'S NIGHT

Valerio Massimo Manfredi

A WINTER'S NIGHT

Translated from the Italian
by Christine Feddersen Manfredi

Europa
editions

Europa Editions
214 West 29th Street
New York, N.Y. 10001
www.europaeditions.com
info@europaeditions.com

Copyright © 2011 by Arnoldo Mondadori Editore
This edition published in arrangement with Grandi & Associati
First Publication 2012 by Europa Editions

Translation by Christine Feddersen Manfredi
Original title: *Otel Bruni*
Translation copyright © 2012 by Europa Editions

Library of Congress Cataloging in Publication Data is available
ISBN 978-1-60945-076-2

Manfredi, Valerio Massimo
A Winter's Night

Book design by Emanuele Ragnisco
www.mekkanografici.com

Cover illustration by Giulia Manfredi

Prepress by Grafica Punto Print – Rome

Printed in the USA

In memory of my grandparents Alfonso and Maria
and to my son Fabio, who has done so much
to redeem the honor of Armando Bruni

Desolina, have you opened the iron gate?
No, madam, I have not.
Desolina, have you opened the iron gate?
No, madam, I have not.
Desolina, have you opened the iron gate?
No, madam, I have not.
—FOLKTALE, Emilia Romagna

A WINTER'S NIGHT

CHAPTER ONE

The night of January 12, 1914, was remembered in our town as one of the coldest that whole winter and perhaps in any winter known to man. The snow had begun to fall towards evening and what happened then was unusual if not actually impossible: the sun turned round—as the old folk used to say—just before it sank below the horizon, and reappeared, for a few short minutes, in that narrow space that separated the western edge of the snowy clouds from the earth's curve. The vermillion rays pierced the thick curtain of white flakes to create a phantasmagorical image, an atmosphere so unreal that the peasants on their way home to dinner stopped dead in their tracks to behold the miraculous vision. Was it a sign from God, and what could He mean by it? Rooted to the spot in their amazement, they became part of a scene they'd never heard anyone describe; one day they would try to tell their children and grandchildren that they had seen it snowing on the sun.

Before long they were mantled in white and the golden light had vanished.

The Bruni family home was an old hipped-roof farmhouse with rusted rain gutters and oakwood shutters whose every last trace of color had been washed down to a uniform gray. It stood at a short distance from the road, about fifty yards away from the stable and hayloft. There was no manor, because the land was part of the Barzini estate, and Barzini the notary lived in his own house in Bologna. The farm was a good five hundred furlongs, if not more, and it neighbored on the east with the so-called Bastards' Foundation set up to care for those poor fatherless babies who had been deposited in a foundling wheel at one of the monasteries or convents in the city.

The stable was an imposing building. Half was used as a loft to store hay in the winter and wheat in the summer after the harvest. The other half was occupied by the cows with their calves, a bull for mounting and four pairs of oxen for plowing. It was there that everyone gathered in the wintertime. Rather than going to bed with the chickens at dusk, it was a place the Brunis could linger with their occasional or habitual guests, with no need to waste wood in the fireplace since the heat given off by the animals was more than enough to keep them all comfortable.

It was going to be a long night, because with so much snow, no one but the cowherds had to get up early the next morning. A night to spend in the stable, telling stories and listening to them. And so after dinner, while the women were washing up, the men wandered over to the hayloft, one after another, carrying a bottle of the new red wine that hadn't finished fermenting yet. There were seven Bruni brothers: Gaetano, Armando, Raffaele, who everyone called Floti, Checco, Savino, Dante and Fredo. Old Callisto didn't take part in these evenings anymore because his back ached and he couldn't get comfortable on the milking stools. He waited instead for the women to ready his bed. They'd fill an earthenware pot—which they called "the nun"—with embers, covered with ash. This would be slipped into a wooden frame, which they called "the priest." Nestled under the sheets, it would heat up the whole bed nicely. The irreverent and rather indelicate analogy had its own logic in that, according to local opinion, putting a nun and a priest to bed together would generate considerable heat indeed. Every night, as he stretched out under the hemp sheets, Callisto would mutter: "What a great invention the bed is!" and he'd be snoring like a trombone in no time.

There was an old man who was more or less a permanent guest in the stable; his name was Cleto and he mended umbrellas to earn a bowl of soup and a bed of straw. He favored a sententious style of speech meant to win him the respect and consideration of the others. He'd also seen that flaming ray of sun streak through the curtain of snow falling from the sky, and as soon as the brothers began to arrive, he opened with a proverb:

"When at dusk the sun turns itself about,
a bad night will follow without a doubt."

Gaetano, the oldest of the brothers and the family cowherd, pointed out that anyone could have guessed that there'd be a bad night, seeing that the snow had already completely filled in the footprints he had just left as he crossed the courtyard. He was still speaking when there was a knock at the door and in stepped Fredo, just back from carting their mother over to the parish church for her Saint Anthony novena prayers. His long *tabarro* cape was pulled up to just under his eyes and a crumpled cap lowered almost to his nose.

"It's snowing to high heaven," he exclaimed as though no one had heard the news yet, stamping his feet on the floor.

"Sit down," said Gaetano, pulling over a stool. "A glass of wine will warm you up."

"I'm thinking," said Fredo, "that tomorrow morning we'll be ass-deep in snow."

"Knee-deep," objected Gaetano. "When it falls so fast it never lasts long."

"That's what you say," broke in Cleto, the umbrella mender. "I remember that in '94, a whole meter came down in one night in Ostiglia."

"A meter is not ass-deep," shot back Gaetano.

"Depends on where you have your ass," snickered Fredo.

When it was the weather they were on about, everyone had something to say, a precedent to call to mind, an incredible event to describe. In their lives everything was always the same, one day like the next, one night just like any other. Only nature could surprise them.

"You know what I say?" said Gaetano. "When it comes down like this, with flakes so big they look like handkerchiefs and the air is so still, that's when an earthquake can strike."

Floti, who hadn't said a word until then, entered the discussion. "I wouldn't worry about that," he said. "If there were an earthquake coming we'd know from the animals. They'd warn us beforehand, you can be sure of that."

He hadn't finished speaking when they heard furious barking coming from the dog outside as his chain screeched back and forth on the wire stretched from the old oak tree to the house. Their eyes all moved up to the crack-ridden vaults on the stable's ceiling, expecting to see plaster dust falling to announce the shaking of the earth's crust. But nothing happened. Nothing at all. The oxen and cows went on happily chewing their cuds and the cat slept peacefully curled up on a bale of hay.

"That's no earthquake," said Cleto. "There's someone outside. Go see who it is."

They all turned towards the door. Checco got up and went to open it. A blade of light projected outwards, illuminating first the millions of butterfly-sized snowflakes settling onto the already whitened ground, and then an unsteady, swaying figure who was making his way towards the stable.

"Is that you, Iofa?"

"It's me," sighed the man. "I saw the light and came into the courtyard."

"You did well. Come on in, then. What is it, have you been drinking?"

Iofa walked in, shook off the snow and tossed his cape onto the hay. "Drinking? Just one glass, at the *osteria*. But I'll gladly have another, if you're offering. I need it."

They'd never seen him like this before: he seemed befuddled, as if he didn't know where to start. They gathered around him as he downed the glass of wine in a single go.

"Well then?" demanded Checco. "What happened to you? It looks as if you've seen the devil in person."

"You're not far from the truth there!" he replied, getting into his story. "I was just at the Osteria della Bassa with Bastiano, Squint-eye, and Vito Baracca, playing a hand of *briscola* with a half-liter of white on the table. Hardly anyone in the place . . . "

"On a night like this, I believe it," interrupted Gaetano.

"Let him finish," said Floti, sure that the man hadn't just happened to wander by the stable in such bad weather. He'd come because he had something inside that he wouldn't be able to keep to himself; not for long, anyway.

Iofa continued: "It was me and Squint-eye against Bastiano and Vito Baracca, and we were even, after two hands. Can you believe that? Sixty to sixty, even though Baracca'd had the ace, the three, the jack of trump. We were just about to lay out our trump when the door swings open and this man we'd never seen before walks in. We could barely believe our eyes. His beard was so long it nearly touched his belt and he had on this big long gray overcoat and a sack slung over his shoulder. His eyes were as red as a demon's! He sits down, then takes a chunk of bread, dry as a stone, out of his bag, and sets it on the table.

"'Where are you coming from, my good fellow?' Squint-eye asks him, calm as can be.

"'From the crossroads, the Corona,' he answers.

"'You should have slept there, at the Corona. It's a long way from there, with all this snow. You could have been buried alive.'

"'I came all this way because I knew that tonight . . . ' and then he stops, with a look in his eyes that had us all scared to death.

"None of us had the guts to say a word. Sitting there with our cards in our hands, looking at one another as if to say, this guy's crazy as a loon. Well, he looks at the barkeep and tells him to bring him a glass of wine and that he has the money to pay for it. He sticks his bread in the wine and then he sticks it in his mouth, chewing on it with his mouth wide open, really disgusting, like the devil himself."

"Must have been the devil himself, then," commented Fredo.

Floti shushed him: "Don't be an idiot, let him talk."

Iofa needed no encouraging. "So in the end I made him finish what he was saying, seeing that no one else would. I said: 'What was supposed to happen tonight, good man?'

"He lifts up his head and he says to me: "I knew that tonight . . . the golden goat would appear."'

Iofa stopped for a moment to take in the faces encircling him, to gauge the effect his story was having.

"Come on, now," Floti said, "don't make us pull the words out of your mouth."

Iofa nodded and went on. "'The golden goat?' I ask him, 'Are you sure you're feeling all right, my good fellow?'

"Well, he gulps down the last chunk of bread, swallows the last drop of wine, and says: 'Of course. I saw the golden goat appear in front of me, just as I'm seeing you now. It was on the highest of the four hills, on the left of the road . . . '

"'That's Pra' dei Monti!' Squint-eye says. 'They've always said the golden goat was hidden there! But how could you know that, if you're not from around here?'

"'It was shining in the middle of the swirling snow," the guy goes on, ignoring Squint-eye, "encircled by a quivering halo . . . '

"'And you? What did you do?' I asked him.

"'I couldn't take my eyes off it. It was all in gold, as big as life, but instead of eyes it had precious gems, as red as fire. You can't imagine what it's like to find yourself looking at something like that. I'll never forget it, my whole life.' That's exactly what the man said."

Gaetano hadn't spoken a word, nor had his brothers, as they silently envisioned the creature that the stranger had described to the card-playing men. He finally said: "I don't believe a word of it. He's some wise guy who comes from lord knows where, out of work and without a penny. He ends up here, hears this story somehow and thinks, I wonder just how gullible these simpletons are . . . "

"Right, he's just looking for someone who will put him up for a few days so he can tell his story again and again, until the roads have cleared up and he can head back to wherever he came from," added Checco.

"That could be," replied Iofa, "but just listening to his voice made shivers run down your spine. He had this rough voice, a voice that . . . sounded like it came from another world. Bastiano, who's big and broad as a bear and not afraid of anything, was trembling like a kid. How do you explain that none of us had ever seen him around here before, and yet he knew about the golden goat . . . "

"So where is he now?" asked Armando, who hadn't uttered a word until then.

"Who knows," replied Iofa. "He disappeared."

"What do you mean, disappeared?" asked Gaetano.

"He asked for another glass of wine and gulped it down, then he left ten cents on the table and walked out. We all ran over to the glass door to look outside but he wasn't there anymore. So what do the lot of you think it means?"

"It means nothing," replied Gaetano. "Tomorrow he'll show up again. He'll have slept it off in some hayloft."

"You're just saying that to set your mind at ease," broke in Cleto the umbrella mender. "The truth is you're afraid."

"Afraid?" protested Floti. "Of what?"

"You know what . . . the golden goat. You know well what it means when the golden goat appears suddenly, on a night like tonight, to a solitary wayfarer. It can only mean that something terrible is going to happen. Folks say that the first time was three hundred years ago. The golden goat appeared and then the next year the plague broke out and carried off five hundred people from this town alone. It appeared again sixty years later to a Capuchin friar who was directed to the monastery in Vignola. He was travelling by night to avoid the heat of the day, it was in August. A few months later the Turks invaded the eastern regions and then Austria and it was a miracle that they didn't invade Italy to take Rome! It would have been the end of Christianity! Twenty soldiers from this very town were killed in the battle of Vienna.

"The golden goat was last seen again just eighteen years ago on a stormy night by a swine merchant on his way back from the market at Sant'Agata. It was pitch dark, and pouring rain, but the goat was lit up like broad daylight by a bolt of lightning. Six months later his three sons died in the battle of Adwa in Abyssinia, along with thousands and thousands of our soldiers . . ."

"Stop that," said Floti. "That's all just idle talk! The superstitious prattle of ignorant people who, when some disaster happens, drag the golden goat into it. That's all it is. It's nothing."

"Really?" replied Cleto. "Well then, if that's the way things are and if you're not afraid of these silly superstitions, what do you say we go to take a look for ourselves? Go to Pra' dei Monti, now?"

"You're crazy," said Floti. "No way on earth! It's too damned cold out there and the snow's coming too fast. We're likely to end up falling in a ditch and freezing to death, and they won't find us until next spring."

"You don't go to church very often," shot back Cleto, "but I remember well what Don Massimino used to say in his day, God bless him. He said that the goat is a symbol of the devil, a symbol that goes way back in time. How do you know that the golden goat wasn't worshipped as a pagan idol around here once, long ago, maybe even right there at Pra' dei Monti? You've heard what they dug up there, haven't you? The remains of an ancient settlement, with amulets, bracelets shaped like snakes, grotesque masks. And people say that it was there, almost two thousand years ago, that a great battle was fought and that thousands and thousands of dead bodies were left unburied in the swamps that covered this territory. Nothing happens by chance, my friend. There's always a reason why certain things take place . . . And while we're on the subject, what do you have to say about what happened here tonight? A ray of sun the color of blood piercing through the falling snow . . . Who's ever seen something like that before?"

Armando, the most easily spooked of the brothers, got to his feet. "Sorry, but I don't like the turn things are taking here! I wish you all a good night. I'm going to sleep myself."

"Go, go," said Cleto, and waited for Armando to leave so he could pick up where he had left off. "Well then? Since you say all this is just idle chatter, why don't we go take a look? We'll cover up well, put on our long-legged clogs and we'll head out. We can be there in less than an hour."

"Come on now," said Floti with a shrug. "You really think the golden goat will be waiting there for you? Aren't sudden appearances supposed to be brief and unexpected? Me, I'm going to bed. Good night to everyone and you, Iofa, be careful getting home. You don't want to meet up with the goat and get strung up on his horns!"

Iofa made the sign of the cross, muttering: "It's nothing to joke about. You should have seen that guy: he would have scared anyone."

Floti left and the other brothers behind him. Iofa lingered, as did Gaetano, who still had a few questions to ask Cleto. He'd always suspected that the man was something more than what he seemed: a wandering handyman who turned up every year at the first snowfall and left again at the end of February, sometimes without having mended a single umbrella. Every Saturday without fail Cleto would wash his stockings, drawers and undershirt and put them to dry near the mouth of the oven where the bread had been baked; not your usual beggar. The Brunis took him in year after year, just as they did with anyone who knocked at their door asking for a place to rest for the night and a bowl of soup. In exchange he told stories of distant lands and extraordinary events that farming men in a small village couldn't even begin to imagine.

"Tell me the truth, now that there are only the three of us here: do you believe those things that Don Massimino said?" he demanded.

"I do. And you should believe them as well, Gaetano. Your brother is a bit stubborn at times; he's convinced that there's a simple reason behind everything. He's wrong. Many things have no explanation. There's a whole world around us that we can't see or hear, but it exists and it can change our lives from one moment to the next. What's more, it's best not to challenge certain . . . forces."

"Then why were you trying to convince Floti to go to Pra' dei Monti with you?"

"Walking in the dead of night under the falling snow on a country road towards an abandoned place where an ancient legend was born . . . would help your brother to understand that we are surrounded by mystery."

Gaetano wasn't sure he grasped what the umbrella mender was getting at, but he felt a chill run down his spine. Iofa's eyes were wide and white and full of fear; Gaetano took one look at him and said:

"Why don't you sleep here, tonight? Tomorrow you can give me a hand with the milking and then we'll have breakfast together: eggs and pancetta and a glass of the new wine."

"Well I'll be sincere," Iofa replied eagerly, "with weather like this out I won't say no. There's plenty of hay here, it's nice and dry, and my cape makes a good blanket. Who could wish for anything more?"

"Then I'll say goodnight," said Gaetano.

As soon as the stable door was shut, the umbrella man started up again: "Don Massimino was no ordinary man. I met him the first time I ever came here, many and many a year ago. I remember once, at the end of June with the fields full of wheat blond as gold and the cherry trees bent with the weight of ripe red fruit, that a storm came up like nothing we'd ever seen before: clouds black as ink but rimmed in white and thunder grumbling in the distance. We knew that hail was coming, and that it would be big as eggs. A downfall that would ruin a year's work and leave our families without bread."

Iofa could feel the winds of the storm chilling him to the bone.

"Well, Don Massimino walked out of the front door of the church," continued Cleto, "and he left it wide open so that Jesus Christ in the tabernacle could feel that icy gale, just like when he was nailed naked on the cross. Then he raised his eyes to that pitch-black sky and he opened his arms as if he could protect the whole town. He was muttering something—I don't know what it was, prayers or exorcisms—and, despite the cold, he was dripping with sweat. His knees were trembling, as if he were bearing the weight of those ice-laden clouds on his own fragile shoulders.

"I hid behind the portico columns to watch, and I didn't lose sight of him for an instant. After almost an hour of that unequal struggle with the elements, Don Massimino won: the sky slowly opened and a strip of blue appeared. The clouds scattered and the thunder vanished in the distance. I saw him collapse to the ground in a faint. When he came to, I was there next to him. He said: 'If I had failed, it would have been a disaster. A catastrophe!' And I had no doubt that he was telling the pure truth. So now you know why I believe everything he said. He knew what he was talking about. Even when he spoke of that image of the devil: the golden goat!"

When Gaetano had crossed the courtyard and reached the door of the house, he turned back to look at the stable. He saw the dim red glow of the lamplight go out, all at once.

Chapter Two

The next day, some time before dawn, the snow began to fall more lightly, and then as fine as powder. It stopped completely as day was breaking. The men got up early, took their shovels and began to clear a walkway towards the road. Iofa helped Gaetano milk the cows and then sat down at the table to have breakfast: eggs and pancetta and a piece of bread warmed on the embers. The man who'd appeared at the Osteria della Bassa the night before was nowhere to be seen in town, and those who had been there playing *briscola* began to doubt whether they had really met him, or heard his words.

The town's children couldn't leave for school until the buzzard had passed, towed by three pairs of oxen, to clear the roads. They called it that because it had two big wooden boards spread wide to push the snow to the edges of the road, just like the wings of a buzzard. The poorest children had had nothing to eat for breakfast and went from house to house asking for alms. They wore wooden clogs made with cowhide that got soaked instantly and then shrunk to squeeze their freezing feet. The lucky ones got a chunk of bread, others a scolding or a kick in the rear. They were happy to go to school because there was a nice clay Becchi stove that radiated warmth and the fragrance of oakwood kindling.

Those were wretched years: the late frosts in the spring and hailstorms in the summer had decimated the harvests, and Don Massimino was no longer around to fight off gales bare-handed.

He was at rest in the old cemetery, in the shade of an oak tree that had sprung up by chance from an acorn. In town, there was a story to be told for every event, and this one was no exception.

Don Massimino had been a poor man his whole life and even in the parish, where he could have enjoyed the generous revenues coming in from its five prebendal properties, he never used a whit more than what he needed, dividing the rest between the diocese and the poor. He'd asked to be buried in a simple shroud, without a coffin, because that amount of money could be used to buy enough wheat to feed a family for a whole week. But the devil, who he had defeated so many times in his life, made sure to give him payback in his final place of rest. Nettles and weeds grew on his grave and a big snake black as ink had burrowed in to stay, so that no one dared to get close enough to clean it up a bit or lay down a bunch of meadow flowers.

Until one day, when a white and black magpie hid an acorn that soon took root. An oak tree grew quickly and spread a dome of green leaves over the grave. The weeds and nettles died, and emerald green grass as fine as cat's fur grew in their place. A hawk nabbed the snake as it left its den and devoured it. And every springtime since then, the humble grave of Don Massimino was covered with daisies.

The people took heart at stories like this one and many others, invented to lead them to believe that there was someone who was thinking of them in their moments of pain, hunger and despair. The poorest families faced the winter as a scourge sent by God, living in hovels where their piss froze in the urinals at night and all the rosaries the women said did not suffice to protect them from malnutrition and disease. Babies were born small and didn't thrive, as their mothers had no milk. Thin, almost transparent, they struggled on until a fever took them away. The women had no tears left. They would open a window so that the little one's soul could fly up to the sky, and whisper: "Saints in heaven!"

At least the child had stopped suffering, whereas they had not. There would be another pregnancy and more trouble and tribulation and more children who cried with hunger until they lost their voices, because men would never give *that* thing up, and it didn't count to close your eyes and say the rosary to stop from getting pregnant. There was never an easy day in the homes of the day laborers, who went into debt in the wintertime for as long as the shops would give them credit, hoping to pay it off in the springtime, when they could earn a day's pay.

The Brunis had lived in the same house and worked the same land for one hundred years, or maybe even more: no one had ever kept records, after all, and no one remembered where the family came from. They had no money but they had never gone hungry: they could always count on enough milk, cheese, eggs, bread, prosciutto and *salame*, because the landowner lived in Bologna, the steward showed up once in a blue moon and the Brunis took what they needed to stay strong.

As times got worse, however, the owner had become more demanding. Just a year before, when old Callisto went into town with the horse and cart to settle the accounts, he had to hear that he'd have to be content with half the wheat and half the corn and from the way things were going, the same could be expected for the year just begun as well. That's why he kept putting off the day when he'd have to go to the city. Clerice asked again and again: "Callisto, when are you going to settle up with the landlord?"

He would answer: "One of these days, Clerice, one of these days."

But they'd nearly run out of white flour and yellow flour and so the time had come for the head of the family to hitch up the horse, to put on his brown velvet suit and white hemp shirt and to pay a visit to notary Barzini. Clerice waved goodbye from the side of the road with a white handkerchief as if he were leaving for the war.

He returned at dusk in a black mood. He sat at the table and ate with his head in his plate without saying a word, until Gaetano decided to break the silence: "Well then, how did it go with the landlord?"

"Badly," replied the old man. "He said it was a bad year and that we'll have to eat cornmeal bread."

"What?" replied Gaetano. "We've worked like dogs, all six of us men, this whole year and he has the courage to make us eat corn as if we were chickens? I'll bet you that he eats white bread and he's never lifted a finger. What kind of accounts did he show you?"

"Accounts with profits and losses. He says we've lost him money."

"And you didn't say anything?"

"What could I say? He's an educated man and we're ignorant. You know what the proverb says: 'When all's writ down in black and white, the farmer sleeps tight.'"

"If you'll allow it, I'll go to talk to him tomorrow. I'll get Iofa to take me with his cart and you'll see me coming back with wheat, as God is my witness!"

"Do as you like," replied the old man. "If you feel up to it, I won't say no. The important thing is to bring home the wheat, but it won't be easy, you'll see." He spooned up his soup in silence and when he had finished he got up and went to bed.

Gaetano was a strapping young man with shoulders as broad as a barn door and he was determined to make good on his promise. The next morning at dawn he got on his bicycle and went to see Iofa the carter. He found him currying the horse and preparing his fodder.

"I need you for a job," said Gaetano.

"Not today. I have a load of gravel to take from the river to the provincial road."

"You'll do it tomorrow. I need you and your cart now."

"And where do we have to go?"

"To the city, to see the notary."

"What do you need the cart for? You've got your new suit on, why don't you go on your bicycle?"

"I can't load two thousand kilos of wheat on my bicycle."

"And who's about to give you two thousand kilos of wheat, your landlord?"

"Yes, I'm going to talk to him. He told my father we're in debt and that we'll have to eat corn all year like the hens. I'll wring his neck like a chicken's if he doesn't give me my wheat. How are we supposed to work ten, twelve hours a day eating cornmeal bread? So then, are you with me? Coming or not?"

Iofa thought it over, added up a few numbers, looked at the big watch he kept in his pocket, shook his head and answered: "You're as stubborn as a mule, but we're friends and I can't say no. Are you ready to go like that?"

"Yessir, I am. Why, don't I look good?"

"Oh, you look very good. Like a fine fellow indeed. Give me the time to hitch him up and we'll be on our way."

Gaetano helped Iofa attach the horse to the cart shafts and fit his collar as he said: "You're not doing this for nothing, you know. I'll give you two bushels of wheat and you'll be making bread for a long time to come."

When the cart was ready they climbed onto the seat and Iofa called out to the horse who started off at a good clip. They went down the Fossa Vecchia road and by the time the sun came up they had almost reached the Via Emilia.

They met up with other carts coming and going because it was Tuesday and Tuesday was market day. They even saw an automobile, a black Fiat Tipo 3, all splattered with mud from the puddles, that was honking its horn trying to get around the carts and pack animals.

"Just think," said Iofa, "that there are people that can afford one of those. Lord knows how much it costs . . . "

"I'll tell you how much," replied Gaetano. "It costs twelve thousand liras, almost as much as our land."

"I can't believe it, swear that it's true!"

"I swear. Our property costs about fifteen thousand liras, but it's more than five hundred furlongs and it feeds a lot of people. If I had the money I'd buy up our land, not an automobile. Then we wouldn't have a landlord to tell us what we can and can't do. My father told us that when we were little and the steward showed up, he'd hide us in the pigpen because the guy was always complaining: 'Too many mouths to feed and too few arms at work,' and he'd threaten to go tell the owner."

"Who knows, maybe one day you will have the money to buy the land for yourself, or maybe something even bigger."

"I don't see how. Ten lives wouldn't be enough to put aside fifteen thousand liras. Only people who have money can make more money. People who don't have anything, they're lucky if they can get enough to eat themselves, and feed their families. Anyway, even if I could, I wouldn't want a bigger plot of land; I'd buy our own because I know it so well. I know what grows well on one part or on another. I know when the wheat is ripe and when the fruit's ready for picking, depending on the year and how much sun it's got. I know how much manure to use and how much water is right for each kind of plant. If you know your land well enough, it will never betray you. If you have land you know you'll never go hungry, that you'll have meat and milk and cheese and eggs, wood to keep warm in the winter and cool water for the summer, wine and bread and wool to spin and hemp to weave. I love my land, Iofa, can you understand that?"

"I do understand that, even if I'm a carter, like my father was and my grandfather before him. I love my cart, and I take care of it and keep it covered so it doesn't get rained and snowed on and, more than anything, I love my horse, right, Bigio?" he said, tapping the animal's rump with his reins.

Chatting to pass the time, at a bit of a trot and a bit of a walk, they were at Borgo Panigale in a couple of hours. Gaetano had only been to Bologna three times his whole life, with his father, but Iofa knew the route well because he'd worked for years transporting the harvest to the notary's warehouses, not only from the Brunis' land but from many other plots that he owned in town. A good fifteen or so, between Via Bastarda, Madonna della Provvidenza and Fossa Vecchia. Iofa stopped at the long bridge on the Reno River so that his travelling companion could admire it. Gaetano was amazed at the series of huge arches stretching over the river and carrying the Via Emilia on their backs, with her load of carts, horses and even automobiles. But what he liked best were the two stone mermaids on the entry columns, with a woman's body and a fish's tail. They were naked from the waist up and had a pair of tits you couldn't help but gape at.

"Don't look for so long!" said Iofa, "or you'll have to go to the priest and make a confession."

"Ah, well," said Gaetano, "what do you think, even priests like to look at tits that beautiful. My father says that even Don Massimino, who was a saint, when a nice ass or a couple of tits like those passed in front of him, his eyes stopped there even if he didn't want them to. And when a pretty lady went to confess her sins he didn't stop at hearing what the sin was, he wanted details before he gave his absolution, like where did he put it and where did you touch it and so on and so on."

Iofa started to laugh and said: "Have you ever been to the city square?"

"No, I never have."

"Well, in the square there's a fountain with a giant: a man almost three meters tall, with a pitchfork in his hand, and he's buck naked and you can see everything, and I mean everything."

"I've heard about that."

"I think it's a scandal: a naked man in the middle of the square and all the little kids, even the little girls, can see him. And then there are mermaids like these that squirt water from their tits."

"Sounds interesting. But we can't go today; we have other business. It's Mr. Barzini the notary we're going to see today."

Iofa called out to the horse and they started up again, crossed the bridge and went on towards the city gate. There were gardens and houses scattered on both sides of the road and, from behind, the Borgo church tower seemed to keep an eye on them from afar.

As they get closer to their destination Gaetano became more nervous and at times seemed to regret having decided to take on the landlord.

"Let's just hope he's there when we get there," said Iofa, "otherwise we've come all this way for nothing."

"We'll find him, all right," replied Gaetano. "He won't get away from me. If he's not there, I'll sit down in front of his front door and I'll wait until he gets back."

"Look, the tram!" exclaimed the carter, pointing at a dark green cable car clattering along on its track.

"I know," replied Gaetano without a smile.

"Well. The notary's office is just after the tram stop, on the right, where the door with the lion's head is."

They stopped. Gaetano got off, smoothed his jacket and pulled on the doorbell handle. The door swung open and the doorman appeared: "Who you lookin' for?" he demanded in the local Bolognese dialect.

"The notary. Mr. Barzini," replied Gaetano in the same language but with an accent that identified him as an out-of-towner.

"You have an appointment?"

"What's that?"

The doorman shook his head: "Have you asked the notary if he wants to see you today, at this time?"

"I live in the country but in my house we're accustomed to seeing anyone, at any time of the day or night. Tell him I'm Gaetano Bruni, Callisto's son. We farm his land. He'll see me."

The doorman nodded and went up the stairs, dragging his feet. Some time and much door creaking later, he called out from the stairway: "Come on up, the notary will see you now."

Gaetano took a deep breath and went up to the second-floor landing, from where the doorman showed him into the office. He asked with-permission and took off his hat.

Barzini was a small, chubby fellow, sitting behind a big desk on a big armchair. Gaetano was shocked. He was expecting someone bigger, with a decent-sized handlebar mustache and a haircut like King Umberto's. Someone who inspired respect and even a bit of fear, someone who you could tell owned fifteen plots of land. It was a real disappointment, from a certain point of view.

The notary was writing on a sheet of paper and without raising his eyes, said "What do you want?"

"I want my wheat."

Barzini lifted his head and took off his eyeglasses. "What did you say?"

"That I want my wheat. You told my father we'd have to eat cornmeal bread this year."

"That's right. You're operating at a loss. I've already explained this to your father and I have no intention of explaining it to you."

Gaetano crossed his arms and his jacket sleeves bulged around his muscles. "All I know is that we loaded up twenty carts of wheat to be brought to your warehouse here in Bologna and Iofa, I mean Giuseppe, the carter, I mean, counted them one by one. You took all of them. I don't know anything about losses, I just want enough to make our bread. To work we have to eat. Thirty sacks, not one less or one more."

"Walk out of that door now! You're nothing but a common lout!"

"Mister landlord, all I'm asking for is what we need to carry on working from sunrise to sunset every day of the year and even Sundays, because the fields won't wait and our work wants doing."

"Leave now or I'll call the doorman!"

"You just called me a lout, but if I don't leave here with what's fair, with what I've asked for politely, you'll see what a real lout is: as God is my witness, I swear that if the doorman takes one step inside here, I'll throw him down the stairs and you after him!" he shouted, and pounded his fist so hard that pens, inkwells and a shiny brass lamp that sat heavily on the table all jumped up at once. Barzini paled, took one long look at the colossus in front of him and understood instantly that he was dead serious. He breathed deep, struggling to quell his fear and maintain his aplomb, and said: "I'm doing this for your father, who is a gentleman. Certainly not for you! And out of the pure goodness of my heart, nothing else. Why, I could call in the forces of order and have you thrown into prison for threatening me like this . . . "

If the look that Gaetano gave him was not enough to stop his blathering, the glance the young man shot at the heavy paperweight on his desk certainly was.

"Thirty sacks, you said . . . "

"Yes, sir."

Barzini scribbled a couple of lines on a sheet of letterhead and signed it. He blotted the ink before handing it to Gaetano.

"And just how are you going to take home those sacks?"

"I have a cart here waiting for me."

"Ah," replied Barzini crossly. "Well then, take this to the warehouse in Borgo and they'll give you the sacks. And don't ever show your face here again."

"Thank you, mister landlord. And if we don't see each other again, have a good death."

Barzini startled, not realizing that those were auspicious words. For people accustomed to expecting nothing but trials and tribulation from life, the idea of looking forward to a good death was at least some consolation. The notary reacted instead by touching his attributes under the desk and mumbling: "Go, get out of here, I've got things to do."

"Somethin' happen?" asked the doorman as Gaetano came down the stairs. "That was one hell of a loud noise I heard!"

"No, we had a little disagreement but all is well now, thank the Lord."

When Iofa saw the smile on Gaetano's face as he came out the door, he couldn't believe his eyes: "Well then, how did it go?"

Gaetano waved the consignment order in front of his eyes.

"You know I don't know how to read," said Iofa.

Gaetano solemnly read out the words: "'I hereby authorize thirty sacks of wheat to be consigned to the bearer of this letter. They will be collected immediately. Signed Barzini.'"

"Oh, now you have to tell me the full particulars!" exclaimed Iofa as he climbed into the cart and turned the horse around in the direction of Borgo.

Gaetano didn't need encouragement, and started to tell his story: "I found him sitting there on his chair in front of me like the king on his throne . . . you can imagine . . . "

"And you?" asked Iofa. "What did you do? And what did he say then?"

The story became embellished with fanciful details as Gaetano's tale spun out. He stopped short of painting too black a picture of the landlord himself, since Iofa knew him well and so did many other people in town, where he'd been seen on more than one occasion.

No one at the warehouse objected to carrying out the notary's signed orders, but Gaetano had to haul all thirty of the sacks on his own back because Iofa was too skinny and what's more, he had a bad leg. The warehouse porters all knew better than to offer him a hand. It was every man for himself. But it was worth it. When he had finished, Gaetano told Iofa to stop at the Osteria del Lavino, where he bought his coachman a plate of polenta with pork ribs because he deserved it, both of them did, and then they headed home so they could get back before dark.

They were greeted in triumph. Almost all the men in the house came out to escort the cart to the loft and they had it unloaded in less than half an hour. Iofa, naturally, was invited for dinner.

When the food had been served, Clerice said prayers and Callisto reminded them to take some soup and a glass of wine out to the stable to the umbrella mender, who still had shown no sign or intention of recommencing his wanderings.

CHAPTER THREE

B efore the end of January it snowed two more times, although little more than a dusting each time. When people grumbled, old Callisto would say: "Don't complain! If it snows there's a reason for it, and under the snow is your bread." He was referring to the grains of wheat sown in the fall that were swelling and swelling, and would soon sprout and push a little plant out of the ground, bright green against the brown earth.

Although it was usually mid-February before the first blade of grass would appear, hope hastened the course of the seasons and on the Feast of Our Lady, the second of the month, the women brought a candle to church and lit it in front of the image of the Virgin. They would say "On Candelmas Day / We wish the winter away."

But everyone knew February was not to be trusted because, as the sayings went, "short but wretched" and "the wolf hasn't eaten up the winter" and "it can always show up again when you least expect it."

And sure enough it started to snow on Candelmas Day. Clerice went up to the bedroom of the two girls, Rosina and Maria, one seventeen and the other fifteen, to make sure they bundled up well and then, all three wrapped up in woolen shawls, they headed off to church. Rosina, who was the quickest, walked ahead of them, and Clerice could see that she'd put together a fine backside and high, wide hips and once spring came around with its light cotton dresses, there wasn't a man in town who wouldn't be turning his head as she passed.

It was every mother's terror: that a daughter might get pregnant. Men were quick at professing endless love to get what they wanted and then, once they'd got a girl in the family way, they'd vanish into thin air or say things like, "If she gave it to me, lord only knows who else she gave it to" and marriage was out of the question. But if the landlord found out, he could give the whole family notice and that was the end of that. They'd have until Saint Martin's Day in November, and then the farmer, his wife and all their children would have to pack up whatever household goods they had on a cart and good riddance.

It wasn't rare to see that cruel scene actually happen. Entire families, men scowling and women weeping, would have to leave a house they'd lived in for many years and wander the country roads in the rain, searching for a vacant plot of land, working under any conditions in order to survive. That's why the mothers never tired of repeating this lesson to their daughters and explaining exactly how and when it could happen: if you let him put it inside of you, nine months from now you'll bring a bastard with no name into this world. Even if he just touches your thing with his, it can happen, understand? The mothers did their best but, although it seemed impossible, there was always some young girl who swallowed the bait.

At the footbridge over the Samoggia, there was an old house that seemed abandoned. It was covered with wild creepers and no God-loving person would ever let himself be seen there during the day. The old woman who lived there was called Malerba, and she would use her knitting needle on girls who needed an abortion. Clerice would point out that house to her daughters from a distance when they were gathering wild chicory on the banks of the river.

"They say that back there, where you see that oak, is where the girls who bleed to death end up," she told them solemnly.

"She buries them in secret, then and there, in deconsecrated ground. That's why that oak is so big, because it thrives on the corpses of those poor girls."

Not that she believed these stories herself, but if they helped to scare her daughters to death and keep them out of trouble, they had served their purpose. Or at least that's what she hoped.

"If a man really loves you he'll have the patience to wait," was another of her lines.

"And you, *mamma*? Did you manage to wait until you married daddy?"

"Certainly," she would reply. "And I did the right thing. We've always cared for each other, comforted each other and helped each other through hard times. That tiny sacrifice was nothing compared to the whole lifetime we've spent together."

She was lying, because she had always known that the heart knows no reason and that when you're in love, waiting is out of the question. But she'd known that her Callisto was a good person from the moment she'd met him; a fine young man who would never get her into a fix: the kind who, if anything happened, would be happy to marry her right away. And she remembered when she was first married, when she would wake up at night and light a candle just to look at him, like Psyche and Eros. He was so handsome she felt it couldn't be true. The priest had explained that her husband's name meant "beautiful" and that's just the way it was. But this was a story that she kept for herself because you can never be careful enough and she didn't want her girls running any risks.

She was a wise person, Clerice was, anyone in town could tell you that. When a woman went into labor they'd always call her to give a hand. Both because she'd had so many children herself and because she was a real expert in bolstering the courage of the first-timers, especially. Clerice was known to have uncommon skills, skills that not even doctors had. She could treat stomach ailments with a glass and a candle, cure falling sickness and shingles and even cast out worms. So many children became infected by playing on the ground and then putting their fingers in their mouths. The worms multiplied in their intestines until their stomachs became as stiff and taut as the skin of a drum and their fevers went so high it would send them into convulsions. Sometimes they died. But Clerice knew what to do. Once she'd put her hands on the child and whispered prayers under her breath, the worms were expelled, the fever went down and the convulsions stopped.

She would often have to leave the house after dark, wrapped in her shawl, murmuring invocations to ward off the spirits of the night.

Sometimes, after she'd helped a woman give birth and was walking back home down the lonely streets fingering her rosary beads, she thought of when she'd brought her own children into the world. She'd remember how she felt when they put the baby in her arms after washing and dressing it. She would look at that innocent creature and think, each time, what will become of him? What will he have to face or to bear in his life? And often, the contrary happened; she'd see a filthy, scabby raggedy beggar walking down the road and she'd think: he had a mother who brought him into the world with great hopes, who had wanted all the best for him and look here at the results of that woman's dreams and her hopes! And she'd carry on praying.

She remembered that each one of her boys, when they were born, gave clues that she would try to interpret. Dante, her firstborn, was an easy, quiet baby, more interested in food than in play, but he would carefully observe any little thing that got into his hands. He would be a sage administrator of himself and his family. Before Raffaele was a week old, he was already grabbing and touching everything around him. He was the first to walk, and to talk as well. His place was certainly at the helm of the family, keeping his brothers together. He was just two when they started calling him by his nickname, Floti. Gaetano was the one who weighed most at birth, and he stayed big and voracious. You could tell from the start what he would be like: strong and fearsome, afraid of nothing. Armando was the first to laugh but then he'd cry for nothing. He would become the funniest, the one who would amuse them all with his stories and jokes, but also the most fragile. And Francesco—who everyone called Checco, because no one in town got away without a nickname—had barely cried when he was born, and when he could, he'd smile instead of laugh. He'd be a good observer of other people's weaknesses and contradictions and never let on his own. And that's the way it was with each one of them; they had their fate carved out for them. In a few years' time, even the two younger ones, first Fredo and then even Savino, would turn twenty and they'd be old enough to be called up as soldiers. The girls in town were already stealing looks at them because, as the proverb says: "He who's good to serve the king is good for the queen as well."

Cleto, the umbrella mender, left one day after mid-March when he saw the first swallow enter the stable to tidy up the nest she'd abandoned in October. He slung his knapsack over his shoulder and said his goodbyes to Callisto and Clerice, the *arzdour* and *arzdoura*, patriarch and matriarch. Terms of archaic majesty that hinted at the Roman origins of their local dialect. The rule of the father and the rule of the mother.

Clerice put a freshly-baked loaf of bread in his sack and filled his flask with wine, pronouncing words with a nearly sacred sound: "Remember us, umbrella mender, when you eat this bread and drink this wine, and much good may it do you!"

"I thank you with all my heart," he replied, "because you give without asking me for anything in return. I'm a man without a trade, a traveler with no destination. I carry heavy memories on my shoulders and I pay with my penury for the errors I have committed and have never dared to confess."

"Why say such a thing, umbrella mender?" asked Clerice with concern. "You have given us so many stories, beautiful ones that make us dream and you know, dreams have no price. Our door is always open for you. And if there's something you have to confess, you know that God Almighty forgives all."

Cleto seemed to hesitate, then said: "You have seven sons and I can feel the shadow of the tempest approaching . . . "

"Explain yourself," Callisto broke in uneasily. "What do you mean by that?"

"A catastrophe is on its way, a bloodbath the likes of which no one has ever seen. Annihilation. No one will be spared. There will be signs, warnings . . . Try not to let them fall unawares. God warned Noah about the flood and he saved himself and his family because he was an upright man. If there's a good man on this earth, it's you, Callisto, and your wife is your worthy companion. She will pray for your family to be spared and I hope that God will listen . . . "

The pearly sky of dawn was getting lighter. From the stable came the lowing of the cows and bulls and finally the rising sun touched the snow-covered flank of Mount Cimone, which blushed like the cheek of a virgin. The scent of violets permeated the clean morning air.

"As far as I'm concerned," continued Cleto, "I already have my mission. Whether you believe me or not, I know that the apparition of the golden goat brings misfortune, and that wayfarer with the long beard who stopped to eat at the Osteria della Bassa said he'd seen it . . . There's only one way to forestall such a dreadful prediction: find the demonic creature and destroy it or . . . " his voice became deep and ragged, "or offer a victim in expiation."

Callisto and Clerice couldn't understand much of their guest's difficult language, but his dark and gloomy mood didn't escape them. They lowered their heads and made the sign of the cross and the umbrella mender walked out of the court-yard. Their eyes followed him as he took off down Via Celeste and then turned left towards the *osteria*. What could he have meant by those words?

They would never see him again.

On Sunday afternoons, on those first days of spring, their boys' friends would come over to play *bocce* in the courtyard. Checco would uncork a couple of bottles of Albana and a good time would be had by all. But at five o'clock on the dot, when the priest rang Vespers, Clerice shooed them all out: she didn't want anyone missing prayers at church because they were play-ing *bocce* in the front yard. And when the church bell tolled for the benediction of the Eucharist, she would make the sign of the cross in the middle of the courtyard and everyone would lower their heads in silence.

As the days got longer and the nights shorter, they had to work longer hours in the fields. The hemp was springing up before their eyes, as was the wheat. At night they began to hear the monotonous croaking of the tree toads and the chirping of crickets. One evening at dinner, Callisto told his children what the umbrella mender had said the morning he'd left, as he walked off towards the *osteria*. Words that had left a weight on his heart that he needed to share with them.

"*Papà!*" protested Floti. "You can't believe such nonsense! He's just a bloke who lives on the charity of others and he has to show he's worth something. This legend of the golden goat has no basis in fact. People see what they want to see."

"So then why, in your opinion, would people want to see a goat all made of gold standing on one of the four hills of Pra' dei Monti under a snowstorm?"

Floti didn't answer right away but he thought to himself that there had to be some kind of explanation. What do poor people worry about if not some kind of catastrophe? It was too easy to prophesy misfortune on its way. He had been an altar boy as a child and he remembered the Latin words of a certain invocation well: *A peste, fame et bello libera nos, Domine!* Deliver us, Oh Lord, from the plague, from hunger and from war! Apart from the plague, which hadn't been around for centuries, hunger and war had always been rampant.

He said: "People need to believe in another world, a supernatural one, a world in which miraculous things occur. Different than the usual things that happen, day in and day out, different than a life where they're doing the same things in the same places, one year after another. That's what I think!"

"That may be," replied Callisto. "All I know is that I've always heard tell of this story of the golden goat, since the day I was born." And he went off to bed without saying another word.

The summer was hot and dry and, when it was harvest time, the Brunis had to bend their backs for ten hours a day in the suffocating heat, cutting the wheat with hand sickles and tying it up into sheaves. Hundreds of them. The women lowered buckets filled with bottles of watered-down wine into the well to keep them cool, and they'd carry them out to fields, where the men were sweating like animals and needed to drink continuously. And when it came time to thresh the wheat, it was even worse. The sun beat down like a hammer on their heads and shoulders. Yet threshing was a celebration, like always.

And Floti was always first, standing at the entrance to the courtyard, waiting to escort the huge thresher inside to the threshing floor. He held the white stable oxen, freshly fed and brushed, by their halters, prepared to come to the aid of the old horses who were struggling to pull the steam engine, as black as the coal at its core. In theory, the engine should have managed on its own, powered by the steam it generated, easily making it up the slight upgrade that led to the courtyard and pulling the rest of the convoy behind it, but it was already pretty winded at this point and it would be no small accomplishment if it succeeded in turning the pulley on the thresher when it was stock still. Floti, who had yoked his champions two by two, hauled the engine into the courtyard followed by the thresher and the baler made of wood and iron, painted an orangey red color and flaunting the name of the company that had built it in big letters. Behind them were at least a dozen farmhands who shouted "Ho! Ho!" to encourage the draught animals to keep pulling.

When the entire train had been hauled into place, the foreman gave a smile of satisfaction at seeing all of the parts perfectly aligned on the threshing floor, then gave orders to mount the transmission belt. The drive pulley had no edges and if the belt was not placed with precision it could fall off. If it fell inwards, towards the wall of the thresher, it was just a question of wasting a bit of time to mount it back in place. If it fell outwards it could kill. Floti had seen an accident of this kind take place once and he would never forget how it ended up. One of the workers was hit full force by the belt and he fell to the ground unconscious. A lesion to his spinal cord left him paralyzed for the rest of his days. That event had greatly impressed Floti, making him aware of the profound injustice that governs the world. He'd long realized that his father's honesty, the balance and justice of his authority within the family, were values limited to a tiny community and that the weight of such values was entirely insignificant in a society dominated by the abuse of power.

When the foreman gave the signal, the engine let out a long whistle, sounding like a steamboat. Four men armed with pitchforks climbed on top of a pile of sheaves of wheat under the ceiling rafters of the hayloft and started to toss them into the threshing drum. There, another worker pushed them towards the mouth of the monster that swallowed them up and then vomited the clean kernels from the front and the hay and chaff from the sides straight into the baler. It always took a little while before the grain started to spurt out, and when the blonde cascade of kernels began to fill up the sacks, the porters greeted them with a cry of exultation in celebration of the miracle that had taken place for yet another year. They opened their big calloused hands to let the kernels flow through their hands and to feel their caress.

They'd have bread, for another year.

Soon the entire courtyard was invaded by a dust as dense and glittery as gold and it became nearly impossible to breathe. The workers knotted handkerchiefs over their noses and mouths and continued their work ceaselessly to the rhythm beat out by the bellowing machine. The ones who had it worst were those working up in the hayloft. When they started there was very little room between the towering stack of sheaves and the sun-scorched ceiling rafters and their sweat soaked through their dust-caked clothing. The bristly awns of the husks crushed by the threshers felt like needles splintering under their skin and created unbearable itching. Then, little by little, as the pile wore down, the air started to circulate a bit better and the distance that separated them from the scorching ceiling began to afford the workers a bit of relief.

The children were the only ones really having fun. They would pour in from all around, awed by the great collective effort and the rumbling power of the machines, which to their eyes looked like fairy tale monsters. Especially the baler, with its big toothy shears which moved up and down at an incessant rate; they called that one the "ass" because its shape reminded them of a donkey's head.

When it was time for the midday break, the foreman slackened the transmission belt and the whole mechanism was shut down, except for the steam engine. The men went to sit somewhere in the shade, under an elm or a fig tree, and pulled out whatever food they had brought with them. The luckier ones were met by their wives, who brought them little pots of pasta. The poorest ones ate bread and onions and that paltry meal would have to suffice for them to continue that exhausting job until dusk, when the foreman would signal the end of the workday.

But the Brunis were generous folk and old Callisto had had the women cook up three or four cockerels *alla cacciatora*, swimming in sauce, that made your mouth water just to look at them, along with an ovenful of fresh bread. It was a great satisfaction for him to see the surprise in the eyes of the workers at the sight of all that bounty. As the men ate, the gleaners went to work, each one with a sack in hand, picking up the ears left behind by the thresher or fallen from the wagons carrying the sheaves.

Clerice always took care that the permission to glean was only given to those who really needed it: the wives of men who were unemployed, or of drunkards who were only good at getting them pregnant. Clerice would always think of the women and, more than to Almighty God, she'd pray to the Madonna, because Our Lady had worried and suffered and she had lost a son and she knew what it meant. Clerice knew what a hard lot women had in life and—as honest and religious as she was—when she heard talk about this woman or that one on the bottom of some dry canal at the hour of the noontide demon wrapped around some worker or day laborer, she'd say: good for her, at least she's enjoying something.

That day, Iofa sent an errand boy to take a message to Floti: he'd be waiting for him that evening at dusk at the Osteria della Bassa. Specifying, strangely enough, that he should come by bicycle.

Floti got there right at the moment in which the sun was disappearing behind the tops of the cherry trees, his curly hair still full of chaff, and went to sit down with Iofa, who had ordered a quarter liter of white.

"What's new?" Floti asked.

"You haven't heard what happened?"

"What should I have heard?"

"A student has murdered the heir to the throne of Austria."

"So? What difference does it make to us?"

"I say it's a very bad sign. The kind of thing that sets off wars. It's always students who make trouble."

"You made me come all the way here to tell me this?"

"Well there's something more . . . " Iofa said with a mysterious air as he poured himself a glass of wine.

"I'm listening."

"Did you come on foot or by bicycle?"

"On my bicycle, since I heard you were in a hurry."

"I've got mine as well. Want to come with me?"

"Where?"

"Pra' dei Monti."

"Ohh, not this stuff again."

"Are you coming or aren't you?"

"All right, I'll come, but let's make it quick because it's already getting dark."

They pedaled one after the other along the creek until they got there. Four little hills in the middle of a meadow that hadn't been cultivated in decades.

"If you start talking about this damned goat I'm going back now."

"I don't want to talk about anything. I just have to show you something."

He started walking up the first and highest hill and Floti followed him up to its top. The place was completely deserted and even though Floti didn't believe a word of the stories they told about that place he felt a shiver run down his spine.

"They say that these hills are made of the bones of the dead from a great battle that happened two thousand years ago on this very spot . . . " said Iofa softly.

"So what? If you think you're scaring me, you are very wrong, my friend. I'm afraid of the living, not of the dead."

The crickets were silent and even the frogs kept quiet so the snakes wouldn't hear them. Iofa stopped at the top of the hill and pointed to something in front of him: a hole at least a couple of meters deep.

"This one was alive until not too long ago."

"This one who?" asked Floti, no longer so sure of himself.

"Someone who came up here looking for the golden goat and ended up not leaving. The dogs have eaten him half up. I saw him by chance when I was out looking for malva, it grows wild up here."

"What are you saying?"

"Look down into the hole."

Floti leaned forward and saw that there was something, someone, curled up on the bottom. The two of them looked each other in the eye without managing to talk for a moment.

"Is it him?" asked Floti finally.

Iofa nodded. "The umbrella mender," he confirmed. "See? He tried to find the golden goat and he didn't get away."

"I'm not surprised. Each one of us prepares his own end."

"You think?" shot back Iofa. "And where are the tools he used to dig this hole, then?"

"You're asking me? How would I know?"

Iofa fell silent while the shadows of the night began to lengthen over the ground.

"Maybe we should tell the *carabinieri*," he said after a while.

"Maybe not. You never know how these things will end up."

"But if someone sees him and recognizes him, they'll think of you right away, and then you'll be sorry. Listen, he couldn't have dug this hole with his fingernails. Let's take a look around, at the base of the hill, maybe."

Floti turned right and Iofa turned left and it was the latter, after a while, who tripped over the handle of a shovel hidden in the tall grass.

"I found it!" he exclaimed. "I knew it had to be here."

Iofa put his back into it and before long he'd covered the remains of the umbrella mender. When he was finished he made the sign of the cross over the hasty grave and threw the shovel into the creek. In less than half an hour they were back at their table at the Osteria della Bassa.

It was the night of June 30, 1914.

CHAPTER FOUR

Floti couldn't get what he'd seen out of his head. Tossing and turning in his bed, he thought of the umbrella mender curled up on the bottom of that hole and asked himself how he'd dug it, and why there, and what had killed him. No one, no matter what, would ever come looking for him, no one even knew who he was, after all. He certainly hadn't carried any documents that declared his identity. He didn't have a family, or if he did, they weren't the kind who would take the trouble of trying to find him.

Actually, there was a possible explanation, seeing as the umbrella mender did believe in that golden goat: the man had gone out one night, got himself a shovel and started to dig, hoping to find it. Maybe he did find it, who knows, in the end? Floti had always heard that the ancients would bury their treasures when there was an invasion or a war, then whoever had buried it ended up killed in some raid and the treasure got forgotten about. So, Floti reasoned, maybe the umbrella mender wasn't alone that night, maybe someone saw him as he was trying to pull the thing out and gave him a hit on the head with the handle of the shovel. At that point, the gold statue was this guy's for the taking and the umbrella man got shoved into the hole.

But the golden goat didn't exist. It had never existed. So who would ever have attacked a wretch like the umbrella mender, covered with rags and without a penny to his name? The only possible motive was revenge: the man had spent his life wandering from place to place, from village to village, hiding for months in a stable like his own and then heading out again because, in reality, he was running from someone. He must have committed some crime, molested someone's daughter or wife, and that someone had finally made him pay up.

Floti fell asleep thinking that they'd done the right thing in burying him and not leaving his body to the mercy of dogs and wolves. May the poor man rest in peace.

Before long, the family turned to other tasks. Harvesting hemp was much more laborious than reaping and threshing put together. Once it had been cut, the hemp was gathered into bundles and thrown into the ponds they used for steeping. Each bundle was weighed down with big river stones so it would remain under water until the fermentation process had detached the fibers from the woody part of the plant. At that point the stones were removed one by one and piled up around the edges. They were covered with algae by now and easily slipped from their fingers and it was twice as hard to fish them out again. Then the bundles were removed; saturated with water, they weighed ten times as much as they had at the start. The men worked inside the ponds, with the water up to their waists. The damp and the stench of fermentation permeated the air all around them, stagnant and fetid, in the intolerable midday heat.

It was like working in a cesspool.

Once the bundles of hemp had dried completely, they were beaten against a wooden board at the hottest hour of the day so the fibers would detach more easily from the woody stem. Only the strongest of men could bear up under such strain; the weaker ones simply dropped. You'd see them swaying, then getting pale and clammy. If the others got to them after they fainted, they were carried under a tree and well water was splashed on their faces and heads. When they came to, they were given water to drink, made tepid by the sun. A little at a time, as much as they could hold, until they felt the need to urinate. There were stories about those who gulped down cold water and ended up kicking the bucket.

Usually the head of the family, or the foreman if there were outside workers, gave these unfortunates the rest of the day off. The women in town, as in the whole province of Bologna, were only given light tasks, like raking the hay or taking care of the garden patch, unlike the women in nearby Modena. In the Modenese countryside, women were sent out with spades and shovels, even when they were pregnant.

By the end of July, their work was finished. The hemp fibers had been wound into balls and were ready to be whitened. The dry, lightweight stems had been bundled up and stored in the hayloft. They were worthless as wood: they'd make a big white flame that crackled and sparked and went out right away, but they were handy for starting a fire. All the men had left to do was give one last spray of verdigris to the grapevines and cut back the shoots so that all the nutrients would go straight to the grapes. They readied the crates and the wine presses and soaked the tubs, the vats and the barrels in heated water until they were as watertight as a glass.

The women picked the leaves from the elm trees used to prop up the vines so they would not overshadow the grapes. They fed the leaves to the cows and oxen, for whom they were a real treat. The elm leaves were tough and scratchy and were hell on a girl's hands, but they had their tricks. A soaking in the whey they got from the dairyman made their skin soft and smooth as a baby's again. Never soap. Clerice had always said that the last time she washed her face was the day she was married. Everyone had nagged her about it: "Wash that mug of yours, before you go to the kneeler!" They convinced her in the end and she gave herself a good scrubbing with the soap they used to wash the sheets. And she was still ready to swear that she'd never been the same since.

The same stories, like a hundred years before, like a thousand years before them. Stories of a life in which the Brunis found many moments of serenity, if not actual joy and happiness. The girls thought of their futures, hoping that one day they'd meet a young man as intelligent and good-looking as one of their brothers. The brothers thought of the girls in town, or—those with the most daring—girls from the next town over, since venturing out involved the risk, or even the certainty, of a fistfight with the young blood there who didn't appreciate the competition. But as one day led to the next, Callisto could feel the approaching winds of the storm the umbrella mender had warned him about the morning he left. Who knows what had become of him, Callisto thought. Perhaps he'd been wise enough to go far away, to Cremona or Treviso, or maybe he'd even made his way to Genova, where he could get on one of those steamers that went all the way to America. He was no longer a young man, certainly, but perhaps there was still a way for him to seek his fortune there. Or maybe he'd be back with the first snows.

Callisto could never have imagined how close he was, curled up on the bottom of a hole inside one of the four hills of Pra' dei Monti, where maybe he'd be found one day by another seeker of the golden demon.

Toward the end of the month Callisto went to the mill to make arrangements for grinding the wheat, and saw the first page of *Avanti!* on display on the notice board of the Working Men's Society. The headline was printed so big you could see it from a distance: *Austria Declares War on Serbia.* He got closer and saw an article entitled *Italy Can't Sit Back and Watch.* But the lettering was too small and the wording too difficult for him to read it. In front of the notice board stood Bastianino, the tailor, with a pair of glasses at the end of his nose, reading out the words one by one under his breath. Callisto, who had been about to ask, "What does the newspaper say?" stood silently and listened, pretending to be reading the article as well. As Bastianino progressed in his reading, Callisto felt a wave of fear and anguish engulf him.

At the end, the tailor read the signature of the journalist who had written the article: "Benito Mussolini."

"But why does this Mussolini want to go to war?" asked Callisto.

"It's not that he wants to go to war, it's not like he's the king," replied the tailor. "He says that Italy should step in to combat Austria, to liberate Trento and Trieste, which are Italian cities."

"But *Avanti* is the socialist newspaper; they're supposed to be on the side of the tenant farmers and workers. Why would they want to send our boys to war? How will we manage? Who will work in the fields? Who will care for the animals? And how many of them will never come back?" As he was speaking he felt a knot squeezing his throat, thinking that he had seven boys of his own, all good to serve the king.

Bastianino turned towards him and saw the tears in his eyes. "Don't fret, Callisto," he reassured him, "we'll stay out of this. Italy will stay neutral. It says so right here, see?"

"What does that mean, neutral?"

"That we're not on one side or on the other."

"That's not easy."

"No. It won't be easy," admitted Bastianino.

Callisto continued on his way until he reached the mill, set up in a little church that had long been deconsecrated. On the back wall you could still make out a faded crucifix though, and everyone was careful not to pronounce the Lord's name in vain while inside. Callisto entered and looked at that poor tortured boy hanging there on the cross and had to turn his eyes away.

"Is it all right," he asked the miller, "if I bring you the wheat tomorrow evening?"

"Not before four o'clock," replied the miller. "I've got lots of work to do."

Callisto walked out, his head thronging with terrible thoughts.

The grape harvest went well and everyone participated, the boys and the girls and even family friends and neighbors because in the end everyone got to take home a demijohn of wine and three flasks of must to boil up into a sweet grape syrup. The young men showed up willingly for another reason: when the women and girls crushed the grapes under their feet in the wine press, they had to pull up their skirts to move more freely and thus show off their thighs.

And then there was the party held on the threshing floor, where everyone danced, with three musicians: an accordion player, a clarinet player and a guitar player. The boys had strung up a rope from one side of the courtyard to the other and hung any number of brightly-colored paper balls with candles inside to create glowing lights. Rosina was so beautiful that all the young men couldn't keep their eyes off her, but even Maria, who was only fifteen years old, found a suitor: a young laborer from a family that came from San Giacomo, in the province of Bologna. His name was Fonso. He went up to Callisto and asked permission to dance with his daughter. "You can dance with her," replied the old man, "but behave like a gentleman."

Fonso was not a looker. His chin was too square and he was already starting to go a bit bald, but he was a great talker, a rarity among the others his age, and the girls listened to him raptly. You could see that Maria was struck by him, although they'd just had a couple of dances together, and she spent the rest of the evening listening to him tell stories.

Floti glared at the laborer with a look of distrust. "Who's that?" he asked Checco.

"A day laborer that the league sent over."

"Do you know him?"

"I've talked to him. Seems like a good bloke. What I do know is that he's one hell of a worker; gets more done than two or three combined."

"But he's getting all lovesick with our sister."

"They're just talking," replied Checco. "He's not going to eat her."

"I don't like it. She's only fifteen. I'm going to tell him to butt out."

"Oh, leave him be. I don't see why they can't talk. Don't worry, nothing will happen. But hey, if they do like each other, what's wrong with that? The important thing is that he's honest and a hard worker."

Floti didn't say anything else, but he continued to keep his eye on the laborer the whole evening, until the musicians got up and passed around a hat, in case their listeners could afford a bit of generosity. The fact that a day laborer was dancing and chatting with his sister annoyed him; it was a question of standing, after all. Floti was the one offering work here, and the other was his subordinate; if a laborer didn't find a job for the day, he didn't eat. In any case, there were no further encounters between the two young men for a long time; there were no more big jobs that required hiring extra help, and if there had been, Floti would have found a way to avoid calling on Fonso.

For All Saints and All Souls the weather was cold and clear, and for Saint Martin's Day as well. The leaves on the grapevines had turned red and yellow and the Lambrusco leaves were violet, a real treat for the eyes. The first snow appeared on the peak of Mount Cimone. Clerice told everyone to thank God that they had a roof over their heads, enough food and good wine, and to pray for those poor souls who had been turned out by their landlords and were now wandering about in search of someone who would take them in to work a plot of land.

"Pray to God that He wards off this war," said Callisto. "The tailor, who reads the newspaper every day, tells me it's a slaughter, everywhere, and that we could be next."

Floti tried to reassure him: "What does the tailor know, *papà*? And those newspaper writers, they can say whatever they want; they're just people like us, you know. I think that seeing what's happening all over Europe, our government will do everything they can to stay out of the war." Clerice watched and listened without saying a word, but her eyes brimmed with tears and in her heart she invoked the Madonna, who knew what it meant to lose a son, asking her to keep them safe from this scourge.

Callisto worried and worried and as winter approached he hoped the umbrella mender would show up, as he had for many years now. He wanted to ask him more, to have him speak about what he saw in the future, but the days passed and he never came.

"What could have happened to the umbrella man?" he would say. "He'd always be here by the first snowfall."

Gaetano shrugged: "What does it matter, *papà*, he was just here to eat off of us. I say, if he never comes back, good riddance. If he had at least given a hand! No, he was always out there in the stable sitting and waiting for a bowl of soup. We haven't lost a thing." But Callisto was uneasy, and kept fretting over the failed appearance of his guest. When Floti was involved in the discussion, he'd try to change the subject, because what he and Iofa had seen was best kept secret. One day, tired of all that talk, he said that he'd heard that the umbrella mender had sailed to America in search of a better life, and they shouldn't expect him back any time soon.

"Ah," said Callisto, "I thought so," but it didn't set his mind at rest.

In the spring, rumors that Italy would enter the war became

more insistent, but they were also contradicted by actual events. The pastor, interpreting the growing anguish of his community, used the homily one Sunday morning to explain just what was going on: the king was willing to go to war to liberate Trento and Trieste which were still under the heel of Austria, but the majority of parliament—and they were the representatives of the people—were contrary to the war. Since the government couldn't go to war against anyone unless the parliament agreed to it, nothing would happen. It was best nonetheless to raise their voices in prayer to ask the Lord to make the atrocious conflict end and to keep their beloved native land out of it.

Even Bastianino, the tailor, approved of what the pastor had said, and this reinforced the common opinion that there was no need for fear.

Until one day the mailman arrived in the Brunis' courtyard, the leather bag tied to his handlebars bursting with postcards marked with the shield of Savoia. He left one addressed to Gaetano Bruni.

It was a registered letter. Floti signed on behalf of the true addressee, who was in the stable, but he sent someone to call him. Gaetano was shocked because he'd never received a letter in all his life and it frightened him greatly.

"What is it?" he asked.

"Read it," said Floti, "it's addressed to you."

"It's written too difficult," said Gaetano, running a trembling finger down the typewritten lines. "You read it."

Floti, who'd already realized what it was, looked into his eyes and said: "It's the king calling you to arms. You have to leave for the war, *Tanein*. In four days."

"Are you sure?" asked Gaetano. "Is that really what it says?"

"I'm sure," replied Floti.

"Can't I say I'm sick?"

"They'll send out a doctor, who'll write that you're fine and then you've got to go. And if you don't go, they'll say you failed to report for military service and the *carabinieri* will come and arrest you. If you're lucky they'll send you to the front; they say there's a special battalion destined for desperate actions. You'd be a goner in no time. If you're unlucky, they'll put you in front of a firing squad."

Gaetano lowered his head, tears brimming in his eyes. Clerice, who happened to be passing by, saw the scene and understood instantly what was happening. She whispered: "Oh Lord, oh most holy Virgin, no . . . "

In a matter of minutes the whole family was standing in a circle on the threshing floor around the two brothers.

"What's there to gape at?" said Floti. "It's the postcard: it's Gaetano's turn to leave, but more will be coming soon. It depends on how many die at the front and need to be replaced."

Callisto looked at his boys one by one, shaking his head with a confused and incredulous expression. The storm clouds foretold by the umbrella mender were gathering over the Bruni home, blacking out the sun and unloosing a boundless disaster. There was nothing he could do to avert the catastrophe. All of the sufferings borne over a lifetime were nothing compared to what was happening before his eyes in that instant.

When the day of Gaetano's departure dawned, Iofa came to get his friend with his horse and cart: he wanted to be the one to take him to the train station, just as he'd taken him a year before to visit the notary in Bologna, the day they brought home all that wheat for the family. Gaetano wore a pair of fustian trousers, a white hemp shirt with a detachable collar, a cotton jacket and a pair of cowhide shoes stitched up for him by the travelling shoemaker. His brothers hugged him first: Floti, Checco, Armando, Dante, Fredo and Savino. Then his sisters, Rosina and Maria, who burst out weeping. Callisto, whose chin was trembling like a child's about to cry, was biting down hard on his lip, and Clerice dabbed at her eyes with the corner of her apron.

"Don't cry, *mamma*, it's bad luck," said Gaetano, embracing her. "You'll see, I'll be back."

Callisto patted his son's shoulder. "Watch out for snipers, my boy," he said, "and never smoke at night because they can see the glow of your cigarette."

"Don't worry, *papà*, I'll make sure they don't get me."

"Write when you can," Floti told him, but he immediately bit his tongue. Gaetano hadn't picked up a pen since third grade. "Find someone who knows how to write for you."

Gaetano got onto Iofa's cart and set off. Everyone stood at the side of the road, waving goodbye with their hands and their handkerchiefs until he disappeared from sight. Then each of them went back to what he'd been doing, still incredulous at what they'd just seen.

Over the next two weeks, Dante left, then Armando, Checco and Floti, and then it was Fredo's turn. Savino, who was only sixteen, remained. The same harrowing scene was repeated, in the same way, for each one of them.

When even Fredo had gone, Clerice knelt alone in the middle of the deserted threshing floor and prayed for her sons.

CHAPTER FIVE

Gaetano got out of Iofa's cart at the station of Castelfranco. He took out the government voucher that
authorized him to travel free to Modena and from
there to Verona where he would have to report to the regiment
headquarters.

"How will I know which train to take in Modena?" he
asked.

"There are timetables that tell you which track to go to."

"But I don't know anything about any timetables," replied
Gaetano, terrified.

"Then you show this ticket to one of the railway officials
and you tell him: 'I'm a soldier and I have to go to Verona,
where's the track?' He'll tell you. The railwaymen have a gray
uniform with a hat like the ones the army officers wear. The
one with the red hat is the stationmaster. You can't miss him."

"And when I get to Verona? How will I find the regiment?"

"Oh, don't worry. They'll find you."

"You know, Iofa, you really know your way around. Where
did you learn all these things?"

"I've delivered goods many a time to be loaded onto train
wagons. The station is like a seaport: there's people and mer-
chandise of all kinds, coming and going."

They heard a whistle and a locomotive soon pulled up, puffing and wheezing and wrapped in a cloud of smoke and steam.
Quite a sight. Like the steam engine they used for threshing but
ten times bigger, and pulling train cars behind it instead of the

thresher. Iofa unloaded his passenger's baggage: a sack with some underwear, a few shirts, a piece of *parmigiano*, a *salame* and a few loaves of bread.

"This is your train, *Tanein*," Iofa said, using the nickname Gaetano's brothers had given him as a child. He handed him the sack. "It's' time to say goodbye."

"How about you, did you get the postcard?" Gaetano asked him.

"No. Can't you see I've got one leg shorter than the other? I'm not good for the king."

"Ain't that the luck? I wish I was you."

"Don't say that. Because no one wants someone like me. I've never had a woman. And when I wanted one I had to go pay a whore on the streets of Bologna. It cost me a fortune and I caught the clap off her. I'll never have a family. I won't have children, much less grandchildren. You really think I'm the lucky one? Go on, get on that train before it leaves. Take care, *Tanein*. Try not to get killed."

"I'll try. You take care too, Iofa."

And so Gaetano Bruni got onto a train for the first time in his life, to go to war.

He got to Modena and then to Verona and from there to regiment headquarters, where a sergeant gave him a uniform and confiscated his *salame*. In a month's time they had taught him to use a gun and then they put him on another train that went to the front.

Things went the same way for his brothers but none of them had the fortune of being assigned to the same unit. They soon lost all contact.

Floti was sent to a regiment of the Fifth Army. Another sergeant lined them up and had them stand at attention and then stand at ease and the commander of the company, Lieutenant Caselli, addressed them: "You are here to liberate the last piece of Italy still under the heel of the foreigner and to drive out the

Austrians who occupy our territories. If we don't drive them back they will brazenly advance all the way to your villages, rape your women and seize your homes and your crops. Many of you will fall, but your children, your fiancées and your wives will survive thanks to you and will remember this forever. *Viva Italia*, long live the king!"

Floti realized that he had no children, no fiancée, no wife, and that the crops and the house belonged to notary Barzini. He felt a lump in his throat and tears rose to his eyes unbidden.

Caselli, a young man with a child's face, noticed him and came close: "What's your name?"

"Bruni, Raffaele. Lieutenant, sir."

"What do you do in your everyday life?"

"I'm a farmer, sir."

"Are you afraid?"

"Yes, sir."

The sergeant shot him a threatening look, as the officer paused to consider the sincerity of that answer.

He continued: "I'm afraid myself, Bruni, but if we can become a free country, united from the Alps to the sea, if we can show the world that no one can trample what is ours, we will be respected and there will be peace and prosperity for all. Ours is a worthy cause. And you should all know," he raised his voice so even those farthest away could hear him, "that every time we're sent to attack, I'll be there leading the way."

Floti lowered his head without a word, but something about the boy had already impressed the young officer: his intelligent black eyes and thick prickly beard and even more so, his Italian; it was very rare for a farmer to speak correctly without a dialectal twang. And so it was that Floti often found himself at Caselli's side for administrative duties, when the lieutenant needed to dictate letters to headquarters or pass on the day's orders. The officer usually spent his evenings alone, reading or writing. Maybe he had a girlfriend, maybe he was writing to his parents who lived in Perugia and had a fabric shop there. He was their only child. And Floti realized then that having only one son was a mistake, because if he dies, that's the end of you, too.

One evening he found the lieutenant's room empty, although the light was on. There was a book open on the table, entitled *The Birth of Tragedy.* The author's name was so complicated Floti couldn't even sound it out; he must have been a foreigner. He thought it might be a book about war.

"Are you looking for something?" asked the voice of the officer behind him.

Floti spun around and saluted. "Excuse me, sir, I wasn't . . . "

"That's all right, you haven't done anything wrong. Being curious about culture is a good thing: it means you want to learn. I'd explain what the book is about, but I'm afraid you wouldn't understand. Go now, Bruni. There's something you must give to the sergeant. In three days' time, we'll be leaving for the front. This is really it, Bruni." A look of melancholy shadowed his eyes as he spoke.

Floti brought his hand up to his cap and took his leave.

He made his way to company headquarters and delivered his commander's orders: "This is from Lieutenant Caselli."

The sergeant practically ripped the envelope from his hands and tore it open. He gave it a quick read and sent Floti on his way. "What the hell are you doing standing there! Get outta my sight," he muttered, and Floti was happy to oblige him.

The night sky was clear and full of stars. The breeze from the mountains carried a whiff of fresh hay and the smell made him feel at home, back at home, for an instant.

They left on the third day at dawn, in double file: the foot soldiers of every corps of the army. The *Bersaglieri* with their red caps, long tassels swinging back and forth with every step, the *Alpini* with lavish black plumes hanging from their hats, the Lancers of Montebello and the Grenadiers of Sardegna. And then the mules, wagons, artillery pieces, trucks. Floti had never seen so many people together in one place, so many cannons or so many vehicles. He tried to imagine how much all of this could be costing, and then wondered how many of those boys would still be alive a month from now.

He fought in the first battle of Isonzo and were it not for a God-given strength of spirit he would have gone mad. On their first attack, Lieutenant Caselli's head rolled beneath his feet, chopped cleanly off by shrapnel. His commander's sad eyes stared into his for a moment before they went blank.

Hell could not be worse than what he was living through. The roaring din of the artillery, the flames, the screams of wounded men, the mangled limbs of his fellow soldiers torn from their bodies. He didn't know where to look or how to move. At first he was practically paralyzed. Then his instinct for survival prevailed and after two weeks of battle he had become another person, someone he didn't know was inside of him. As a child he couldn't bear to hear the shrieking of a pig under the butcher's knife; when it was time he'd cover his ears and burrow deep under his bedcovers. Nor could he stand the smell of blood. Now blood was everywhere and it was the blood of twenty-year-old boys. He had learned to shoot, to use a bayonet, to crawl through tall grass, to interpret the whistle of a mortar bomb. But he still couldn't understand anything of what was happening around him. It was like being in another world or inside the nightmare of a madman. At least the umbrella mender, buried head down like they'd found him, wouldn't be seeing any of this slaughter. Lucky him.

Once he saw the enemy. An Austrian or Croatian soldier, blond as a corncob, white as a washed rag, stone dead at the bottom of a cannon's crater. He didn't look much like Floti, who was shorter, with black hair and a tough beard, but he didn't look so terrible, either. He looked like a kid who'd grown up too fast.

At the end of every offensive, when the battlefield was strewn with dead bodies, there would be a period of weeks on end where they'd settle into the trenches and wait for a sign of the enemy or for orders for a new operation. It was almost worse than attacking. The heat was insufferable, the stench of sweat and excrement, the flies that fed on that filth and then got into your eyes, your mouth, your ears, the fleas and lice that never let up, neither day nor night, the impossibility of washing, the futility of scratching, the revolting food and scant water . . . Floti realized that there was a lot worse in life than beating hemp in the midday sun or tossing sheaves of wheat with a pitchfork under the scorching roof of the hayloft. The worst jobs were tolerable when you knew how long they'd last and when they were followed by a dive into the Samoggia and dinner with freshly-baked bread and cold sparkling wine.

Floti's intelligence and his ability to read and write correctly soon helped him shift into tasks involving more responsibility and less danger. By winter he found himself working in an office, and the full accounting of that massacre began to flow across his desk: thousands, tens of thousands of deaths, boys like him mown down by machine guns, riddled with bayonet wounds.

One of his jobs was to write the letters that announced that "first name" and "last name" had fallen in the line of duty on "day, month, year" and to send them to the army postal service, which would see to getting them delivered. Every letter finished with a stamp: "Signed by General Cadorna."

As if Floti were the supreme commander of the army.

He'd write letters of his own at times, to his parents and his sisters: "Dear mother and father, I am keeping well and I hope the same is true of you at home . . . " but he never spoke of the battles and the butchery at the front; the censors would never let his letter through. They had to safeguard the morale of the civilian population, after all.

He thought of his brothers and wondered where they were. If they were still alive. As the ledgers of death piled up, the statistics became clear: out of the seven of them, three or four would die and one or two more would be wounded. Who would it be? Who among the seven brothers would be the only one to come through unharmed? Who would be writing up the first and last names of the others?

He saw many requests for information from parents desperate over their missing sons, and he sorted out the bureaucratic replies of the military authorities: "Corporal Martino Munaretto does not appear on the list of soldiers killed in action." Who was this Martino, anyway? A boy from Veneto, blond as a corncob himself? A craftsman? A shoemaker or a day laborer or a carpenter? There was a story behind that name, a story that had come to a sorry end. On the other hand, the same thing could have happened to him when he was at the front. You had to try to keep going somehow.

The bond that joined the brothers was plain and straightforward, with no room for sentimentality. Meaning that, if they could, they helped each other, but each one of them knew how to get by on his own. If Floti was partial to anyone, it was his sisters, towards whom he felt tender and protective. He doted on the younger one, Maria. He was worried that the women would be stuck with the tough jobs, now that nearly all the men in the household were gone, and hoped that they wouldn't get hurt doing heavy lifting or using a shovel or hoe. Savino was still home, but they really couldn't rely on him too much since he wasn't even fully grown yet.

He tried assiduously to contact other administrative offices in the other army corps for news of his brothers but his letters often went lost; any answers took months to get back to him, and by that time the troops had been moved, transferred, sent out as replacements to units that had been decimated. The only one he knew anything about was Checco, who was the brother he felt closest to, and that was only through their parish priest who read the boys' letters to Clerice and Callisto and wrote back their answers.

Floti knew well that seventy divisions with nearly a million men were deployed along the Isonzo River, from the sea to the Dolomites. Trying to find anyone was like looking for a needle in a haystack. He had made his parents promise that any message they got from his brothers be sent to him through the parish priest, since his office was stably positioned at a distance from the front and could provide a certain point of reference.

Little by little, this strategy began to work: by the end of 1916 he'd heard from Gaetano and Armando, who had both written home with another soldier's help. They were alive. He used any free time he had to search for them. He learned to use a telephone and to communicate with the other offices. As time passed, the slaughter only got worse, and the number of deaths could not be calculated. The troops were sent to attack the enemy in their trenches, the logic being that there had to be more soldiers than the number of rounds that their opponents' machine guns could fire. When there were no more bullets, the survivors would take out the enemy emplacement.

One day, when he was given the job of transferring certain papers to division headquarters, he met up with a unit of special soldiers called *Arditi*. Their very name meant "daring," and he'd heard speak of them any number of times: they were shock troops, sent out on the most dangerous missions. They were trained in hand-to-hand combat with a dagger and in the use of grenades, and they carried an automatic pistol that not even the officers could boast of.

The uniform they wore was different than his, with a high-necked sweater instead of a shirt, and a cap like the ones the

Bersaglieri wore, but black. Their battle flag greatly impressed him: black again, picturing a skull with a dagger between its teeth. They spoke softly and smoked fragrant oval-shaped cigarettes instead of the strong-shag Milits the ordinary troops smoked. They never sang.

In the late fall, a lad from Romagna was sent in to help with office duties. The dialect he spoke was a bit different than Floti's but they managed to understand each other quite well without making themselves understood to their officers, who were from Abruzzo and Sicily.

His name was Gino Pelloni and he came from Imola, a friendly fellow. His grandfather had stood with Garibaldi in the pine forest of Ravenna as they made their way towards Venice, besieged by the Austrians in 1849. The things he said were unheard of:

"War is a dirty trick invented by the ruling classes to kill off proletarians while they earn a ton of money on weapons and equipment. Have you ever read Marx?"

Floti was dumbfounded. "Who has time to read?" he protested. "I barely know who the guy is."

"Wait, are you telling me you've never heard 'workers of the world, unite'?"

Floti shrugged.

"Well, he's a guy who studied how the world of the bosses works; how they exploit the workers and use what they earn to buy new factories so they can exploit new workers and just get richer and richer, because what they earn off the labor of their workers is daylight robbery. Now do you understand?"

"I do. I know what you're saying. But I think that if one guy is the boss of a big factory and the other guy is a worker there, there must be some difference between them."

"That the boss is a thief."

"Would you be capable of running a company like Ansaldo?"

"What does that matter? The bourgeoisie have the money to send their children to school, while the proletarians do not."

"Well, all right, but even so, there's no saying that the son of a worker is necessarily bright."

Pelloni would lose his patience at this point: "Oh, come on; whose side are you on, anyway?"

"On the side of the poor, but that doesn't mean I can't think it through. You, if you got rich, what would you do? Would you think the way you do now?"

That was all Pelloni needed to hear. The conversation would heat up considerably, but their dialects were hardly the ideal instruments for speaking about such complicated economic and philosophical concepts. In any event, Floti, who had great sympathy for the socialist cause, learned over the months about industrial systems, trade unions, company profits and the organization of labor. Not that he always agreed with Pelloni. From his vantage point, the grim accounts of the war had demonstrated to him that, proportionally, as many officers died as foot soldiers, and sometimes even more. He couldn't forget Lieutenant Caselli's eyes as they glazed over in death, and he was convinced that even a man of humble origins, who had his wits about him, could improve his life without resorting to revolution.

"I've seen enough blood in all these months," he said. "There has to be a way to improve things without killing."

"You're a fool," replied Pelloni. "You have to fight fire with fire. Country, bravery, honor: all hogwash invented by the rich. You mark my words: their sons will find a way to hide out while ours are being sent to die."

"What do you do in your normal life?"

"I'm a bicycle mechanic. Why?"

"Then you were worse off than me, because where I live there was always plenty to eat and to drink. And yet here you are hiding out in an office while our comrades are out there charging the enemy twice a day and are dying like flies."

"What about you, then?"

"Me, too."

And that's when silence fell.

In the meantime, the offensives followed one after another and the carnage grew more horrific with every passing day. Floti was afraid that they'd soon be calling up the seventeen-year olds and that meant Savino as well.

Just before Christmas, Captain Cavallotti called Floti into his office to entrust him with a special mission. "We have no more couriers and the telephone line that connects us with the forward command is out. You have to take this message to Colonel Da Pollenzo. Can you handle a motorcycle?"

"Nosir, Captain, sir."

Cavallotti had become long accustomed to doing without almost everything he needed. He stood and walked over to a gray-green Frera, laying a hand on the saddle. "I'll try to find someone who can drive this. You'll ride on the back." Floti couldn't understand why there had to be two of them; if some-one else was already driving the motorcycle, he wasn't really needed. The captain seemed to read his mind.

"I trust you because I know you're sharp, but you don't know how to drive. I have to find a driver, even if he's no genius. So the two of you together make one who's up to the task. And if one of you dies, the other can continue, in one way or another. Isn't your friend Pelloni from Romagna? The *Romagnoli* are crazy about motors. Anything that runs, runs on an engine, whether it's a car or a tractor or a motorcycle. I'll bet you he's up to the job. Wait here and don't move."

Pelloni ran up a few minutes later, saluted and belted out a "Reporting for duty, sir."

"Can you drive a motorcycle?" asked the officer.

"Yessir."

"See? What did I tell you?" said Cavallotti to Floti, handing him a map of the area and pointing out the route that would take him to the forward command.

"This message is of fundamental importance. It can save the lives of a great number of our boys, if you get it to him in time. If you should fall into enemy hands, destroy it immediately."

Floti realized, looking at the map, why the captain had said he needed someone who was sharp. He'd never read or tried to understand one before.

"Sir," he said, "give me a few minutes to figure this out. It isn't easy."

"I know. Lieutenant Cassina will show you how to read the map: you'll find that it's less complicated than it looks."

The route was marked in red and crossed an area of rough terrain; the road was out at several points and the countryside was ravaged by bombings. Cassina pointed out that certain stretches were very close to the front lines, and they couldn't rule out contact with enemy reconnaissance patrols on this side of the river. In all, the route covered a distance of thirty-two kilometers. The journey's end would bring them very close to the Isonzo. In the end, that's why Floti accepted the job. He wanted to see the river, because he imagined it flowing red with blood. There had been sixty-two thousand dead in the last battle. How much blood could pour out of sixty-two thousand boys? Did the earth just drink it all up or did it spew into the river?

When he got to a point where the river was very close he had to get a look at it, at whatever risk.

It was green. As green as a meadow in springtime.

CHAPTER SIX

The earth was devastated by bomb craters, the air poisoned by the smell of cordite that made your eyes water. The ground was a wasteland without grass or plants. The trees which had once grown there were charred stumps and the roots, burnt as well, looked like skeletal hands reaching up to curse the sky and bear witness to the hell below.

Everything was gray, perhaps because the smoke had spread out all over and killed all the other colors. The noise of the motorcycle was the only sound in the middle of all that desolation and Floti was afraid that it would call attention to them, that there was a sniper lying in wait, taking aim, and then boom, he and Pelloni would be killed and be added to the list of casualties. Pelloni was proceeding at a snail's pace because the road had practically disappeared and they had to be extremely careful not to slash their tires on the scraps of metal and splinters of glass underfoot. Then he stopped.

"Get off," he said, "we have to walk it. I'll hold the handlebars and you push from behind."

Floti obeyed. The two of them weighed too heavily on the tires and they would go flat in no time.

"How much farther, do you think?" asked Pelloni after a hundred meters or so.

Floti looked at the map and tried to estimate, although neither of them had a watch and there were no shadows on the ground. Daylight was fading and it would be dark soon.

"I think we're close. Less than half an hour. If we can get back on, half an hour, maybe less. Look . . . "

"What?"

"There, on that stone. It's a blackbird. A baby one. It must have lost its parents."

Pelloni shrugged. "Who gives a shit about a blackbird. Let's go, it's getting dark."

"No. Wait," said Floti again.

"I told you I couldn't care less about some damn blackbird."

"Down, we have to get down. The motorcycle too."

Pelloni finally understood, lowered the Frera to the ground without making a sound and stretched out beside it. On a hill they could make out a couple of shapes moving slowly.

"Austrians," mouthed Floti, putting a hand on the carbine slung over his neck.

"Don't. They're proletarians like we are."

"You'd let a proletarian stick it up your backside," hissed Floti. "If they come this way, I'm shooting. You can do what you like."

Pelloni pushed deeper into the furrows in the ground. "How can you tell they're Austrian?"

"Because they have a helmet that looks like a piss-pot," replied Floti.

He counted them: there were four.

"Don't be an idiot," warned Floti, "they're coming this way. Ten more steps and they'll see us. I'll shoot first. Then you shoot while I'm reloading. I fire, you reload and then fire again. In one minute's time, we'll have taken out all four of them. Got it?"

"Got it," mumbled Pelloni, and checked that his rifle was ready.

The patrol halted, as if the soldiers had heard the Italians talking. The sergeant leading them muttered something; they were so close his voice could be heard clearly. Then they turned and cautiously made their way back to the river. A splashing noise: they were fording the Isonzo to get back to the other side. Floti let out a sigh and whispered, "Thank God."

"Why, you would have shot them?" asked Pelloni. "You would have killed another human being?"

"I sure would have," replied Floti.

"Not me."

"Listen, so much the better. No one can say what he'd do if put to the test. Maybe you who didn't want to would have shot at them and I who thought I could wouldn't have pulled the trigger. Let's get moving."

Pelloni straightened up the Frera and gave the pedal a kick to start the engine. They proceeded very slowly for a couple of kilometers, Pelloni in the saddle and Floti on foot, until the roadbed became smoother and they could both get on the motorcycle and increase their speed. It was soon dark and they were forced to switch on the headlight to avoid holes and debris. It was blinded so it lit up the ground just a couple of meters in front of the wheel, but it turned them into a target nonetheless.

"In the distance I can see a yellow light moving back and forth," said Pelloni.

"How do you know?"

"Because I saw it," he replied.

"So did you shoot at it?"

"No, thank God."

"Why, you believe in God?"

"No," replied Pelloni.

A flash and then an explosion. Then a voice: "Halt! Stop or I'll shoot. Who goes there?"

"Courier."

"Come forward."

Pelloni stopped the Frera and Floti held up the folder with

the message inside. The sentry, a Sardinian no taller than the king, tried to grab it, but Floti stopped him. "I have orders to deliver it personally to Colonel Da Pollenzo."

Pelloni remained with the motorcycle, while Floti was taken to the base headquarters. They passed in front of the field hospital and he saw a medic standing outside the tent smoking a cigarette and wearing an apron so bloody it looked like a butcher's. His face was gray and expressionless. Like a stone.

Floti continued to the command tent. Da Pollenzo was a man who inspired awe: nearly six feet tall, with a neatly groomed beard, perfectly pressed jacket and mirror-finish boots. He was standing behind an improvised desk, with a topographical map draped over it like a tablecloth, lit by an oil lamp. The stiff visor on his cap shaded dark eyes topped with bushy brows. To Floti it seemed impossible that a man on the front lines could maintain such an impeccable appearance, and he would have liked to ask him how he did it. He hastily patted down his own uniform, saluted, and handed him the sealed folder.

"Sit down, you must be tired," said the colonel as he opened the folder with the tip of his bayonet.

Floti was surprised at such thoughtful attention, but stayed on his feet: "Thank you sir, I'm not tired."

"Do you know what it says here? It says that in one hour's time there will be a massive attack by the Eighth Hungarian Division camped directly opposite us on the other side of the Isonzo," he said, extracting his pocket watch from inside his jacket and glancing at it. "And in half an hour they'll start firing their heavy artillery."

"Just now, at about ten kilometers from here, we saw a group of Austrians or Hungarians on this side of the river, sir."

Da Pollenzo drew closer and looked straight into his eyes. "What were they doing?"

"I couldn't say, we saw them at the last minute and we took cover, ready to shoot at them if they came closer. They came within a few steps, but then turned around and crossed the river. We jumped back on the motorcycle so we could get here as fast as possible."

"You did well. If you'd gotten here any later, thousands of your fellow soldiers would have died in the bombing. You've accomplished your mission and you could turn back, but I fear that's too dangerous now. The artillery could start up at any moment."

"Begging your pardon, sir," replied Floti, "we'd like to go straight back. We have to get back to our unit and report to the commander that we did as we had been ordered. He'll be worried about us."

"Go then. But be careful. You're running a considerable risk."

"Yes, sir. Thank you."

Da Pollenzo left him and immediately summoned his officers, ordering them to pull their men back as far as possible beyond the range of the Austro-Hungarian artillery. "Sound the alarm and muster the men. Every minute gained will save the lives of thousands of men, including our own. Move."

Floti caught up with Pelloni who was filling the tank with a jerry can. "Hell is about to break loose here. We have to get out now."

"Right. Get on."

The Frera started up at the third kick and Pelloni deftly wove between potholes and debris, skirting the wreckage of bombed-out vehicles. The blinded headlight showed them the road one meter at a time, suddenly illuminating the unexpected objects in their way.

"Do you think we're being watched?" Floti asked loudly to make himself heard over the sound of the engine.

"Maybe," replied Pelloni, turning around.

"Maybe one of those four guys we saw before is taking aim right now."

"No, stop worrying. All they can see is a reflected light going on and off. They can't see us, and even if they could, by the time they drew a bead on us we'd be past them."

That made sense to Floti and he did stop worrying for a while but then he thought that a rifle barrel would only have to move a few centimeters to follow their movement from a kilometer away and that got him worrying again, but he didn't say anything so as not to be a nuisance.

Time passed and the sputtering of the slow-running engine began to seem like a friendly voice. Then a thunderclap ripped through the silence of the night. Pelloni stopped and looked back. Floti got off.

"There," said Pelloni, "it's started. Who knows if they had enough time to retreat, out of range. How much time has gone by, would you say?"

"Half an hour."

"Will you look at that!" said Pelloni. "It looks like the end of the world." The echoes of hundreds of explosions filled the air. The noise was quite loud, even at this distance.

"Let's hope they got away," said Floti, and Pelloni could see the flashes of cannon fire reflected on his face and in his eyes.

"You can move quite a ways in half an hour," he replied. "And even if we managed to save just a couple of hundred lives, it was worth coming out here. For the big brass, the life of a soldier is nothing. They have thousands, tens of thousands, hundreds of thousands of men to send in as cannon fodder. But for me and you, for us, even one single life is precious. Let's get out of here, Floti, there's nothing more we can do."

They had covered another hundred meters or so when a shot rang out and then another. Pelloni fell over on the saddle. The motorcycle rolled forward for a few more meters and then fell over, and Floti rolled onto the stones at the side of the road.

"Pelloni!" he screamed as soon as he had struggled to his feet. "Where are you?"

There was no answer and he started to feel around for his friend in the dark, listening for his gasping breath. When he found him, he saw that Pelloni couldn't move and when he tried to pull him up, he realized that his hands were wet with blood. The life of his friend was flowing through his hands and soaking into the dry earth.

"Damn it, Pelloni, don't die now, we're almost there!" he shouted between sobs. "My god, what do I do, what do I do now . . . we were almost out of this." But his friend wasn't listening anymore. His body was dead weight, and Floti lowered him carefully on to the ground. He snuffed up hard and dried his tears on the back of his sleeve, then took Pelloni's dog tags and his wallet and tried to lift the Frera which was still running, the rear wheel still spinning and spinning . . .

Once he'd gotten it back up, he grabbed the handlebars and took off running, then jumped onto the saddle as if it were a horse. He didn't know how to use the clutch or the gears, and he went forward all night without ever shifting the gear that Pelloni had been using. It felt somehow that his friend was bringing him home.

He didn't know where he was and he couldn't see, he didn't recognize anything around him in the dense darkness, his back hurt, all his muscles were tight as knots, the damp night air stuck to his hands and face and he waited for dawn with mounting anxiety. He had begun shaking uncontrollably. He was afraid he would fall off, afraid he would be shot, afraid he would crash into something.

The first glimmer of light reached him on a country road. Soon after he saw a Fiat 18 BL loaded with supplies heading south. He thought it might be carrying ammunition and replacement parts to headquarters, and he pulled over behind it thinking he could follow the truck in. He couldn't stop to check the map because he didn't think he could start up the motorcycle again, and this seemed to be a good strategy.

The truck proceeded slowly because the road was unpaved and full of holes and he managed to stay behind it.

The sun rose, finally, and its clear light stung his tired eyes, red with strain and tears. He rode past a couple of small towns, then saw a railway crossing and heard the bell announcing the lowering of the bar. He'd learned how to open the throttle to accelerate and he pulled as close behind the truck as he could; it was racing forward to beat the bar.

He managed to get through as well, by the skin of his teeth.

He kept going, pushing on, pushing through the cramps that were seizing at his muscles. He was hungry and thirsty and tired. And above all, he felt an overwhelming need to urinate. His bladder hurt so much he felt like he was sitting on a stone. But he didn't want to give up. He wanted to take the Frera back to headquarters and tell them that the mission had been accomplished. Finally, overcoming his natural restraint and the sense of dignity that had been instilled in him since his boyhood, he urinated in his pants. The hot, strong-smelling liquid that ran down his leg and filled his boots disgusted him, but he felt better and knew that he could continue his journey. It wouldn't be much longer, and he'd be able to wash up.

He was right. In half an hour's time, he was back at the camp he had departed from. He recognized the guard post and prepared a strategy that would allow him to touch ground. He closed the throttle all the way. The engine gave a couple of hard knocks and then, starved of fuel, died with a bang so loud it sounded like a gunshot.

"Is that any way to treat an engine, you goat!" yelled a corporal who happened to be passing by at that moment. "Do you know that thing costs more than you do?"

"I don't know how to drive it," replied Floti. "I did what I could. I have to talk to Captain Cavallotti right away."

"He's in his tent, down that way," said the other churlishly. "You smell like piss, you goat."

Floti felt a strong urge to punch him, but decided to drop it. He put the motorcycle on its kickstand and walked to the captain's tent.

Cavallotti recognized him: "It's you, Bruni. How did it go?"

"Your message was delivered just in time. Half an hour before the cannon fire began. Colonel Da Pollenzo meant to have his troops retreat beyond the range of the Austrian artillery. I don't know if he managed to do so. We left immediately to report back to you, sir."

"You did all you could do. I'm proud of you both. Call your friend and have them give you a bowl of soup and some boiled meat in the kitchen, with a flask of wine. You deserve it."

"Private Pelloni died, sir, in carrying out his duty," replied Floti. "These are his personal belongings." He placed his friend's identification tag and wallet on the table. He raised his hand to his forehead in a salute and added, "Request permission to be dismissed, sir," and walked out.

The officer's eyes followed him out, perplexed at this boy who talked like a printed book and stank of piss.

CHAPTER SEVEN

Floti was completely unnerved by Pelloni's death and, in a certain way, he was surprised at himself. What was the death of one man in the midst of all that slaughter? Hadn't he personally certified the deaths of thousands of young men? The answer was not difficult to find: people care about who they know, not who they don't know. If someone were to get all upset every time he heard about anyone dying, life would be nothing but grieving. It was only right, he thought; each person should cry for the people he was close to. Somewhere else, other people were crying over someone they had cared about. A bit like when you went to the cemetery for All Saints and All Souls. At first everyone follows the priest in the procession, then once you're beyond the gate, everyone goes their own way and has their own grave to attend to. Widows say the rosary over the graves of their husbands, children gather around the tombs of their parents, a younger sister might have the task of tending to an older brother who'd already passed on.

Although usually, thought Floti, it's the young who bury the old, whereas in time of war it's the opposite. Boys that leave home healthy and full of life come back in a casket and the mothers and fathers who brought them into this world have the job of burying them.

Things continued more or less the same for several months, and Floti kept searching for his brothers. He found Dante thanks to a quartermaster stationed at Colloredo in Friuli. He was part of a regiment of *Bersaglieri*, the ones with the red cap and tassel. The discovery put him in a good mood and for a while he stopped suffering over Pelloni. So it was him, Gaetano, Checco and Dante, four out of six accounted for, not bad. He still had to find Fredo and Armando, he had no idea where they were. Savino luckily was still at home, the only one of them still too young to be called up.

Towards the end of the summer he received a letter from the parish priest with news of his father: he'd had to hire a farmhand, because he and Savino couldn't handle everything on their own. A good lad named Secondo who came from a very poor family up in the Apennines. Those mountain families didn't have much imagination as far as names went. When a child was born, those who went to church, those who could read, that is, would look at the calendar and give him the name of that day's saint. Those who weren't so faithful went by the numbers: *Primo*, *Secondo*, *Terzo* and so on, although at some point they usually stopped. Calling a son *Dodicesimo*—Twelfth—or *Quattordicesimo*—Fourteenth—was a little much. Floti had met a boy whose name was *Ultimo*. His mother and father must have had enough of children and were hoping that by giving him that name he'd be the last.

The most important bit of news came at the end of the letter: Rosina had married! A revenue officer from the south of Italy. They had gone to live in Florence. On one hand, he thought, this was a good thing, because she had a husband with a fixed salary, who made good money every month, even when it rained or snowed, and that was a great privilege. On the other hand he was sorry because Florence was so far away, and he didn't know when he would see her again. As he mulled it over, he thought that a fixed salary was really no great thing, after all, and that there wasn't enough money in the world to buy a beauty like Rosina.

He replied:

> *Dear Mother and Father,*
>
> *I'm well and hope you are too. Here every day is tougher than the last but life goes on and there are those who are much worse off than me. I've found Dante. He's alive and well, and so are the others, as far as I know. No news is good news, as the saying goes. And in a war like this one, it's pretty lucky for us. You've told me that you've taken on a farmhand. You did the right thing, but why now, at the end of the season? Aren't there enough moochers out in the stable during the winter? It would have been better to hire him on at the beginning of the spring.*
>
> *My captain is a good person and he treats me well. He gives me packs of cigarettes and even coffee, the real stuff. I think he might even send me home on leave and that would be a wonderful thing, but I don't want to get up my hopes or yours. Last week he was about ready to let me go, but then he changed his mind. Every now and then I think about harvest time, how we'd sing and then all have dinner together and drink the new wine and it makes me cry.*
>
> *I hear that Rosina has married. Let's hope this husband of hers treats her well. If he doesn't, I'll go looking for him as soon as I get back, all the way to Florence or wherever he is.*
>
> *I hope you stay in good health.*
>
> *Your son,*
>
> *Raffaele*

He signed his name Raffaele instead of Floti like everyone called him at home to show them that since he'd been in the soldiers he'd learned to do things right.

Everything changed suddenly in the fall. One night in October, the Austrians and their Germans allies carried out a surprise attack, with an amazing show of firepower. The

Italian forces were not expecting it and were overwhelmed. Terrain which had been nibbled away from the enemy meter by meter over two years of hard fighting, at the cost of tremendous loss of life, was gone in a matter of hours. More than half a million men abandoned the positions they had held for months and months, and scattered down roads, country lanes, paths, running from the enemy in pursuit. Entire field armies were surrounded and tens of thousands of soldiers were taken prisoner. Panic, confusion and terror reigned and not even the officers knew what to do. The lines of communication were interrupted, the enemy artillery strafed roads, bridges and fords. It was like doomsday. Many tossed away their weapons, and thought that if the others did the same the war would be over.

Floti retreated with the others in his unit but they all stayed together, without losing sight of one another. Captain Cavallotti knew what he was doing: he had had them collect all available ammunition and load the machine guns, gasoline jugs and provisions onto the trucks.

"If we stick together," he said, "we can make it. If we split up we're lost. The Austrians will capture us and send us off to rot in prison camps, off to die of hunger and hardship and humiliations. They hate us, because we were their servants and we had the courage to attack them, and they'll make us pay dearly for it. There's even worse: if the *carabinieri* catch up with you, they'll put you in front of a firing squad for deserting. As long as you stay with me—as long as you have your uniforms, your insignia, your weapons and your commanders— you are a unit of the Italian army in retreat and any citizen is bound to provide you with aid and assistance. If we run into the enemy, we'll take up position and show them who we are. If we're stopped by our own, they'll let us know where we have to go and what we have to do. Let's get moving now. The Austrians could be upon us at any moment."

There wasn't enough room for all the men on the trucks, so about one hundred of them had to walk, but every six hours, the captain halted the column and those who were marching switched places with their comrades on the trucks. This system eliminated the need for rest stops, and when you were riding you could even get a little shuteye.

About four in the morning they saw a stronghold on their left with a unit of *Bersaglieri* who were taking heavy fire and Cavallotti said: "Those boys are going to lose their lives to allow us to pass and get to safety. Remember this when you're out of harm's way, and again when it's time to prepare the counterattack."

Floti knew he would remember this, even though it seemed completely senseless to him. It was bedlam, a furnace that devoured everyone and everything, a storm of fire and sword with no way out for anyone.

The boy sitting next to him on the truck was just a little over twenty. His arm was in a sling and his eyes were glazed over.

"Where are you from?" Floti asked.

"From Feltre, province of Belluno," he replied.

"What's wrong with your arm?"

"A mortar fragment, two days ago."

"Is the bone all right or did it break?"

"I don't know. It hurts a lot."

"If it's broken maybe you can go home."

"Let's hope," said the boy with a wispy voice and fell back into silence.

There was a Sicilian on the other side of him and two Sardinians opposite them. You couldn't understand a word of what they were saying, worse even than the guys from Bergamo. They almost always advanced at a crawl because the road was jammed with vehicles and soldiers, and sometimes they didn't move for hours, but the sound of the cannons never ceased. Instead of getting farther away it seemed closer and closer.

When it was time for them to switch places, Floti went to the captain, who was sitting in front next to the driver. "Sir, there's that boy from Feltre who's wounded. Can't he stay on the truck? I don't think he'll be able to walk for six hours in his condition. He's white as a ghost and he can hardly get a word out."

"All right," replied the captain. "Let him stay on the truck."

One of those who'd been walking for six hours found himself without a ride and he began whining and complaining.

"Cut it out," Floti told him. "What are you moaning about? When it's time to switch again, I'll do a double shift walking."

And he started to march, careful to stay within calling distance because it was too dark to see. Three hours later, the truck had to stop because the road was blocked by a vehicle at the head of the column that had broken an axle and couldn't go forward or backward. Floti went over to the boy in the truck and put a hand on his forehead: it was very hot. He went back to the commander.

"Sir, that kid's burning up. A bad sign, from what I know."

"Yes. It means there's an infection."

"Isn't there a hospital around here?"

"A hospital? You're joking. We won't find one before Udine. And even if we manage to get that far, can you imagine how overrun they'll be with casualties coming in from the front?"

"Then there's nothing we can do for that poor boy?"

"We can bury him, when it's time, and write to his family; there's nothing else we can do, Bruni. You can see that yourself."

He could see that himself.

But he couldn't believe it. There the kid was, sitting on the back of the truck, his face red with fever and his eyes glistening in the glow of the taillights. He was moving and thinking and breathing and yet in just a short time he would be nothing.

Finally the column started up again and the trucks, with their retinue of foot soldiers, rolled forward. Fatigue was setting in with every step for the walkers, because the food they had was distributed very sparingly, just enough to keep them alive and moving. It was running out nonetheless and soon they'd have none left. In the middle of the night, when they had almost come within sight of the plains and the lights of distant convoys glittered in the darkness, there was a moment of near silence. Not a voice could be heard in the cold night. The truck had stopped once again and the engine was idling, when the still air was rent by the tolling of a bell, like hammer blows from the sky: one, two, three strokes, then two shorter, shriller ones. It was three thirty.

"There's a town here," said Floti. "What town, I wonder."

"Who knows?" replied the soldier closest to him, a young man with curly black hair and a Neapolitan accent.

"Anyone live around here?" called out Floti a bit louder, turning around. A sergeant of about forty with reddish hair and whiskers stepped up.

"We heard the bells tolling: what town is near here?"

"Sant'Ilario? I might be wrong."

"Is there a hospital?"

"In Sant'Ilario? I doubt it," replied the sergeant with a shrug.

"Wait, see those lights down in the valley? That looks like a big town."

The sergeant nodded. "That's Cividale."

"Is there a hospital there?"

Captain Cavallotti suddenly appeared out of nowhere. "Bruni, I know what you're feeling. I've felt the same way myself many a time, but there's nothing to be done. If you don't resign yourself to that, you'll go mad. We're trying to break out of the Austro-Hungarian encirclement, and we can't afford to stop. Set your heart at rest, boy: there are no hospitals, there are no doctors or medicines, there isn't a damn thing. It's time to get moving again."

They continued without interruption down the long mountain ridge, and then the long snake of men and vehicles stretched out into the valley heading towards Cividale. The cannon salvos behind them shook the mountains and filled the sky with lightning, like a storm. The boy with the bandaged arm was leaning against the inside of the truck as if he were yielding to sleep. Every turn and pothole jerked him around like a puppet.

They continued in this way until close to dawn, when there was another forced halt. Cavallotti appeared again: "No fear, men, we're past the worst. I believe we've distanced them sufficiently so that they won't catch up to us."

Floti approached the wounded boy and touched his brow with the back of his hand: he was burning up, and when Floti felt his pulse there was a constant throbbing instead of a steady beat. He had begun ranting as well. Confused sounds came from his lips: curses, perhaps, or prayers. Nothing that made sense.

Floti jumped off the truck and walked ahead of the convoy for a while to clear his mind. After a short stretch of road, behind a rocky outcropping, he spotted a tent with a light on inside. There was a red cross painted on the canvas. He immediately turned back at a run: "Captain! There's a field hospital just a hundred meters from here!" Without waiting for a reply, he got the others to help him unload their feverish comrade from the truck. They placed him on a stretcher and ran him over to the tent. A number of wounded men were piled up at the entrance, several of them more dead than alive. Bone-chilling screams, weeping and cursing could be heard from inside.

The soldiers stared at each other in that first pale light of dawn, seeing faces the color of mud, sunken, darkly-ringed eyes, dry, cracked lips and bewildered expressions.

"I'll go," said Floti. "You wet his lips with a little water," he added, leaving his flask with them. He went in.

There was a big table covered with blood at the center of the tent and, behind it, a man wearing an apron so soaked with blood it was dripping. A couple of nurses were laying a semiconscious man whose leg had been amputated onto the ground. The limb was sticking out of a wooden laundry tub.

Two soldiers and a nurse were depositing on the table another soldier whose abdomen was ripped open; he'd lost his voice with screaming but hoarse noises were still coming out of his open mouth. If the sight was unbearable, the smell was worse, and Floti had to swallow hard to stop himself from retching.

"What the hell do you want?" shouted the doctor. "Piss off, can't you see what we're doing here?"

Floti nodded and turned back towards the exit, mumbling a swear word in dialect under his breath.

"What'd you say?" yelled back the doctor in the same dialect.

Floti stopped in his tracks without turning around and answered in good Italian: "I think you know if you asked me that question, sir."

"Come over here," said the doctor. "Where are you from?"

"Province of Bologna."

"Me too. You're the first one I've seen. What d'you want?"

Before Floti could answer, the patient on the table gave one last gasp and went limp.

"This one's gone," said the doctor. "Take him away. We'll stop for a minute here. I have to catch my breath."

He handed Floti a bench, took a pack of cigarettes from his vest pocket and held it out to Floti. He lit one up himself and took a long pull.

"Lieutenant, sir," began Floti, having checked the rank on the doctor's shoulder, "outside there's a boy who's just twenty years old. He's got an infected wound and he's at risk of dying. Can't you do something for him?"

"You know that if I stop to look at him, someone else will die in his place, don't you?"

"Each of us is concerned with those who we're close to and who we care about, sir. And that's a good thing."

"Right. *Mors tua vita mea*," said the doctor, quoting in Latin.

"In three minutes, you've spoken three different languages, sir," commented Floti, "but one is enough for me, you can answer me in dialect if you want. Can you give this kid a look, yes or no?"

The doctor ground out the cigarette stub under his boot and replied: "Have him brought in."

Floti motioned to his fellow soldiers, who lifted the stretcher and transferred the boy onto the table, just after a nurse had thrown a bucket of water over it to rinse it off. The doctor cut the bandages with scissors and exposed the wound. The boy's arm was swollen and inflamed and the infection had obviously worsened; the stink it gave off was unmistakable.

"I have to amputate," said the doctor, "or he'll die of gangrene."

The boy had heard everything and terror filled his eyes as they spilled over with tears.

There was a bottle of strong grappa on a nearby table. "It's all I have," said the doctor, "have him drink as much as he can." He wiped his brow with the back of his sleeve, then told his assistant to give the boy a piece of leather to bite down on and to hold him down.

"Blindfold him," he added. "It's better he doesn't see this."

Floti had the courage to watch while the doctor cut through the boy's flesh to the bone, then set down the saw and with a single thrust snapped the bone right above the elbow.

The boy's scream, muffled by the leather stuffed in his

mouth, sounded like the moaning of a butchered animal. The doctor clamped the veins that were spurting blood a meter away, disinfected the cut with alcohol and tincture of iodine and started to stitch up the wound. When he had finished he turned the boy over to the nurses and walked outside, exhausted, to breathe in the morning air.

Floti watched him while he lit up a cigarette; it was hard to believe that a human being could be capable of so much.

"How much of a chance does he have?" Floti asked him.

"Of surviving? Fifty, maybe sixty percent . . . depends on when he'll be able to get to a hospital. Without amputating, zero."

Floti nodded as if to approve the decision that had been made, then took his leave. "Maybe we'll see each other back home . . . after this is over. My name's Bruni, Raffaele Bruni. Who have I had the pleasure of meeting, sir?"

"Name's Munari," replied the officer. "Alberto Munari."

Floti looked back into the tent and caught a glimpse of the white bandages swaddling his comrade's fresh wound. He remembered that he didn't even know the boy's name, but what did it matter anyway? He looked at Lieutenant Munari again and saw that he even had blood on his mustache, which was neatly clipped.

"Good luck, sir," he said, and turned to get back to his unit.

"Good luck to you," said the doctor. "You'll need it."

Captain Cavallotti welcomed him back by hurling swear words his way. "Where the fuck did you go off to, Bruni? Half the army has passed this way already! Move it, for Christ's sake."

Floti jumped into the truck because he knew he couldn't take another step and he lay down on the floor at the feet of the other soldiers. He put his haversack under his head, covered himself as best he could with his cloak and tried to get some rest. He was so tired that despite the jolts, the din of the engine and the racket inside and outside the truck, he sank into a deep sleep, but then awoke with a start: the nightmare he'd just witnessed flooded his mind and spirit with pain. He couldn't start to imagine how he'd feel if he found himself from one day to the next without an arm, and his only consolation was thinking that he'd heard of soldiers who stepped on a landmine and lost both of their legs. This boy would surely pull through, otherwise why would destiny have put him on the path of someone like himself? Raffaele Bruni, known as Floti, someone who would find him a field hospital with a doctor who spoke Bolognese and could operate on him just in time, just before the infection had killed him. Why else?

They reached Cividale del Friuli the day after, at about one in the morning. An ocean of men, of trucks, of mules, of artillery pieces, soldiers from every corps and unit chasing frenetically from one end to the other of an enormous muddy clearing filled with tents, improvised fences and patrols of *carabinieri* crossing back and forth to prevent the general confusion from degenerating into chaos and panic. They would shoot on sight at the least hint of insubordination. Here and there, wherever it was possible to string up a power cable to provide some light, groups of officers huddled, intent on reorganizing the chain of command.

In the midst of that bedlam, Captain Cavallotti managed to find the pennant of his battalion and to report to the colonel. He returned just before dawn, visibly upset.

The Austrian army had cut through the Italian front like a knife through butter. There was talk of entire divisions encircled on every side with no possibility of escape. Fifty thousand, a hundred thousand, perhaps two hundred thousand prisoners: disastrous figures on the extent of the catastrophe were rife.

"We have to set out again immediately," said Cavallotti. "The entire front, from the Bainsizza to the Carso, has collapsed. The Austrians and the Germans are at our heels. General Cadorna is trying to organize a line of resistance at the Tagliamento. That's where we're going. That's where we'll stop running and we'll turn around and shoot. Good luck, boys."

CHAPTER EIGHT

C aptain Cavallotti's small army continued their retreat until not a drop of gasoline remained in the tanks. Then, having abandoned the trucks, they continued on foot, stopping now and then to rest and get a little shuteye curled up right there on the ground. Their food supplies had run out; all that was left were a few bottles of grappa, but Floti had never been able to drink on an empty stomach and he would have sold his soul for a hot *crescente* fritter stuffed with a slice or two of prosciutto. He remembered how that transparent rim of fat on the coral-red slice would melt on contact with the steaming freshly-fried surface of the *crescente*, releasing all the sublime essence of the cured pork. Dreams and memories of the rustic banquets enjoyed with his family filled his thoughts. Food fit for a king on their modest country table, set out on a lavender-scented hemp tablecloth.

He'd completely lost contact with anyone who could give him news of his brothers. The information that did filter through from overheard conversations among their officers bode nothing but ill: tremendous losses, tens of thousands of prisoners and many more than that missing in action, which meant slain or captured anyway. Since he was still alive, Floti reasoned that it was increasingly probable that any or all of his brothers were dead, wounded or imprisoned.

Whose turn had come? Checco? Or Armando, who'd been skin and bones his whole life? Dante or Fredo, or Gaetano? Or all of them? He got goose bumps just thinking about how

Clerice, and his father Callisto, would take it. There was no way they could survive the shock.

After travelling about thirty kilometers in a westerly direction, they came across another clearing center packed with soldiers and refugees. Dispatch riders sped around on their motorcycles and Red Cross nurses fluttered like white butterflies over a sea of gray-green uniforms. And yet the center reminded them of another life: there were automobiles in circulation, trucks loaded with bread and other provisions, and even a mail van.

Floti found a scrap of paper at the bottom of his haversack and a pencil that he sharpened with the blade of his bayonet and took advantage of the stop to write a letter to his parents. He informed them that there had been a great defeat, that the Germans and Austrians were still at their heels, and that he would be moving on with his unit to escape capture by the enemy. He also wrote that he'd had no news of the others and that since the telephone lines were out, like every other means of communication, he was not sure when he'd be in touch again, but not to worry, that he would try to manage somehow. He didn't have an envelope, so he folded the piece of paper in three, sealed it with the stub of a candle and wrote his parents' address on the back. He deposited it in a red mailbox with the Savoia coat of arms, hoping that it would reach its destination.

By the time they left the clearing center, the enemy were just a few hours behind them and were proceeding at a forced march. They proceeded towards Udine, but it soon became apparent that that city was lost as well. Floti realized immediately that they wouldn't be stopping when he saw the trucks coming with food, tents and ammunition. No one knew where they were headed, when their unceasing flight would end. One of the soldiers in Floti's battalion came from the mountains near home; his name was Sisto. Floti barely knew the fellow, because he wasn't the type of person he normally sought out, but Sisto, on the contrary, was always trying to strike up a conversation. That day he had started out by saying that the war was lost and so why not just toss your rifle and go back home. Floti nearly came to blows with him. "You damn idiot!" he said, pulling him aside, "you want to face a firing squad? If they hear you, you're dead." Sisto turned white; he hadn't had a clue of the risk he was running, and from then on, he never mentioned the topic again. It wasn't long before he saw for himself what Floti meant by those words.

It happened when they were near Codroipo, shortly before reaching the Tagliamento. As they were moving along the provincial road, trucks in the center and foot soldiers on either side, the soldier from Naples shouted out: "Look, an airplane!"

"It's ours!" shouted another.

"No, it's Austrian!" shouted the captain. "Take cover, everyone!"

Some of the men dove into the ditch at the side of the road, others sought shelter behind the trucks.

"It's on a reconnaissance mission," said the captain. "They're observing us, our conditions and our strength, to report back to their superiors."

"Let's shoot him down," said the sergeant, raising his carbine and taking aim.

"No!" Cavallotti stopped him. "You mustn't! If he dips down and you're following him with the barrel of your gun, you risk hitting one of us. It's happened before. Let him go, someone will show up to take care of him. Look, up there, that one's one of ours."

They all stopped in their tracks, noses in the air, to witness the air cavalry duel about to unfold. The Italian fighter plane homed directly in on the other frontally as if it meant to engage, then at the last minutes veered to the right and tried to put itself on the enemy's tail. The soldiers on the ground cheered the pilot on but the captain reprimanded them: "That's enough! Get back into line, we have no time to lose and they'll handle this one on their own. Sergeant, give the orders to march!"

No sooner had he said these words than they heard more shouting. It came from a nearby farmhouse, which appeared to be abandoned. As they got closer, they saw two *carabinieri* with their gray three-cornered hats and carbines slung over their shoulders escorting a young man out of the building with his hands tied behind his back. He must have been a soldier, although he couldn't have been any older than twenty. He was bawling at the top of his lungs. Cavallotti stopped with all his men behind him. The soldier was taken to the barn behind the house where a firing squad was standing in formation with their rifles at their sides.

Just then the crackle of machine gun fire could be heard and one of the two planes went into a spin and plunged to the ground, leaving a wake of smoke behind it.

"What's going on, sergeant?" asked Floti.

"Can't you see? They're executing him. He's a coward who shed his uniform and tried to escape."

"They're going to execute him? Just like that, without a trial?"

"It's called a court martial, Bruni," said Captain Cavallotti. "Ten minutes are all that's needed to find a man guilty of desertion." Floti, who already knew all this, nudged Sisto so he'd understand the lesson was for him.

The *carabinieri* tied the boy to a chair, facing the wall.

"He's to be shot in the back," observed the sergeant. "The punishment reserved for cowards and traitors. Maybe he's both."

The boy began weeping even louder as they blindfolded him. He cried out: "Mama, mama, help! Mamaaa!" calling for his mother like a little boy afraid of the dark.

The *carabiniere* officer ordered: "Platoon. About . . . face!"

The soldiers, who had been facing away from the barn, turned towards the prisoner.

"The squad never sees the condemned man," commented the sergeant, "and he never sees them."

Floti ignored him and turned to the captain. "But he's just a kid who's lost and terrified, they can't just kill him like that. Isn't there anything we can do, captain?"

Cavallotti did not answer, but it was clear that he'd had them stop for a reason. Funny how they weren't in a hurry anymore, the enemy wasn't right there at their heels. He wanted to give all of them a lesson. Show them what happens to someone who tries to get away.

The commanding officer drew his sword: "Platoon. Atten . . . tion!"

Floti lowered his eyes to the ground. The same voice rang out again, brusque: "Load!" That boy had only seconds left to live: he'd heard the metallic click of the rounds being pushed into the barrels. What was going through his head?

"Aim!" The rifle barrels converged towards the target.

He had stopped crying.

"Fire!"

He collapsed onto the chair. As the guns thundered, Floti felt his own heart stop for an instant.

He thought of Clerice waiting for him at home, fingering her rosary beads, awake at night in the dark, in her bed. He was sure that somewhere, someplace on the plains or in the mountains, the mother of that boy had heard his last silent plea, the words that never found their way out of teeth clenched in a spasm of terror. She must have collapsed as well wherever she was, out in the fields or in her house, her back sliding slowly down the wall as her eyes stared wide onto nothing.

Floti turned around and saw that Sisto had tears in his eyes. Cavallotti didn't say a word. He glared at the sergeant to ensure he would stay silent as well as they resumed their march.

Towards Codroipo. Towards the Tagliamento flowing gray and swollen between its banks. Entire divisions were heading towards the bridges, with their baggage trains and artillery pieces. The pounding of boots trudging wearily forward was the dull backdrop to that unending march. And yet that multitude of men, looking more like a herd than an army, carried their weapons and wore their uniforms and obeyed orders. The unrelenting discipline, paired perhaps with the conviction that there was no alternative to closing ranks, kept together the hundreds of thousands of soldiers in retreat.

The first to pass was the Third Army, under the command of the king's cousin, the Duke of Aosta. They could be distinguished at a distance because they were formed in rank and file and were marching in step, unit after unit, their officers at their head and flanks. They had lost none of their equipment and as soon as they crossed the Tagliamento they took up battle positions in order to cover the others who still had to pass. But that was not to be the main line of resistance. The king had personally decided that the front was to be established on the Piave, and declared that he was prepared to abdicate if that line of defense were to fall.

Floti and his comrades passed Udine as well on the night of October 30th, and it was there that Captain Cavallotti was informed by a message from the High Command that the new line of resistance would be the Piave river, while Mount Grappa would be the stronghold from which the artillery would keep the Austrians at bay if they attempted to break through.

Towards evening, when they had already set up camp, Floti saw a colonel arriving in the sidecar of a Frera. He had the captain summoned immediately and Floti was close enough to hear their conversation.

"How many men do you have, Cavallotti?"

"Six hundred and fifteen, sir."

"Arms?"

"Light arms and seven machine guns with ammunition."

"Good. This is the position your men will have to secure between the Priula Bridge and Mount Montello: this is a crucial point because Mount Montello will be one of the main objectives of the Austrian army. You'll have to hold them off, at any cost. The English and French commanders have arrived and are promising reinforcements."

"About time," replied Cavallotti.

"Yes, right, but don't be expecting too much: they have their own nuts to crack. Cadorna has ordered the Fourth Army to fall back from the whole region of Cadore beyond the Piave, so they can join up with the rest of our defensive front. Di Robilant won't be very happy but he'll have to comply. There's desperate need of his artillery to hold Mount Grappa."

Cavallotti nodded. "When?"

"Tomorrow at five you'll have to set off. Don't stop until you've reached your position. As soon as you arrive, dig in. Expect the Austrians to attack immediately. They won't give you a moment's respite."

"Yes, sir."

"I also wanted to tell you that we'll be calling two more years to arms: 1898 and 1899."

"'99? But they're children!"

"You have a son born in '99? Well, so do I, but we have no choice, Cavallotti. Good luck."

Floti felt his heart sink. 1899! Savino would be getting his summons from one day to the next. His parents would be alone, with just Maria and the farmhand. All seven brothers, whoever was still alive, would be lined up on the Piave.

But where?

He thought of those men with their fancy sounding names—at least they sounded fancy to his ears—deciding the destiny of hundreds of thousands of fellow human beings just by signing a line on a sheet of letter paper, those manicured fingers moving a pen over paper and moving entire divisions. It reminded him of the talks he used to have with Pelloni.

The next morning they started their march and didn't stop until they saw the Piave. It was much bigger than the Samoggia back home; it was in flood and its waters were raging and foaming. It must have rained a lot up in the mountains.

"Men, look!" exclaimed the captain. "The river is on our side! We'll blow up the bridges after we've crossed them and the Austrians will never get across with the water so high."

Floti couldn't help but think that the Austrians and the Hungarians hadn't done anything wrong. They were shooting at them because they had been ordered to, just like him, and if someone didn't want to shoot they'd execute him, just like that poor boy they'd seen before arriving at Codroipo. He thought of what the captain had always told them, and it did seem right that each population should be independent and not ruled by foreigners who spoke a different language. But in the end, the only thing that really counted was saving your life and he hoped that his brothers would be spared as well. Not just for their sake, but for their parents, who would never be able to bear such a terrible loss.

Before mid-November, the rumor got out that General Cadorna had been dismissed and that the king had put a Neapolitan general named Armando Diaz in his place. Floti waited until he had the opportunity to ask Captain Cavallotti what kind of man this new general was, struck by the fact that his name was Armando like his own brother's.

"He's a good person," replied Cavallotti. "He has had a lot of experience on the field, and he's a man who thinks that soldiers are not animals, and that it doesn't help to beat them down. That their courage will not falter if they are given good reasons for fighting."

Floti would have liked to say that he didn't know any good reasons, but he thought it better to keep his mouth shut under the circumstances. Cavallotti, however, seemed to have read his mind. "I know what you're thinking, Bruni," he said, "and you're right, in part, but you don't know what's really at stake here; you have to take a step back, and understand how the Italians have suffered for centuries over the loss of their liberty and independence. A nation is something like a family, you have to stick together. And when a stranger comes into one of our houses he has to ask permission, doesn't he, and behave like a guest, not like the boss. What's more, the fruit of our labor must remain here at home. And those of us who are better off must help those who are worse off."

Floti nodded without saying a word and Cavallotti concluded his speech: "I know we've seen too many deaths, far too many. I don't sleep at night over it, don't think otherwise. But I never send my men into danger's way if I can help it."

"That's a good thing, sir," said Floti, plucking up his courage, "because it's not like their mothers bought them at the market. Their mothers conceived them and gave birth to them and stayed awake with them at night when they were ill and fed them the best they had, so they could grow up and live as long as possible. Let's hope this new general thinks the way you do."

Cavallotti dropped his head in silence for a moment, then went outside to check the cannon stations. Before nightfall he promoted Floti to corporal.

For at least their first two months there, they had no contact with other contingents and Floti could get no news about his brothers. From one day to the next, new soldiers were constantly being added to the line of troops along the Piave to comply with the king's orders that no enemy be let through. As soon as the new year started, the latest recruits began to report for duty, boys of eighteen and nineteen. Floti continuously scanned the units to see if he could spot Savino, but it would have been easier to win the lottery. That didn't dissuade him and, whenever he could, he'd stop one of the new boys and ask: "Have you ever met a lad called Savino Bruni?" And it didn't discourage him if they looked at him like he was crazy or if they replied with a shrug or with a "what the fuck?"

Once Floti saw that even the impossible can happen. An *Alpino* of about forty-five wearing a sergeant's stripes, at the head of his company, was returning from the trenches, covered with mud from head to foot except for the black raven feather on his cap. Under the rain that had begun to fall from a gray sky, his boots were beating time as all his men marched behind him, formed into rank and file. Dead tired as they were, soaked to the bone, some of them wounded, they kept the pace like a single man. All at once, as they were crossing paths with their replacement unit—all *bocia*, as the Alpine soldiers called the youngest troops—one of the foot soldiers cried out: "*Bepi! Bepi!*" Half a dozen of them wheeled around as if they'd been ordered to perform a half turn to the left, but he was interested in just one, the one with the light blue eyes and the freckles. Bepi too abandoned the ranks, heedless of the cursing of his sergeant and the two of them embraced in the middle of the field. Both units stopped and the non-commissioned officers who commanded them did not have the heart to separate father from son.

As time passed, the pressure continued to mount: the cannonades were continuous and the Austrians were forever attempting to cross the river; in the end, they succeeded, managing to establish two bridgeheads on the right bank of the Piave.

One day, Captain Cavallotti, who had struggled to set up a tent which provided some semblance of an administrative office, gave his men orders to pack up everything and send all the documents over to the engineers' headquarters.

"We have to take up our rifles, Bruni," he told Floti, "all of us, down to the last man, because if we don't push them back this time, it's over. Venice will fall, and all the rest with it. Do you know how much sacrifice it took to create Italy? We've been fighting for almost one hundred years. We have to finish the job once and for all, and then we'll be done with it. I know what you're thinking: 'France or Spain, who gives a damn, as long as there's food on our plates,' but only a nobody reasons that way. Only animals and slaves have masters: are you an animal, Bruni? No, you're not. Are you a slave? No." He was answering all of his own questions. "Now we can finally afford to be free men, all of us, cost what it may."

"To tell you the truth, sir, I do have a master back at home. He's a notary named Barzini. We work his land, he does nothing and takes more than half of everything."

"We'll take care of that, too, Bruni, but now let's worry about this army that's invading our country. I've armed even the members of the band, Bruni: guns instead of trombones and clarinets."

That was true. Floti had seen the guys from the band in the trenches, and they weren't half bad as shots.

From the two bridgeheads, the Austrians were battering Mount Montello and Mount Grappa incessantly, and from his post Floti could see hell being unleashed over the dominion of those two peaks. Cannons rumbled in the distance and columns of smoke rose with fire inside. The volcanoes in the south of Italy must be something like this, he thought. Everyone was expecting the Italian front to collapse all at once, like at Caporetto, and then that would be the end of everything.

Instead, that's not the way it went.

Assault after assault, the Austrians were pushed back. Could the fear of a firing squad alone be a sufficient explanation for all of this, Floti wondered. Why didn't all those proletarians rebel and start shooting at the *carabinieri* instead of at their comrades of the Austro-Hungarian proletariat, as Pelloni would have suggested. Apparently this whole thing was not very easily explained, but Floti had come up with his own idea while fighting at the front: he'd seen that the Neapolitan general who was commanding now and whose name was the same as his brother's didn't send his men to the slaughter, his soldiers; he asked them to hold fast but not to get themselves massacred by charging the machine guns bare-chested. The food was better, the shoes were sturdier, the grappa and the cigarettes were better quality. It didn't take much, all told, to stop them from feeling like cannon fodder: a little respect and a bit of consideration. And then there was the river, so big and so beautiful, that had to be defended at all costs, and before you knew it you ended up believing in it and doing your part.

One evening Floti crawled over to a derelict building near the riverbank to see if he could see for himself any traces of this offensive everyone was talking about. But it had become too dark and he couldn't make out much at all. Then he heard a light lapping of waves along the shore, and saw dark shapes intent on sliding small boats into the water; one man to a boat, they stretched out inside and used their arms as oars. There were a number of them: two, three, five, all dressed in black. Maybe half a dozen in all. They were crossing the river to the opposite side, where Franz Joseph's empire began. Well, not his any longer, the old man was dead, so his son's empire. They were using the current to their advantage, cutting across on the diagonal until they touched land.

All at once, as he was getting ready to turn back, he felt a boot crushing down on his back and something hard like a gun barrel pressing into the nape of his neck.

"What are you doing out here, handsome? Shouldn't you be asleep?"

"Listen," replied Floti. "I'm from the thirty-eighth. I just wanted to take a look because I heard there was going to be a big offensive."

The man with the boot, a big burly fellow, black as ink, flipped Floti over with his foot and planted the rifle in the middle of his chest instead. "You wouldn't be a spy, would you? Figuring how to make it across? If I wasn't afraid of making noise, I'd shoot you here and now just to be on the safe side."

"Are you crazy? I can't swim and all I know how to say in German is *kartoffen*."

"It's *kartoffeln*, you cunt."

"Right, okay, but let me up, will you? I have to get back to my unit. My commander is Captain Cavallotti, I'm Corporal Raffaele Bruni and I'm no cunt."

"Then get the hell out of here. Let's say you were lucky this time. If I catch up with you again I'll put you to bed with a shovel. Got that?"

"You bet," replied Floti. He got up, dusted himself off and headed back to the camp.

He told the captain what he had seen as he was bringing him a cup of coffee the next day.

"Those were *Arditi*. Special assault units," the officer explained. "They more or less swim across the river and when they get to the other bank, they take out the sentries with their daggers, lay mines and blasting gelatin, sow terror and mayhem, and then cross back over. You saw the Caimans of the Piave, Bruni, not everyone can say that," he concluded.

Time passed. Days and months. Whole seasons. The trenches filled with muck up to your knees became dusty instead as spring turned into summer, but Floti still had no news of his brothers. He received a letter from his parents once, three months after they'd asked the parish priest to write it, saying that they hadn't heard from anyone and that his father Callisto could find no peace, could think of nothing but where his sons were, whether they were alive or dead. Floti wrote back, but got no answer. Who could guess at the destiny of a single sheet of paper in this hellish situation.

One day at the beginning of June, Captain Cavallotti told him that something was in the air, another offensive, most probably, starting very soon. The Austrians already had five bridgeheads on the right bank of the Piave and were trying to consolidate them. The rumor was that they wanted to push all the way through to the Po.

In the following hours, one courier followed another and soon the whole camp was seething with activity. A great number of airplanes began to cross the sky—it was astonishing to see so many all at once—and armored vessels could be seen on the river. The groundwork for land, water and air battles was swiftly being laid. They had never seen anything like it.

Then the attack began in earnest, on June the 15th: the Austrians, from their bridgeheads, opened their big guns to prepare the way for their infantrymen who were meant to storm Mount Grappa and Mount Montello, the Italian strongholds which stood in the way of their advance and still had the firepower to hammer thirty kilometers of territory all around.

In a short time the din from the mouths of twenty thousand cannons made the air quiver all along the flow of the Piave, and two hours after the start of the offensive Floti's unit was sent to the attack, with rifles first and then with their bayonets. Once, twice, three times on the same day. And again the next day. They returned at night with barely enough energy to force down some cold rations. Three days later, Floti could not believe he was still alive. It was a miracle he was still steady on his feet, because he hardly ever slept. He would nap when he could, leaning on a tree or propped behind a wall, when there was a lull in combat. The Austrians had crossed at a number of points, by laying footbridges on the shores of the river, and they launched wave after wave of powerful, head-on attacks in an attempt to break through, but the front continued to hold fast.

That evening there was an assembly of the regiment and the colonel told them that their mates on Mount Grappa and Mount Montello had fought like lions, driving back the enemy and putting them to rout. As long as the mountain strongholds held, the whole line of the front could count on being protected from behind. The enemy had suffered tremendous losses, because the air force had done its part by machine gunning the fleeing soldiers from the air. The French and English allies had made an important contribution on the high plateau of the Seven Communities, and had seen for themselves how bravely the Italian soldiers were fighting.

"We can do this, boys!" shouted the colonel finally. "We can do it! All of Italy is talking about you. Your families will learn of your valor and they will be proud of what you've done here."

The troops responded this time with shouts of enthusiasm, and Floti was surprised to find himself yelling with the others. "There's no accounting for what's in your heart," he thought to himself as the officers gave the order to fall out.

The Austrian offensive continued incessantly until the 20th of June and then little by little began to wane. By the 24th, the enemy army started to retreat. The Italian aviation and artillery gave them no respite and then even the infantry set off in pursuit of the Austrian troops as they attempted to flee over the footbridges they themselves had built to cross the Piave. It was a massacre.

Corporal Raffaele Bruni played his part, leading the company into the attack. He strove forward, his strength unbelievably holding out until, suddenly, he felt a burning pain on the left side of his chest and fell to his knees. His vision fogged over into a red cloud and the roar of the battle ended, all at once.

CHAPTER NINE

C hecco had dropped out of sight ages ago; no one in the family had received any word of him. No one knew that his regiment had been transferred to France to provide support for the French who were having a hard time of it. His unit had taken up quarters at Bligny, and Checco, an artillery private assigned to ammunition provision and transport, drove a Fiat 18 BL loaded with mortar rounds and 320s, machine gun belts, and tubes of gelatin for blasting holes in the German barbed wire entanglements.

He knew that he could be blown to high heaven at any moment: all it would take was a gunshot, a stray bullet, a deep pothole taken at high speed and goodbye Checco. But he hugely preferred this work to serving guns, loading rounds into barrels, breathing in cordite fumes day and night under an unrelenting downpour of metal and flames as the thunder of artillery fire rent the air. He thought he'd been lucky. If it was his turn to die it would be in a single go; he wouldn't even have the time to realize what was happening. And at least this work gave him plenty of time to gab with the fellow assigned to drive with him, a bricklayer who had emigrated to France. Sitting next to a friend, listening to the rumble of the engine and enjoying the scenery: not a bad job at all. At just twenty kilometers or so from the front, the countryside was just beautiful. The land dipped up and down in gentle slopes covered with vineyards lined up in perfect order, the grapevines low to the ground and much smaller than any he'd ever seen. How many grapes could they grow with such small vines? They certainly must have been easy to harvest, not like those back at home, more than two meters high, with shoots so long you had to keep moving the ladder to make sure you got everything, down to the last cluster.

What made him most curious was that there were no houses to be seen no matter how far you looked, and there weren't even any hedges marking boundaries. Where were the farmers? Just how big could those properties be? And how many harvesters would they need to pick all those grapes?

His travelling companion told him that the wine produced from those grapes was called "sham-pane" and that it was so precious that the row on the border between two plots, marked with a red rose bush, was harvested one year by one neighbor and the next year by the other. "What you can learn by travelling the world!" thought Checco.

He realized that sooner or later a replacement would arrive and he'd be sent up to the front line, where every day the war was killing thousands, and wounding or maiming thousands more who'd have to spend the rest of their days hobbling around on a wooden leg or hiding the stub of an arm in their shirtsleeve, unable to work and bring home bread for themselves and their families.

And this is exactly what happened, not two months later. He got an order signed by Captain Morselli, a Tuscan who was full of piss and vinegar but had a heart of gold, transferring him to a field battery twenty kilometers from his supply base.

"Oh, you," said the captain when he reported to headquarters with the order in hand, "you have to take turns like everyone else, Bruni; everyone wants to drive the truck and no one wants to serve the guns. But cheer up, the Austrians and Germans didn't succeed in breaking through at the Piave. Our men are holding the line and not letting those bastards make a move. If things continue this way, we may have good news soon . . . who knows, maybe even before Christmas."

Checco wasn't sure what the captain meant by that last phrase, but he thought of his brothers there holding down the bank of the Piave. If they were still alive, that was. Who knew how many of them were left. And whether his parents knew anything, or were in the dark like him.

The next day, at five in the morning, he was already at the front with his battery. The cannon rounds were so big it took four of them to pick each one up and load it. Then the gunner pulled the lever on the breech block, everyone covered their ears and off went the shot. The deflagration was so powerful it shook the ground under their feet and knocked the gun carriage backwards. Then Checco counted one, two, three, four and there was a second explosion as the projectile made contact, producing a blast even louder than the first, a blaze of fire then a huge cloud of smoke and dust that rose for dozens of meters. Cannon shot was falling thick and fast all around them, making the earth shudder painfully as if wounded to its deepest core. Maybe, before the war, that desert of holes, that blackened mess of stones that he saw before him, had been a field of wheat dotted with poppies or a pretty vineyard, like the one he used to drive his truck past every morning, down the little dirt roads that crisscrossed the countryside.

This went on for ten or twelve days, with continuous salvos from both sides, a rain of fire that never left him; it kept thundering in his head even after he'd returned to camp for the night.

Then, one day, he saw the advance of the tanks, iron monsters as tall as a house that spit flames and fire and roared and groaned so loud it burst your eardrums and turned your blood to water. A scene that he'd never forget, for as long as he lived. There was a space perhaps three hundred meters wide between the two battle lines, bombarded from one side and the other by an incessant artillery barrage. A heavy cloud of smoke hung there permanently, but that morning, from inside that cloud, Checco—who was on forward guard duty—could have sworn that he was hearing an intermittent sound that was getting closer and clearer with every passing moment. He could barely believe it, but he was listening to the words of a song, warbled out at a full yell:

"My darling Spanish songbird
Lovely as a flower in bloom . . . "

Then the source of those notes appeared and Checco was sure that he was seeing things. A two-wheeled wooden cart drawn by a pair of mules was lurching forward, sinking left and right into the holes left by the bombs, at risk of being over-turned at every bump. The unlikely vehicle was being driven by none other than Pipetta, a carter from his town who worked transporting gravel for making roadbeds and who was now approaching his position, getting nearer and nearer to the tanks and the no-man's-land being pounded by the artillery.

As soon as he had gotten over his shock, Checco took advantage of the dense curtain of smoke covering everything; he jumped out of the hole he'd been crouching in and ran over to a burnt-up tree stump. As Pipetta continued to wail his song, Checco started calling out: "Pipetta! Pipettaaaa! Stop, for god's sake, it's me, Checco!"

Pipetta tugged at the reins on his mules and, just as if they had run into each other one Sunday morning in the town square:

"Well, well, well. It's good to see you, milord!"

"Pipetta, what are you on about?" replied Checco. "Can't you see we're at the front?"

Pipetta had a laugh at this and turned his cart towards the tanks, in the midst of the crashing bombs, singing his song.

Checco started shouting: "Stop! Pipetta, stop, you idiot!"

But Pipetta wasn't listening anymore. He continued singing about a beautiful Spanish maiden at the top of his lungs and heading, completely unawares, into the mouth of the dragon. Checco left his shelter and dashed off behind him, but a grenade exploded almost immediately between him and the cart, and Checco was buried under a hill of debris. He had just enough time to think that at least he'd be making the journey to the next world with someone from his hometown.

Gaetano took part in the counterattack of Pederobba with his regiment, and since he was hefty and strong as an ox they had paired him up with others like him to lay the planks on the pontoon bridge being installed to allow the Grenadiers of the Sixth Army to cross over to the other side of the Piave. They were mounting a counterattack and the word was that the Austrians were in bad shape. They had also heard that the Duke of Aosta, the king's cousin, was launching an offensive on the other side of the river with the Third Army, the troops who had taken Gorizia the year before and had kept everyone hoping they would reach Trieste.

The weather was getting worse as the autumn neared, but who cared about the weather? Gaetano had fought four battles on the Isonzo, the battle of Ortigara and then Mount Montello. Two of his comrades had completely lost their hearing thanks to the pounding of eight thousand cannon mouths. Another had lost his sight, and now his eyes were only good for crying.

At first Gaetano had been scared to death and he'd often pissed his pants at the moment in which the lieutenant would shout "Forward, Savoia!" to order an attack. But then he learned how to stick the enemy with his bayonet before they stuck him. He, who had always refused to slaughter a pig because he felt badly for the poor animal that was squealing and struggling to get away, now killed people without batting an eye; he'd killed so many of them it really didn't matter much one way or the other.

He wanted out. He cared nothing about anything anymore. He wanted out and that was all, and the only way to get out was to win the damned war and to kill as many Germans and Austrians and Croatians and Hungarians as he could, even though they'd never done anything to him. They were trying to do the very same thing anyway, although none of them really knew why.

When the moment finally came, the artillery upstream of his position started laying down enough firepower to frighten God himself, while the bulk of the army crossed on the pontoon bridge further downstream at Pederobba. Gaetano had installed a great number of the heavy ash boards, freshly cut and still smelling of the sawmill where they had been made, that the infantry were now crossing on. They advanced in silence under the pelting rain, not marching in step, treading lightly so they would not give themselves away. All that could be heard was a confused scuttling, not easily noticed against the rush of the current, as the Piave pooled up for a moment amidst the pontoons of the bridge before breaking and running free and fast towards the sea.

Gaetano was one of the last to cross so he and his team could ensure that the bridge was still usable. But not because they would be crossing back, there was no going back anymore. Because the bridge would be needed for guaranteeing supplies and ammunition to the advancing army.

All at once he thought he heard voices, a whispered song. A battalion of *Bersaglieri*, you could tell from the clusters of feathers perched on their helmets. They were singing in such low voices he had to strain his ears. It wasn't a war song, or who knows, perhaps it was . . . It sounded like certain songs sung at harvest time in an old dialect that you couldn't understand entirely. Something about a girl's heartache because her fiancé had left for the war and she'd heard nothing from him since. Gaetano thought it would be nice to have a fiancée who was waiting at home pining away with love for him, but he didn't have anyone. Once he got back he'd have to look for a girl and start up a family.

The advance lasted six days in all, without ever stopping. Sometimes entire units of the Austro-Hungarian army, surrounded on every side, surrendered along with the officers who commanded them. They'd had enough of the war as well; they didn't believe in what they were doing anymore. Every man for himself and God for all. Everything around them was gone; there was nothing but rubble, razed houses, whole towns where the only thing left standing, barely, was the church bell-tower. A few emaciated chickens still strutted around abandoned farmhouses, and a rare cow witnessed the soldiers' passage with her big damp eyes, unmoving under the rain.

As they proceeded, a sort of excitement was spreading among the troops and the officers. Victory was suddenly seeming altogether possible, and with it, the end of the war. Even Gaetano felt caught up in the mood. After so many months of bloody battles, of slaughter and destruction, he'd come to the conclusion that wars should never be fought because they only bring havoc and ruin and they don't solve anything, but that if you had to make war, it was better to win than to lose. Not much is gained, but at least you feel like you'd fought for something. A bit like at home in the winter in the stable when he used to play a hand of *briscola* without stakes. He would rather win, anyway.

The third of November—he would remember this for the rest of his life—the Austrians surrendered. On the fourth the war was over.

CHAPTER TEN

C hecco woke up on a hospital cot and for a few minutes couldn't tell whether he was dead or alive. He soon realized it was the latter, because there wasn't a single inch of his body that didn't hurt. He felt like a whole truckful of stones had been dumped on him.

"Well, it's about time!" said a voice. "You're finally awake, you worthless bag of scum! I've always said that layabouts have all the luck."

Checco recognized the medical officer who was looking at him and chewing on a Tuscan cigar stub. "What happened, sir?"

"What happened is that you saved your ass. Your regiment was decimated while they were trying to stop the Germans. They fought like lions, while you were comfortably stretched out in a bed, you slacker."

"But sir," Checco tried to explain, "I don't even know how I got here." He sat up and brought a hand to his forehead, sighed, coughed, spit and started to touch himself all over. He was full of bruises, his skin looked rubbed raw, and his feet were burnt as though he'd been walking on live coals. "All I remember is that Pipetta was driving his two-mule cart straight into a tank, singing that 'darling Spaniard' song. And that he'd just called me milord."

"What the fuck . . . what on earth are you saying?" burst out the doctor.

"No, really," replied Checco. "And then a bomb went off and I said 'I'm dead.' And that's all."

He looked around him: he was in a big, open room full of cots like his own with hundreds of the sorriest looking fellows he'd ever seen. Some were missing legs, some arms, some both. They were swaddled in bloodstained gauze, heads bandaged, many were groaning, some asking for water, others yelling "Nurse! Nurse!" Some were cursing loudly and others were calling for their mothers, Jesus Christ and the Madonna. As he slowly began to regain awareness, Checco took in the hell, or the purgatory, that surrounded him. In the meantime, the doctor had put a bottle of grappa to his mouth and swigged down a good mouthful, and had disappeared down the main corridor, swearing, hawking and spitting.

Then a volunteer nurse stepped in, wearing a snow white apron and a stiff, starched cap sporting a red cross, her chest thrown out like a *Bersagliere*'s, carrying a tray with a syringe and some phials. She walked straight to his cot, told him to roll over and before he knew what was happening stuck a needle in his rear end.

"There you are," she said, "You're cured. You can go back to your regiment tomorrow."

Checco rubbed his butt for a while, then turned on his side and tried to sleep. He thought that, after all, he was luckier than those other poor devils who were suffering the pains of hell in that bare, cold room. He thought of Pipetta who certainly was not singing anymore and it brought a lump to his throat.

The morning after, a nurse gave him his release papers. He collected what was left of his uniform and his shoes and received instructions on how to reach regiment headquarters. He got dressed, put his feet on the ground and, one step after another, made it to the exit. It was sunny outside.

His comrades had indeed stopped the Germans but many of them had met their ends doing so. His captain was gone:

killed in combat. Another arrived and called them to assembly, to tell them that the French general thanked them and praised their courage because their sacrifice had served to stop the Germans from opening the road to Paris.

Next to Checco was his emigrant bricklayer friend, his partner on the munitions delivery truck. He turned to Checco and said: "That's no small thing; the French never thank anyone, least of all the Italians. They feel entitled to everything that comes their way."

The officer went on to say that the worst was over and that the Germans would no longer be able to break through, and announced the Italian counterattack on the Piave.

"What day is it today?" Checco asked his friend.

"The 25th of July," the other answered.

Checco did some figuring in his head and realized he'd been in the hospital for more than three weeks, meaning that he must not have been in very good shape when they had taken him in, and if they hadn't sent him home on sick leave they must have been banking on more trouble in store, and no small amount of it.

There were about three more weeks of trouble and then, almost suddenly, they got the news they'd be going home.

Home.

Unbelievable. He tried not to think about it, afraid that the next thing they'd hear was that there had been a mistake, that it wasn't true. But no. One morning he said goodbye to his emigrant bricklayer friend because he was staying in France where he had a family, with a wife and son who spoke French.

"So long, Beppe!" Checco told him. "If you come back to Italy someday, come visit me. When you get to my town, just ask for Hotel Bruni, that's what they call our place. Anyone will be able to tell you where it is."

"So long, Checco," replied the other, slapping him on the back. "Good luck!"

Then each went his own way.

Checco was taken to a station and put on a train all full of tricolor flags: some with blue and some with green. For hours and hours, and for dozens of stops, the station names were French. It was night and then it was day and the names became Italian: Ventimiglia, Albenga, Genova. There you go, Genova was a place he'd heard of and he even knew someone who'd been there. Was Genova where the ships that sailed across the ocean to America left from?

As the convoy proceeded, soldiers got out, some in one place and some in another, to change trains and head to other cities, other countrysides, in the mountains or at the seaside, back to the towns they'd abandoned to come to the front. And what would they find once they made it back? What would Checco find at home? It made him shudder to think about it. After the enthusiasm for the end of the war came fear, panic even, at the sole thought of the misfortunes that must have befallen his family since he'd left, roosting like crows on the roof of the house.

The entire nation was full of flags because that last piece of Italy had been reunited with the rest of the country. It had cost them dearly but what's done is done and it was time to look ahead. In many stations, there was a band playing the royal march and rendering honors to the returning soldiers. Those who were hobbling on crutches, those who were still walking, those who wept and those who were struck dumb, incredulous at setting foot on the land where they were born. Another day and another night passed and when the train stopped, a voice shouted: "Modena! Modena Station!"

Checco startled and looked around him: many of his travel companions were getting out and stumbling, still half-asleep, past the band playing the royal march and an ode to the river Piave. He stayed on, waiting for the next stop, where there certainly would be no band to greet him.

The train started up again and the music faded away behind the last car. Checco began to recognize the places they were passing and he felt his heartbeat quicken: Fossalta, the bridge of Sant'Ambrogio; it would only be a few minutes now. A soldier with a haversack on his back walked past him. For god's sake: it was Pio Patella! A day laborer who lived on Via Menotti.

"Hey, Pio!" he called out in their local dialect. "Pio, where you goin'?"

Pio turned. "That you, Checco?"

Of course it was him, who else could it be? Not that they had ever been great friends, but running into each other like this, after three years of war and both of them headed to the same town seemed like a miracle. A wonderful miracle. They'd walk the last kilometers together.

The train came to a halt and they got out, but Pio decided to stop in on his sister, who lived close to the station. So Checco set off on his own with his haversack on his shoulders. It was just after All Saints and All Souls; the scent of maple leaves was in the air and the red hawthorn berries sparkled amidst the rust-colored leaves of the hedges. The robins and wrens hopped from one branch to another and regarded him curiously with eyes black and bright as pinheads. Every now and then a dog would bark at him and run back and forth on his chain strung up on a line extending from the house to the shed. Once he had walked past, the dog would stop his barking and settle down with a whimper, resigned to the same old life. A dog's life.

The air was fresh and the sun shone cold in a clear sky.

He passed in front of Pra' dei Monti and glanced over at the four hills dug up here and there by the occasional treasure hunter. He wasn't worried; the golden goat wouldn't be putting in any more appearances, because no disaster could be greater than the war that had just ended. And if it ever did reappear, it would be on a night of tempest with thunder shaking the earth and lightning rending the black clouds, or in a snowstorm, with flakes falling fast through the night sky. Certainly not on a clear morning in November.

He got to the sluice on the creek and then to the spot the women favored for washing, and there they were, beating the laundry against the stones and singing to take their minds off the cold that was numbing their fingers. He reached the footbridge and then the path lined with lindens that led to Signor Goffredo's villa. As he got closer to town, just past the San Colombano mill, he began to run into people, but no one made a fuss over him; just a little nod, or a half smile, if that. This made him very uneasy, and he took it as a sign that the end of the war had brought little joy to his town. A sign that a lot of men were still missing and perhaps would never come back, a sign that those that had made it back were not the same as when they'd left: wounded, disabled, maimed.

He finally reached the square: Poldo's brick wall was still there, on the left, with vine shoots curling over the tiles at its top, and there was the fountain with its piston pump at the center. The church was there on the right, with its image of the Sacred Heart on the lunette over the door, as was the bell tower that marked time for the whole town: births, weddings, deaths. And right at that moment, the big bell began slowly ringing a death knell. At that same instant, four gravediggers left the oratory carrying a litter made of wood. Walking behind them was the priest, wearing a purple stole and white lace surplice over his black cassock. An altar boy carried the holy-water bucket and sprinkler.

They passed alongside the tower and then went past the People's House and Checco had the impression they were about to turn right along the ditch, but they headed straight on instead, nearly as if they were opening the path for him. They passed the pharmacy and the Osteria della Bassa, and Checco was sure they'd continue towards Madonna della Provvidenza. He realized instantly that, more than conjecture, his thought expressed hope. Instead they turned right, walking through the fields and continuing towards the fork and Checco tried to convince himself that it would be there that they would part ways. At this point, he was less than half a kilometer from home. He would soon be hugging his mother and his father; maybe some of his brothers had already returned, Gaetano, or Floti . . .

The little funeral procession turned left precisely where he would soon be turning left himself, and he realized with great relief that just before the Via Celeste crossroads lived old Signora Preti, who had already been in sad shape when he'd left. Surely they were going to fetch her body.

Instead they turned into the Bruni courtyard.

The first one to see Checco was Maria, who was in the farmyard feeding the chickens. She ran towards him and threw her arms around him, weeping. She couldn't manage to say a word. Clerice arrived almost immediately. She hugged him and kissed him and then lowered her head to dry her eyes with the corner of her apron. "Your father, Checco. He didn't make it. Such a long time without hearing anything about you boys, so many terrible stories from the front. He was convinced that at least half of you wouldn't come back because those were the numbers we were hearing from the front. Or worse. I tried time and time again to tell him we mustn't lose heart, but he wouldn't listen."

"*Mamma*, where are the others?"

"They're not here, Checco. You're the first to return, and you've found this awful welcome. Come now, come and say goodbye to your father before they take him to the cemetery."

They went inside. Checco looked at his father and tears filled his eyes. They had arranged the body in a coffin, four elmwood boards nailed together, dressed in the only good suit he had, with a white hemp shirt buttoned all the way up and a rosary intertwined in his ashen hands. He had a two-day beard because no one had shaved him for fear of cutting his skin.

"He tormented himself. Every night I'd hear him sighing, 'Where can our boys be, Clerice? Who knows where on earth they are.' And he would twist and turn in his bed. He could find no peace. He hardly slept at all. How often I heard him weeping! When he saw soldiers passing by, with their haversacks and guns, looking dead tired and worn out, he'd call out to them: 'Come inside, boys, eat and drink!' and when they'd left, he'd say, 'Maybe someone's doing the same with our sons.' Your father was a good man, Checco, I couldn't have found a better one. He loved you boys as if he'd given birth to you himself. He died of a broken heart because you were gone."

The gravediggers were waiting to nail on the lid and take him away. Checco put a hand on his icy forehead and said: "Why didn't you wait for me, *papà* . . . at least one day, so I could say goodbye." Clerice gave him a kiss and covered her face with her hands. The priest sprinkled holy water on the elm box and murmured some prayers, then the gravediggers put the coffin on the litter and walked out the door as the priest began loudly reciting the rosary.

Meanwhile, the courtyard had filled with people from town, friends, relatives. Clerice took off her apron, patted down her hair and began following her husband's coffin, arm-in-arm with Checco and Maria. Behind them walked the women, kerchiefs on their heads, then the stable hand, and last of all the men wrapped in their long cloaks and carrying their hats. In church, the platform was ready, covered by a black cloth edged in yellow. The pastor said the mass and added a brief eulogy, saying that Callisto was a good Christian and that the Lord would certainly welcome him into heaven.

The procession headed to the cemetery and the gravediggers didn't even need to be relieved of their burden, because old Callisto was skin and bones and didn't weigh a thing.

Checco didn't have the heart to watch them put him in the ground, his father, and he left. He wandered through the fields for a long time. A bit of fog was beginning to rise, and he realized that he would be the one to worry now about who was or wasn't coming back. He thought of when the postman would arrive with a letter carrying bad news and how he would have to tell his mother. That would be tough; as the proverb said, "A husband gets into your dress, but a child gets into your heart."

When he got home he had a bowl of soup brought out to the stable, as if he were a traveler who had happened upon Hotel Bruni for the night, and he stretched out on the hay because he knew he wouldn't be able to fall asleep in his bed. It was late when he heard Clerice come in. She pulled his army overcoat up so that it covered his shoulders, like when she would come to tuck him in when he was little, but he said nothing and pretended to be sleeping.

A week later Gaetano returned. He was all in one piece but he was dumbfounded to hear that their father had died and that they'd just buried him. He wasn't expecting it; he'd long dreamed of the moment in which he would set foot in the courtyard and embrace his parents again before he went to see the cows and oxen in the stable, and instead it was a very sad moment, sadder than any he'd had in the war. He took it out on Secondo, the farmhand, who was not to blame, and told him he wasn't needed anymore. When he learned that the boy had fallen in love with Maria and was crazy about her, and noticed how yellow his ears were, a sure sign that he was whacking off, he told him to pack up and get out the next day.

Checco took his brother aside: "Let it go, Gaetano, there's nothing wrong with falling in love, and he's never been disrespectful towards our sister. You know she's in love with Fonso the storyteller, and she won't even look at anyone else. Sending him away now at the beginning of the winter is dooming him to cold and hunger. His family up in the mountains is so poor that they can barely scrape by and all they eat is chestnuts. We've given food and drink to so many vagrants even if we didn't know who they were. Think about it, while we were away at war he helped our parents get by here, for just a bowl of soup and a chunk of bread. He'll give you a hand in the stables; he knows how to bottom a chair with straw and fix the tools . . . We'll decide in the spring, all right?"

Gaetano muttered something under his breath that meant all right and they carried on. Clerice went to the cemetery every other day to pray on her husband's tomb, and since there were no flowers to be had she put two hawthorn branches in a jar, which looked nice anyway with their red berries. When she finished praying she would let Callisto know how things were going, sure that he would be listening. That Checco and Gaetano were back and that they were well. Checco had a bit of a limp, but it wasn't too bad. She couldn't complain. "You can see them all, our boys, from where you are now. Help them if you can; the Lord will surely listen to you because you were always a good man and you never hurt anyone. You always acted rightly. Let them all come home to me." Here she had to stop for a moment because she got a lump in her throat. "If . . . if by chance some of them are there with you, better for you and worse for me." Then she blew her nose, dried her tears and step after step, went back home.

Even with all this worry and distress, there was a laugh to be had at times. Like when, a week after Checco's return, Pio Patella showed up in the courtyard wailing like a banshee. "Clerice, Clerice, open that door wide! I've been cuckolded and the horns I'm wearing are so big I can't fit through!"

Clerice knew well that when men stayed away for years, there were always some of the ladies in town who sought solace with someone else, but she also knew that horns were the least of their problems and that it was best to forget the past and start anew.

"Why would you say such a thing, Pio?" she asked.

Pio replied that when he got home he found that his family had grown without any help from him. Not one, but two children, and he was having none of it.

Clerice had him sit down and poured him a glass of wine to lighten his spirits. Goodness, a extra child was one thing, but two? She had to find a solution and a way to comfort him.

"How long were you away, Pio?"

"Eighteen months."

Clerice's face lit up. So? Where's the problem? Nine plus nine is eighteen, she figured. Since one pregnancy lasts nine months, two pregnancies doubles the time. All fine and dandy.

Pio Patella looked puzzled for a moment but, considering that Clerice was a woman of experience and she knew everything there was to know about such things, he hugged her, thanked her and told her that she was the wisest and the best person in the whole town and that she had taken a weight from his heart. He returned home in an excellent mood and, now that he knew his honor was not at stake, he apologized to his wife for having thought badly of her and he pointed to the stairs that led up to the bedroom, the place where all problems were solved, or at least those that can be put right.

After Gaetano, Dante came back. Then Armando, then Savino, then Fredo and, last of all, Floti. His lung had been pierced by shrapnel during the Battle of the Solstice and he'd been kept in the hospital for a month until he was capable of travelling. None of them knew that their father had died and each of them thought it was a cruel trick of fate that poor Callisto had tortured himself to the end thinking that out of seven sons he would surely have lost two or three or maybe even more. He'd heard about battalions that were decimated, entire divisions annihilated. Why would the Black Lady spare his own, why hadn't she swept her scythe over the field of the Brunis?

Clerice reasoned, instead, that the Madonna had listened to

her and that in some way, the sacrifice of her husband had served to allow his boys to come home, one after another, none of them left behind.

Truly, all seven had survived: even Savino, the youngest and greenest. Only Floti had returned disabled, but you couldn't see anything from the outside; he was still the good-looking boy he had always been, who girls turned to look at when he walked down the road. It was only that the doctors had prohibited him from overexerting himself or doing heavy labor of any sort, since they hadn't been able to operate on him and the fragment, a very small piece of metal, was still stuck in his left lung.

At first no one noticed much, because it was only natural that Floti would spend his time looking after the family's business, which meant going to the market, eating out in the *osterie* with livestock dealers or negotiating with the landowner. He was the brightest, after all. But as time went on, the others began to feel that he was taking advantage of his position, while they did the hard work in the fields, the stable, the farmyard. And thus the seeds of envy were sown, or at least of malcontent.

One day Floti came back from the market with a worn-out, skinny mare. Her eyes were glazed and her coat was bristly and dull, her tail smeared with excrement.

"Why on earth did you waste money on this nag?" Gaetano demanded. "She'll die before the month is out and we won't even be able to sell her hide."

"No she won't. She's only been mistreated by a mean, stupid owner."

"Well, I don't know how you can say such a thing. You don't know the first thing about livestock."

"A horse is not a cow. But you can see it's true; look, here and here, the signs of the whip, and these wounds at the sides of her mouth. Someone who flogs a horse and jams the bit that way is not only evil, he's an idiot, because he's damaging his own property."

Gaetano clammed up but you could tell from his expression that he was skeptical.

"What's more," concluded Floti, "she cost me practically nothing. Give her a month and you'll see a miracle."

Floti saw to all her needs himself. He gave her clean well water and alfalfa hay which he knew was the most nutritious. When she started regaining strength, he started giving her a mix of fodder he made himself: barley, spelt, wheat, oats, vetch and horse beans. He even added dried peas when he could find them. After a week, her ears had straightened, her eyes were wide-open, dark and glittery, and her muzzle had become as soft as velvet. Her coat got shinier and denser day by day, and her mane and tail seemed made of silk. A miracle. Even Gaetano had to admit he'd never seen anything like it.

In a month's time, Floti was able to saddle her up to the shafts of a little carriage he had bought from a secondhand dealer and fixed up a bit at a time. He'd sandpapered all the wood and puttied the cracks, then painted it a rich black and shined up the shafts until they gleamed. A jewel. When he hitched up the mare, everyone was speechless: a real high-class ride! Floti's six brothers, along with Clerice and Maria, stood in a semicircle around the magnificent carriage, their hands on their hips, astonished. Not even Signor Barzini's steward had anything like this.

"But isn't this too much?" asked Clerice. "You're not thinking of actually riding around on that contraption?"

"Why not, *mamma*?" answered Floti. "Sunday morning I want to take you to mass on this, like a real lady."

Clerice shook her head, scandalized. "You're not in your right mind, Floti. I won't even consider it!"

Gaetano was even more alarmed: "When this reaches Barzini's ear, he'll say we stole his money."

Floti let his head drop, irritated by the negative reaction to his success. "Signor Barzini won't say a word when he sees that we're increasing production and profit, for him and for us. As far as this carriage is concerned, yes, I will use it. Not only will I enjoy it, seeing all the work I put into it, but most of all, the people who I do business with will see who I am. They have to get the idea that it's them who need me, not the other way around. If you have little, you do little. You can't achieve anything on a shoestring. Trust me. I learned a few things in the war, I thought things through and what's more, I talked to people who knew what they were on about, because there's all kinds in the army."

The words slipped out of his mouth easily and earnestly, summoning to mind his friend Pelloni and what he used to say about socialism, justice and injustice, and the rights of the working class. Floti had seen a lot during the war, and he was afraid that the victory that had cost so much blood would bring no riches to the foot soldiers who had defended the Piave and chased the enemy back to the other side. If they wanted their rights, they'd have to win them in peacetime, like they'd won back the last pieces of Italy in wartime. As he was thinking of all this, the image in his mind's eye was Pelloni's Frera on the ground, like a horse wounded to death, the wheel spinning and spinning . . .

CHAPTER ELEVEN

E ven the dead came back home, at least those who had been identified, and they were turned over to the grief-stricken parents who had watched them leave healthy and full of life, and who had to welcome them back now inside a fir-wood box ready to be buried. Others never came back, because their bodies were simply destroyed by the bombs, carried away by raging rivers, wedged deep in some mountain crevasse. Whatever was left of them was all mixed up with the scattered remains of other soldiers, waiting for big cemeteries of stone and marble to be built in those places where the most ferocious battles of the Great War had been fought.

But people wanted to forget. The men wanted to return to their old occupations, to the trades they'd left behind, to the rhythms of a peaceful life, without the screams of pain, the groans of dying soldiers, the explosions and blinding bursts of fire. They craved a life lit by the moon and the sun, sustained by regular, hard, day-to-day work.

In the early spring of the following year, Gaetano began to see a girl from town called Iole who mended clothes for a living. One day, his mother had asked him to accompany his sister Maria to have a few dresses hemmed, since she couldn't see very well anymore and Maria was never very good with a needle. His sister would much rather tend to the calves in the stable, or go looking for nests in the spring so she could raise a pretty blackbird or a goldfinch or nightingale and listen to them sing when they grew up. She didn't like sedentary work.

And so Gaetano went with his sister, carrying the bundle of clothes to be mended. As the two girls chatted, he couldn't take his eyes off Iole because she was really beautiful: dark haired, with green-blue eyes, a nice full bust and wide hips. The kind of girl he'd always dreamed about. She had noticed and had met his gaze without lowering her eyes, a sign that she wasn't shy. When it was time to pick up the mending, Gaetano went on his own, and he asked Floti to borrow the horse and carriage. Floti gladly let him use it, because he was pleased when Gaetano cut a fine figure, wherever he was going, as long as he left the whip home because they needed it there.

Iole couldn't hide a glint of pleasure in her eyes when she saw him, or her curiosity for that posh, shiny carriage that contrasted in no small measure with the image of the farming family she knew so well, and the young farmer before her.

"What a lovely carriage you have, Gaetano," were the first words out of her mouth.

"I'm glad you like it," he answered.

"It must have cost an arm and a leg."

"It cost what it cost," replied Gaetano, respecting the rule that the family's interests should never be aired openly, "what's important is that it looks fine and that it does its job."

"You're right! I didn't mean anything by that."

"Maybe you'd like to have a ride, now that the weather is getting nicer. The fair of San Giovanni will be starting soon. We could go together; people would be impressed."

The girl looked at him with a sparkle in her eye: "We'll have to see what my mother says. She might think you're a bit . . . cheeky!"

Gaetano gave an embarrassed smile, but inside he could barely believe that he was talking to Iole face to face, and that she was smiling at him and leading him to believe she was happy to be in his company. Just three years ago, before he left for the war, he never would have dared to set eyes on such a prize and now it all seemed so easy and spontaneous! As she was calling him cheeky, she came close and he could smell the lavender scent of her linen blouse that made his head spin like a glass of Albana on an empty stomach.

"Your mother knows that I'm an honest person and that I hold you in respect."

"If that's the case, I give you my permission to ask her. She may even say yes."

Gaetano thought that he'd already gone a long way in a short time, at least talking-wise, but perhaps it was best to strike while the iron was hot. He realized that Floti's carriage and the mare with the shiny coat and intelligent eyes had been a good investment and that, if all went well, he'd be asking to borrow them again, for the fair of San Giovanni.

"Where is your mother?" he asked.

"She's inside shelling peas. Go on, then, what are you waiting for, for me to change my mind?"

Gaetano entered, asking permission.

"Come in, young man," replied a voice from inside.

"I've come to ask how much I owe you for your daughter's work."

The mother, whose name was Giuseppina, replied: "It'll be four cents in all."

Gaetano counted the coins onto the palm of her hand and before she could finish thanking him, he continued: "I also wanted to ask you . . . "

"Go on, young man," she encouraged him.

"I wanted to ask if you would be pleased for me to accompany your daughter to the fair of San Giovanni, eight days from now, in my carriage."

The old lady got to her feet, setting the basket with the peas on the table, and she went to the window to look outside: "Is that your carriage?"

"Yes, Signora Peppina," replied Gaetano, confident that hearing herself called "signora" would nicely endear him to her.

"Well, you'd certainly make a fine figure, you and my Iole."

"Then I can take her to the fair?"

"Certainly, if you give me your word of honor that you'll behave properly."

"My word is my bond, Signora Peppina," replied Gaetano and he ceremoniously took his leave.

He walked out and towards Iole who had gone near the horse. "She said yes. I can come and collect you and take you to the fair of San Giovanni. If you're still happy to come, we'll go together."

"I'll be waiting for you, Gaetano," said the girl, with a tone of voice and two eyes that would have weakened the knees of the fiercest of brigands. Gaetano would have turned somersaults in joy, but he knew well, or rather, he'd often heard, that you should never let a woman know how much in love you are. You didn't want her thinking she could twist you around her finger. He felt happier than he ever had his whole life, and everything around him looked radiant. One moment had wiped away all the horrors he'd seen in the war, and he thought of nothing but Iole as he returned home with the bundle of mended clothes.

Floti could see from a mile away that his brother was floating on air. "How'd it go?" he asked.

"Well. I've brought home the mending and didn't spend much at all."

"Oh come on, don't give me that! You know what I'm talking about. You've fallen for Iole, haven't you? All she had to do was smile at you and now you're head over heels."

Gaetano turned bright red. "So what? Maybe I do like her, what's wrong with that. And anyway . . . "

"Anyway what?"

"She said she'd come to the fair of San Giovanni with me."

"So you need the horse and buggy . . . "

"Well, only if you don't . . . "

"And to think that I'd done something so stupid, and that I'd let myself be duped, that I'd brought home a nag whose hide was not even good enough to make the skin of a drum . . . "

"You were right," said Gaetano. "And you have no idea how good it felt when I pulled up with this wonder on wheels: she couldn't stop looking at the horse or the carriage."

"Listen to me: appearances can be deceiving. One swallow does not make a summer, and a carriage does not a gentleman make. As far the girl is concerned, be careful. She's beautiful, very beautiful and she knows it. She's used to men courting her. She looks at you with those bedroom eyes today, and tomorrow she'll be looking in the other direction. A girl like that is waiting for the day when she'll be noticed by a man of property, by the son of a lawyer or a notary. If she marries someone like that, she knows she'll live the rest of her life like a real lady, with a maid, a cook and all the rest. While she's waiting, she might not mind giving in to a whim now and then, like installing someone at her feet who adores her as if she were the Madonna of San Luca and is easily fooled into doing her bidding."

Gaetano lowered his eyes and turned red again. "I'm just taking her to the fair of San Giovanni . . . "

"Yeah, right. Go ahead and use the carriage, but I still have to tell you to watch out. If a woman like her takes to you and then leaves you, you'll go crazy. You'll never get over her: you'll dream about her day and night, smell her on your own skin. You'll do anything to catch a glimpse of her even though she doesn't want to see you anymore, you'll convince yourself that she'll come back to you some day and that day never comes."

Gaetano was perplexed, and perceived something rather unpleasant in his brother's words, as though he'd gone a bit too far, but he tried not to think about it. He reached the stable, unhitched the horse and let her free in her pen, then shined up the carriage and stored the shafts up against the wall.

From that moment on, all he did was count the days until the fair. When the time came, he showed up in his best suit, a fresh shirt, polished shoes and the carriage that shone like a jewel. He helped Iole up, called out to the horse and they departed at a trot.

It had been windy the day before, and the clean air carried the delicate scent of the invisible wheat flowers. The green fields were dotted with yellow buttercups and red poppies and the road was flanked on both sides by a row of ancient cherry trees laden with red fruit. Gaetano would veer to the side of the road now and then and rise to his feet to pick a few cherries and offer them to Iole. She smiled and he watched her lips stain with vermilion red juice as the succulent fruit melted in her mouth. There was a moment when the carriage jolted slightly and a drop of juice fell from her lips to her breast, a drop red as blood, and he felt suddenly dizzy, like just before they were sent into an attack during the war.

At the fair, he held out his arm as they strolled among the stalls, and when she paused in front of a cotton candy stand he bought her two cents' worth and had them add a piece of almond crisp. He noticed the old women stealing little looks at them and exchanging knowing smiles and winks, and he could almost hear their comments.

When evening came, he asked: "Are you hungry, Iole?"

"Don't trouble yourself over me, Gaetano," she answered, "you've already spent enough!"

"Don't you worry about that," he replied. "Come with me."

He took her back to where the carriage was parked, helped her up and took a basket from the back with two pieces of focaccia stuffed with prosciutto. Then he opened a flask of the new red wine and poured some into two sparkling glasses.

"It's not much," he said, "but it comes from my heart."

She bit into the focaccia and ate eagerly, washing it down with long sips of wine. Then she stopped to dry her lips and she laughed happily. They waited until it was time for the puppet theatre and then the fireworks that colored the sky and her cheeks with wondrous metallic reflections.

It was time to return home. The night sky was brightened by a nearly full moon, so the horse made easy progress on the dirt road. At a certain point, while they were in the middle of the countryside, Iole leaned onto Gaetano's shoulder as if seeking his warmth in the cool night, or as if she were afraid of the shadows that the moonlight cast across their path. His heart skipped a beat and a wave of heat rose from his chest and reddened his face. He'd never felt this way his whole life. The scent of the wheat flowers and the fragrance of her skin mixed into a single soft and indistinct perfume, so light that perhaps no one else could even perceive it. He did; ever since he was a child, this was the smell of springtime for him. He wanted to share the sensation with her: "Iole, can you smell that?"

"Yes," she said, "I think so . . . "

"Do you know what it is?"

"Some flower?"

"A very special kind . . . they're wheat flowers."

"Oh, you're teasing me. Wheat doesn't bloom into flowers; it just grows into ears."

"No, it does flower: all plants bloom before they come to fruit. It's only that some you see, and some you don't because they're so little. Wait," he said.

He stopped the horse, jumped off the carriage and approached the ears of wheat rippling slightly in the breeze wafting down from the hills. He picked one and held it out to her: "This is what we're smelling in the air."

"You're right! I'd never realized it." She took his big calloused hands, along with the ear of wheat they held, into her minute and delicate ones and brought them to her nose. Gaetano was afraid that the odor of the stables might still be lingering on his fingers despite his vigorous scrubbing with laundry soap, but she gave no sign of smelling anything nasty. She breathed in deeply: "You're right. And it's the loveliest thing I've ever smelled. So this is where the scent of springtime, and summer too, comes from. Who would have guessed?" She gave his hands a little kiss and Gaetano felt his heart beating like crazy but also a subtle, ineffable sense of exhaustion. Is this what love was like? A sensation as fleeting as the scent of wheat flowers?

She drew even closer until her lips were a whisper away from his. She kissed him.

Gaetano had never kissed a woman and he responded in an awkward, clumsy way but his hands touched her, seeking out the curves of that body that he'd only ever imagined. She didn't stop him, not until he tried to put them between her thighs. And he remembered then that he'd made a promise to her mother to behave like a gentleman. But he wasn't displeased by Iole's refusal, because it meant she was a good girl who cared about preserving her chastity.

They went on seeing each other that whole summer and it became harder and harder for Gaetano to control himself. Iole had gotten into his blood and he dreamt of nothing else than the day when he would be able to stretch out next to her in bed, with the blessing of God, his own mother and hers, of course. He envisioned her nude body and him blowing out the bedside candle and taking from her everything he wanted, even what he dared not confess to himself.

What would be the right time to ask her to marry him? In the fall or in the spring? The fall, for sure, so then they could plan for a spring wedding; he would be the first in his family to marry after returning from the war. Every time he thought about it and decided it was time to speak up, he would get cold feet and put it off for next time. In the end, he resolved to ask for her hand on Saint Martin's Day. He practiced often for the crucial moment, looking at himself in the mirror as he shaved and talking out loud in a self-confident, natural way: "Iole, I love you and want to marry you. If you feel the same way, I was thinking that Saint Joseph's Day would be a good time." How could anyone say it better? Not even Floti could do better than that.

Sometimes he considered the idea that she might say no, but he didn't even want to think about it, because that would be exactly what Floti had guessed would happen, and he really would end up looking like a fool.

When the day came, he rode up in the carriage with a basket in which he'd put a *salame*, a chunk of *parmigiano* cheese, a dozen fresh eggs and a piece of focaccia straight out of the oven. Who could resist? In fact, Iole, and even more so her mother, were overjoyed at the sight of such abundance. Signora Giuseppina, with the excuse of emptying the basket so she could give it back to him, disappeared into the kitchen, leaving Gaetano alone with Iole. He said: "Would you like to take a walk? there's something I wanted to talk to you about."

"Why, sure," replied Iole, putting a shawl over her shoulders.

They sat outside on a wooden bench at the side of the house, where they'd spent hours chatting on the long summer evenings. The November sun was tepid and the grapevine creeping up the wall was covered with big scarlet leaves.

"You look well," started Gaetano.

"You too," replied Iole.

"I meant to say that you look marvelous."

"Thank you for the compliment, but I don't deserve it."

"I have to ask you something."

"Happily, if I can."

Gaetano swallowed hard, the moment had come. "I love

you, Iole, I do nothing but think about you all day, and every night before I fall asleep . . . " He was surprising himself; words that he had not even prepared were flowing spontaneously. "I love you and I want to marry you. I was thinking that St Joseph's Day would be perfect . . . "

"Not so fast, Gaetano! You've already decided the day?"

Her words turned his blood to ice.

"I'm sorry, it doesn't have to be then. For me any day is good, and if you'll marry me I'll be the happiest man on earth. You choose the day, the month . . . the year. I don't want to hurry you."

Iole looked up at him and he saw a total indifference that made his heart sink. In that moment he thought of everything she'd let him do to her, how she'd taught him to kiss with his tongue, how she'd let him touch her breasts and thighs and everything else except for that one thing. Wasn't that love?

"Gaetano, I don't feel I can."

"But why? I thought that you . . . " but he couldn't go on because of the knot in his throat.

Iole bowed her head, but not out of embarrassment or for any other reason. She looked like she was trying to come up with an excuse.

"Because . . . because you plant too much hemp, you Brunis."

Gaetano's courage came rushing back. "Too much hemp? No, no, you don't need to worry: it's true, we do plant a lot of hemp but the men take care of it. There are seven of us and we don't mind hard work. Women are respected, in my house. They only do light work, like holding the lead on the oxen, gathering eggs in the morning, feeding the hens and rabbits. And when a woman is pregnant she stays comfortably at home to prepare the baby's diapers and blankets, three months before and four months after. Honestly."

Iole put a hand on his shoulder, as if to interrupt his heartfelt pleading. "They all say the same thing. And then it's one pregnancy after another and the washing and the ironing and the chickens and the pigs, the hoe and the shovel. Your hands end up looking like shoe leather and your face fills up with wrinkles . . . No, Gaetano, seriously, I just can't."

Gaetano got up and said: "But after everything we've done together . . . I thought you loved me."

"We haven't done anything, Gaetano," she replied in a tone of voice that might have been saying, "Go ahead, cut your throat for all I care." The matter was closed.

He left on the carriage while Giuseppina, who had appeared on the threshold in the meantime, shouted: "The basket! Your basket!"

CHAPTER TWELVE

G aetano was miserable as miserable could be: he acted completely stunned, as if the roof of the hayloft had caved in on him and hit him square on the head. Clerice stole sidelong looks at him during the day. She imagined all too well the source of his grief, because nothing going through her children's minds escaped her. It went without saying that in such a small town what had happened became public knowledge in a matter of days. Not that Clerice felt offended that her son had been rejected; like Floti, she had always known that it would end up this way. It was hardly customary for a woman to leave a man, and when such a thing happened it meant that she was one of those who didn't mind having more than one man, and had no problem going back and forth between them.

"You haven't lost a thing," said Floti when he found Gaetano in the hayloft one day with his head against a column, weeping silently. Gaetano didn't answer and Floti was intelligent enough to avoid adding that loathsome phrase, "I told you so." "She doesn't deserve you," he started up again. "She would have made you suffer and she might have even betrayed you. She would have betrayed you, Gaetano. You are a good man, you're good-looking, strong as a lion, not afraid of the devil, and the most big-hearted person I know. There are lots of women out there and every one of them would be happy to have you. You're a man of few words, but your word is your pledge; a woman feels protected and respected and safe with you. Try not to dwell on her, *Tanein*. It hurts a lot now, but that will go away. You know like when the hammer slips and you pound it into your finger? It hurts like hell and you feel like you're going to die, but then little by little the wound heals and your nail grows back. That's just the way we are. You really suffer over something but then, with time, you get over it.

"Death is the only thing there's no remedy for, *Tanein*. You know something? Sometimes I go to *papà's* tomb and I stand there looking at the photograph on the gravestone. He looks alive, but there he is, under the ground, decomposing, until there will be nothing left but his bones. Now that's a terrible thing. You know how many times I say to myself, 'If *papà* were here I'd ask his advice about this or that,' but instead he's not here and I can't ask him anything, while all seven of us were spared, thank God. Just think of what we went through in the war: the wounds, the bayonet attacks, the corpses of our buddies rotting under the rain for days and days because no one could bury them, because if you tried you'd get a bullet hole in your own head. It's a pity that we've lost *papà* but we're fine, otherwise, aren't we? We're doing well, Gaetano. Come on, buck up. When you want to talk, you know I'm around. And you can take the carriage any time you like."

Gaetano snuffled noisily and mumbled something like "thanks." He started cutting up chard for the animals, with enough vigor to be chopping off heads.

The summer was a scorcher. The sun beat down on people's heads like a blacksmith pounding an anvil. It made some people sick, some went off their heads and some even went raving mad. The son of Martina Cestari, a widow who had fifteen or twenty furlongs of land to plow, hung himself on a mulberry tree one August afternoon when the air was still and overcast, so hot and suffocating that not even the cicadas were saying anything and the leaves drooped lifelessly from the trees.

Fortunately, Don Giordano, the new pastor of the parish, would bury them in sacred ground even though they were suicides, because he knew that those poor people hadn't taken their lives to offend God, but only because they couldn't bear the tedium and despair of their daily existence. Because life could be a much heavier burden than death. He would bless them anyway and recite *"Requiescat in pace, amen,"* sprinkling a liberal amount of holy water.

He made a point of visiting the lad's mother and said: "Have faith, for God will not abandon you." Pretty words, but Martina wept like a fountain and would not be consoled.

"It's easy to say that we'll see them again on the other side," observed Clerice, who was there to console her, "but in the meantime, they're gone."

Martina cried and cried, and kept saying, between one sob and the next, a phrase in her bizarre mountain dialect: "My poor little bastard!" "Bastard" for them was an affectionate way of saying "son." There was a reason behind it; young girls would come down from the mountainside where their families had nothing to eat, and take positions as servants on the plains. In no time, they'd find the landowner in their beds and they'd soon find themselves pregnant and sent back home to give birth to exactly that, a bastard. But that wasn't true in Martina's case, she'd had a husband for as long as the Lord had left him with her, and he had been a good sort at that.

Floti and Gaetano and Fredo and Dante carried Martina's son on their shoulders to the cemetery, because they were his friends and because they were the same height, so the casket travelled on an even level. He didn't weigh a thing, poor devil, reduced to skin and bones by all the hard work he'd had to do alone on all that land. Their brother Armando never came to funerals because he was afraid of the dead, despite all the ones he'd seen during the war; he just didn't want to think that one day it would be his turn. Savino, on the other hand, who'd learned to kill at the front when he was only nineteen, was not afraid of the devil in person. He was even a bit too cocky at times, and Floti had to raise his voice with him sometimes, as their father would have done.

From then on, whenever there was work to be done in the fields, two or three of the boys would go to give Martina a hand, seeing that there was no way she could handle the farm on her own. When it was plowing time, they showed up with two oxen as big as houses, strong enough to pull down a church. In three days the work was done and the soil turned by the plowshares let off a light steam that smelled of dead leaves.

Winter that year cut cold as a knife blade. The soil hardened and all the leaves fell off the trees in a single night. Luckily, firewood was not lacking, but Floti said it was best to sell it so they could make money on it, and to use as little as possible for themselves. On the long December and January nights everyone would gather in the stable. The fire that Clerice would keep going in the hearth was barely big enough to heat the "priest" that would warm their beds.

They whiled away the time playing cards or listening to stories. After the first snowfalls, wayfarers began to show up, and they had a host of tales to tell, since that was how they earned a bowl of soup and a straw mattress to sleep on. One day, a knife grinder happened by. A stranger who spoke a strange dialect, which only Floti could recognize because he'd spent months in Friuli. He was very good at his trade, sharpening knives until they cut like razors, but he also knew how to make really nice chairs. He'd take a piece of acacia wood and with four or five strokes of a bill hook he carried with him, he'd make the legs and then the rails and then last of all the spindles, and then he'd add a straw seat that was made just right. But his stories were really scary ones. And sometimes you had the impression he was a little crazy. Maybe it was the war, and what he'd experienced. Everyone said that in the house where he lived all alone up on a mountaintop he heard things and saw things. More than once, he'd seen his wife who'd died three years earlier walking across his bedroom carrying their child who'd died as well in an artillery bombing. The child was as limp as a rag doll and the woman stared at him with eyes red from weeping, but if he tried to talk to her she would not answer.

Everyone fell silent at that point because no one felt like saying, what a bunch of nonsense, or giving him a reason to go on with his tale. Clerice said, however, that maybe what he said was true and what he was seeing were souls from purgatory.

"But what about the baby?" Maria would ask. "What could such a small child need to atone for, mother? What sins could he have committed, poor creature?"

"Even if he didn't do anything, he has to stay with his mother. He's too little to be on his own," Clerice said, making the sign of the cross and murmuring prayers under her breath.

Even Fonso, the storyteller, had survived the war and there was no one who could spin a tale like him. The Brunis were always happy to see him, except for Floti, who didn't want him courting his sister Maria. He was not handsome in the least and he was just a day laborer. What's more, he'd come back from the war half deaf, because he'd been at the Battle of Mount Montello, with those eight thousand cannons firing all together and making a horrible din, and his hearing had never been the same.

Even so, when he arrived in the evening wrapped in his long *tabarro* cloak, even the women started to drift into the stable, with the excuse of spinning hemp. Maria sat and listened openmouthed and his stories were so beautiful that he became beautiful as he told them. At least in her eyes. When he started up, using the set phrase, "You should know that once upon a time . . . " the silence that fell was so complete you could hear the oxen slowly chewing on their cud. Sometimes he'd come accompanied by friends who hoped to share in his privileges: a few glasses of wine or even, when he'd finished his story, a cockerel fried right then and there, with a loaf of crusty bread. But this happened rarely and anyway, when the gang that showed up wasn't too numerous.

And then there were certain conventions to look forward to: if the narrator, for any reason, named the king, that was the sign that it was time to down a glass of wine. So that every so often one of his buddies would lean in and whisper: "Name the king, name the king!" so that they'd all get the chance to raise their elbows.

While he had been away at war, he and Maria continued to keep in touch. When he could, he'd send her a postcard with a little rhyme:

Daisies are wild
And I love you more than
A mother loves her child

Clover grows low
And for you I'd even jump
Out of the window!

From the man who's always thinking of you,

Alfonso

Maria would never tire of reading and rereading his words, keeping them well hidden from her parents.

The storyteller's earnings always depended on the wealth of his listeners or of his hosts: it might be a bottle of wine, a chunk of *parmigiano* or even a thirty-kilo bag of wheat that he'd heave onto his shoulder and carry home in the dead of night and toss down at the threshold. His fame had spread to the nearby towns as well, and he was called upon from places far and wide, from San Giovanni and even farther out if he'd wanted to. Fonso was one of the few people in town who read books, besides the pastor, the doctor and the pharmacist. He'd read *War and Peace*, Salgari's *Son of the Red Corsair*, *The Count of Monte Cristo*, and Ohnet's *Ironmaster*, and he would retell them in the local dialect. Sometimes the whole story would take more than a single night, especially with long novels. *War and Peace*, for instance, took up three nights running.

When spring returned, Gaetano began to feel a bit better and he even began to resign himself to the fact that a girl like Iole would never have agreed to marry someone like him. She'd surely settle for nothing less than the son of a notary or a pharmacist or a landowner like Barzini, for instance. He'd let himself be fooled. There were worse things in life. But sometimes he couldn't help but think of the last time they saw each other and the awful things she'd said. Her words had left him with no hope whatsoever but, for an instant, he would think of the look in her eyes and wonder if they were trying to say something different. Or maybe once again, he was just fooling himself.

For a long time he'd acted like a dope, just as his brother Floti had predicted. More than once he'd hidden behind the hedges to catch a glimpse of her when she went into town to do the shopping or stopped to chat with her friends or with a suitor.

He finally decided to cast off the past and one day as he was returning in the carriage from the cooperative, where he'd taken the accounts for the milk they'd delivered, he met up with a girl who was walking home along the Finaletto with a basket of linens that she'd washed at the sluice on the creek. She was a tiny thing and the basket must have been really heavy because her left hip looked like it might give out under the weight of it. But she had a certain grace about her and beautiful black hair gathered into a braid that nearly reached her waist.

"Good evening, miss," he called out. "That basket must be awfully heavy. If you'd like I could take you to where you're going in my carriage."

The girl answered sharply: "Go on your way, good sir. I don't need any favors and I'm not accustomed to talking with people I don't know." A bit brusque, but that was a good sign: she was surely well brought up and accustomed to hard work.

"I don't want to be any trouble to you," he replied, "I'm just offering to give you a hand with that heavy basket. Please, let me help you."

The girl drew up and looked straight into his eyes: "You can't imagine that I'd accept a ride from you just because you have a fine carriage."

Gaetano smiled: "It's not even mine, it belongs to my brother. But just to prove that my intentions are honorable, here's what we'll do. We'll put the basket into the carriage and I'll get out and walk you home. It's on my way, anyway."

He was lying since he had no idea where her house might be but he was very interested in the girl and she surely must live somewhere nearby. She accepted.

"I'm Gaetano," he began, "and I live not far from here. Will you tell me your name?"

"Silvana," she answered. And in the time they spent walking towards her house, she realized that he was a good man, simple and honest. She'd already admired his strong build, from her very first glance.

As far as Gaetano was concerned, he understood instantly that Silvana would be a good wife and a good mother. He was also pretty sure, from the stealthy glances he managed to take, that he would find reason to be intrigued and attracted by her intimate charms, when the right time came.

And so they continued to see each other. Gaetano helped at first with transporting the wash, but soon asked to be introduced to her parents. That was an important step, nearly akin to an engagement, because it meant that, in one fell swoop, he would enter her home, meet her family and make it clear that his intentions were serious. After that day, he came calling every Tuesday, Thursday and Saturday, and sometimes even on Sunday, after he'd tended to the animals and shoveled the manure out of the stable. The days were getting longer, giving him more time on his own. He would wash in the tub, and Clerice would scrub his back and head with the laundry brush to get rid of the stable smell. Then she'd give him a hemp shirt, pressed and scented with lavender so that he'd make a good impression. Clerice was as eager for him to become engaged as Gaetano was himself, since she had asked around and learned that Silvana was a decent girl and very sensible.

Gaetano was preparing to ask her to marry him at the end of June. They had already spoken about it and there didn't seem to be any hindrances, so it was time to make a decision.

"I'm getting married, *mamma*. Are you happy I've chosen Silvana?" he said one day to Clerice.

"I certainly am. The sooner you have children the better it is, so you'll have time to see them grow up and get settled. The girl is a pearl, you couldn't have found any better, not like that other . . ."

"Please, *mamma*," Gaetano interrupted her, "let's not talk about that. It's personal."

"Don't be ridiculous: boys your age don't understand a thing. She would have swallowed you up and spit you out in a single bite."

"Mother, as I've said, that's my own business. Stay out of it, please."

Clerice was surprised and disappointed at getting such a rude reply from a son who'd always been kind and respectful, and she became even more convinced that certain women poison a man's blood and get them to do whatever they want them to do. Thank goodness it was over. She didn't say another word, because she would only have made the situation worse; talking about her would bring her even more to his mind.

Some time later, one morning at the end of April while he was returning from the Sant'Agata market, Gaetano saw her walking along the ditch where the old oak was, gathering wild chicory with a little knife and a wicker basket. She was first to say hello: "*Buongiorno*, Gaetano."

He slowed down so he could answer: "Hello, Iole."

· "Long time no see."

"Don't say that: you were the one who never wanted to see me again."

"That's not true. All I said was that I didn't feel like getting married. It wasn't about you. I've always liked you, and I proved that to you, didn't I?"

Gaetano felt his blood boil at such a direct reference to something only the two of them could remember. Very cheeky, and all the more seductive.

"I was expecting you to offer me another life, at least. We could have moved to the city, opened a shop, for example, and then once we'd earned enough, we would have gone to the theatre, walked arm in arm under the porticoes . . . "

"How was I supposed to take you to the city, open a shop, buy things to sell? You need a lot of money to do those things: who on earth would have given me all that money?"

"That's not my affair. That's men's business. I know lots who have started from nothing and done well for themselves. But you didn't feel up to that, and I can't blame you."

Gaetano fell silent, tormented by thoughts he couldn't control. Iole's mere presence, after so much time that he hadn't seen her, erased every other image, every other event, every other person. How lucky that he was wearing his good suit and a clean shirt; he would never have forgiven himself if she'd seen him looking unkempt. He swallowed and spoke again: "Is it true that you've always liked me?"

"Oh, what a question. What do you think, that I let you kiss me and caress me and touch me because I'm a bad girl? It was because I liked you. But I just couldn't face that kind of life. When we saw each other you always looked so fine, with your shirt freshly washed and ironed, on this beautiful carriage. But then I would have seen you shoveling manure in the stable, sitting down to the table with that smell on you. I would have become a mess myself, always out in the chicken coop with the hens and the geese, trudging through the mud in the winter and the dust in the summer, having one baby after another like you peasants do, because you need more hands in the field . . . and that's what you call light work."

Gaetano was wounded by her merciless appraisal. Just a few words from her had upset him deeply: Iole had dangled the vision of another life in front of him; a life with her at his side, beautiful and maybe even in love with him. A life he knew he could never have: a man born a farmer had to be a farmer and that was that. Iole got closer and he felt drunk. She got even closer, close enough to brush his lips with hers: "Think of what you're losing, Gaetano," she whispered. And she walked off down the lane that cut through the meadow. He stood there stock still with tears brimming up, next to his horse who regarded him with big moist eyes as if trying to understand.

He was so shaken by the encounter that he could not bring himself to call on his fiancée. Days passed and she became so worried that she sent him a message through a relative of hers who was a friend of the Bruni boys: his name was Tonino.

Gaetano was in the stable milking the cows when Tonino approached him: "Gaetano, Silvana has sent me to let you know how worried she is that she hasn't seen you. She's wondering if you're not feeling well, or have some other problem.

She says you shouldn't have qualms about talking to her directly and telling her the truth, no matter what it is. Do you understand what I'm saying?"

Gaetano stopped, moved the stool and the milk bucket and walked over to the unannounced messenger: "Tonino . . . I'm sorry, I've had a bit of a tough time lately . . . tell her I need a few days to pull myself back together and then I'll go see her myself and explain all this."

"Aren't you feeling well, Gaetano?" the young man asked.

"Yes . . . no, no. Just go now, go tell her what I've just said."

His friend got onto his bicycle and went off to do as he had been told. A week later, it was Gaetano who entrusted a message for Silvana to Iofa, because he regularly went by the girl's house in his cart: Gaetano asked to meet with her the next evening at the chapel of San Firmino, a quiet, isolated place not far from her house. Silvana arrived at the appointed time, just before dusk, and found her fiancé sitting on a stone bench built into the wall at the side of the front door. The air smelled of roses.

"How are you, Gaetano? I was so worried; I've been hoping every day that I'd hear from you."

Gaetano got up and gave her a kiss on the cheek: "Forgive me, Silvana. I wasn't . . . well."

"Not well? What was wrong? Tonino told me he found you working in the stable. What kind of sickness kept you away from me?"

Gaetano realized that the reason he'd gone missing was written plainly on his face. It was just as well to be honest. "The other day I saw my old fiancée, Iole, by chance."

"By chance?"

"Yes, by chance. I was coming home from Sant'Agata and there she was at the ditch, the one by the old oak tree, gathering wild chicory. Since we've been together, I've never gone looking for her, I swear it."

"Well then? What happened?"

"Nothing. We just talked, but that was enough to get me all worked up. Since then all I can think about is her and what she told me."

"What did she tell you, Gaetano?" asked Silvana, her eyes shiny but her voice firm.

"She led me to believe that . . . if I was willing to change my way of life, she'd have me back." He lowered his head, reddening. He could feel Silvana's pain and humiliation.

"Change your way of life? Why, what's wrong with your way of life?"

"Well . . . it's that I'm a farmer, a cowherd, and she wants a different life, she wants to live in the city and if I . . . well, if I did as she asked, she would take me back again."

"I see . . . now, listen to me well, Gaetano: if you want to go back to her for any reason, if you've found the way to make her happy, I will not stand in your way. I will release you from your promise. You owe me nothing. Nothing has happened between us, has it? You've kissed me a few times on the cheek, nothing more, and so you can consider yourself free. I'll still remember you fondly. I'll remember that day that you walked me home with the basket of the wash on your carriage. What I'm going to say now is something I've never said before because I'm not used to saying such things and because I'm shy. I love you, Gaetano. You are a good man and in my eyes you are handsome and gentle and I'm sure you'd be a good father if we had children. Since we've been seeing each other, I've often thought of how our life might be together. I'm not afraid of hard work, I'm used to it. And if I'm tired when I go to bed at night, all the better for me. I'll feel like getting close to you," and now it was her turn to blush, "so you can warm me up, and we can talk about the day we've had together and about our future and our hopes for our family. That was my dream, and that dream made me happy, but now things have changed. I understand that you've never forgotten Iole and that maybe I'll never manage to make you forget her: I'm not beautiful like she is, I don't have her charms. But most of all, Gaetano, I would never want you to be unhappy or to have regrets. Because I love you."

Gaetano started to speak but she stopped him: "No, I just have a few more words to say and then I'll have finished. Think about what you really want. I'll wait for seven days. If you don't come back to me by then, don't try afterwards, because I'll have to refuse you." She brushed his cheek with her fingers and got up, setting off down the little road that flanked the Finaletto, towards home.

Six days later, Gaetano, dressed in the finest clothes he had, called upon her parents and asked them for her hand in marriage.

CHAPTER THIRTEEN

One Saturday morning in mid-June, the day before his wedding, Gaetano hitched the mare to the cart to go to fetch his bride's dowry: sheets, linens, towels, curtains, embroidered fabrics, everything an accomplished, respectable girl prepared for her marriage. As he was on his way, perhaps accidentally or perhaps deliberately, he drove past his old girlfriend's house. Iole, as beautiful as always, was sitting at the threshold, shelling peas, and when she saw him passing by, dressed in his Sunday best, she said hello: "*Buongiorno*, Gaetano. Where are you going all dressed up?"

Gaetano slowed until he came to a stop. Everyone knew that the next day he was going to be married and surely she did as well. So she was asking the question for some other reason. He replied: "I'm going to a place where you could be too, if you had said yes."

Iole stopped shelling peas all at once and shot a withering look at him: "May God not even let you enjoy the first night," she hissed. Then she overturned the basket of peas, which went rolling in every direction, and went into the house, slamming the door behind her. Gaetano froze. He felt a chill filling his heart and snaking its way down his spine. Why so much hate? Why did she curse him when it was she who had rejected him? He would never understand what was going through her head, never understand that Iole, in her own way, had shown that she felt something for him, but had such a high opinion of herself that she thought she deserved much more than the henyard, the stable and the pigpen of the Brunis.

Gaetano tried to shake off this sudden feeling of foreboding and called out to the mare, who took off again at a trot. It was the height of the most beautiful season of the year and nature was triumphing, the roses curling around the pillars of the Madonna found at every triple crossroad, and the wheat just ripening. He took heart and by the time he reached the Finaletto he felt much better. He told himself that her words were meaningless, that they could not have had any consequence. It was all envy, because he was marrying Silvana, while she—biding her time while she waited for someone to take her to the city—was turning into an old maid.

When he had loaded the dowry onto the cart, he returned home, where wedding preparations were in full swing. Clerice, ladle in hand, was giving orders to the women who had come to help fix the wedding lunch: friends, daughters, relatives. This was one of the most eagerly-awaited occasions for chattering, gossiping, indulging in all sorts of idle talk. Some of the women, those who had the warmest hands, kneaded flour with eggs until the dough was as smooth as velvet and was ready to be rolled out with the *mattarello*. They'd start from the edges with short, rhythmic taps, proceeding in towards the center of the huge sheet of pasta they'd rolled out, then back out again.

When the sheet became thin enough, it was lightly rolled like a piece of fabric around the *mattarello* and pressed out again, with a back and forth movement of the long pin, until it became as fine as a bride's veil, transparent and golden, so light that it fluttered over the breadboard when they lifted one end of it so that a long wave would ripple across the sheet and settle it flat and wrinkle-free on the wooden surface, ready to be cut. Others prepared the filling for the tortellini, chopping up pork filet, prosciutto, chunks of mortadella and the thinnest slice of *salame*, just for flavor. Then, just before they lightly browned this opulent mix in a pan, they'd add salt, pepper and just a touch of nutmeg.

The broth was also bubbling away, the pot filled with fat-marbled beef ribs, a capon, an old boiler hen with her eggs, just the yolks, still inside, and the livers and gizzards, peeled and cut in half, along with onion, celery and carrots. The roasts were also well on their way: tender young roosters, pork, guinea hen and a couple of pheasants that Floti had shot down three days earlier while hunting in the hills near Savignano.

Other women were busy with the sweets: *zuccherini* sugar cookies shaped like wedding rings, a chocolate and almond cake made especially for weddings called *torta secca*, and nut brittle assembled to form a church, with two sugar dolls on top representing the bride and groom. Last of all, the *zuppa inglese* made of ladyfingers soaked in Alchermes liqueur layered with pastry cream and chocolate custard. The smell wafted out of the kitchen into the courtyard and all the way out to the fields, causing the men to stop in the middle of their work to comment on how their mouths were watering at the thought of the wedding lunch. A banquet so rich was commensurate to the unique importance of the event; not even at Christmas or Easter did they enjoy such a repast, nor even during the festival of La Madonna della Provvidenza, the town's patron saint. The festivities lasted seven days, and the inhabitants of nearby towns were so impressed by the continued feasting that they'd made up a teasing rhyme:

Ding dong, ding dong
Three days of tortellini
Three days of *tortelloni*
Then polenta and cucumbers all year long.

In truth, what you could look forward to on these holidays was a bowl of tortellini, some of the soup meat with savory *salsa verde* on the side and a slice of plain cake to dip into your wine.

Gaetano was the first son to marry, after the return from the war, and it was such an important milestone that his sister Rosina, who had wedded a Sicilian revenue officer in Florence, decided to return home for the occasion, defying the ire of her famously jealous husband. She was due to arrive in Bazzano on the eleven o'clock train and Floti had been waiting for Gaetano to get back so he could detach the cart and hitch up the carriage.

Rosina stepped off the footboard dressed in a beautiful long gown with a fringe that danced over the toes of her boots. She was carrying a purse and wearing a hat with a veil and looked like a real lady. Floti hugged her, took her suitcase and led her to the carriage. "Oh this is lovely!" she exclaimed at the sight of the sparkling vehicle and the shiny-coated mare, and she settled in next to her brother. Travelling those few kilometers in the sun and the air of her native land filled her with indescribable joy. She didn't stop talking for a moment and Floti had a really tough time keeping up with her: look at this and look at that and that house wasn't there when I left and who lives there and what do they do and what don't they do. Then she told her brother about the marvels of Florence: her strolls along the Arno, the church of Santa Maria del Fiore that had a dome so big that their whole town would fit inside and was topped by a kind of tabernacle as big as their whole church. She told him, with a little giggle, that in the main square there were two giants made of marble, taller than their house and as naked as the day they were born, and you could see just everything.

"You think that's something," replied Floti, "we have a giant of our own in the square in Bologna, naked himself, holding a fisherman's trident in his hand. He represents Neptune, the god of the sea, because people used to believe in gods instead of in Jesus Christ."

When they arrived in the courtyard, Clerice, Maria and all the women came rushing out with their hands and aprons full of flour to greet the beautiful Rosina. "How are you, *Rusein?*" Clerice said, as if she'd just seen her the day before, using a pet name that sounded like a boy's.

Rosina embraced her and got big tears in her eyes. She was easily moved, but Clerice knew well that there was another reason: that her daughter's husband, being Sicilian, was terribly jealous and kept her under lock and key like some fine wine, and Rosina just hated that; she wasn't used to it and suffered over it. If she dared to complain, he beat her.

"Now you enjoy the party," her mother told her, "and don't even think about him. Maybe, with time, he'll get over it."

"Right," said Rosina, "but not before I'm old and wrinkled and no one wants me anymore. Not before then."

In just a few minutes' time she had changed and put on an apron and there she was in the middle of all the others, chatting away and busying herself with the pots and pans. She felt happy and carefree, at home, where maybe there wasn't much money, but lots of good cheer and singing.

Bettina, Pio Patella's wife, urged Clerice to have a nice bath in the wash tin, since the next day she would be accompanying the groom to the church door, but Clerice was reluctant and told everyone the same old story: "When I married poor Callisto, my neighbor kept nagging me, 'wash your face with soap, Clerice, you're going to the altar tomorrow!' I didn't want to, but she insisted so much that I listened to her, and I've never been the same. I had skin as smooth as a plum just picked, I did, and now look at me!"

"It's not the soap's fault, mother!" replied Rosina, laughing. "It's your age that's to blame and there's nothing you can do about that!"

The next morning Gaetano went with his mother to wait for the bride in front of the church, while the bells chimed out and people gathered to watch. He was wearing a fustian suit in a gun-barrel gray color and a pair of patent leather shoes that hurt like anything but sure looked nice. His mother stood next to him, wearing a dark cotton jacket and skirt, a white blouse trimmed with lace at the collar and sleeves and, around her neck, three strands of garnets red as fire. Checco, in a gray fustian suit and black trousers, shirt and tie, was his best man. As he was standing there waiting, the words of Pipetta came to mind, calling him "milord" as he was charging to his death against a line of tanks. Silvana, wearing a light-colored cotton dress and a crown of braided daisies in her hair, arrived right on time with her father and brothers on a little cart polished to a high sheen with furniture oil, its hubs painted a brilliant black. Her father helped her down, walked her to the door of the church and turned her over to her fiancé so they could walk together down the aisle to the kneeler draped with a red cloth in front of the altar.

Silvana couldn't hold back tears when the archpriest asked her if she would marry the here present Gaetano Bruni and did she promise to serve and honor him for the rest of her days. She said, yes, I do, and they exchanged rings. When they walked out into the bright sunshine, one of her bridesmaids handed her a little basket with the *zuccherini* sugar cookies and a few sugar-coated almonds to pass out to the children who were waiting impatiently. She tossed out a few handfuls and the children dove in and scuffled among themselves. Then Floti had both of them get into the carriage and, on his feet like an ancient charioteer, he slowly accompanied them home.

When all the guests had arrived, it was time for lunch in the courtyard under the grape trellis, with Iofa playing the accordion and belching out a song about a chimney sweep that was full of double meanings, but Clerice didn't so much as say a word, since you only get married once in life and you can't deny people a little fun. Gaetano, strangely enough, didn't eat much; his bride, surprised at seeing him pick at his food, asked: "Aren't you feeling well? Where's your appetite? Everything is so good!" Gaetano replied evasively that he was a bit tired. He tried to joke and laugh with his friends, but you could tell he wasn't his normal self.

The guests, on the other hand, ate and drank for hours, until dusk, helping themselves to seconds and thirds of each course. They all got a bit tipsy and some were downright drunk. Sandrone Burgatti, who everyone knew as Piziga, a lad who went hungry almost all year long, had gorged himself so thoroughly that what he'd eaten would not go down or come up. He'd become white as a sheet and was muttering: "Oh good lord, I'm dying, I'm dying."

"Go call the doctor," said Clerice, "this one here's really about to burst." Floti didn't wait to be asked twice: he hitched up the horse and took her out at a gallop through the court-yard and down the road that led to town.

Everyone thought they'd be back in no time but, waiting and hoping, Floti failed to show up and no one knew where he'd gone. Maybe the doctor had been called away and he'd gone off looking for him, but in the meantime Piziga had taken on a greenish cast that made everyone fear for the worst. What to do, what not to do, until one of the old men, a certain Anselmo Borzacchi who seemed to know what he was talking about, said that the only way to save the poor wretch was to bury him in the manure heap up to his chest. Their eyes widened: the cowplop? Yessiree, the manure heap, because it was very hot underneath and the heat would cure his indiges-tion. No sooner said than done: Piziga was stripped from his belt down, stuck into a hole dug into the cowplop and sealed in all around. Borzacchi was satisfied at their effort and men-tioned that the man's plight reminded him of a character in the Divine Comedy although he couldn't remember which one. They waited patiently for the cure to take effect. In a very short time, Piziga's natural skin color was restored. "Good sign," said the old man. "What did I tell you?"

In the meanwhile, Floti came driving back at full tilt with the doctor in tow, who surprised everyone by saying that old Borzacchi's therapy was spot on. He had them bring him over a chair and a plate of guinea hen with roast potatoes and a bottle of Albana, and sat by his patient's side, chatting with the other guests sitting around the manure heap. When it got dark, Piziga was extracted, filthy as a pig and stinking to high heaven. He immediately asked to be excused so he could relieve himself. When he returned from the hemp field, he was dumped just as he was into the cows' drinking trough and scrubbed down until he looked like new, and then he went home on his own two legs.

That same night, Gaetano fell ill.

The town doctor was called only a couple of days later because everyone hoped that he would get better on his own. Young Bruni was a strapping sort who'd gotten through the worst of the war unscathed; he was capable of lifting a sack weighing a hundred kilos from the ground and hoisting it onto his shoulders without help. What could possibly bring down a man of his mettle?

Neither the doctor nor anyone else had an answer. Different cures were attempted, both those prescribed by the doctor and the ones Clerice pulled from her vast stores of wisdom. Without any success, unfortunately. Armando and Fredo took over for Gaetano in the stable, while he continued to worsen until he couldn't even get out of bed anymore. Silvana stayed at his side day and night. When he nodded off, she prayed to the Madonna to save her husband because she loved him and didn't want to lose him, and because she was pregnant and didn't want their child to be born without a father. Sometimes she couldn't bear the anguish and she'd curl up in a corner of the bedroom and burst into tears, hiding her face between the two walls. Clerice would come up with hot broth, or a brew of herbs or a special unguent to rub on his chest that she alone knew the composition of. But any small improvements turned out to be fleeting. He would come out of a swoon uttering strange expressions and once Silvana was sure she heard the name of her rival. She went straight to her mother-in-law, the matriarch and ultimate authority of the family, to ask for advice. Clerice lowered her head, looking stricken and deeply disheartened.

"That's why, then," she whispered. "It's her. She's making him die . . . "

"What are you saying, *mamma*?" asked Silvana.

"Nothing is more terrible than a woman's spite, daughter."

"You can't believe in curses?"

"The Church tells us we mustn't, but I know things that no priest knows. Have you ever heard of scorned or betrayed women who lift footprints? We call it the *pedga*, I don't know how you say that in your town: it's that mass of mud which sticks to a man's shoes when he's working in the fields, in winter when the ground is damp, or even in the summer after a sudden storm. When it gets too heavy, it drops off his shoe and gets left behind on the ground, conserving the print of the foot that it dropped from.

"If a woman has evil intentions, she'll gather up the *pedga* and put it at the spot where the main branches of an oak tree join. Little by little, the wind, the rain and the sun start to crumble the lump of dirt and the man who left it begins to waste away. When there's nothing left of the lump, the man dies. Before your wedding, there were several storms, and Gaetano often went into the fields to bring home grass for the animals."

Silvana brought her hand to her mouth and gasped: "Oh, no!" Clerice stared at her, eyes brimming, and nodded. "Isn't there anything we can do?"

"If you can find the *pedga*, you must collect it, taking great care so that it does not crumble, cook it in an oven and then hide it in a place where no one can find it. If you do, the victim of the curse will start to get better and finally regain his health completely."

Silvana wept disconsolately with her face hidden in her hands, and Clerice looked at her son, so big and so strong, lying in bed limp as a rag. For a brief moment, she thought that she would do anything she had to do to save him. Anything. Before she could speak, Silvana broke out: "I'll find that woman, and I'll force her to talk, to tell me where she's hidden my husband's footprint, I'll torture her if I have to, rip out her nails one by one . . . "

Clerice raised her hand to stop the delirium. "No, you won't. What if our minds are being clouded by our despair? Acting against her could be the gravest injustice of all. We know nothing, we've seen nothing; you only heard, or thought you heard, a word from the lips of a sick man who was delirious with fever. We'll pray to the Madonna: she who saw her son die can understand us."

Gaetano died, six months after marrying, nothing but skin and bones. His brothers carried him to the cemetery and buried him next to his father. Before dying, he had told his wife what name to give the baby if it were a boy, and what name to give her if she were a girl.

Silvana gave birth to a girl who died before she was six months old, and she closed herself up in mute, brokenhearted grief. Clerice never stopped praying and appealing to the Madonna: if She hadn't been able to grant her the blessing of saving her son and the little one, could She at least give her the strength to bear such pain and to carry on, with faith and a strong will, in the certainty that one day they would all be reunited in heaven.

For several months, Silvana remained in the Bruni house, and she would often accompany her mother-in-law to the cemetery to pray on the graves of their dead. Then one day, she said: "*Mamma*, I've decided to return to my own family. You are a good woman and I love you dearly. All of you here treat me with respect, like a sister, but this is not my home any longer because I've lost my husband and my daughter."

Clerice touched her cheek: "You're right, and I understand you, daughter. If it were up to me, I'd keep you here happily because you are the wife of my son and you gave birth to his child, but it's only right that you return to your family. If you can, make a new life for yourself. Remember, though, that whatever may happen, the doors of this house are always open to you, by day or by night, in good weather and bad. May God bless you."

The day of her departure was decided. Floti hitched the mare to the cart and loaded it with his sister-in-law's dowry and her personal things. Silvana held Clerice tight in a long embrace and both women wept in silence. She hugged Maria and said goodbye to her brothers-in-law one by one. Floti helped her up, called out to the horse, and they were off.

Silvana never came back. Her family moved to Piedmont for work and the Brunis lost touch with them, but Clerice never forgot her; she kept the girl close in her heart and her thoughts, because Silvana had loved her son with a strong, sincere love and, had God willed it, she could have made him happy.

Gaetano's death, so sudden and unexpected, cast a shadow of deep sadness over the family, and the death of his little daughter seemed to be a further sign of ineluctable destiny. The good fortune of the Brunis, who had all seven escaped the scourge of the war, had evaporated all at once. The inconsolable pain which was always present in Clerice's eyes and in all of her gestures made it hard for any of the others to even think of forgetting. Savino, the youngest of them all, was the one who took it best. He was handsome and full of life; girls liked him so much he was invited to enjoy their charms even without promises of eternal love. Floti, born with a strong will and personality, tried to persevere and instill courage in the others as well and, most of all, he looked out for his mother. He took her for rides in the carriage, to visit relatives or to the market where she could buy a few little gifts. He talked to her as much as he could.

"*Mamma*, these are things that happen, sadly, in every family. You still have six sons and two daughters who love you and who want to see you smile again. You who have faith know that you'll see Gaetano again in the next world, because he was a good boy and wouldn't hurt a fly."

"A mother can never resign herself to losing a child," she answered. "It's a pain that won't kill you but it will never leave you. I pray every day that God will give me the strength to carry on and still be a good mother to all my children."

As time passed, Clerice managed, at least in part, to return to her old life, to take care of the everyday chores and the housekeeping. Fredo and Dante married and her daughters-in-law recognized, through their behavior, the role of authority that was due her. It was customary, when a daughter-in-law first entered her husband's home, that she not speak at the dinner table unless her mother-in-law invited her to do so, but Clerice wanted the two girls to feel at ease and asked them to join in the conversation from the start. She treated them with affection, but in her heart Silvana remained her favorite, perhaps because she'd lost her, perhaps because she'd watched her care for her son with such loving devotion.

Before a year and a half was up, both girls gave birth. Clerice called a midwife, even if that meant spending money, because she didn't want to embarrass them by assisting them herself. One had a girl, the other a boy and life seemed to smile on the Brunis again.

Until one day an event occurred that was destined to radically change the life of the whole family.

CHAPTER FOURTEEN

The season of the grape harvest had just begun when the mailman came by with a registered letter addressed to: "Esteemed Mrs. Clerice Bruni, née Ori." The addressee was quite flustered at receiving such a missive, which brought to mind state offices and incomprehensible language. She immediately called Floti, who she knew was capable of handling such a situation. He signed for the letter, since any member of her family could do so, and opened the envelope. The mailman had, in the meantime, mounted his bicycle and was loudly ringing the bell to warn carters and cyclists that he was on the road again.

Floti's expression changed considerably as he read the letter.

"Bad news?" asked Clerice, expecting nothing less.

"On the contrary, *mamma*. Let's go in, it's cold out here."

"Well?" asked Clerice again as she shut the door behind her.

Floti sat down and laid the letter on the table: "Mother, you've come in to an inheritance."

"What?!"

"That's what it says here. This letter comes from a notary in Genova who is summoning you to his office so he can read you the will of one of your relatives. It seems that this person has made you his universal heir."

"What does that mean?"

"It means he's left you everything he had."

"How much is that?" asked Clerice.

"It doesn't say in the letter, and that's why they sent it to you. You'll find out when you're before the notary. He'll read the will in the presence of two witnesses, so no one can dispute what's written there."

"So I have to go to Genova?"

"I would say so."

Clerice, who was still on her feet, sat down and fell silent as she thought about what Floti had just said, her elbows planted firmly on the table.

"How far is Genova?"

"*Mamma*, it's not like you have to walk there. You get on the train and you go. At every stop, the stationmaster calls out the name of the place. When you hear: 'Genova! Genova Station!' you get out, otherwise the train will take you some-place else and it won't stop until it gets to the next station."

"I have to think about it," she said, after having thought about it for quite some time.

"Mamma, there's nothing to think about! We're talking about an inheritance; this could be a very important opportunity for our family. Try to remember which relatives of yours might have been living around Genova. There must be some way we can figure it out. Your parents, or your grandparents, must have mentioned them to you. Someone who set off to seek their fortune . . . "

Clerice was looking more and more confused. She said again: "I have to think about it, and then we'll talk."

"Take your time," said Floti curtly, "but keep in mind that if no one shows up to claim an inheritance, after a certain time, the government will take the money and the land."

For several days, neither Floti nor his mother mentioned it again, and neither of them spoke with a living soul about it, not even with the family. It was Clerice who broke the silence. She stopped Floti while he was leaving with a cartload of milk cans to take to the dairy.

"I've thought about that letter, Floti, and I have decided that it's best to talk to the whole family about it. Tonight."

"The best thing, mother? I'm not so sure. What if one of us talks to someone in town about it? Armando, for instance: have you seen him lately? I haven't. But I bet that if I wander over to the *osteria*, I'll find him shooting the breeze with the loafers there."

"He's still your brother," replied Clerice, "even if he is weaker than you are. He has a good heart and he wouldn't hurt a fly. Tonight, Floti, after dinner. All of you must be there."

Floti left the house and headed towards the dairy. The fact that his mother hadn't trusted his judgment, despite the fact that he knew more than his brothers did, annoyed him, and so did having to take orders from an old woman who had never left town her whole life long. But she was his mother and he had to respect her wishes.

That evening they all gathered around the table, even Maria.

Clerice waited until everyone had finished dinner before she began talking. They'd been chatting about the weather, the stable, about Lola who'd just had a calf three days before, about when they'd have to start pruning the grapevines, about Checco who had plans to marry in the fall and needed to organize his wedding.

At about nine o'clock, Clerice spoke up. "Something has come up," she began, "and I want all of you to listen to me carefully. I received a letter five days ago. Only Floti knows about it, because he was there when it arrived and he helped me to understand what it said."

"A letter?" demanded Fredo. "What letter?"

They all stopped to listen, even Armando who had been telling Savino the last joke he'd heard at the *osteria*. It wasn't often that a letter arrived.

"Good news or bad news?" asked Checco.

"More good than bad, certainly," replied Clerice, "but things are not so simple. You tell them, Floti, you can explain better."

Floti, thus invested with the duty that in effect put him in the role of their dead father as the family patriarch, although he was not the eldest, spoke up. "It's a letter that a notary wrote to mother," he told them, "saying that a relative of hers has died and left everything to her in inheritance."

"How much have we inherited?" asked Dante.

"It's mother who has inherited," specified Floti. "We haven't inherited anything."

"Yes, but . . . " Dante protested.

"But nothing. It belongs to mother."

"The inheritance is mine," said Clerice, "but I won't live forever and when I die it will be divided up in equal parts for each of you. Parents always live for their children."

The thought of an inheritance, that is, money and land falling from the sky instead of being the fruit of long, hard labor, was so unsettling to the brothers that it may even have caused niggardly thoughts to worm their way into the minds of those present; for instance, that Gaetano's death had left a richer share for those remaining. It was neither evil nor cynical on their part, probably just automatic. But Clerice must have seen a glimmer in the eyes of some of her children that she didn't like, although she continued without a moment's hesitation.

"Our feelings are the best part of each one of us and no one must forget that we are a family before anything else, and that money is not everything in life, although it may often come in handy. Remember that money creates envy, jealousy, disagreement and malice. Many people have found themselves ruined because they couldn't be happy with what they had."

Floti started up again. "There are problems, in any case. To get the inheritance, mother has to go to Genova. She'll have to sign, in the notary's presence, that she accepts the inheritance and whatever else is involved . . . "

"What does that mean?" asked Fredo.

"That you can inherit debts as well, and you have to decide if you want to do that or you don't."

"What!" exclaimed Dante. "What kind of an inheritance is that, anyway?"

"That's the way it is. Whether you like it or not. But if you think about it, anyone who comes into an inheritance is usually happy about it, right? It almost always improves your lot in life . . . "

Some of the brothers, in trying to understand what Floti and Dante were saying, had already gotten lost along the way and they only thing they had clear was that it was all very confusing, stuff that you needed an education to understand. Everyone knew that if you were poor and unschooled that made you an easy mark and you could be easily fooled by notaries, lawyers, counselors and the like. They'd bleed you white if you didn't watch out. So when Floti finally put the decision to his assembled family, reminding them that if no one went to claim the inheritance within a certain amount of time, the state would take anything there was to take, he was met with a long silence.

Armando tried to lighten things up by cracking a joke—he had one for every occasion—but he was shushed by the others. "Stay serious, we're talking about the family interests," Dante chastised him.

Armando shut his mouth, but not before he could get in a fast, "Too bad because it was a good one."

"Then you tell us what you think, Dante," Floti urged, calling on the second eldest brother to provide an opinion.

"It doesn't seem so rich to me," said Dante. "First of all, Genova is quite a ways away. She'd have to take a train, find a hotel, eat at an *osteria*. How is she even supposed to find the office of this notary and how long will it take her, unless we hire a carriage? And all of that costs money. Then, as you just said, we have to see if there's something to be had, like money or land, or just a pile of debts. It wouldn't be the first time! And what about the notary? He'll want to be paid as well. And

174 · VALERIO MASSIMO MANFREDI

just how do we calculate if we stand to lose or to gain? We'll have to hire an accountant to add things up for us, and there you go, another expense. There's nothing certain about this. I would forget about it. After all, things aren't going so badly for us: why should we go out looking for trouble?"

Floti listened without letting out any feeling or emotion and continued making the rounds to gather his brothers' thoughts.

Fredo was of the same opinion as Dante. The city was far away, they'd never been there, everyone knew that city people can't wait to make fools out of country folk, to trick them and make them look like idiots. It was all much too complicated, and the only sure thing was that they'd have to spend money. Best to let the whole thing go.

Armando made a little speech that was actually quite sensible, and mirrored their mother's: as long as there was nothing to split up, they all got along fine, but as soon as money and property were in the game, they'd kill each other for a dime. This inheritance didn't seem all that great after all, and who had the money for all those expenses? None of them did, so that settled the matter, didn't it.

Floti expected that at least Checco would favor giving the endeavor a try, but instead he was very cool, leaning towards no rather than yes. He was more fatalistic than anything else: if you're born poor you die poor and you'd better get used to the idea. Thinking that you can better your lot in life holds more risks than advantages. And he was honestly perplexed about how Clerice would get along in such a distant city: what if she got sick? Or if she had some kind of accident? How would they find her? How would they get her back home?

"That makes four," Floti thought to himself and he realized that he'd already lost, unless their mother herself spoke out in favor of the idea. He was sorry he'd thrown out both the pros and the cons; he should have emphasized the pros, certainly.

It was his turn to talk, and he knew it would take great skill to get his mother and the others to change their minds. He hoped to sway Checco, at least, who was such an intelligent lad.

"I think you are all mistaken: you, Dante, and you, Armando and Fredo and most of all, Checco; you've seen the world, you've been in France, I'm surprised at you! How can you say such a thing? I've heard of a considerable number of people who have managed to change their lot in life: some who have started out without a penny to their names and have built a fortune in a foreign country, others who have gone into debt to make an investment and earned it all back tenfold. Risk is the spice of life! Why is it that all of you only see difficulties and problems? If no one had ever dared to try something new, we'd still be savages. There are problems, I admit that, but they can be solved. Money? We can always go to a bank, show them this letter, and say: 'This is an inheritance. If you, the bank, lend us money to go and get it, we'll give you five percent.' Can't you see that?"

"Mother may have inherited land, farms, for instance. Can you imagine us finally working our own land without having to turn over a share to anybody? Or starting up another kind of business? Always with our mother's permission, of course, that's clear. Just letting it go, allowing the government to scoop it all up, that's madness, to my mind. My opinion is that we should scrape together enough money for the trip and for a hotel for mother in Genova, so that she can collect her inheritance. If you like, I will go with her. I'm sure we can do this."

That's where he made his mistake. Him taking over the role of the patriarch, without being the eldest brother, had already irked some of them. They had never said anything in the past because the results were good, but a sense of envy was already rife among them. When he offered to accompany their mother, more than one of them felt that Floti, underneath it all, must have had some personal interest of his own at heart. Had he convinced her to favor him in some way? Had he already made a deal with the notary? In a matter of moments, the idea that "better nothing for anyone than too much for one alone" spread like wildfire among the brothers. Ignorance, always the companion of diffidence, did the rest.

Savino, on the other hand, spoke openly in Floti's favor. He was still too young to have certain thoughts and he was fascinated by his older brother's personality; Floti always knew what to do, seemingly without having any doubts. Or, if he did have doubts, he got rid of them by grabbing the bull by the horns. He also admired how his brother was so attractive to women, but didn't let himself fall for a girl easily. Floti could make them suffer, all right; when he accepted a relationship it was him in the lead: he never succumbed to a woman like poor Gaetano had, destroying his own life in the bargain. The girl who would pull the wool over the eyes of Raffaele Bruni, known as Floti, hadn't been born yet!

"Floti is right!" Savino cried out as soon as his turn came. "He's the one who should go with mother. He knows how to handle himself; a lawyer or a notary can't fool him or lead him by the nose like a chump. He's our brother: who can we trust if not him?"

Floti even tried to pull Maria, always his favorite, over to his side. Whenever he went to the market, he'd always bring back a little something for her dowry: a bit of lace, an embroidered towel, sometimes even perfume. But Clerice stopped him: "In this household, or in any other house I've heard of, it's never the women who decide the affairs of the family, except for the *arzdoura*; as the matriarch, I will speak for her, and you already know how I feel about this."

Talk was finished, the decision made. They'd do nothing.

That nonevent became legendary: for years in town everyone spoke of a fabulous inheritance that had been tossed to the winds due to the Brunis' stubborn simplemindedness. No one would ever learn how much it amounted to.

There was never any doubt that it had truly existed, because precisely one year later, another letter arrived from the notary in Genova to inform them that, since no one had appeared to claim the inheritance, it had been turned over to the state's coffers. Armando said that this Mr. Coffer was a very fortunate guy and that they had been idiots, but it was too late to do anything about it. Floti said nothing, because just thinking about it made his blood boil.

It wasn't long at all before life picked up again as if nothing had ever happened.

CHAPTER FIFTEEN

C hecco married a young woman from town called Esterina. Intelligent, affectionate and uncomplicated, she immediately entered into Clerice's good graces. They had a happy marriage because they were well suited to each other and happy with what they had. Checco didn't want to be a farmer his whole life, and decided to learn a trade that would allow him to make ends meet, while his wife tended to things at home without wearing herself out too much. And that would leave him a bit of time to spend with his cronies in town. He knew he'd have to be careful about having children, because once they moved into a rented house, there wouldn't be much room. Destiny gave him a hand here because once his wife had had their first son, she never remained pregnant again.

They called the boy Vasco, a name they'd heard in the pirate stories that Fonso told at night in the stable. The war and the battle of Bligny were much more distant in Checco's memory than they were on the calendar, although he never quite forgot Pipetta belting out his song so he could be heard over the cannon fire and calling him "milord" as he merrily turned his cart in the direction of the steel monsters in a head-long race to meet his fate, like Amphiaraus in *Seven Against Thebes*, another of Fonso's tales.

Floti had also begun seeing a girl, seriously and with the most honorable intentions. But once again, as in many other ways, his behavior set him apart from all his brothers: he was the only one to break with the age-old adage that it was better to stick to your kith and kin when seeking a bride. She hailed from a nearby town on the Samoggia. Better to mix up your cards than stay local, Floti declared. Her name was Mafalda and she was lovely without being showy, the kind of beauty that lets itself be discovered and appreciated a little at a time. Only her eyes shone outright: they were black as coal, shadowed by long lashes, quick and intriguing. They spoke much more openly than her mouth did, which she often kept closed, especially when she found herself in talky company.

This was a quality of hers that Floti liked instantly; he read it as a sign of her intelligence. When he finally saw her unveiled, the first night of their marriage, her shape softly revealed in the light of a candle that she had distractedly forgotten to blow out, he reveled in her sensual perfection. Her breasts were firm and round like those of the bronze sirens in Bologna's main square. She had stepped out of her clothing, like a butterfly from a chrysalis, and the shapeless gray folds of the material contrasted with the sinuous curves of her body.

Floti, who had been brought up to be proper, was still in his underwear at this point, but encouraged by the sudden and unexpected immodesty of his bride, stripped to the buff as well. Holding her close in bed later, he said: "Why were you always hiding in such big, shapeless dresses? I could never have imagined that you were so beautiful."

"Why would I want to be admired by men I'm not interested in? So I could go to the trouble of spurning them? I was waiting for this moment, to show myself only to you."

So this was the kind of love, the kind of lover, that rich, powerful men could seek and hold for themselves! Floti felt that a kind of miracle had happened to him. He resolved to love her wholly, fully, deeply, and to stay beside her his whole life. He realized that he wanted that body, those eyes and that smile all for himself; he would not let her be disfigured by an endless series of pregnancies, nor worn out by toil, nor burned by the sun and the frost. He would cherish her and defend her like wheat ready to be harvested, like a cluster of ripe grapes.

But even this fact, of having a beautiful wife who remained that way, ended up sowing envy, among both his brothers and their own wives. Floti ran his life well and lived well. He didn't dirty his hands in the stable, nor did he soil his shoes with mud or dust. When he left the house he always wore a clean, pressed shirt and jacket, cotton trousers in the summer and wool ones in the winter. Practically no one remembered that he'd returned from the war with shrapnel in his lung and that the doctors had admonished him not to do heavy or tiring labor. Despite this, the well-being of the family had always depended largely on him. He sold their cheese at the best price, paying attention to the trends of the market, his hay was untouched by mold, his fruit blemish-free, his wine without a flaw. He managed this by choosing the right men for each job. All in all, he never put on airs, he treated everyone with respect and when he'd made a good deal he always remembered to bring home some prettily patterned material for his sisters-in-law and some toys for the children.

Life continued as usual that whole winter on the farm, and the big snows didn't fail to bring the usual guests to Hotel Bruni. Wanderers and wayfarers, even several pilgrims on their way to Rome to pray at the tomb of Saint Peter. The house was always open to anyone suffering from hunger, cold or solitude, as it had been for time immemorial.

Fonso told his stories and one peaceful night slipped into the next as everyone listened. He and Maria were engaged by now, in secret, because Floti was against it. The Brunis were enjoying, it might be said, a moment of grace. They had absorbed the terrible blow of Gaetano's death, which mostly Clerice had borne the brunt of, and were going about the quiet business of forming their own families.

Despite appearances, Floti was no dandy. He was a farming man, dedicated to improving the conditions of his extended family and his own stock. The first child born to him and Mafalda was a boy, whom they called Corrado, and then a girl he decided to call Ines, a Spanish-sounding name that had an exotic touch and an aristocratic one at the same time.

That was, perhaps, the best moment in the history of the Bruni family, but it didn't last long. Shortly after the birth of little Ines, Floti suffered a terrible blow: he lost his wife. Perhaps the pregnancy had weakened her, or an infection had struck; one day Mafalda fell sick and a week later she was gone. Floti never left her side for a minute and held her hand until the very last moment, hoping and trusting that she would pull through. He hung onto her every word, as if saving them up for a time when he wouldn't be able to listen to her voice ever again.

It was unusual for men of his type to be so tender with their wives. It smacked somehow of a lack of virility, but Floti was gentle and solicitous, caring for her and serving her like a princess. He even brought her fresh oranges, which cost a fortune.

"Do you think we'll see each other in heaven?" she asked him in her last moments.

Floti couldn't lie to her at such a terrible moment. "I don't know," he answered. "Maybe I should say yes, I believe we'll see each other, if that's what you're hoping and what will make you happy. To me it makes no difference. I've already known heaven: the moments I've spent with you in this room have been the most beautiful of my life and I'll never know anything like this again. I'll keep thinking of you, for all the rest of my days, and even if we do see each other again, I can't believe that we could ever take more delight from our love than we have right here in this bed, or that we'll ever be able to look at each other with such desire."

At these words her eyes welled up with tears and when she felt that her time had come she squeezed his hand with all the strength left to her and said: "Take care of our children. Give me a kiss, and then go, because I have to die now."

Floti gave her a kiss, walked down the stairs and said to Maria: "Go upstairs and take care of her body, please. Dress her in her most beautiful gown. I can't."

Other people died that winter, in town, of starvation, of the cold and of tuberculosis, and the big church bell tolled often, filling the streets with its death knell. Clerice was called to many a death bed, to recite the rosary after the person had passed. Maria would go with her, and when the struggle was a long one and lasted through the night, she would shiver as she heard the hooting of an owl, a syncopated moan which sounded to her like a hiccup.

"It's really true that owls bring misfortune!" she told her mother.

"Misfortune happens even without owls, daughter," her mother whispered in her ear, but she wasn't convinced. From then on, whenever Maria found an owl nest while she was picking elm leaves for the animals or gathering cherries, she would destroy it. If there were nestlings inside, she would kill them, so less misfortune might befall the town.

When the winter lightened its grip and the townsfolk had wept over their dead for long enough, work in the fields began again. Many families were starting to earn a bit of money, and could afford to buy food, but quite a few children would still be sent out to beg for alms early in the morning before school.

Change was in the air, and soon the people who owned the land and those who worked it were at loggerheads. Hard negotiating by the unions had procured better conditions for tenant farmers, who were now able to keep sixty percent of the harvest for themselves, and turn over only forty percent to the proprietor. The land owners had all united to depict the socialists who were fighting for workers' rights as revolutionary sub-versives, like the Bolsheviks in Russia who had overturned the czar and slaughtered his whole family.

In order to achieve their goals, these land-owners' coalitions had for years been financing and supporting the Combat Leagues led by Benito Mussolini. His so-called 'action squads' beat, intimidated and terrorized anyone who dared to sympathize with the laborers and farmers.

Savino was practically the only one in the family to take interest in such things, and one day he asked his brother Floti what he thought of this Mussolini.

"He's a man who has dashed the legitimate hopes of a great number of people," replied Floti, "He's chosen to side with the people who can offer him power. At the start of his career, he was championing a work day of eight hours and a retirement age of fifty five. He was active in the socialist movement and wrote articles for *"Avanti!,"* the party newspaper. Now, not only has he become the head of the government, but he's bent and determined to go it alone. It's called a dictatorship when one man rules alone, and that can only end badly."

Savino listened eagerly, although Floti took too much for granted when he spoke to his brother. No one had ever talked to Savino about certain issues. Floti himself had slowly become convinced that he could not stand and watch while the rights of men who worked from morning till night were systematically trampled upon. The loss of his wife had pushed him even further into politics, in no small part because it took his mind off her. He decided to run for councilor in the local elections, even though Clerice had begged him not to, not to get mixed up in things, because only trouble could come of it.

One spring morning Savino found himself walking along the drainage ditch that separated his property from his neighbor's when he noticed a group of people assembling on a strip of unplowed land between two big cornfields. Two or three of them were farmhands who worked on the adjoining plots of land. They provided their labor free of charge, in exchange for food and a place to sleep. They weren't on his land, so he stopped and looked on curiously, until one of them noticed him and beckoned him over. Savino recognized him and he recognized another man as well, a friend who had been in the war with him and had fought on the Piave, one of the "Boys of '99" as they were called. Savino jumped over the ditch to join them: a gesture he would long remember as the moment he took sides.

The friend was named Antonello, but everyone called him Nello. He'd proved to be a great soldier in the war, as brave as a lion. The man who had motioned him over was from Magazzino, a little town just about a kilometer away; his name was Graziano Montesi and he was a blacksmith. He had a high, wide brow and fine black hair that he slicked straight back with a hand of brill cream. He wore a fustian suit, a hazelnut colored cotton shirt and a grey tie. Not fancy clothing by any means, but it gave him an air of distinction and elegance, as if those assembled laborers deserved the same respect as the Senate of the Realm.

"You're a Bruni, aren't you?" he asked.

"Right. My name's Savino."

"You're welcome here with us. Your brother Floti is running for councilor, isn't he? Well, I'm here to advise all these men to vote for him because he's a socialist like us. I hope you'll vote for him too. We're working men, and we should be respected. As citizens of this country, our rights should be recognized."

Savino had never even thought of himself living in a "country," only in the town where he'd been born. This man was talking about the whole of Italy! The speech of this impromptu tribune went on for nearly an hour, and Savino didn't miss a word of it. Montesi spoke in inspired tones of liberty, of rights, of equality. He spoke of the irremediable damage and loss caused by the war that had actually been turned to the advantage of big industrial groups and landowners, their bosses, who were now preventing laborers, workers and farmers from achieving more humane living conditions.

"We don't want to start a revolution," he concluded, "we've already seen enough blood. All we want is to be treated like human beings, to have the value of our work and our toil recognized. We're asking that our dignity as citizens be recognized. And we want a State that makes people who have more property and money pay taxes, so as to help people who have less. No gifts, no alms, which are only another way of humiliating us. Only what is legitimately ours.

"It won't be this government that gives us what we ask; they're well on their way to becoming a dictatorship. They're filling the city squares, and Parliament, with their empty, pretentious words, but we can see the truth here in the countryside, where we are suffering violence and humiliation. The king is doing nothing to defend free institutions. But we must not surrender, we will continue to fight, until we win."

The silence that followed seemed interminable, then everyone started expressing their opinions at once: some wanted to cut the throats of the landowners, because they were all bastards anyway, others felt that the key was abolishing private property, like in Russia. Everyone should be treated the same, receive in accordance with their needs. It was not right for a few to live in luxury and the rest to live in misery; the big estates should be confiscated and farming cooperatives instituted.

As each man spoke his mind, and Montesi tried to respond as best he could, Savino and Nello walked off together, jumping the ditch back to the other side. "I think he spoke well," said Savino.

"Sure, nice words, but for pity's sake, can't you see that he's just fueling hate? Weren't you listening to the others? All

186 · VALERIO MASSIMO MANFREDI

mouthing off as if we were at the barber's shop. No one even considering that if one guy is a farmer and another guy is a head of state there must be a reason for that. Who was Mussolini only three or four years ago? No one. And now who is he? The most important man in Italy, with grand projects for this country. Too many people run off at the mouth without any idea of what they're saying."

"Well, maybe, but the fascists we know are arrogant bullies. They thrash anyone who doesn't agree with them. They caught up with a trade-union rep in Sant'Agata and beat him to a pulp; when he came to, they made him drink half a bottle of castor oil in front of his wife and kids. He spent the whole night on the toilet. And this was a good guy, a father . . . if someone tries something like that with me, I'll go after him and kill him dead, so help me god. Castor oil? I'll show them castor oil . . . "

"Calm down, Savino. Fine, they may be hot heads but what's important is that they're restoring law and order . . . "

"Whose order? Mussolini's?"

"Why, are you telling me that the Russians know what they're doing?"

Savino stopped and looked his friend in the eyes: "Are you a fascist, Nello?"

"What if I were?"

Savino fell silent for a while, thinking, then replied: "You're right, a friend is a friend. We fought together in the war. Side by side. When any minute, any second, it was a matter of life or death. You're more than a brother for me, but be careful, Nello, if you go down that road you don't know where you'll end up. They're bad people. Bandits, blustering cowards, running wild."

"That's not true! They're patriots."

"We're the patriots! We are the ones who pushed back the Austrians at the Piave. We could have given up, turned tail, run back home. We were only eighteen years old. Do you remember how many of our companions we saw fall?" Tears came to Savino's eyes as he was speaking. "Just think of the *Arditi*, Nello, who vowed to protect the population after the war; they defended Parma against the fascists, saved her people from their violence and abuse. The *Arditi*, Nello! You and I saw them during the war, attacking with a dagger between their teeth, as many as three times in a single morning, remember? Balbo and his fascists didn't have a chance against them. They were driven out of the city.

"They're the real patriots, because our country is not some fancy lady dressed up in green, white and red like you see in our schoolbooks; our country is us: the farmers who make bread for everyone, the workers who keep the factories going, and all the rest of us . . . why can't they get that into their heads?"

Nello dropped his head. "I understand what you're saying, Savino, but your leaders are poisoning you with their theories so they can sic you on what they call the bourgeois class that is ruling the nation. They're filling you up with hate so you'll start a revolution; they want to turn all of you into a bunch of rioting fanatics. Even that Graziano Montesi that you were just listening to and liked so much. There are many others like him. But they will not succeed. Mussolini will make this country great and he'll make sure everyone gets help: he'll give us land and seeds to sow in that land, he'll help the women and their children, he'll build railways and ports, he'll open new construction yards and make work for everyone, here or in our colonies. But right now we can't avoid this violence. We can't allow defeatism and subversion to take hold."

"That's the difference between you and us," shot back Savino. "Almost every day, we have to suffer the abuse that you inflict on us because you continue to accuse us, in your sick minds, of intentions that we do not have. Even though we

188 · VALERIO MASSIMO MANFREDI

would have every reason to rebel against this slavery. No, your way of thinking is warped, Nello, and I'm afraid that we'll never be able to come to any agreement on this. Certainly not now. All I can hope is that we never find each other with guns in our hands, against each other this time, on opposite sides."

"That won't happen. We'll never be one against the other, I swear it . . . Do you trust me?"

"I do."

"Good. See you around, Savino."

"See you around, Nello."

They went their separate ways.

Floti was successful in his bid for office; he was elected to the city council and became deputy mayor. He began working in favor of those who were the most disadvantaged: the day laborers and the tenant farmers who were living under the harshest conditions. He sought to create job opportunities for the farmhands in public works and to encourage the farmers themselves to form associations so their products could be sold at a better price on the market and generate higher profits. In his enthusiasm for his new role, he committed a number of mistakes. One was certainly that of positioning his men on the road to waylay the wheat-laden carts of the big landowners on their way to the warehouse and steer a number of them towards the houses of destitute, hunger-stricken families. His friend Pelloni would have been proud of him if he'd seen that. In general, however, he tried to apply the same criteria he'd used to improve the well-being of his family members to improving the lot of the townspeople. On one hand this made him very popular, but on the other it branded him as a "Red" and made him the target of the fascist squads.

Threatening slogans even began to appear scrawled on walls: "Death to Bruni!"

Clerice was terrified and set about trying to convince him in any way she could to leave his post, and politics as a whole. All she could see was the likelihood of losing another son, after the war had miraculously spared them all. It seemed too much to ask the Madonna to save Floti's life, as She already had when he had been wounded in the war. Especially considering that the first time around he'd had no choice, but this awful situation here was a problem of his own making.

"You can always say you're not well, that the doctor told you not to overtax your strength, which is the pure truth. They'll surely find someone else who wants to be the deputy mayor, you're not the only person in the world."

"Mother, the people elected me because they trust me and I certainly can't abandon them now, just as the situation is becoming more and more difficult by the day."

"I don't want anything to happen to you. I've already lost Gaetano and I've cried all my tears. I don't want to lose you too; I'd rather die myself."

"*Mamma*, nothing will happen. They won't kill me. There's still the police and the *carabinieri* and the judges. The fascists are good at ganging up on someone ten to one and beating the hell out of him, but killing a man is a whole different thing: you go to prison for that. Prison for life, and there's no getting out. And they know that."

"That may be, but they are hot-tempered and once they get started, the most violent ones can become dangerous: all it takes is once. You fall badly, you hit your head and there you are, dead. And with your wound, you're made of glass! If they beat you, that fragment that you have in your lung can tear it and make it bleed . . . oh, dear God! Do not challenge fate, Floti, listen to your mother."

"Mother, I've told you, you mustn't worry," he answered. "I'm not alone. My friends keep their eyes open and they're always passing me information. When they notice a band of fascists getting together at night, they warn anyone who might be their target, so they can hide and stay safe. We don't wait around to be slaughtered like sheep. And if worse does come to worst, we know how to defend ourselves: we've been in the war."

"See? It's true! You're already thinking of using a weapon! Dear God in heaven, help me!" Clerice invoked the Madonna and all the saints to change the mind of that obstinate son of hers.

One evening towards the middle of March, a boy ran into the Bruni courtyard asking for Floti. He might have been ten or twelve years old; he was thin, his hair was dripping with sweat and his eyes were as frantic as if he'd seen the devil himself. Floti was coming out of the stable, where Guendalina had just given birth to a calf, and he found himself face to face with the child.

"I'm Graziano Montesi's son," he said, panting. "Last night, the fascists came to our house and they beat my father; they punched and kicked him and caned him. They spit on him and told him that if he doesn't stop sticking ideas in the heads of the villagers, they are going to kill him."

Floti tried to calm him down. "Were you there?" he asked.

"Yes. They closed me into a room but there was a crack in the door and I could see everything."

"Did you recognize anyone?"

"I think so. My father said they were from Sogliano."

"How is your father?"

"He's in bed. His face is swollen up and it's all black, his lip is split and one of his eyes is completely closed. It hurts him everywhere. He looks scary; if you saw him you wouldn't know it was him. Grandma's crying. My uncle tried to defend him but they locked him in the pig sty and they said they'll kill him if he says a single word. I got him out after they left."

"Wait, I'll come back with you." He hitched the horse to

the carriage, helped the boy up and took off at a fast clip towards Magazzino.

"What's your name?" asked Floti as they were on their way.

"Bruno."

"Do you go to school?"

"Every day."

"Good. You have to learn to read and write if you don't want people to trick you. Read a lot of books; they'll teach you what life is about. What do you want to be when you grow up?"

"A blacksmith. Like my father and my grandfather."

As soon as they arrived, Floti jumped out, tied the mare to the iron ring hanging on the wall and went up the stairs behind the boy. Graziano, stretched out in bed more dead than alive, looked like Christ on the cross. His mother was at his side, holding his hand and weeping.

"Look what they've done, Floti!" she said as soon as she saw him. "Tell him yourself that as soon as he's able to stand, he has to leave here. If he stays they'll kill him, understand? They'll kill him," and she starting sobbing again, dabbing at her eyes with a handkerchief.

"Can you talk, Graziano?" asked Floti.

Montesi nodded.

"Your mother's right. I'll have my men take you someplace where they'll help you get back on your feet and where you can stay hidden and protected until this storm is over with. Has the doctor come?"

"Yes," he said, pointing at the bandages around his head.

"Did he give you medicine?"

His mother broke in: "He said to put cold compresses on the swelling and to take these pills to help with the pain."

"Tomorrow I'm going to report this crime to the *carabinieri*, but you have to go," Floti repeated. "We'll take care of you."

Montesi shook his head weakly and motioned for Floti to come closer. Floti leaned over the bed.

"I can't run. Who will help our people here? I can't leave them at the mercy of these thugs."

"Don't be an idiot. You look like hell. Tomorrow, after I talk to the doctor, I'll get you out of here myself. And then I'll make that report to the *carabinieri*."

Montesi put a hand on his arm. "I'm not leaving, Floti. We can't give them a free hand. You go home. I'm staying."

There was no way to convince him and Floti returned home fuming.

CHAPTER SIXTEEN

Floti went the day after Montesi's beating to the municipal *carabiniere* headquarters and, as deputy mayor, was immediately received by the commander himself, sergeant Curto, a good man although something less than lionhearted.

"Sir," Floti began, "the night before last, Graziano Montesi was brutally beaten by a fascist squad from Sogliano, and he is in serious condition. Have you heard about this?"

Curto replied with another question, a sign of his evident embarrassment: "Are you reporting a crime?"

"Yes, if you're not already in the process of taking action. That's why I asked you if you knew anything."

"Of course. The *carabiniere* chief in Sogliano called me that night to tell me that a squad was heading towards Magazzino. Their target was easily identified."

"So why didn't you do anything about it?"

Curto sighed. "My dear Bruni, I find myself in the middle of two violently-inclined factions on the verge of war with each other and all I have at my disposal are five officers and one corporal. You expect me to take action against the fascists who beat Montesi, but have you ever asked yourself why I haven't taken action against you? How often have you and your friends halted carts of wheat belonging to Ferretti, Borrelli, Carani and I can't say how many other landowners, seized these vehicles and taken possession of the goods being transported?"

194 - VALERIO MASSIMO MANFREDI

"Since we're laying our cards on the table, chief, I can tell you that those carts were not seized, but rather relieved of a sack or two of wheat or flour which was given to the families of workers or farmhands who were starving. The drivers were then left free to arrive at their destinations. If you don't believe me, question the people who were involved."

"I have done so, and that's the only reason why the authors of this prank, and you yourself, haven't been arrested on charges of theft."

"Don't tell me you're comparing these two things. Those were delinquents who took a man who had never done anything wrong and beat him nearly to death. We were trying to help people who were suffering."

"By committing a crime. The fascist action squads are supported by the government, the government is legitimized by the king. Do you really think that one single *carabiniere* sergeant, in a small town in Emilia Romagna, could sally forth on his own and take on such powers? There's simply a tacit agreement: no dead on their end and none on ours."

"Sounds like connivance to me."

"Watch your words, Bruni. We're trying to save what we can and to prevent the worst from happening. We've sworn allegiance to the king and cannot fail this oath, unless we want to set off a civil war. Listen to me: give Montesi some sound advice. Tell him to leave, at least for a while, and then we'll see. He's propagating ideas that are seen as subversive, especially when connected to the thefts that your men have been responsible for, Bruni. Understand what I'm saying? It's like a snake that's biting its own tail."

"Agreed, sir. We'll stop requisitioning the wheat, and you'll do your job with the fascists."

Curto lit a Tuscan cigar and let out a big cloud of smoke, as if he wanted to hide his embarrassment behind it. "If you cease the requisitions, that will make my job easier," he replied, "but

I can't promise anything. Do tell Montesi to get out of here, at least until the waters have calmed."

Floti managed to convince his men to let up in their campaign against the wheat producers, at least for a period of time, but he did not succeed in persuading his friend to go. As soon as Montesi was better, he was meeting up again with laborers and workers and organizing *la Resistenza*. The fascists didn't give up either, but changed their tactics. Instead of canes and crowbars, they came armed with more underhanded, but even more devastating, weapons. They tormented and humiliated him without leaving any signs of violence, until he fell into a state of total prostration. He no longer spoke with anyone and locked himself in his room, in the dark, like in a tomb. One morning they found him hanging from a beam at the foot of his bed.

He had decided to go that way instead of running away.

Floti realized that he would be the new target, but no one could have imagined what was to happen next.

One evening at dinner time, as he was eating dinner with the family, there was a knock on the door. It was the *carabinieri*.

"Raffaele Bruni," said the corporal commanding them, "I hereby declare you under arrest and order you to come with us."

"I don't understand," replied Floti, alarmed, "what have I done?"

"You'll be told when the time comes. Follow us."

Clerice wailed in despair: "Why are you taking him away? He's done nothing!"

His brothers were in shock as well: the *carabinieri* never set foot in the home of an honorable family.

Floti tried to calm his mother: "Don't cry, *mamma*. There must be some misunderstanding, you'll see. I'll be back tomorrow."

Instead, the charges were quite serious.

"Attempted homicide," said sergeant Curto when he was brought to headquarters.

"What is this, a joke?" asked Floti. "You know full well that that's not possible."

"You'll have to convince the judge, Bruni, and I'm afraid that won't be easy."

"Who was it that I'm supposed to have tried to kill?"

Curto, who was chewing on a nearly burnt-out cigar stub, replied: "Renato Marassi. Does that name mean anything to you?"

"Of course. He's a bastard, one of the worst fascist squad . . . "

"Careful of what you say! Marassi has accused you of shooting him."

"That son of a bitch! How can he say such a thing?"

"He does have a wound in his thigh, and he says you're the one who caused it, with a pistol. And that if you were a better shot, you would have killed him."

Floti flew into a rage, but there was nothing he could do about the charges. Curto advised him to find himself a good lawyer if he could, surmising that this was a trap the fascists had cooked up to keep Bruni out of circulation.

The next day he was transferred to the jail in Reggio Emilia and the judge, who had in the meantime read a police report that described him as a subversive, was intent on keeping him there at length.

Clerice went to visit every two weeks. She had Checco take her in the cart to the station at Castelfranco and she and Maria took the train to Reggio Emilia. They would bring bread, a *salame*, a few chunks of *parmigiano*, half a *pancetta*, a couple of bottles of wine, clothes that she had mended, washed and ironed, and they'd stay as long as possible to hear how things were going, whether there would be a trial and what the lawyer had said.

Floti was locked up with other "political" prisoners coming from a number of towns in the region, including some who spoke with the same accent as poor Pelloni. Floti shared with them everything his family had brought him.

The whole ordeal was a nightmare for Clerice. She had no doubts about her son's innocence, but she was deeply saddened by a situation that had shaken her life and that of the entire family. Being involved judges, policemen, *carabinieri* and lawyers was the worst thing that could happen to you, and all this because Floti had refused to listen to her advice. She thought that youngsters always think they know more than old folk, even though the older you are, the more things you've experienced. But they never believe you until they've smashed their own heads. And when they finally do realize what's best for them, the damage is already done.

In addition to their troubles with the law, there were also problems at home: no one was capable of replacing Floti in running the family affairs and things were going very poorly. His misadventure had managed to give the whole family a bad reputation, and their relationship with the community was no longer the same. The other brothers, in Floti's absence, tended to argue more often and it was up to Clerice to try to keep the family together and defend her missing son: "Remember," she'd tell them, "he always looked after the interests of the family before his own; when he came back from the market he always had a gift for your wives and he never treated them any differently than his own sisters. The fascists and the landowners have managed to put him in prison, but if you gang up on him as well, well, that's truly scandalous."

The complaining around the dinner table stopped only to pick up again in the fields where their mother could not hear them. The only one who abstained from criticizing Floti was Checco and, from a certain point of view, Armando as well. He wasn't even around much; skinny as he was, he wasn't usually much help on the farm, but he also didn't have what could be called a very strong work ethic. Sometimes he would disappear early in the day and not show up again until nightfall, especially when it was time to beat the hemp at mid-day under the scorching sun. On the other hand, he was the only one of them who still enjoyed good relations with the town's people. His stories were famously entertaining and his jokes were memorable. He was unmatchable at creating and spreading good cheer, and in such miserable times, his innocent, silly banter was a relief for the people around him, sometimes even a blessing. Folks loved to be in his company because he was so amusing, but he didn't command their respect because he was so weak: the strong and the arrogant had him under their thumb, and anyone who offered him a drink had him in their pocket.

Otherwise, just about no one in town continued to keep company with the Brunis. Iofa, the carter, would show up now and then for a question of work or to get some information. Despite his failing health, his hobbling walk and his bizarre looks, he wasn't afraid of anybody, nor was anybody afraid of him.

The summer that year was even hotter and more suffocating than usual, making work in the fields tougher and more tiring. The water in the steeping ponds rotted and let off a nauseating stench which spread on the thin mist that hovered above the surface when it got dark and the air cooled down. The only things that could survive in that turbid sewer water were the catfish who hunkered down on the muddy bottom without ever moving.

When, towards the end of the autumn, the heat finally let up, they started the harvest. Golden, ultra sweet grapes that produced an extraordinary wine. The Brunis still sang as they picked, in part to forget their worries, in part because the colors, the fragrance and the light still seemed a blessing from God.

The swallows left the third week of October. By Saint Martin's day the wine was already in the barrels and the wind scattered the red and yellow leaves among the grapevines, making them swirl like butterflies. Now Armando too had decided to marry and Clerice was quite surprised indeed. What woman would agree to marry this peculiar son of hers?

"Lucia, *mamma*, Lucia Monti," explained Armando. "Do you know her?"

Clerice regarded him with a perplexed expression: "Lucia Monti? Where's she from? Not those Montis who live at the Botteghetto?"

"That's her!" exclaimed Armando, satisfied.

Clerice scowled.

"She's beautiful, mother."

"She is beautiful, but you do know, don't you, why no one else has chosen her yet?"

Armando dropped his head and said only: "I like her. I don't care about anything else."

"The Montis are a tainted breed, my son. That woman may be beautiful but she'll bring you trouble. Leave her be, let someone else have her."

"*Mamma*, I know her very well. It's true, she's a bit strange at times, but nothing more. As long as you don't get her angry."

"You're a grown man, son, and you don't need someone to tell you what to do or what not to do. Remember, though, that I'm warning you: forget about her now, while you're still in time. She's not the only one with a nice bum and bosom! And anyway, you'll see, in five or six year's time the spell will be broken and you'll have a creature on your hands that you won't know what to do with."

Armando would not listen to reason and he married Lucia Monti at the end of November, on a cold, gray day. He was afraid that she would change her mind and he didn't want to risk losing her by waiting for the spring, the season in which just about everyone got married. He knew that he'd never again find another girl so beautiful.

He was given the bedroom that had been Gaetano and Silvana's, because no one else had wanted to sleep there even though space in the house had been running out and they'd had to convert part of the hayloft into a bedroom. The wedding lunch was plain and unpretentious because with Floti gone, there wasn't much hope for anything finer. Floti's absence weighed heavily on the festivities, but there was occasion for merriment nonetheless. To make sure of this, Armando took it upon himself to tell a number of spicy stories having married life as their common theme.

"Have you heard the one about Lazzari, the hunchback?" he began. He was talking about a blacksmith who lived in town. "Well, old Lazzari gets into a fight with his neighbor, who did something to annoy him, and now he's bent on giving him tit for tat. He knows that every morning, when this neighbor gets up to go to work, it is still dark out. So Lazzari waits until he leaves, sneaks into the house behind him and, quiet as a mouse, slips into the wife's bed, with her still sleeping! While it is still dark, he does what a wife could expect from a husband in bed and then, with her all relaxed and just about to fall back asleep, Lazzari the hunchback sticks her backside with a fork and runs off in the dark before she can see who he is.

"When her husband gets back that night, dead tired, she's waiting for him behind the door with her rolling pin and she clobbers him so hard he can't go to work for three days!"

Roaring laughter and the guests, tipsy by now, added their own stories until the cake and coffee were ready to be served. The bride laughed as well, but in a coarse, unbecoming way that embarrassed the others and put a frown on her mother-in-law's face. By dusk the party was breaking up.

Clerice served some of the leftovers for dinner and then

everyone retired, the men first of all, while she and Maria and a couple of the daughters-in-law cleared the table and began to wash the dishes. No sooner had they begun than they heard a scream of terror coming from the floor above them, as if someone were being murdered.

"Mercy!" exclaimed Clerice, dropping the soap into the sink. "What's happening up there?" She took off her apron and rushed up the stairs, stopping in front of the door to the newlyweds' room.

"Armando, what's happening?"

Armando came to open the door dressed in his nightshirt and looking all disheveled. Clerice could see the bride standing in a corner on the other side of the room, half-undressed, eyes wide, shivering with cold and fear.

"Out," she said to Armando, "but what on earth did you do to her?"

"Nothing, *mamma*, I swear it, I just got close to her, to . . . "

"I understand, I understand. Just go now, this one here is out of her mind." She entered the room, muttering, "What did I tell him?"

Armando went into his mother's room because he was cold and he lay there under the covers waiting wide awake to be able to go back to his rightful place, but time passed and not a thing was heard. Finally Clerice appeared with a candle in hand: "Where are you?" she asked, raising the candle and looking around the room for him.

"I'm here, *mamma*. I just got into bed because I was cold."

"Listen to me, are you sure you didn't do anything strange to her?"

"No, are you serious? I just got close and well, you know, I was ready . . . " Armando tried to explain, embarrassed.

"I understand, I understand. You can go back to your bed now. I've told her that you won't do anything to her and you'll both sleep and that's all. Then you'll have to see, a little at a time . . . you have to treat her like a child, understand? Not jump on her like a goat."

"*Mamma*, I didn't do that, I . . . " Armando tried to justify himself, but Clerice stopped him.

"I'm afraid the problems are starting even sooner than I expected." She refrained from adding 'I told you so,' because it seemed completely useless.

The next day it snowed.

CHAPTER SEVENTEEN

That winter, Fonso was invited to tell his stories at a number of different farms, some of them quite far from the town, but none so far that he couldn't get there on foot. He was happy to go: first of all, because he liked having an audience who were enchanted by listening to his tales, and then because they always gave him something, especially food, wine and wood for the fire, and in those times that was a lot. Some gave him a *salame*, others a plucked rooster, and others a big oak or elm log to burn in the fireplace. The most generous offered him his choice; they'd say: "Fonso, any trunk that you can manage to hoist to your shoulders and carry home is yours." This was said with a sly smile, as if to say let's see if your shoulders are as good as your tongue. And when Fonso had finished telling his story and everyone said goodnight and went to bed, he went out into the courtyard in the moonlight and picked up the biggest trunk he could carry on his back and away he would go, trudging through the snow for as far as a kilometer. Every so often he'd lean one end on the ground, so he could rest a bit, then he'd ease himself under the trunk again until he had it solidly on his shoulders, straighten up and go on.

But he'd go to the Bruni house for nothing, because there was another, greater reward waiting there. He was crazy in love with Maria. And that year, more people had shown up seeking lodging than ever before. There was one fellow who claimed that he'd been part of the band of Adani and Caprari, the two famous bandits who, in the saddles of their Frera motorcycles like knights errant, robbed the rich to give to the poor. He'd worked with them as a highway robber for four years before his two bosses were brought down in a gunfight with sergeant Capponi's *carabinieri* in the plains north of Modena. When he'd had a couple of glasses too many, the Brunis could hear him screeching in the middle of the night:

"When the moon sets sail over the hill
That's when we're ready to kill, kill, kill!"

Maria was terrified of him; when she brought him food he would look at her and roll his eyes and say, just like some ogre in a fairy tale: "I'm starving for a bit of the nice, tender meat of a Christian!" He would burst into hysterical, burbling laughter while she swiftly put his plate of soup down on the ground and took to her heels.

No one else, obviously, gave him a second thought. Except Armando, lying still in his bed with his eyes wide open next to his cold, numb wife. When he heard the shrill voice of that braggart piercing the night, he would shiver:

"The first attack was all mine:
We saw a lady dressed very fine
My knife went into her neck so white
We got her money without a fight!"

It was bitter cold that winter. Icicles hung from the gutters like crystal daggers for weeks and the hoar frost dressed the trees in white lace that the pale foggy sun couldn't manage to melt. It was winters like this that Hotel Bruni offered shelter to a full house. The cowherd would open two or three bales of hay and spread it out in a corner of the stable where wayfarers could stretch out comfortably and warmly. At meal time,

Clerice sent each of them a steaming bowl of soup and a small flask of wine, convinced that Our Lord himself might be hiding in any of those poor creatures, roaming through the night to test whose heart was hard and who instead had compassion for their fellow men.

Some of the guests even did something to deserve all of that benevolence. They helped to care for the animals or took out the manure or fixed the chairs or put a new handle on a shovel or hoe. In that case, they had dinner with the family because it was only right that someone who pitched in to help should be able to put their feet under a table.

It sometimes happened, in seasons like that one, that a woman came knocking at their door. It was very rare, but sometimes it happened. In that case, Clerice opened the little room where the vinegar was kept, because she didn't want trouble of any sort. There was one woman in particular, not all there in her head, who had come several times; that year she had shown up at the beginning of December and gave no signs of wanting to leave, although January was almost over. When they asked her who she was and where she came from, she would always answer with the same sing-song phrase: "Poor Desolina, her mind is unsound, poor thing . . . " She seemed to be mechanically repeating a diagnosis that she had been given lord knows where. One of those rare times that she seemed to be clear-headed she told them that, before she discovered Hotel Bruni, she had knocked and knocked at the door of the presbytery, back in Don Massimino's day, but that no one opened the door for her.

"I believe you!" replied Clerice. "Priests can't be having women in their house at night!"

Some claimed to know her story: she was a widow who had lived up in the hills with her only daughter, working an unproductive plot of land, all weeds and stones, from morning till night. One day her daughter seemed to fall ill: she was pale, subject to sudden fainting, nausea and vomiting.

"You're not pregnant, are you?" she'd asked the girl. "Look, if you're pregnant, I'll kill you. I told you that the owner of this land will drive us off if he hears of such a thing. We'll end up begging on the streets. We'll die of starvation!"

The girl was terrified by those threats and could find no rest. She felt she was to blame for of all of the misfortune that would befall them and finally, no longer able to bear the sense of guilt that was crushing her, she drank some mercury salts and died a horrible death. Her mother went crazy and the village doctor had her shut up in the insane asylum in Reggio Emilia. Whether she escaped or had been released, no one knew. That's where she must have learned the phrase: "Poor Desolina, her mind is unsound . . . unsound insane . . . "

Nobody knew whether such a cruel story was true or had been made up, but the perennially bewildered look in the woman's eyes made you imagine she was fighting a perpetual battle against herself. As if she were forever trying to forget or to repress intolerable memories. In any case, despite it all, Fonso's stories seemed somehow to quiet her, acting like a balm to soothe her frantic thoughts. She listened raptly without batting an eyelid. If she could, she would sit there for hours and hours. You could see that she was escaping the reality of a past that would not let her be; the voice of the narrator transported her to another time and another place.

When the stories were over and she had to reach her room by crossing the courtyard, she pulled her raggedy shawl tight around her shoulders and her body seemed to shrink until it nearly disappeared, prey once again to memory.

One night late in January, as Fonso was weaving his tales and had paused for dramatic effect, a hard knock at the stable door interrupted the deep silence.

"Who's there?" asked Checco.

"It's me," replied a voice hoarse from the cold. Checco went to open the door and there was Floti. Pale, his face gaunt and unshaven, his eyes shining, perhaps with fever. Maria leapt into his arms and Clerice dried her eyes on the corner of her apron. The others, both family and strangers, were struck dumb by the sudden apparition. His brothers, especially, did not know what to say. It was Fonso who had the presence of mind to break that stony silence. He jumped up with the flask to pour Floti a glass of wine.

"How's it going, Floti?"

"Much better, now that I'm home," he replied. He drained the glass and held it out again. "Give me another," he said, "and you go on, I didn't want to interrupt your story. It was your favorite, wasn't it, Fonso?" and he started reciting:

"From beyond the sea I have come
to collect the waters of the river Ossillo
that heal any kind of malady."

There was a moment of embarrassment. The circumstances would have called for everyone to leave, returning to their own homes or their own straw beds to allow the Brunis to speak with their brother who'd been released—or had escaped?—from prison. But no one made a move and Fonso understood that they truly expected him to continue. And continue he did.

"Go on, Fonso, you're just getting to the good part, if I remember well," repeated Floti, beckoning to Checco to follow him outside. His brother wrapped himself up in his *tabarro* and followed Floti out.

They faced each other in the icy courtyard while the sky sputtered fine snow at them.

"How are things going, Checco?"

"Badly. It's every man for himself, mother can't keep the family together any more. Savino wants to go. He has a girlfriend, and a job at the Ferretti farm. They're going to get married."

"We've all gotten married. That's normal."

"Yes," answered Checco, "that's normal."

"What else?"

"We bought a new bull for mounting the cows."

"I noticed, last stall on the left. Beautiful animal."

"Right, I paid a good price for him. Name's Nero."

"I want to know whether you spoke badly of me while I was inside."

"Why, Floti, what does it matter?"

"I want to know who organized the trap that sent me to prison."

"Prison has turned you bitter, I can understand that, but you have to try and forget. Revenge won't get you anywhere: the way things are going, it would only make them worse."

"I'll find out anyway. What about the storyteller? He's more here than at his own house, it seems."

"Maria in is love with him, and he with her. What's wrong with that, Floti? He's a good man, a hard worker, he's always come to help when we've needed a hand."

"He does that so you'll accept him. But that's something I'll deal with later. Do you know who betrayed me?"

"Floti, it's damn cold out here. Can't we talk about this tomorrow? What's the hurry? Is there some reason you want to talk now? How did you get out?"

"I was acquitted of the charge. The idiot who accused me wasn't even smart enough to get rid of the jacket that his pistol put a hole through. The judge sequestered it and the experts established that the shot came from inside his own pocket. This guy accidently shot himself and they decided to put my name on it."

"It's turned out all right for you this time, but this may not be the last you hear from them. If they've tried once, they'll try again. Go to sleep now, your bedroom is waiting for you. Mother has always kept it clean and neat. She was sure you'd be back."

Floti nodded gravely.

"Good night," Checco told him. "Welcome home."

They entered the house together and Floti went up to his room. From the window he saw Fonso saying goodbye to Maria in front of the stable door; the storyteller threw his *tabarro* around her and drew her close. Floti felt the blood rush to his head and he felt like running downstairs, but Fonso was already walking off.

Floti was convinced that, now that he was home, things would go back to the way they were before, but he was wrong. In his absence, the family situation, which had already begun to show its cracks, had further deteriorated. The inclusion of so many women had multiplied the occasions for tension and disagreement. Each of them thought she saw her sisters-in-law enjoying privileges and advantages that she didn't have, or felt that her own husband wasn't receiving the right amount of respect, or that some of the brothers were expected to do too much while others did too little. As for the husbands, they wanted to appear attentive and worthy in their wives' eyes, and thus tended to attach importance to imagined snubs or perceived acts of discourtesy that they never would have even noticed in the past. On top of everything else, Clerice was becoming worn down by all of the knocks life had given her, and no longer had the spunk she once had, nor the energy to manage such a numerous tribe.

Floti took the reins in hand again, but the family's bad habits had already become entrenched and it wasn't easy to go back. He needed a stroke of luck to help him regain his undermined prestige. The opportunity unexpectedly presented itself towards the end of that spring. Barzini, the notary who owned their land, had gone to meet his maker, and since none of his heirs was interested in agriculture, they had decided to sell the plot and to split up the proceeds equally among themselves. The Brunis were given the chance to buy the land that the family had been farming as tenants for over one hundred years, and what was more, at deferred payment conditions.

The family council was immediately convened: Clerice and her six sons. All of them participated, including Armando, who in the meantime must have convinced his wife to grant him her favors, since she was pregnant. The meeting took place in the kitchen, around the table where they had their meals, and Floti immediately took the floor: "You all know the reason we're here together today. The last time we met, it was to decide whether to pay for mother's trip to Genova so she could claim her inheritance. You all remember how that turned out: the inheritance was handed over to the government. Now we've been given another opportunity and I don't think we should this one slip: the landowner's heirs are willing to sell us this property.

"We've been farming this land for more than one hundred years, but the fruit of our labors has always gone to Barzini. At first, he barely left us enough to live on until, thanks to the cooperative league, we managed to get him to agree to more humane conditions. But whatever we had to turn over to him was still too much, considering that all the labor was ours and he never came to help us a single day, for a single hour."

Dante was afraid that his brother would start up on politics, and said: "Get to the point."

"I will," replied Floti, without hiding his irritation, "what I want to say is that we should buy our farm. The heirs have proposed that we pay for the property a little at a time over the next ten years. This is a positive gesture on their part: it means that they recognize that we've always worked the land and that we deserve to own it. We have a bit of money set aside in the bank . . . "

"We have money in the bank?" asked Fredo.

"That's right," replied Floti, "everything I managed to save was put into an account in mother's name, and we've even earned interest on it."

"I didn't know we had money in the bank either," broke in Dante.

"How much?" asked Armando.

"Enough to pay the first two installments of the debt we're going to incur, while allowing us to get along comfortably."

Floti realized that each one of his brothers was mentally calculating how much he would get if the money were to be divided up equally, and he thought it best to interrupt the process: "I know what you're thinking, but you're wrong. If we use that sum of money together, we'll all stand to gain. If we split it up, each one of us will have some money in our pockets but it won't get us anywhere. Strength lies in unity, you know that. They want thirty thousand liras, payable over ten years' time, which means that they're giving us the land for a song, even though the figure may seem high to you now. If we stick together we can do this, I promise you. Once we've bought the land, we'll be our own bosses, no one can tell us what we can do and what we can't do, no one can send us packing from one day to the next. And the forty percent that we've been turning over to Barzini will be ours to split up every year. Or we'll use it to buy more land and build a future for our children."

Floti concluded his plea without realizing that all of the enthusiasm and energy that he'd put into his speech, rather than convincing the others, had made them suspicious. When he noticed their reaction, he could have bit his tongue. He understood what they were thinking: if Floti is getting so excited about this, he's hoping to get something out of it himself. The atmosphere around the table felt heavy, and the silence that greeted his speech promised no good. If they wanted to buy the land, they would have said so right away.

But Clerice supported him this time: "Floti's right. Land never betrays you. If you have land, you're sure you'll never suffer hunger, no matter what happens. If you need to, you can always sell it again, and make a profit. Think about it, boys, Floti's never been wrong about things like this. I can barely believe it myself: the Brunis, who have been working someone else's land for a hundred years, becoming property owners!"

No one responded. Armando cracked a joke that made no one laugh.

"What's wrong?" asked Floti. "Don't you trust me? Are you afraid we'll sink into debt? That won't happen. If you borrow money without any capital, you've got a problem waiting to happen, but if we have capital, that is, our own land, we can always sell it and make our money back, if we need to. We can do this, together: we can set up a company, so that each one of us is protected and no one is running a risk. Think about it, please."

The brothers said they would think about it, that it wasn't something you could decide on the spur of the moment, that thirty thousand liras was no small sum and, finally, that they'd give him an answer in a couple of days' time.

Two days later, when Floti went to market with the cart to sell a sow, his brothers took advantage of his absence to meet and discuss the matter amongst themselves. After they'd hashed it out for more than an hour, each of them went to talk to their own wives, which further worsened the situation. Clerice realized what was happening and it saddened her greatly because it meant that the family had split apart and would perhaps never be like it once was.

Floti heard their verdict when he returned home for dinner. Dante spoke on behalf of the others: "It's too much money and we'll have to make too many sacrifices to pay the installments. And what if something goes wrong? The toil of a farmer is at the mercy of the weather. What if a hailstorm comes up and destroys the whole harvest? Or if the season is too damp and the wheat and hemp get moldy before we can pick them? I say, let's go on as we have been. After all, we've always had what we needed."

Floti made a last ditch effort: "But can't you see that if we don't buy the land someone else will? And it might be someone even worse than Barzini who, if nothing else, at least left us alone. When the land is sold, we'll be sold with it, in a certain sense, and you know that. If we buy it we'll own ourselves and our destiny."

Nothing doing. The true reason for their refusal was another; each of them, some more than others, thought that in reality nothing would change for them: they'd still be slogging away in the fields, milking the cows, emptying out the stable, hoeing and shoveling, spreading manure, beating hemp in the heat of summer, pruning the vines with freezing hands in the winter. While Floti couldn't do any of all that, poor thing, he had a piece of shrapnel in his lung. And so he had to go to the market, eat at the *osteria* with the brokers and the dealers, wheel around in a carriage, dress in a suit, shirt and tie because he had to make a good impression, especially when you go to the bank to deposit your money. He would have become the real boss, he would have decided the family interests, and this didn't suit them in the slightest, not them and not their wives, for whom every occasion was good to fan the flames.

When he learned about what had happened, Fonso, who had studied in books, said that this sorry state of affairs was exactly what had happened in the fable told by Menenius Agrippa, but no one paid any attention because no one had ever heard mention of any *Meno Grippa*.

Word got out in town because Armando couldn't keep piss to himself, let alone a secret. Many attributed the family's failure to buy the land to the envy Floti's brothers felt towards him and the influence that their wives had on those boys. But Dante and the others weren't all wrong. A debt of that size and an investment so important could certainly scare people who were used to conducting a life that was harsh but predictable, always the same, a life where the only surprises came from nature.

Whoever was right or whoever was wrong, the truth was that this was the last opportunity that fate offered the Brunis to deliver themselves from a state of eternal subservience and prepare a different future for themselves and their children. Now it was just a question of time: the time that it would take for the Barzinis to find a buyer. Then the Brunis would, of necessity, have to make a decision.

CHAPTER EIGHTEEN

F loti had got it in his head that he didn't want Fonso to court his sister Maria. He had nothing against the man personally, on the contrary, he was a serious lad who didn't mind hard work and enjoyed a good reputation in town.

It was a gut feeling. He felt that Fonso wasn't suited to Maria, ugly as he was, with that big, prominent jaw of his. And half deaf to boot. He knew that he and his sister had already been talking, and that talk might already have gone pretty far. He needed to break things up now if he didn't want to find Fonso in the house one day asking for Maria's hand in marriage.

As for Fonso, he knew that he needed to offer his fiancée and her brothers some assurances, and that meant a steady job, something that was not easy to find in that day and age. It was simply a question of supply exceeding demand; physical labor just wasn't worth much. But that didn't frighten Fonso: the important thing was getting an in and then showing the boss just what you could do.

An employment exchange existed, but the bosses preferred the do-it-yourself approach, which involved a visit to the "wall." This was a brick parapet that overlooked the now dry medieval moat which surrounded the town. Four artificial mounds marked its four corners. All of the laborers looking for work would gather there in the morning and lean against or sit on the wall, chatting with the others and waiting for someone to come along and hire them for a day or two or, if they were lucky, for the entire season. Fonso didn't go too often because if he wasn't already working someplace, he preferred to help someone who needed it, free of charge, rather than loiter around with the others. Even if he worked for free, there was some recompense at the end of the day: a flask of wine, a piece of loin, a slice of lard to make a tasty *soffritto* for pasta, or some chicken feet, neck, wings and innards for broth.

One morning, as he was passing by the wall, a couple of friends who were there looking for work stopped him and just at that moment, the steward of the Baccoli estate showed up. Baccoli was a lawyer in Bologna, and he owned vast tracts of farmland just outside town. He pointed his finger at six of the men, one after another: " . . . you, you, you and you go to over the farm on Via Emilia, there are ten furlongs of stubble to be turned over so we can sow the alfalfa." Those who'd been called upon got onto their bicycles and rode off in a group towards their destination. At that same instant, the overseer noticed Fonso's sturdy build and added: "And you go with them!"

Fonso thanked him and jumped on his own bicycle, pedaling hard to catch up with the others, who had a few minutes' head start. Given his experience, he already had an idea of why they had been recruited. To prepare a stubble field for planting alfalfa, it wasn't necessary to dig up ten furlongs of soil: a couple of oxen with a plow and then a final go with the harrow would accomplish the task much quicker and much better. This was certainly a test of strength, and Fonso knew very well what it entailed: the diggers would be lined up at the starting line and each would have to dig as fast as he could under the careful eye of the steward, who would be checking from behind whether anyone was cheating by not digging the shovel in deep enough so as to make quicker progress. In the evening, the slowest would be eliminated.

And that's just how it went. By dusk, Fonso was a length beyond the rest; the second guy was at least twenty meters behind him. It was a ruthless test, but everyone accepted it: it was right that the best man win. But in many cases, the problem was that some of them were undernourished and didn't have enough energy to sustain such backbreaking work. They had all figured that there was something important being tested here and had participated with all the strength and stamina they could summon up. The weakest of all proved to be a fifty-year-old farmhand named Mario. He collapsed twice that first day, pale and sweat-soaked, and when he got to the end, he had tears in his eyes, knowing that he would never be able to win the job.

He was, in fact, let go the next day. Another was sent home the day after, a third the next day, two on the fourth day and another on the fifth. On the sixth day, Fonso was the only one left.

"We need a foreman," the steward told him, "and you're it. We're hiring you at a fixed salary, you'll be paid by the week. If the landowner likes you, you'll even get a bonus at Christmas."

Fonso thanked him, hiding his satisfaction but, once he was out on the road, he started singing his *stornelli* at the top of his lungs, because he'd finally had a stroke of good luck! If his friends hadn't stopped him in front of the wall exactly at the moment that Baccoli's steward showed up, no one would have noticed him and he certainly wouldn't have been called upon to dig up the land on Via Emilia. Now he was a man with a sure salary and a steady job that could last him his whole lifetime. Now he could maintain a family and he could ask for Maria's hand in marriage, knowing that he'd be able to offer her a decent life.

Should he talk to Floti first, or Clerice? He thought it would be best to start from the toughest. If her brother said yes, the others would certainly fall in. But you could see from a mile away that Floti wasn't thrilled about the situation; he was jealous of his sister, somehow. Clerice, on the other hand, was very fond of him and would almost certainly accept his proposal without opposition. He decided to wait a couple of days, plucking up his courage and waiting until the news got out in town that he had become the foreman of a big estate, a stable job with a fixed salary, ready cash at the end of the week.

It was a Thursday evening in late April when he walked into the Bruni courtyard and asked if Floti was there so he could have a word with him.

"He's in the shed," replied Fredo, "unhitching the mare from the carriage."

Fonso went in that direction and met up with Floti as he was coming out of the shed.

"Nice evening, isn't it, Floti?" he said.

"It's a fine evening indeed, Fonso. What brings you here at this time of day?"

"I'd like to talk with you."

"I'm listening," said Floti.

"It's about Maria."

"Maria's not here."

"She's not here? Has she gone to do the shopping?"

"No, she's gone to Florence and she'll be there a long time."

"Florence? Without saying a word?"

"You know I have a married sister in Florence. She's not well just now and needs company. We thought that it would do Maria well to have a change of air, to stay in the city for a while. In Florence, everyone speaks Italian, so she can learn some there; it may come in handy."

Fonso lowered his head and frowned: "'Far from your eyes, far from your heart.' Is that what you're aiming for, Floti?"

Floti sighed, "It's no use playing games here, Fonso. It's true, that's one of the reasons I sent her to Florence. It's not that I have anything against you, you know. You're a good, honest man, a hard worker. I know what you're thinking: that when I was in prison you were always here helping in the fields, beating hemp at midday when the heat and the strain are enough to kill you, pulling the water-soaked hemp out of the pond when it's slippery and heavy as lead. See? I haven't forgotten and I'm no ingrate; I'll find a way to make good on my debt. You don't have any vices, Fonso, but I don't think you're the right man for Maria, and there's no way I'll let you marry into this family. Women don't understand a thing when they're in love, but then . . . if someone had pointed certain things out to them while they were in time . . . "

Fonso held up his hand: "Stop, Floti. That's enough. I don't understand, although I already knew you felt this way about me. You lost your own wife: she was beautiful and you were in love, just like me and your sister. It's not our fault! We love each other and we want to marry, to have a family. It's true, she's much more beautiful than I am handsome, but what does it matter? And now I'm a person with a steady job and a pretty good salary that will come in regularly. You're making a mistake here. Who says that she'd be happier with another man? You could ruin her life by giving her to someone that you like but that she doesn't. We'll be happy together. Why do you want to separate us?"

Floti scowled: "That's my business, Fonso, don't get mixed up in it. Maria's in Florence now and we'll see how that goes. As they say, 'if they're roses, they'll bloom, if they're thorns, they'll prick you.' Time will tell. But I'm against you marrying her and there's nothing I can do about that."

Fonso could not resign himself: "You're taking on a big responsibility, here, Floti, and I'm surprised at you. You, who have suffered the death of the woman you loved and were put into prison, an innocent man. You know what it means to be unhappy, to suffer. Why take it out on us? What have we done to you?"

"Nothing," said Floti. "That's it and there's no changing it."

Fonso wanted to insist, but he understood it was useless. There was nothing more to be said. His voice was trembling and he didn't want to break down in front of Floti. He left with tears in his eyes.

He walked his bicycle out to the street and started towards home, his heart swelling, as it began to get dark. After just a few dozen meters, he heard a whispered voice calling out to him: "Fonso, Fonso . . . "

"Who's there?" he asked.

"It's me, Maria," replied a voice on the other side of the hedge.

"Maria? But then you haven't gone to Florence!"

"Come over to this side, here, there's a hole in the hedge."

Fonso leaned his bicycle on the side of the ditch and leapt over to the other side.

"Where are you? I can't see you!"

"I'm up here on the elm tree. I was picking leaves for the cows and I saw you. Wait, I'm coming down."

"No, don't move. I'll come up, that way no one can see us."

He pulled himself up swiftly along the enormous trunk and found her in the middle of the foliage. He embraced her. "What is this? Ten minutes ago your brother told me you were in Florence."

"Well, it's not far from the truth. I'm leaving tomorrow. He's taking me to the station in Bologna and from there I'll take a train to Florence. He told you I'd already left because he didn't want us to say goodbye. He's worried I'll change my mind."

"Can't you change your mind? You know he doesn't want us to get married, don't you?"

Maria lowered her eyes. "I know. And he thinks that if I go to Florence I'll forget you. Listen to what I'm saying, Fonso: I can't disobey my brother, because he's the head of the family and he loves me. He thinks he's right in doing this, he doesn't realize what a mistake it is, but if you wait for me, I'll be back, sooner or later, and we'll get married because I will never forget you. Whatever happens, I will never forget you, do you understand?"

"But maybe, if your mother . . . "

"No, it won't work, believe me. There are already enough reasons to quarrel in my family, it's terrible and I can't bear it any longer. I don't want to add to them. I hope I'll be back for Christmas, and all the time I'll spend in Florence will be like hell and purgatory put together."

"It will be the same for me. I swear to you that I will never look at any other woman. I'll wait for you. And I'll write you as soon as you send me your address."

Both had tears in their eyes, even if no one could see them because it was dark by now, and they made love on the tree like a couple of sparrows. Then they wept, embracing each other and swearing that nothing and no one would ever separate them, like the star-crossed lovers in Fonso's fables.

The next day Floti drove off with his sister, who was crying like a fountain. She'd never been away from home and going to Florence was like going to the ends of the earth. She didn't manage to say a word the whole way to the station, and Floti was scowling and taciturn as well.

"Why are you sending me away, Floti?" she asked him when they got to the train.

"For your own good. You deserve much more than that storyteller. One day you'll understand."

"No," sobbed Maria, "I'll never understand." Then she got on the train and watched as her brother got smaller and smaller . . .

The summer passed and so did the fall, and the winter began but Fonso did not come to Hotel Bruni to tell his stories because he didn't want to embarrass anyone, and so the nights went by tedious and sad.

Word had gotten out that Floti had been acquitted and was home again scot-free. There were plenty of people who had sworn they'd get another chance at that subversive, make him pay, him and everyone around him. It wasn't long before the day of reckoning and that was the greatest disaster in the whole history of the Bruni family. It happened just a few days before Christmas, when the novena was just rounding up. Clerice had just come home from church, all bundled up in her woolen shawl, and had started to prepare the batter for the Christmas bread and *raviole*: flour, honey, raisins that they'd dried from their own grapes in a warm oven, quince jam and *saba*, a jelly they made from red grape juice.

Since Fonso no longer came around, Hotel Bruni had lost its main attraction, and so that night everyone had already gone up to bed. Clerice was still awake, perhaps she had some presentiment or perhaps she simply wasn't tired, because old people knew in their hearts that no matter how little they slept now, they'd soon have even too much of it.

In the deep silence, she thought she heard voices: shouting, it sounded like, or singing, or both, and the distant roar of an engine coming closer. Now she could hear them well, they were singing in unison, and they were so close now she could hear the words:

"To your weapons, men, we're fascists,
We'll strike terror in the souls of the communists!"

Her own heart jumped into her throat as she whispered: "Mother of God, help us!"

Clerice had never had any interest in politics, but she'd long grown used to watching squads of hotheads who would go around beating, caning and humiliating in every way possible those they considered troublemakers, defeatists and enemies of the nation. She was sure that this time they were coming for the Brunis and, in particular, one of them: her son Floti. She ran up the stairs, as fast as she could with her candle in hand, to wake him.

"*Mamma*, what's happening? What are you doing here?" Floti had barely the time to say before he heard the shouts for himself and saw the look of terror in his mother's eyes.

"Get dressed and go out the back way, now, the fascists are coming! Can you hear how close they are? They'll be here in minutes. They're coming for you, get moving!" She was right, and the beams of his bedroom ceiling were already echoing with their song. Floti slipped into a pair of trousers and a sweater, threw an overcoat over his shoulders and flew down the stairs. Clerice ran after him with a scarf because it was cold outside and it looked like snow. She tied it around his neck like an embrace and opened the back door for him, so he could escape into the open countryside. She stood watching for a moment as he ran off; the last thing she saw before he disappeared was the scarf, waving in the wind like a flag.

She closed the door up again and chained it and then went to the front door and did the same. She soon heard the sound of a truck stopping and a confusion of voices. It sounded like there were a lot of them and Clerice tried to peek out from a crack in the shutters. They'd left the engine running and the headlights on because it was pitch black outside. Men she'd seen before, from Sogliano, she thought, maybe the same ones who had beaten Graziano Montesi.

"Bruni, come out!" one shouted. "We know you're in there!"

There was no doubt which Bruni they were looking for.

"Hand over Bruni!" shouted another and Clerice counted Floti's steps in the night to figure how far he might have gotten by then.

"He's not here!" she cried out from behind the closed window. In the meantime, all the others has woken up. The men had come down to the kitchen while the women, shivering and covered up as best they could, took the children down to the cellar, trying to get them to stop crying.

One of the wives, who had heard the fascists' shouts, said out loud: "What does she mean he's not here? I saw him go to bed."

The men shut her up with a look: "If mother says he's not here, it means he's not here."

"Turn him over to us or we'll set fire to the house and roast you all inside!" shouted the same man as before, brandishing a lit torch. His companions, one after another, lit their own torches from his and before long the courtyard was all lit up. They wore black shirts and boots with leather or gray-green felt jackets. The shouted threat could be heard all the way down in the freezing-cold cellar, terrifying the women who had begun crying themselves.

"For the love of God!" Fredo shouted back at them from inside the house, "if the man you're looking for is Raffaele Bruni, he's not here. He never came home."

"Bullshit!" shouted one of the besiegers. "Send him out or we'll set fire to the house. This is your last warning."

Checco looked around at all of his brothers and, apart from Savino who seemed quite calm, all he saw were terror-filled faces. "What shall we do?"

"There's little we can do," said Clerice, "seeing that Floti's not here. We can only hope they believe us."

"If he were here, he'd come out of his own free will!" shouted out Checco. "There are women and children here."

"Then open up or we'll break down the door and destroy the whole house. We won't even leave you eyes to cry with!"

"All right," said Checco. "I'm opening the door. Check for yourselves." He pulled back the chain, but before he even had time to turn the handle, a violent shove pushed the door open and sent him rolling to the ground. Eight or ten men poured into the house, practically walking on top of him, and spread out to search every room. They went down to the cellar where the women were clinging together and shaking. The children began to cry out and scream, absolutely terrified by the uproar.

They found nothing and this made them even more furious.

"Do we want to let these subversives make fools of us?" one yelled. "I'm sure that that coward is in here someplace. Let's set fire to the house, and he'll come out, you'll see!"

"Right, let's give him a lesson! That way they'll learn they can't play games with us."

"All right," approved their leader. "Everybody out! This time you'll save your skins, you bastards."

The family came out the front door and Clerice, who had only been on the defensive until then, started to attack instead. She'd recognized some of them and treated them like a mother whose sons deserved a scolding. "Shame on you! You come here at night armed with clubs like the jailers of Jesus Christ! Taking it out on peaceful, unarmed men, with women and children. And you!" she said, pointing her finger at one of them. "I know you! I was with your mother in the Company of the Most Holy Sacrament. That poor woman, I am so sorry for her. Go back home with all these headstrong dolts and never come back!"

"*Mamma*, stop," said Fredo, pulling her back by an arm. "You're only making it worse."

Savino recognized Nello, who lowered his eyes, unable to meet the shock, dismay and sorrow in his friend's gaze.

Checco put one arm around his mother and the other around his wife, who was carrying little Vasco in her arms, and led the family in their brief exodus to the middle of the court-yard.

One of the fascists carrying a lit torch ran towards the open door and was about to throw it in when Nello stopped him: "Wait."

"What's wrong?" asked the man, turning towards him as if to light up his face.

"We can't throw women and children who have no blame into the street. There are good people here, who've done nothing but work in the fields their whole lives without bothering anyone. It will be Christmas in a few days, do you want innocent children to be without a bed and without a home?"

"Then we'll burn down the stable!" replied the other.

"Yes, right, let's burn down the stable!" they all started yelling as if intoxicated, and turned with their torches towards the barn which rose, a dark mass, on the other side of the courtyard.

The Brunis looked at one another appalled and incredulous, their eyes full of tears: they wanted to burn down the place of fables and of fantastic tales, the shelter of the poor, of beggars and derelicts. They wanted to burn Hotel Bruni!

CHAPTER NINETEEN

Under the petrified gaze of the Brunis, the Blackshirts approached the stable and tossed their torches into the hayloft which was packed with bales of straw. The fire spread in a matter of moments, shooting up a gigantic flame that crackled at the old wooden roof beams.

Certain that at this point not even a miracle could put out the fire, the arsonists got back into the 18 BL which was still running and drove off, singing and swearing.

The Brunis stood there for a while, stunned and practically paralyzed in the middle of the courtyard, faces reddened by the reflection of the fire and already feeling the heat of the blaze. The roar of the flames blended with the bellows of terror from the animals chained up inside the stable: ten cows and four pairs of monumental Modenese bulls, the family's pride and joy at fair time and during the plowing season.

"The bulls!" shouted Checco. "We have to free them or they'll burn alive." He lurched forward into the blinding globe of fire and light.

Clerice, horrified, tried to stop him. "No, Checco, for the love of God! There's nothing we can do for those poor animals. The stable will collapse on your head!" But her cries were completely useless: the idea of letting the animals burn alive was not even conceivable for someone who had spent his whole life working the land. Checco had already reached the drinking trough, broken the ice with a shovel, dunked his *tabarro* in the water and was wrapping it around his head and shoulders and rushing through the door of the burning building.

Checco's fearless example roused his brothers who, after a moment's hesitation, ran in after him while their mother, shaking, dropped to her knees in the middle of the courtyard, moaning: "For the love of God, for the love of God, Mother Mary, help them!"

The stable itself had not yet been damaged by the flames because they had been sucked upwards and were devouring the hayloft and the roof above it but licks of fire had already penetrated between the beams and the entire place was full of smoke. The bulls, crazed with terror, were pawing the ground and kicking, and bellowing desperately. Some were trying to free themselves, yanking at the chains that secured them in their stalls, but the ground under their feet was slippery with their own excrement. They slipped, got up and then stumbled to the ground again.

Fredo and Savino ran to open the back door to create a draft and disperse the smoke, then all the brothers rushed to the stalls to unchain the bulls. It was an almost impossible endeavor, because the animals were pulling back so hard that it was practically impossible to get the bar at the end of the chain through the iron ring so the chain could be freed. The bulls' long horns slashed out right and left, with the risk of goring the men at any moment. But then, by dint of shouting at them and hitting them with sticks, the animals were pushed against the hayracks and then, acting swiftly and instinctively, the brothers were able to unloose the chains and set the bulls free.

They took off at a gallop, charging into the courtyard which was lit up bright as day by the fire, running furiously past the women who stared speechless as they shot off into the fields.

By this time, the roof beams over the hayloft had been burnt to a crisp and they gave way all at once, collapsing one after another into the raging fire, raising a red hot cloud of swirling sparks that rose up into the cold starry sky.

Clerice went to the door of the stable and began to cry out, calling her sons out of that inferno: "That's enough! Enough, now! Get out of there, you're all going to die!" Other animals galloped out as the last beams sank into the blaze, feeding the vortex that swelled up like a ball of fire and was then dispersed in a thousand flaming tongues against the dark of night.

Blackened and choking on the smoke, her sons stumbled out. Checco, who had been counting the animals they'd released, realized that one was still inside. "Nero! He's still in there!" he shouted.

"No, no," implored his mother, crying. "If you go back in, this time you're dead!" Checco paused, disconcerted by his mother's pleas, but Savino pulled the *tabarro* from his brother's back, dipped it in the icy water again, dunked his own head and trunk into the trough, then wrapped the wet cloak over his head and shoulders and disappeared through the open stable door.

Nero was a magnificent ungelded specimen weighing over a ton with a very dark coat. He was taller than a man at the withers and endowed with incredible strength. When he was mounting a female, she had to be put in a trestle so his weight wouldn't crush her. Now Nero was struggling in an inferno of smoke, flames and sparks. His rear legs were planted against the hayrack and he was pulling back with great yanks, making the whole wall shake. The chain was already halfway out of the wall but, by pulling so hard, the bull was strangling itself. Savino understood immediately that if he put his hands on that chain to try to extract the iron bar from the ring they would certainly be crushed or ripped to pieces.

He yelled as loudly as he could: "Ohhhh! Ohhhhh! Good, Nero, good boy!" and tried to get closer. From the ceiling over the door a sinister crackling could be heard. Savino was about to run out the back door but right at that instant a figure stood out against the glow of the flames, holding a solid iron crowbar: "Move over. This is what you need."

"Floti!" gasped Savino. "We have to get out of here, it's going to all come down." But Floti had already jumped onto Nero's stall. He hooked the crowbar into the ring and with a hard yank pulled it out of the wall. Nero wrenched away with a last tug and took off at a gallop down the corridor. He came out bellowing, with the chain hanging from his neck between his legs and Savino close behind him. An instant later the whole building came crashing down, with a final eruption of flames, smoke and sparks that was seen by everyone for miles around.

Savino got to where his brothers were: "Where's Floti?"

They shook their heads.

"Where is he?" he shouted more loudly. "He was in there with me a minute ago."

"He must have gone out the back," replied Fredo, and ran around to the other side to check, but he saw no one.

Clerice had started to sob.

"Mamma, don't do that," said Checco. "He'll be back, you'll see. He's out there in the fields somewhere. He doesn't want them to see him." But in his heart, he feared that his brother was there, under that heap of beams and rubble burning like a huge bonfire.

"The Brunis are burning!" The first to see were the latenighters on their way home from the Osteria della Bassa.

Their shouts got people out of bed and brought them to their windows: "Who's burning?"

"The Brunis! Hurry, let's give them a hand!"

But very few put their noses outside their doors: it was late and very cold out there, "and then," many of them thought, "by the time we get there, the fire will have destroyed everything." Fonso did hear the call and, even though he lived at quite a distance, hurried over as fast as his bicycle would carry him with a bucket in tow. But there was nothing he, or anyone, could do. The Brunis stood there in silence, still as statues in the courtyard, in the glow of the dying flames. The women wept, holding their trembling, frightened children close. From the fields rose the mournful lowing of the bulls wandering in the darkness.

Fonso noticed that besides himself, the only ones who had come were Iofa, Pio, and another eight, ten people. He dropped the bucket on the ground and said: "Don't despair. They left you your house and your lives and you saved the bulls. For the rest, there's always a remedy. Tomorrow I'll be back, after work, to give you a hand. Be glad that you're all still alive."

"Floti's missing," said Savino. "He helped me free Nero and we haven't seen him since." He stared at the huge smoking heap of ashes.

"He's not there," said Fonso. "I don't think he's dead. He's too smart and too fast. He'll show up sooner or later. But not now." He wrapped his *tabarro* tightly around him, got on his bicycle and rode off. Almost no one had come to help the Brunis, he thought, none of those who every Sunday in the summertime were there drinking and playing bocce, none of those who would loiter in the stable eating and sipping at that good red wine that foamed in your glass.

"Fonso's right," said Checco. "Floti's far off by now, off in the countryside, hiding in the stubble of an alfalfa or maize field. Let's go to sleep if we can, we'll worry about it tomorrow."

That night Fonso arrived home with a heavy heart and tears in his eyes: not just because Maria was still so far away, in Florence, and who knew when she'd ever come back, but also because Hotel Bruni had burned down. That stable as big as a church where so many poor people slept every winter; it was a miracle that no one had been there that night. That stable where he'd spent so many long hours telling fables, where he had fallen in love with Maria, and she with him. He felt that the destruction of Hotel Bruni marked the end of an age, poor but maybe happier, and that the town, its people and maybe the whole world would never be the same.

He went to bed late and had a hard time falling asleep, especially because Maria hadn't written him for a long while, not even a postcard, and he was afraid that she had forgotten him. Who knows, some smooth-talking young man from the city, with a Tuscan accent and elegant, fashionable clothes, might have turned Maria's head. But then he remembered the last time they'd made love, up in the branches of the old elm tree and how they'd sworn they would always be faithful to each other. She couldn't have forgotten him. Especially without saying a word, not two lines, not a hint of anything wrong. He tried to imagine what could have happened but couldn't come up with an answer. He tossed and turned, sighing, before falling into a light, agitated sleep.

If the atmosphere of the night, the blinding glare of the flames, the dramatic escape of the galloping bulls, the shouting, the weeping and the bellowing of the animals had created the perception of a nightmare and thus of an unreal event, the gray, opaque dawn that followed, with the black, smoking ruin of the stable that wounded the gaze of the first who dared to wander out into the courtyard with such harsh violence, obliged them to face the bleak reality.

The church bells sounded the Angelus and Clerice, who had not slept a moment all night, joined her sons in the courtyard and looked each one of them in the eye.

"On your knees," she ordered. Most hesitated.

"On your knees," she repeated, setting the example herself.

One after another, the Brunis knelt, and she prayed: "Lord,

you were born in a stable with a bull and a donkey to warm you and protect you from the cold. Look with compassion on us poor souls who have lost our own stable because of the cruelty of unjust men. Look upon the ruins of these walls that once welcomed the poor and the derelict. We shall forgive those wretches for they know not what they do, but you help us, give us the strength to begin again, show us that you are on the side of the weak and the offended. Do not abandon us. Amen."

"Amen," responded some. Others said nothing.

"I'm not forgiving anyone," said Savino.

"Me either," a second voice echoed.

"Floti!" shouted Clerice.

Floti walked towards the ruins of the stable and looked at the crumbled walls as if he couldn't believe what he was seeing. He felt the weight of disgrace and the responsibility for what had happened. He turned towards his brothers. "It's my fault," he said. "If I could, I would repay you for everything you've lost. Unfortunately, what's done is done. Forgive me, if you can. I did what I did in good faith . . . "

At that moment another figure emerged from the fog: "Floti . . . "

"You damned son of a bitch, you traitor!" screamed Savino, hurling himself at the man.

"Stop," said Floti.

Savino drew up short just inches away from Nello's face and shot him an unbowed look of challenge. Nello was pale and had dark circles under his eyes; he seemed worn out and demoralized.

"What nerve you have showing up here! And to think I thought of you as my friend. Get the hell out of here, and don't ever come back."

"Let him talk!" said Floti. "He must have come here for a reason."

"If they didn't burn down the house it's because of me,"

said Nello, "because I made sure I came with them, but don't tempt fate, Floti. I'm talking to you. I'm here to tell you that they've sworn to get you. Your life is in danger. Get out of here, go someplace else. If the situation gets any better I'll find you and tell you. If you leave, your family will stand to gain. They'll be able to rest easy. I did all I could do, Savino," he said, turning to his friend. "I couldn't do any better. Don't call me a traitor. I've always kept my word. Goodbye. I hope we'll meet up in better times."

He disappeared.

"Maybe what he says is true," said Clerice, "He was the one who came to our defense, remember? If it hadn't been for him they would have set the house on fire. But did you hear what he had to say, Floti? He says they've vowed to kill you. He says your life is in danger. You have to leave this house or you'll meet a terrible end. I don't want to lose another son." Tears poured down her face as she spoke.

"If you all want me to go, I will," replied Floti, looking into his brothers' faces. "But I don't know if I can do it, just like that. I don't have a place to go and I don't know how I'd survive with no work and no house. I don't think it'll be so easy for them to kill me: I'm no sheep, they'll have to catch me first. I'm asking you if I can stay until I find someplace else and then I promise I'll leave this house and you'll never see me again."

Savino stepped up and Checco joined him: "Floti, they're after you because you're the only man who's had the guts to stand against them, and none of us can fault you for having that kind of courage. As far as we're concerned, you can stay here as long as you want and you can count on us for anything you need."

The others mumbled something, but no one else was forthcoming and so Floti, who didn't want any trouble, moved to a room next to the cellar, from where he could run straight out into the fields if he had to, without anyone seeing him. As soon as the weather got better he'd think about leaving. Moving out of his bedroom meant that a double room would be freed up and someone could certainly get good use out of it, so he imagined there wouldn't be too much grumbling.

Later that evening Fonso came by. His *tabarro* was drawn all the way up to his eyes but he was in a good humor, in keeping with his natural disposition. He had come to ask what they intended to do. "Are you thinking of rebuilding the stable? I'll bet you that some of the walls are still good and you can find used beams at a good price, or new ones for that matter." It seemed that he'd come to encourage them to roll up their sleeves and not fall prey to discouragement, but the reaction to his words was quite lukewarm. Each man for himself and God for all, is what the Brunis seemed to be thinking after that catastrophe. Maybe some of them already had an idea, or even the concrete possibility of working on their own, independently. Maybe the only one still interested in keeping the family together was Armando—given his gregarious nature and his lack of inclination towards hard work. His wife would be having their first child soon.

That spring, it was announced that the Barzini heirs had sold the property and this too was seen as the hand of fate. The new owner was called Bastoni; he was a livestock dealer, a coarse, presumptuous type who had always been full of himself. It didn't take much to imagine what he'd be like now that he'd become a landowner and could give orders and make people obey them. Floti had completely abdicated his position as administrator except for dividing up the common funds they had deposited in the bank. Clerice was too downhearted over recent events and worried about the future to stand up to Bastoni. Unlike Barzini, who used to come by maybe once or twice a year, the new owner was there all the time because, he said, you have to keep an eye on farmers or they'll steal everything from under your nose, they'll hide the wheat and sell chickens and eggs on the sly. The Brunis knew it was better not to say anything, if they didn't want a fight. The man would often complain: "There are too many of you! Too many mouths to feed! You're having kids left and right and I'm the one who has to support everybody!" Once Fredo found him making a pass at his wife and it was all he could do not to stick the pitchfork in his rear end. In short, the situation had become unbearable.

Nello showed up at the beginning of the summer to tell Savino that Floti was in danger again: they'd found out that he was still at home and wanted to teach him a lesson. That's when the fugitive moved to a toolshed in the countryside and then even started to sleep out in the open, on a bed of straw, in the middle of the cornstalks. Not that he ever slept, because he knew he couldn't let his guard down, and he had become thin and pale, with deep rings around his eyes that looked frightening. And so Clerice would remain outdoors with him, awake all night with his head in her lap so he could sleep. Every time she heard a noise, a flutter of wings in the darkness, the hooting of an owl, she had to force herself not to cry out or jump up. She didn't want to wake him.

At dawn, at first light, Floti would wake up and get to his feet. He would look at his mother and she would look at him, in silence, and then they would part. She returned home to sleep a few hours and he wandered through the fields like a soul in torment. Adding to his worries, Clerice had told him that for the last couple of months she hadn't heard from Maria, if not through her sister Rosina, and this bothered him tremendously; were they hiding something?

One day Fonso brought Clerice a book so she could give it to Floti. It was called *The Brothers Karamazov*, and it was by a Russian writer. Floti always carried it around with him, on those long summer afternoons, and he'd stop to read it in the shade of an oak or along the bank of the hemp-steeping pond, under a poplar tree. When he finished he gave it back to his mother, along with a few lines written in pencil on a wrinkled sheet of paper, addressed to the person who had lent it to him.

Dear Fonso,

I haven't written many letters in my lifetime, but I wanted to write you this one to say that I'm sorry that I sent Maria to Florence. She hasn't written us in three months, although her sister sends us letters, and this means that there's something they don't want us to know. If something bad happened to her I could never forgive myself. Because I've hurt both you and her, with the intention of doing the right thing. Your book wasn't easy but I read the whole thing. The part where its talks about God and evil in the world I'll never forget. Almost everything depends on fate, our life is a mystery.

Floti

CHAPTER TWENTY

M aria had not fallen in love with anyone else. What
had happened was something very different.
When she first got to Florence, she didn't so much
as look at the place. All she did was cry, because she felt terribly homesick; she missed her town, her house, her brothers
and most of all Fonso. She thought of him day and night, terrified that the distance between them would make him fall out
of love. Worst of all, there was no grass in Florence; you didn't
hear the crickets and tree toads at night or the cicadas during
the day and the trees were closed up between walls and stones.

She hardly ever saw her brother-in-law, but Rosina was
always there trying to console her. Don't think I was any different, she'd say, at first I felt the same way you're feeling now
but then I got used to it and I learned to like the city. It's really
wonderful, she'd say, trying to cheer her up. Everyone speaks
Italian here, you know, not like up by us where only the fancy
folk speak Italian and the poor ones speak dialect.

As time passed things did get a little better, especially after
she started getting letters from Fonso. It took her a while to
read them because she had only gone as far as fifth grade at
school, but she didn't want anyone to help her because what
her fiancée wrote her was her own affair; it was just between
the two of them.

Rosina began by taking her to the market so they could do
the shopping. The first time left her speechless. There every
day was like the Festa della Madonna back at home, a long row

of stalls decked out in every color of the rainbow that stretched all the way around the square and sold absolutely everything: bolts of cloth, ladies' bags and blouses, jackets and trousers, underwear and an amazing array of fruits and vegetables. There wasn't a pear or an apple with a single blemish; they were all perfect and exactly alike. And then the two sisters went for a walk in the big square where there were marble men as tall as a house and naked as the day they were born. Maria looked away because she was embarrassed, but Rosina teased her: "What are you doing, silly? They're just pieces of marble, not real men!"

"Why don't they put pants on them?" asked Maria. Rosina started to laugh and a lady who was passing by commented out loud in her Florentine accent: "Oh will you listen to this one, she wants to put pants on Michelangelo's David!"

Rosina tried to explain to Maria that if the great artists wanted to make those statues naked, there must be a reason, and that they'd look absolutely ridiculous with pants on, but Maria wasn't convinced. A little at a time, though, she was beginning to understand that this was a place like no other and that there was something magical in those streets and towers and belfries. And that river! In the evenings the lights of the houses above would be mirrored on the waves, quivering and glittering like precious stones. Sometimes the two girls would take a stroll at dusk, or else at night to see the moon and the stars and to listen to the bells that chimed all together, like a chorus, playing the Ave Maria.

Rosina had also taken her to see the cathedral, which was the most important church in the city. But even there, there were paintings with naked men and women that seemed scandalous inside a church.

"When you go before God, you go naked like the day you were born. How would they look with underpants on?" replied her sister. "And anyway, those up there are already damned, they're in hell, look! See that woman up there with the devil who's sticking a burning firebrand in her female parts? That's because she acted like a whore when she was alive. And that other devil that's sticking it in the rear end of that man there? Just a little to the right; he must have been one of those who . . . " But her words dropped off there; Maria probably wouldn't have understood anyway.

But Maria had understood perfectly: that the people who went to mass, looking around and seeing what would happen to them if they ended up in hell, would get scared and try to behave well. She also thought of how many stories she'd have to tell when she went back home. She realized that, little by little, she was taking up the habits of a city-bred lady and she didn't mind that at all. For example, the fact that her shoes were polished and that every day she changed her clothes. A different blouse and skirt every day, and sometimes even a shawl.

But the moment she most looked forward to was when a letter would come from Fonso. Not too often, stamps were expensive! Postal cards of a light gray color with the king's head on the stamp. She even learned to like the king!

Things did not always go well at her sister's house. Her Sicilian brother-in-law was often cross and quarreled with Rosina; it was as if Maria didn't exist. Although once she had had put her ear to the bedroom door and had overheard them arguing about her. He was saying: "That sister of yours, when is she going home? She eats and drinks and I pay."

Rosina had answered: "But she's my sister and she helps me in the house: she does the washing and the ironing, makes the beds and sometimes she even cooks . . . " but that didn't shut him up. He went on saying that a wife should stay at home, and not take walks around the town while he was at work. Once Maria even thought she heard him slapping Rosina and the next day her face was bruised.

"Was it him?" she asked. "Did you husband hit you?"

Rosina said nothing but her eyes welled up with tears. It didn't take Maria long to understand what was at the root of all their quarrels. Rosina was as beautiful as the sun, while he was small and ugly with whiskers like a mouse's under his nose. He was crazy jealous, that's what he was, he knew that men turned to take another look when Rosina passed. He didn't want her wearing tight dresses, or low-necked blouses; she wasn't allowed to wear lipstick or makeup, and he accused her of blackening her eyelashes. What was worse, they had no children, and where he came from, that was considered humiliating because it was like being impotent. But who knew who was to blame there; maybe it wasn't Rosina at all!

"You know?" Rosina told her once. "In the south of Italy they think that all the women up north are whores because we like pretty clothes and wearing lipstick and going for a walk around town. What's wrong with that? For example, I like the theatre and he doesn't. It's not like I go alone, I always go with a lady friend, but does he believe me? No, he's always only thinking of one thing. Do you like the theatre, Maria?"

"Oh yes, I love puppets."

"Puppets! What are you on about! Tomorrow night at the Verdi Theatre they're putting on Mascagni's *Cavalleria Rusticana*."

"What's that?"

"Opera. It's like a comedy, but it makes you cry, too, and instead of talking, they sing. They all wear beautiful costumes and the women warble like nightingales."

One night Rosina decided to take her sister to see *La Cavalleria Rusticana*. They dressed up and fixed their hair. Rosina wore something she'd made herself: a clingy dress in organza that rustled when she walked and a little hat with feathers that was gorgeous. She wanted Maria to remember the evening for the rest of her life, and she even called a landau to pick them up. The city was all lit up and people were strolling up and down the streets and Maria felt like a real lady, in a beautiful dark dress with a bow on her behind and new shoes that squeaked as she walked.

At the entrance to the theatre no one could help but take an appreciative glance at the two new arrivals, especially Rosina, who the men were eyeing openly as if their wives wouldn't notice.

"If you had lived here when you were a girl instead of in town," Maria whispered to her sister, "you could have married a real gentleman; can't you see how they're all eating you up with their eyes? Why did you marry Rizzi in the first place?"

"We were so poor back then, and a man who brings home a steady salary every month wasn't someone to sneeze at. At least that's what our parents and our brothers thought. What should I have done? At least you have Fonso; he may not be that handsome but he's very well-built and he has that way of talking that would make any woman fall in love with him."

They were walking up a staircase, as they chatted in this way, from one floor to the next, until they went through a door that ended up on a big balcony that circled around the theater. You could see everything from up there: the grand red curtains with their yellow fringe and a chandelier so huge and so heavy you couldn't understand what made it stay up.

"What if it falls?" asked Maria.

"It's not going to fall."

"How do you know that?"

"I just do!"

"Shh!" someone said at their left.

"We have to stop talking," whispered Rosina, "because it's about to start. Look, the curtain is opening!"

The conductor raised his baton and the orchestra began playing the overture.

"Who's that man with the baton?" asked Maria, whispering this time.

"That's the maestro. He uses the baton to direct the musicians, otherwise everyone would be playing something different. But quiet now, we're annoying the others; they want to listen."

Maria stopped talking and tried to understand what was happening but she soon grew weary of looking at those singers shrieking words that didn't make any sense. She leaned close to her sister and said: "I can't understand a thing; why don't we go see the puppets doing *Pia de' Tolomei*?"

Rosina glared at her and put her finger to her lips as if to say "shut up before someone hears you!"

Maria shut up and tried hard to figure out what was going on. She thought it had something to do with cuckolds but then she fell asleep on her chair and when the fateful cry exploded: "They have murdered Turiddu!" she opened one eye and said: "Who did they murder?"

"Never mind," said Rosina, "let's go to bed." And that was the end of their unforgettable evening.

The young Bruni's Florentine sojourn continued with its ups and downs, but at a certain point Rosina had to reveal to her husband the reason for her sister's prolonged stay: their brothers wanted her to forget a fiancé who wasn't to their liking.

"What do I have to do with any of that?" grumbled Rizzi, visibly irritated. "Let them take care of it!"

Rosina was a bit embarrassed because in truth, the situation had gone beyond any reasonable limits. Instead of helping around the house, her sister actually spent most of her time reading and rereading her boyfriend's letters and trying to answer them, which was quite an ordeal in itself. Between the ink spots she spattered the paper with, trying to get her thoughts written out, and copying them over again in her best handwriting, a good week would pass before she had a letter finished. Some were never even sent off. In any case, the strategy behind her Florentine exile was clearly being thwarted.

Rosina had just about decided to take a pen in hand and write Floti to convince him to desist in his intent to keep the two lovers apart, when an epidemic of lethargic encephalitis broke out in the city. Maria fell ill and was immediately taken to hospital. The disease was better known as "sleeping sickness" and, in fact, she slept seven days and eight nights without ever waking up. A telegram was sent off to the Brunis with a few essential words:

> *Maria has sleeping sickness stop if she wakes up she will want to come home stop Rosina*

Meanwhile, the sender of this message decided, against her husband's wishes, to pay for one of the most important professors in the city to examine Maria. Once he had seen her, the doctor announced that he could take no responsibility for the prognosis, but that it was reasonable to believe that the girl, being so young and of such good constitution, might snap out of it.

"I could have told you that myself, and for free," commented Rizzi with considerable irritation, and you couldn't really fault him on that.

In the end, Maria did wake up, but she had been so weakened by the illness that her convalescence would certainly be lengthy, and Rosina informed her family back in town about this.

When the Brunis learned that their sister's life was at risk because of the epidemic that had struck the city of Florence, they became very worried. But while Clerice prayed to the Madonna and all the saints, the brothers quarreled because some of them believed it was Floti's fault for having capriciously sent her away from home.

Meanwhile, Maria was trying to regain her strength in Florence. Rosina brought cups of hot broth to her in bed with a glass of good Tuscan wine, sure to give her energy and put her in a good mood. As soon as the days began to get longer, she helped Maria outside into the garden and sat her under an umbrella that she'd bought especially so her sister could get some fresh air. As soon as she felt strong enough, Maria asked for paper and pen and wrote to her family and Fonso to tell them that what had happened to her was like a very long night without dreams and that she'd woken up weary and exhausted, as if she'd been working for days and days instead of sleeping! Fonso replied:

> *Dearest Maria,*
> *I am well and I hope you are too. Your letter was of great comfort to me. For the whole time I didn't hear from you, my life was like hell on earth. I thought of you from morning till night and I couldn't sleep. I hope that what has happened will convince your brother Floti that no one can go against destiny and that we should be married. At the edge of the town, workers' houses are being built and I've applied for one, so if we're married we will have a house to live in. I think of nothing but the day I'll see you. Take care of yourself and know that I still want you and I will always want you until the day I die.*
> *Alfonso*

Maria couldn't stop reading it, and each time she did she ended up crying. Neither Fonso nor her brothers had told her about the stable burning down, because they didn't want to worry her.

After Easter, Maria's convalescence drew to an end and her health seemed to be completely restored. The only symptom of the illness that stuck with her was an intense sleepiness that would come over her at about seven in the evening; it was so overpowering that she'd have to go and lie down. Rosina wrote to her mother that she thought the time had come for Maria to return home; perhaps getting back to town would help her to heal completely and restore her appetite. It had become a chore to get her to eat anything!

The great day arrived. Maria packed her suitcase and Rosina gave her another one for all the clothing she'd bought for her while she was in Florence. Maria put on the prettiest dress she had, and a pair of high heels that perfectly matched her shiny brown bag. Who knows what they would say in town when they saw her! And Fonso, what would he say when he saw her looking like such a lady? Rizzi was so happy to be rid of her that he called a landau to take her to the station. It was a tearful farewell for both sisters; after all, they'd never left each other's sides the whole time Maria had been in Florence, chatting, strolling, confiding in one another. When she was the saddest, Maria had always found comfort and support in her sister, who often seemed to have moments of deep sadness herself, although she never spoke about it.

Everything about Rosina made Maria think that there was no joy in her wedded life. In the whole time she'd been there, Maria had never seen her enjoy a gesture of affection from her husband, a compliment, a courtesy. And Rosina was so pretty and so sweet. Maria had never had to courage to ask her directly about what her marriage was like, but she left with the memory of a shadow in her sister's clear gaze.

"I'll write you," she promised, "and when I marry I want you to come to my wedding. It will be the best gift I could ever receive."

"I'll do everything I can, absolutely everything, to come," replied Rosina. "But if I don't make it, don't take it badly." Tears were streaming from her eyes as she said this.

Maria hugged her tight. "I love you, *Rusein*," she said in her ear, using her pet name for her sister.

"Get on the train! The stationmaster has already whistled," said her sister, breaking away.

Maria went into the carriage and stayed at the window wav-

ing her hand for as long as she could see the white handkerchief her sister was agitating in response. Then she sat down
and began to watch the countryside. The train soon started up
the hillside and then the mountains as it neared the pass. Every
stop was another little town, with some who got off and others
who got on. It took more than an hour to get to Porretta, and
a lot of people got off there. On the station walls, she saw a
poster with an image of a beautiful woman in a little hat and a
close-fitting corset drinking a glass of water from a fountain
and the words underneath said "Porretta Springs, your source
of health." That reminded her that Fonso sometimes went to
the salt water spring near Bazzano and drank from the font to
purge himself. Sometimes he'd even take two or three flasks
home with him.

The train started up again puffing and clattering and began
its descent. The light poles were sailing by faster now, a sign that
they were going much faster and that they would soon arrive at
their destination. But even going downhill, the train had to stop
in dozens of stations, so people could get on or off, and it took
another good hour, if not more, to get to Casalecchio, where
Rosina had instructed Maria to get off the train and catch the
bus that would take her to town. Rosina had explained exactly,
step by step, what she needed to do, but Maria was soon confused and she thought of asking a passing gentleman for information: "Sir," she asked him, "could you kindly tell me where I
can catch the bus that will take me home?"

"And just where would that be?" he asked back, suspecting
that, despite her elegant dress, bag and high-heeled shoes, this
was an inexperienced country girl.

She explained it to him and he gave her instructions on how
to reach the bus station. There she would find a timetable with
all the different destinations. The whole endeavor was getting
much more complicated than Maria had imagined and she was
tired of asking questions and embarrassing herself. She saw a

signpost pointing towards Bazzano and decided to set off on foot in that direction; it couldn't be so far, after all. Once she got to Bazzano she knew she wouldn't have problems because from there it was just a half-hour walk to her town. Maybe just a tiny bit further.

So she started walking, even though what she was wearing was hardly the ideal gear for a journey of that sort on foot, with high heels and two suitcases in tow. But she was so eager to arrive home and see her family and her fiancé again that nothing could stand in her way.

She took the road that skirted the hills, certain that, sooner or later, she'd arrive at her destination. She found herself teetering on her shoes almost instantly, but she tried to take her mind off her physical discomfort by enjoying the view of the surrounding fields and watching the farmers at work. If she turned around, she could see the Madonna di San Luca church on the hillside behind her, and she made the sign of the cross and said three Hail Marys to thank Our Lady for having brought her back home safe and sound.

After five or six kilometers her feet were full of blisters. After another three or four her shoes were damp and blood-stained and her ankles were killing her, but she hadn't taken her shoes off until then because she wanted to be sure that she made it home well dressed and in her high heels, like a real city lady. In the end, however, her pain exceeded her stubbornness: she stopped, took off her shoes, laced them together and tossed them over her shoulder. But it had been so long since she'd walked barefoot through stubble that the calluses under her feet had disappeared and the gravel on the road hurt like anything. She started walking on the edge of the road where it was grassy and that felt a little better, but her suitcases were getting heavier with each step and she was forced to stop more and more often to catch her breath and massage her aching shoulders and arms.

A man passed by driving a cart full of fava beans and, seeing her in such a sorry state, offered her a ride: "Where are you going on foot like that, young lady?"

"I'd be happy to get to Bazzano. From there on I can take care of myself."

"You're lucky," replied the carter, coming to a stop. "That's just where I'm going. Would you like to ride with me?"

"I won't say no," replied Maria. She heaved her suitcases onto the cart and went to sit next to the driver.

"Where are you coming from?"

"From Florence."

"On foot?"

"No. I took the train to Casalecchio and then I walked. I'm dead tired."

"I believe you, with those shoes and two suitcases."

They drove on, chatting, for a while, and Maria asked for news about what had been going on in her absence, just to keep the conversation going. The driver began glancing her way with increasing interest, seeing how pretty she was. At some point, he must have convinced himself that the girl was so exhausted that she would have done anything rather than start walking again with two suitcases and her feet bleeding like that. No sooner said than done, he took off down a little country lane between two rows of poplars that stretched off into the countryside, and stopped alongside a dense cluster of locust trees.

"Why are we stopping here?" asked Maria.

"I'll tell you right away," replied the carter resolutely in his Bazzanese dialect. "Either you let me have some pussy or you get out and walk home." As he turned towards her, Maria was quick enough to let him have it across the face with her bag, making his nose swell up instantly, as big and red as a pepper. While he was cursing and shouting she got out, took her suitcases and stalked off down the road.

250 · VALERIO MASSIMO MANFREDI

"Where do you think you're going? You're as crazy as they get!" he shouted after her.

"I'll go wherever I please, thank you very much, you disgusting pig!"

And so she started her journey again under a sun that was getting hotter and hotter. She had only gone a couple of hundred meters when she heard the sound of a cart coming up behind her and the shuffling of a horse. When it was almost at her side, certain that it was the nasty carter she'd just escaped from, she shouted out without even turning around: "Steer clear of me, you ugly pig."

"Maria, what are you saying? It's me, Iofa!" Finally, a friendly voice! "I can't believe it's you. How did you get into such a state? What are you doing on foot with two suitcases?"

"I'm just getting back from Florence," replied Maria. "Which way are you going?"

Iofa was heading to town, thank God. He helped her up and that was the finishing stroke to her city-girl finesse: after the elegant shoes which had been worn out by her long march and tossed over her shoulder, now it was the turn of the new dress bought for her in Florence. Already soaked with sweat, it stuck nicely to the flour that coated the sacks in the cart, but she couldn't care less. At that moment she had a person she knew, nearly one of the family, beside her and she was sitting on something soft and even rather comfortable instead of walking on her wounded and aching feet. That gave her so much satisfaction that nothing else mattered.

Iofa stopped to unload the sacks of flour at La Compagnia, the farm where he'd picked up the wheat that morning to bring it to the mill. They started off again and, of his own initiative, he took Maria all the way to the Brunis' courtyard. Maria hopped down and thanked him. She wanted to invite him in for a glass of wine, but the unexpected sight of the burnt-down stable stunned her, leaving her confused and dismayed. She shook the flour off her dress, smoothed it down with her hands as best she could and walked almost hesitantly into the courtyard: the pillars still raised their blackened bricks towards the sky and the straw was piled up in a rick because there was no longer any shed where it could be kept dry. She burst into tears. The stable was almost more important than the house itself, in her eyes. It was there that she had learned, on those long winter nights, to spin hemp on a wheel, it was there that she'd chattered about boyfriends and husbands with the other women.

There was no one around; everyone was in the fields. She went into the house, where she found Ersilia, one of her sisters-in-law, preparing lunch.

"The stable burnt down!" she said. "How did it happen?"

"The fascists did it," replied Ersilia. "It was all Floti's fault, for getting into politics."

Maria dropped her head in silence, not knowing what to say, then asked, "Where's mother?"

"She's sleeping in her room," replied Ersilia sternly, "because she stays up all night keeping watch over your brother."

CHAPTER TWENTY-ONE

S pring came late that year and they didn't see the first swallows until the first half of April. They had taken to flying low over the ruins of the stable, twittering constantly like lost souls because their nests had been burnt along with the barn. They continued to soar around the ruin for hours, as if they couldn't resign themselves to this disaster then, at dusk, they finally scattered.

Fonso arrived in the Bruni courtyard two days after Maria had returned. He found her feeding the chickens. She was so shaken at seeing him after so long that she let go of the corner of her apron and let the corn scatter all over the ground. Then she ran towards him and threw her arms around his neck. Fonso was embarrassed, knowing well what her brother thought about him, and whispered into her ear: "Maria, if Floti sees us . . . "

"Floti won't say anything. He knows what I've been through because he sent me away. This time I decide: you can come see me on even days, that's in keeping with tradition, right? Until we get married. If you still want me, that is."

"Of course I still want you. You've read my letters, haven't you?"

"Many times. And did you get mine?"

"Yes, of course I did. That was the only time I was happy, all these long months. But where is Floti?"

"Somewhere," said Maria, and she said nothing else because it didn't matter anymore.

When May came, Clerice—who hadn't been seen in town
for ages—couldn't miss her appointment with the rosary ladies
at the intersection of Via Bastarda and Via Celeste. After the
last Hail Mary, the neighborhood women gathered around her
to ask if she'd had news of Floti, since no one had seen him
around for so long. She replied that he'd gone away and that
she rarely heard from him.

Young Montesi, the son of ill-fated Graziano, was Clerice's
informer. He told her continuously that they were still looking
for Floti and that he had to stay out of their way if he cared
about staying alive. Nello had also let her know that it didn't
look good for him in town and that he shouldn't do anything
rash. And so, now that the weather was so mild, Floti never
spent the night in the house anymore, in the windowless room
by the cellar. He stayed out in the fields, sometimes in the
toolshed but most often out in the middle of the corn, sleeping
with his head in his mother's lap after she brought him his dinner in the mess tin he'd used as a soldier.

He could never fall asleep right away; he would lie there at
length with his eyes wide open and staring, and every now and
then he exchanged a few words with her. They were moments
of intense heartache which embarrassed them both, and so
their silences were even more moving than their words. When
Floti finally abandoned himself to sleep in the warmth of his
mother's lap, Clerice, her head high and back straight, watched
over him, alone, sitting erect against the night sky like a dark
mater dolorosa. She turned to that sky with a fervent, anxious
prayer that lasted until the Angelus bell chimed at dawn, when
they separated and Floti began wandering around the countryside again, along the drainage ditches and the rows of
maples and grapevines, hiding from the eyes of those who
wished him ill. A good number of farmers knew who that solitary figure was crossing their fields with his slow steps, but they
would never have betrayed him for all the gold in the world, so

secretly satisfied were they at being able to protect a rebel, a man of honor and courage. Nothing could match that.

Trying to go on this way would be impossible, and Clerice herself told Floti that he would have to go where no one could find him. "You're still young, you'll make a life for yourself. I'm getting older every day. I'm not the woman I used to be."

"That's not true, *mamma*, you're a strong woman. Now that Maria's back and we're all together again, things will get better."

"The worry I have for you is killing me. There's nothing that can make me happy. If you love me, go."

Floti reflected on her words, his head low. "It's hard for me to go. Everything I have is here. My memories, my family, my friends. It's easy to say, just go. For me it's like pulling my arm out. But maybe you're right. I've already started talking to some people. I'm waiting for their answers, then I'll make a decision."

Maria was rinsing out the dishes in the sink and overheard their conversation, which brought tears to her eyes. Floti was the brother she loved most, even if he didn't want her to see Fonso.

Clerice, already at wits' end with worry and dread, felt that she would faint when she heard that her son was actually planning to leave. She tried to control herself and sat down at the table, leaning her head on her left arm.

"Are you all right, *mamma*?" he asked with concern.

"I'm fine. You take care of yourself, you have more than enough to worry about."

Floti nodded slowly and walked out the back door into the fields.

Clerice had just begun to prepare for the arrival of the Madonna della Provvidenza, for the yearly eight-day-long festivities. She had a prayer that needed granting and she ardently hoped the Virgin would not deny her. On the morning of the second-to-last day of May, she set out early in the morning, dressed in her finest clothes, accompanied by Maria who had on the dress she'd worn home from Florence, washed and freshly pressed. The entrances to all the courtyards that found themselves on the route of the procession of Our Lady had been adorned with images or words in honor of the Virgin Mary, all created using rose petals. Banners of embroidered cloth in red, yellow and white were stretched across the roads and the bells were ringing full peal. Clerice and Maria turned in the direction of the sanctuary of the Madonna just as the sun rose over the tops of the age-old cherry trees laden with luscious fruit as red and shiny as garnets. When the breeze picked up a little, you could smell the delicate scent of wheat flowers. It was going to be a splendid day.

The two women reached the Osteria della Bassa and turned right. It only took them a few minutes from there to get to the Cappacella, the little chapel just outside town. They nodded to greet the older women who were there in a group waiting for the procession to pass so they could fall in and accompany the Madonna along the last stretch of road that led to the parish church. Those whose houses were along the route put out chairs so the elderly could sit and take a rest when they needed to. As Clerice and Maria continued on towards their destination, countless small groups gradually joined with others, streaming together until they had formed a single assemblage in the little square in front of the sanctuary.

The parish pastor was already there waiting, wearing his surplice and stole, surrounded by altar boys wearing the red satin robes taken out only for the most important ceremonies; with their white lace surplices, they looked like a lot of little cardinals. Then the image of the Madonna della Provvidenza was carried out of the sanctuary: the enameled terra-cotta bas-relief depicting Our Lady was mounted on a panel covered with deep red velvet and was completely surrounded by a ring of beautiful silk flowers. The image was placed onto a wooden base fitted with two shafts designed to be carried on the shoulders of the bearers, a role that all the young believers yearned to be chosen for.

The procession started up. It was led at the front by the cross bearer, a burly young man wearing a leather harness and straps which allowed him to bear the weight of a fifty-kilo cross for the first half of the route; he was flanked by a similarly sturdy friend who would relieve him halfway. At their sides were two more youths carrying a pair of rigid standard banners depicting the Madonna and Saint James, who was the town's patron saint. They were followed by two long lines of men, then the band and, last of all, the sacred image preceded by the celebrant himself. The women came next, heads veiled and rosary beads in hand, bringing up the end of the procession.

The most well-to-do did not mix with the regular townsfolk, but waited in church sitting in the choir behind the altar: they had always followed this custom, which placed them in a position of superiority and separated them from the ordinary workers and peasants. They even had their own side entrance which crossed the sacristy and which no one else dared to use.

When the procession came within sight of the Cappacella, the procession's official governor, who was the Credito Romagnolo bank accountant, signaled a slowdown, to allow the elderly who had been waiting there all this time to unite with all the others. At that very moment, a man parted the hedge that marked off the fields on the left of the road and stepped in between the barber and the mailman. Floti.

The news that the man wanted by the Blackshirts had dared to step out in the light of day and that he—notoriously a freethinker—had joined the ranks of believers in the procession of the Madonna della Provvidenza, immediately flew up and down the left-hand column from top to bottom. It reached the pastor, who widened his eyes in shock. The long wave travelled down the row of women and came back up the other side, intercepting Clerice and Maria, who were stunned at his audacity.

"Floti is in the procession!"

Clerice thought she should try to catch up with him, to talk with him, but she realized that such a gesture would have drawn even more attention and curiosity. Instead, she went on reciting the rosary, in the hope of convincing the Madonna to protect her irresponsible and foolhardy son, and to help him to act with wisdom.

By the time they reached the Cappacella, the news had inexplicably preceded them, and the ranks of elderly believers craned their necks to catch sight of the Scarlet Pimpernel of the cornfields who was calmly strolling between the barber and the mailman and chatting, first with one and then with the other, as all the men were wont to do on such occasions.

When the tower of the eastern gate of the town walls appeared, the accountant stepped out of line and, like an officer of the Grenadier Guard, signaled for the procession to halt and for the band to begin playing. They all realized that, next, Floti would be swept up with all the rest of them towards the House of Fascism, under the eyes of those men in their fezzes and black shirts. But anyone in the procession was under the protection of the impenetrable mantle of the Madonna della Provvidenza, and no one would dare to lift a finger against him. Especially taking into account the two *carabiniere* officers in full dress uniform who were there as Our Lady's honor guard but also to maintain law and order. The fascists had also already been advised of Bruni's intrepid appearance and they could do nothing but watch helplessly, although they certainly didn't miss the opportunity to put him under surveillance so they could close in on him later.

In the end, the procession broke up in the town's central square in front of the parish church and, as Floti slipped away, the Image made her triumphal entrance into the nave, greeted by the organ with the full-orchestra pedal down and the choir, singing:

"Beautiful Lady, look upon your people
Who honor you today full of joy.
I, too, join their festive ranks and run to your feet,
Pray for me, oh Virgin most holy!"

Then the Image was carried behind the altar and placed on the flat bed of a wooden machine that was cranked up to slowly raise Our Lady up to the very top of the altarpiece and hold her there. The effect, seen from the nave and aisles, was something of a miracle, a sort of brief ascension that allowed all those present to see the Madonna, crowned in gold, rise to the highest point of the presbytery. For a whole year she'd been closed up in her votive chapel and now, finally, she had returned to visit her people, to hear their prayers and invocations.

Clerice waited until the Mass was over and everyone had left the church. She told her daughter to wait outside for her and she went up to the first pew so she could be all alone with the Virgin Mary, just the two of them. She knelt.

"Holy Mother," she prayed silently, "you know what it means to lose a son and, unfortunately, now I do as well. I could not endure the pain again, and so I supplicate you, let my Floti find a way to leave this place where everyone wants him dead, especially now that he has taunted them by walking in this procession before your holy image, and certainly not out of devotion for You. Forgive him! His leaving will be very painful for me, but at least I'll know he's alive and perhaps, every now and then, I'll even be able to see him. I beg you, Madonna, grant me this prayer and I promise that every month I will make an offering in your name to the hospital of the poor."

She lit a candle and genuflected, made the sign of the cross and then, greatly relieved, she headed towards the exit. She was struck by the blinding light of May which flooded the square, and the festive ringing of church bells. Maria took her arm and they walked home without even trying to keep an eye out for Floti, knowing full well that they were being watched.

In the meantime, her son, surrounded by a group of friends, had managed to reach the door to the forge belonging to Lazzari the hunchback, another freethinker, who Floti followed into the cellar and from there down an ancient underground tunnel that led outside of town, where a cart was waiting for him. In just half an hour or maybe a bit more he was already inside an abandoned farmhouse over by Fossa Vecchia. Lazzari left him with a couple of loaves of bread, a *salame* and a chunk of *parmigiano* to sustain him, but Floti gently refused: "Don't worry, humpback, I can take care of myself. You keep this stuff for yourself, you need it more than I do. Everyone thinks you're a devil but you are in truth an extraordinary person. See you around, then."

"I don't think so," the hunchback replied, "you can stay here for a couple of days but then you have to go."

"Why, dammit? I've never done anything wrong. I was born here, I've always worked here, I fought in the war, don't I have the right to stay in my own home?"

"No one has rights anymore," replied the hunchback. "Goodbye. And don't dream of moving until I give you the all-clear. But why on earth did you do such a thing? How did you get it in your head to join the procession?"

"Because I wanted to demonstrate that I can go wherever I want and that I won't be intimidated by anyone."

The hunchback repeatedly shook his head, grumbling to himself, then went back to the cart they'd used to transport Floti, hidden carefully under a load of brushwood.

Maria and Clerice had meanwhile arrived home. Savino

rode up on his bicycle with his little boy in a baby seat hooked to the handlebar.

"You'll stay for lunch, won't you? Your wife is coming too, isn't she?" asked Clerice.

"I'll be glad to stay with the boy," said Savino. "Linda can't come; she has to watch the house because there's no one else home."

He sat down in the kitchen with the baby on his knees, watching his mother and Maria setting the table for twenty people. They put the pot of broth on to boil for the tortellini.

"Where's Floti?" he asked in a different tone of voice.

"Who knows?" replied Clerice, her eyes welling up. "After what he pulled today, if he understands anything at all, he has to get out of here, as soon as he can. Until now, your sister would take him something to eat in the fields, but now . . . You heard what he did, didn't you?"

"Who hasn't heard, *mamma*? That's all anyone's talking about in town. I'm still ready to give him a hand. I'm armed and I'm not afraid of anybody."

"Hush up, for the love of God! I don't want to hear such words. You're married now and you have a child, you have to have enough sense for you and your brother together. We'll eat without him today. What a terrible Festa della Madonna!" she said. And she dried her eyes on the corner of her apron.

Three days later, Bruno Montesi, Graziano's son, went to the abandoned farmhouse at Fossa Vecchia to give Floti a message.

"This one's from Nello," he said. "He says to tell you that you really blew it this time . . . "

"So what else is new? Like I don't know that already."

"He says there might be a way out."

"Oh, really? And what might that be?"

"Nello says they wanted to kill you off and make it look like an accident . . . "

"Well then?"

"Well, then . . . " the boy hesitated.

"Well, what? Have you swallowed your tongue? What are you trying to tell me?"

"He says that now they're talking about an exemplary punishment instead. They'd be willing to accept that, if you agree, afterwards, to act sensibly."

"And just what would this exemplary punishment consist of?" sneered Floti.

"I don't even know if I should . . . but rather than see you killed dead . . . nobody would criticize you if you accepted, Floti; everyone cares about saving their skin."

"Come on, spit it out. As they say, you don't shoot the ambassador. Look, I'll turn around, it'll be easier for you to tell me."

"You ridiculed them in front of the whole town by joining the procession in broad daylight like that. And they want to pay you back, in spades. It would be at the Osteria della Bassa. They'd make you drink castor oil, a bottle or two, until you shit your pants, in front of your friends. There, that's the price they want you to pay."

Floti spun around, his face red and his eyes lit up with ire: "Never! You understand me, boy? Never! I'd rather they murdered me. These humiliations are what killed your father, more than any beating he ever got, you know that, don't you?" The boy nodded. "Tell Nello that he really doesn't know me at all if he thinks he can propose something like that. Go. Tell him."

"That's exactly what I expected from you," replied the boy. "Nothing less. In an hour they'll hear your answer, the only answer that Raffaele Bruni, known as Floti, could give!"

He went back out and ran off across the fields.

CHAPTER TWENTY-TWO

T wo days later, Floti sent word through Bruno Montesi that he'd found a way to leave and that he would like to meet with the family on Wednesday, to say goodbye. Checco sent Bruno back with the message that they were expecting him.

That next Sunday the Madonna left the parish church to go back to her sanctuary. Clerice said farewell and thanked her with a lump in her throat. Her prayer had been heard, but it was a bitter satisfaction. She would have to say goodbye to this son of hers; who knows where he'd have to go to escape danger and who knows when she would ever see him again. She accompanied the Image all the way back to the sanctuary on foot and when the band at the end struck up the first notes of "Mother Of Love", "It's the hour that, piously, the faithful call . . . ", Clerice wept all her tears as the Madonna turned her back to her, entered the sanctuary and vanished into the darkness.

Wednesday, she thought, Wednesday would be the last time in the Lord only knew how long that her whole family would be together. She thought of times past, of the celebrations, the weddings and baptisms, of the long winter nights listening to stories, even of the funerals that had pierced her heart and, looking forward, she saw no reason to hope for better times than those she had behind her. Her sons' wives were all pushing to move out, to go live on their own, without realizing that they had everything to lose, that strength lies in unity and that in such harsh times, each isolated family would find it much more difficult to make ends meet. By the time she got home it was already dark and she started to prepare dinner with Maria's help: a bowl of bean soup followed by *crescente* with prosciutto.

"Always this same old stuff!" Armando blurted out, seeing that the menu didn't tend to vary much.

Clerice didn't let the comment go. "You'll remember," she replied, "this same old prosciutto when you're out on your own."

On the appointed day, they sat down all together at the table to wait for Floti, who didn't show up until long after dark. When Clerice went to open the door, she saw another couple of dark figures leaning against the elm tree, both with rifles slung over their shoulders.

"They're friends, *mamma*, here to watch my back," said Floti, and entered.

They sat down at the table together, each one of them wondering whether this might be the last time they'd see each other. Clerice had saved some broth and tortellini from the Festa della Madonna, because Floti hadn't had any yet, and Maria served, passing around the table to pick up the bowls and bringing them back one at a time, filled to the brim and steaming.

"What a treat!" Armando said this time, adding an abundant sprinkle of grated *parmigiano* to his bowl. "Tortellini on a weekday!" he marveled, and plunged his spoon into the soup.

They didn't talk about much, besides everyday concerns like the weather, the hemp crop and the wheat. Luckily, Maria amused them by recounting her Florentine adventures, some of them familiar by now, others new. She never left out the story of the two marble men, tall as a house and naked as the day they were born, with Rosina saying that she shouldn't attach any importance to that, because they were works of art and artists could do as they please. But not even that topic lasted very long. They all continued eating with their heads in their plates because it was evident that the person who should have done the talking wasn't.

"What are you thinking of doing?" asked Floti at a certain point, as if to say "after I've gone?"

"Each man for himself and God for all," replied Dante

"Yes, that's the only solution," confirmed Fredo.

Savino didn't say anything, because he'd already made his choice and no one could blame him. Checco had already started a little business venture on his own and it must have been doing well, for he always seemed to have money in his pocket.

Floti turned to his sister: "I've heard that you're still seeing Fonso. You still want him."

"Of course I still want him. And he wants me."

"No kidding," commented Armando, "where's the story-teller going to find another girl like you?" forgetting that Fonso had a stable job and that they paid him every week.

"Good," said Floti, "that's good. Maria will be getting married and the rest of you will strike out on your own . . . every man for himself and the devil take the hindmost. As for me, I've found a job in the Garfagnana, at Camporgiano."

"What's that?" asked Fredo.

"It's a place in Tuscany. There was an earthquake there a couple of years ago, and a lot of houses fell. They still need bricklayers."

"But you've never held a trowel in your hand your whole life!"

"It can't be too hard to learn."

A leaden silence fell over the table. Floti wanted to ask: "Who will take mother?" but he said nothing because the answer didn't depend on him. He looked over at Armando, who was so frail and unaccustomed to hard work. How would he find work with that weakling's build? His own thoughts echoed his mother's; Armando would certainly remember the same old prosciutto he was served nearly every day in the Bruni household.

The atmosphere was oppressive and no one felt like talking. Eventually, Floti broke the silence: "Well then, I'd better go before it gets too late. I don't want them catching up with me tonight since it's going to be my last. Goodbye to all of you. Good luck."

"Good luck to you too," said Checco, "you need it."

Dante and Fredo took the cue to get up to go to bed, and just then, each of them realized that with the family breaking up this way, the soul of Hotel Bruni would vanish. They both gave Floti a nod, as if to say, be careful, but they couldn't speak a word because they felt a deep sense of sadness, and if they had spoken their voices would have trembled.

Savino walked up to him and slapped him on the back, "Stay well, Floti. I'll always be here. Just say the word and I'll be there for you, count on it."

"I know," said Floti with a tired voice.

Maria got up and threw her arms around his neck saying, "Write me as soon as you get there! I'll come to visit you, even to the ends of the earth. I've been to Tuscany and I made my way home on foot from Casalecchio. I'll find you for sure. And I'll always love you because when I love a person it's for always."

"I'll always love you too," replied Floti. He dried her tears with the clean, pressed handkerchief he kept in his pocket and he touched her cheek: "Will you forgive me?"

"I have nothing to forgive you for. You only did it because you loved me too much."

Floti's own eyes became shiny at those words. "You're exactly right. Marry your Fonso. He's a good man and he tells beautiful stories. Listening to a good story is like dreaming, but then you have to wake up, and life . . . well, life is another thing. Don't ever forget that."

"I won't forget it, Floti."

"My children." Tears were running from his eyes down his bristly cheeks now but his voice was firm. "You take care of my children, Maria, I'm trusting them to you. They have no one. But one day, I'll come back for them."

He left out the back door and disappeared into the dark.

After dismissing the friends who had been standing guard, Floti cut through the property and headed towards the Samoggia, jumping over all the ditches and drainage canals until he could hear the voice of the river in the distance. He tumbled through a hedgerow in the dark, pricking himself on the thorns, and ended up on the road that flanked the ditch on the other side of the bushes. At that same moment, a galloping horse burst onto the road from a curve at his right and nearly trampled him. He rolled to the ground to avoid being hit and was caught by a blinding light.

A voice cried out: "Damn you, what do you think you're doing?" as Floti heard the horse's hooves pounding the ground just a footfall away from his head. He got up, aching all over, shook the dust from his clothing and walked in the direction of the voice. The man sitting upright on the saddle eyed him: "Look, I'm armed. Make a move and I'll put a hole through you. Is that clear?"

Floti tried to invent an excuse, "Forgive me, I hadn't seen you coming,"

As he spoke, he studied the man who was holding the horse's reins in one hand and a carbide lamp in the other, which lit up his face enough to suggest to Floti that he'd already seen him. "There's no need for weapons," Floti continued. "I know that you don't meet many gentlemen out at this time of night, but sometimes appearances can be deceiving: I'm out here in the dark, jumping over ditches and startling people, but I've never hurt anyone, while those who are after me are safe at home in their beds and they're the true delinquents."

The man got off his horse and approached him: "Who are you?"

Floti shook his head.

He held his lamp up to Floti's face: "I've seen you someplace before. I know your face."

"And I know yours. All right, let's say that you took me for a highway robber, I can see why. But who could you be, out at this time of night and on this road, but a priest or a doctor? Priests don't travel armed and on horseback, so you must be . . . a doctor . . . Oh yes, the lieutenant! Sir!" He raised his hand to his brow in a military salute.

"Codroipo del Friuli, the field hospital: that's where I saw your face!" remembered the doctor. "You broke my balls until I sawed off that lad's arm!"

"That's exactly right. You were all covered with blood, like a butcher. What happened to that guy?"

"Who knows? What's your name?"

"Bruni, lieutenant, sir, Raffaele Bruni. And you're Doctor Munari, if I'm not mistaken."

"Good memory, dammit! And I was a captain when I left the service."

"What are you doing here, captain?"

"I've been named the town physician. What about you?"

"I'm escaping. The Blackshirts are looking for me . . . "

The doctor raised his hand: "Not another word. It's not necessary. The only thing that counts is that you and I passed through hell and we survived. And we're still human beings, it seems. It's a pity you're leaving."

"Yes . . . it is a pity. I would never be doing this unless I was forced to. It's sad to have to leave home."

"You'll make it. After what we went through, we can't be

afraid of anything. When you do come back, come by to see me. We'll have a cup of coffee and chat."

"I'd like that, but it won't be easy. But you know, doctor, I'm taking this meeting as a good sign. Good night, then."

"Good luck, Bruni, and let's hope the night won't be too long. You know what I'm saying."

"Let's hope, doctor."

Doctor Munari spurred on his horse and rode off in the direction of town. Floti continued walking towards the Samoggia, until he saw the water sparkling in the moonlight. There he found a hiding place, tucked under a tangle of locust trees, that he'd used in the past. He covered himself with an old *tabarro* that he'd left there and tried to sleep.

The next day a friend gave him a ride on a cart that he used for transporting crushed stone and took him to the station of Modena. Floti took a train from there to Parma and then to Lucca, from where he could catch a bus to Camporgiano. He'd heard that the town had been partially rebuilt, but many of its buildings were still in ruins. That's where he was headed.

For a while, the Brunis bided their time working the land they had farmed and turned, clod after clod, for over one hundred years. In the meantime, each of the brothers was wondering who Clerice would choose to go and live with. It was an honor and a privilege that each one of them aspired to in his heart, but it was also true that there were objective impediments for some of them. Savino lived in his father-in-law's house and came, now and then, to give a hand. It certainly wouldn't be easy for any of them to convince their mother to live in someone else's house, after she'd wielded the soup ladle her whole life in her own home. Fredo had found work as a cowherd on the property of a landowner in Zola Predosa, too far from all the other brothers. That would be a bit like kidnapping her. Poor Floti had ended up living at the back of beyond somewhere; who knows whether he'd be able to make a living for himself, let alone support someone else. Armando, poor thing, didn't have many prospects. He hoped to work days if someone would have him and to settle his family in the hovel that the parish priest had set aside for the homeless in the old part of town. A miserable solution which he nonetheless took philosophically, laughing that "even the mice, in that place, go around with tears in their eyes."

Checco and Dante were left, and Checco was the first to step up at the beginning of fall. "*Mamma*," he said, one day that there were just the two of them in the chicken coop, "wouldn't you like to come live with me and my wife? For us it would be a great pleasure. I've found a house at the other side of town, near the Morandi villa. It's nice and big, it's dry and there's a bedroom all for you, with the commode right in the hall, opposite the door of your room, because the house used to be annexed to the villa and the estate foreman lived there. I'll be earning well, because I've started up a wholesaling business with a friend of mine who buys and sells feed flours for pigs and cows. You'll live like a countess."

Clerice looked into his eyes. "Thank you, Checco, I'd like very much to come and stay with you, but you know I've always lived in the country, with my chickens and rabbits. I like waking up to the rooster crowing and going to bed when the church bell chimes for the last time. And I'm used to having a lot of room around the house. Living in town, where everyone is so close together and so interested in other people's business, that's not for me. I'd be happy to live with you because you're a good boy and your wife is a respectful, virtuous woman.

"But my place is with the child who needs me the most, without me being a burden for him. I think it's best I go and live with Dante. He's found work as a tenant farmer on a property near Cavazzona that's one hundred and fifty furlongs. He already has three children and his wife is pregnant. I can still be useful to them; I can cook, feed the chickens, heat the water for the pigs, take care of the little ones while their parents are in the fields . . . They need me, Checco.

"You're talking to me about a life that I've never lived, and at my age it's not easy to change. I wouldn't know what to do with myself all day; I've always been accustomed to working. Please don't take it badly. I'll come to visit and we'll have a cup of coffee together on Sundays after mass. And you can come to visit me whenever you like."

Checco dropped his head without managing to say a word, and Clerice understood that he had taken it badly. He must have been hoping she would accept and her refusal had hurt his feelings. All he said, finally, was, "Whatever you wish, mother."

Fonso wanted to get married right away, at that point, because the new public housing development was almost ready. The windows weren't in yet, but that wasn't a problem. The problem was Maria, who felt responsible for her niece and nephew. One day at the end of October, Floti finally sent word: he had found a place to live and a job and he wanted his children to join him. He asked Maria to bring them to the station of Bologna, since he still couldn't set foot in town. One foggy morning, Maria dressed them in the nicest clothes they had, tidied them up, put a pretty ribbon in Ines's hair, had the farmhand hitch up the horse to the cart, and headed to Bologna. She had begun to feel like they were her own, and she wept during the whole journey, at the thought of separating from them. Corrado, the elder of the two, kept asking her: "What's wrong, *zia*?"

By the time she got to the station, Maria was almost hoping her brother wouldn't be there. Instead, she soon saw him emerge from the fog and steam of the locomotive and come towards them. Floti embraced the three of them tightly, then brought them to a café where they could have something hot to drink. They spent a couple of hours together before it was time to go. The children kept looking at the ground because they were a bit afraid of their father, who they hadn't seen in so long and didn't really feel at ease with. Maria kept her eye on the big clock hanging in the station. The hands clicked forward, marking, minute after minute, the approaching moment of separation. It was even worse, sadder, than when she had left Fonso to go to Florence.

When the moment came, Maria burst into endless, inconsolable tears, and stood watching while they got onto the train and rode off. The fog swallowed them up instantly and she went back to the cart, pulling her shawl tight over her shoulders. She couldn't say a word the whole way back and the farmhand, who'd always been in love with her, said now and then: "Cheer up, Maria." But he had a lump in his throat as well: he knew that no more obstacles lay in the way of Maria getting married. He was right.

The wedding was soon celebrated. This time it was Maria asking her fiancé to hurry things up, because she didn't want to be there when the time came for all of her brothers to leave their ancestral home. She and Fonso didn't have a penny more than what they needed to live, and they had to take out a loan to pay for the bedsprings and mattresses. They did, however, have a brand new house: a little apartment in the public housing project that had just been built, which to them seemed like a royal palace. There was even a little sty in back, so they could raise their own pig. Their first few days there turned out to be nice and cool, because the carpenter hadn't fitted the windows and shutters yet. With that excuse, they spent all their time in bed, and thus Maria made up for all of her many heartaches.

When the windows were ready, Fonso's mother and unmarried sister came to live with them.

On Saint Martin's Day, the Brunis took their leave, each one of them going their own way because there was already more that divided them than what united them. It was said that it was the wives who had broken up the family. None of them had ever been fond of the farmer's life, and renting a place in town already seemed like a step up on the social scale. The men, on the contrary, left with heavy hearts because, if the truth be told, they'd been happy living all together for so many years. Some of them had tears in their eyes as they left Hotel Bruni, more than one hundred years after the family had entered for the first time.

Checco was the last to leave the courtyard and, although a more comfortable life awaited him, he was full of melancholy. He looked at the blackened skeleton of the stable and thought of those long winter nights when the snow would fall in big flakes and the oxen would peacefully chew on the fragrant hay. He thought of the big cellar, spacious as a parade ground, where the good red wine fermented in the big vats. He thought of the joyous, bloody ritual of butchering the pig, of those crisp days in January when they seasoned the pork to make salami, sausages and prosciutto. He wasn't sure whether he was mourning the happiness that a stroke of ill fortune had swept away, or the end of his youth.

He moved to the new house with his wife, his young son Vasco and all of their household goods. The Bruni house had emptied out.

From then on, Checco and Dante stopped speaking to each other. No one ever knew why; the fact that Clerice had chosen one of them over the other didn't seem sufficient reason to generate such discord. Perhaps Checco blamed his brother for not having any qualms about allowing their mother to continue working, old as she was, while he could have offered her an easy, comfortable life. He could have taken her to the market in Spilamberto and to eat at the *osteria*, to Bologna to see the Sanctuary of the Madonna di San Luca, who she was so devoted to, instead of watching her slave away until the day she dropped. Someone even said that Checco and Dante had met up one day, just the two of them, and they'd had a terrible fight after which they had never spoken another word to each other again.

A long time after that, two or three years before dying, Checco was said to have written his version of the truth in a letter to his sister Maria. But the letter, in moving from one house to another, was lost and never found again and Maria, who was the only one ever to have read it, never revealed what it said.

CHAPTER TWENTY-THREE

Floti had arrived at Camporgiano at the end of June, after a full day's journey. Although it was evening, he went immediately to introduce himself to the person who his friends had told him about and who had helped in finding work for him. He was a old master builder and Floti caught him in the middle of his supper.

"You must be Bruni," he said, sizing him up. Floti had a suitcase with him and a bag slung over his shoulder with a few personal belongings.

"Come in," said the builder. "Have you eaten?"

"Yes, a little."

"Sit down, there's a bowl of soup left and some bread. You must be tired."

Floti thanked him and sat down. The soup made him feel better, as did being welcomed into his home, the smell of cooking and the scent of chestnut blossoms which he wasn't familiar with but that reminded him of apple blossoms.

"You're safe here. No one will come looking for you. Have you ever laid bricks?"

"No, but I'm willing to do anything to earn a living."

"I've been told you were wounded in the war and so you can't work as a hodman. You'll have to start as a master bricklayer. You can learn with me; you'll help me build the henhouse and the boundary wall. For the time being you can stay here with us, and when you start working you can pay me back for the board and lodging a little at a time. I expect you'll find people here to be a bit mistrustful at first; you know how mountain folk are with strangers. But if you earn their respect, they'll become your friends and you'll always be able to count on them.

"No one knows who you are or why you've come to live here. But I can see that you speak Italian well and that will be to your advantage. I've found you a place to live as well, a little abandoned house on the outskirts of town. It belonged to an old woman who died without leaving heirs. It was damaged by the earthquake. You can move in as soon as I've taught you the trade. That way you can fix it up as you like."

"I can pay you board and lodging. I have my savings with me. Anyway, I don't know how to thank you," said Floti, "you don't even know me."

"Of course I know you," replied the master builder, "you're a person who earns his living by hard work, you are being persecuted because you acted like a free man, you were wounded in a war you didn't ask for, but you did your duty, with courage. Your name is Raffaele. I don't need to know anything else about you."

Four months after his departure, before All Saints and All Souls, Floti wrote Maria a letter in which he told her that he had settled in, had a regular salary and had managed to transform a temporary shelter into a comfortable home. It was then that he announced that he would come to collect his children at the station of Bologna.

After their initial bewilderment, the children got used to the place and were happy there. Corrado went to school and little Ines to the nursery where she was cared for by gentle nuns who didn't mind letting her stay after hours when her father came home late at night. They ate dinner together and it was Floti who cooked the meal, something he'd never done in his whole life. Sometimes he even made fritters from chestnut flour, which was so abundant there, and the children loved them.

In that tiny town, lost in the middle of the mountains, with chestnut forests thousands of years old all around them, with the moss laying carpets of velvet at their feet, with the river crashing down from one crag to the next, seething its way down the mountain only to finish up in quiet, crystalline pools, Floti had started to breathe again and to form a bond to a land so wild and barren yet capable of engendering true, strong emotion.

One evening in February, near dusk, he had gone to fill a bucket with water at the fountain for the washing up, and he'd felt embarrassed at being the only man in the middle of so many women carrying out that task. It wasn't the first time he'd gone, but it had always been at different times of day. In the end, just he and a thirty-year-old woman were left in line. She wasn't pretty, but she had very light, clear blue eyes and a graceful figure. He insisted that she go first and she accepted with a smile. While she was filling her pail, she spoke to him: "You're the stranger who has moved into the abandoned house outside the village, aren't you?"

"Yes, miss, you're right."

"And I see you have to do a woman's work as well."

"I'm a widower, unfortunately, and I do what I can."

"Do you have anyone helping you?"

"No, of course not! I couldn't afford it."

"I understand. If you won't take offense, I'd be happy to give you a hand. I do most of my work in the afternoons. If you bring me the children in the morning, I can get them ready and take them to school and then collect them again in the evening. They can stay with me until you can come for them. I live in that brick house down there, the one with the trellis. It's not too far from your place."

At first Floti didn't know what to say, but then he realized that this was a true act of generosity on her part, and he accepted. "You are really too kind. I don't know how I can repay you."

"Don't worry," she replied. "A person's always in time to die, and to pay his debts!" she said, with such an open smile that Floti was enchanted.

"Thank you very much, then. And . . . let me introduce myself: I'm Raffaele."

"I'm Maria, but everything calls me Mariuccia."

"Thank you, Mariuccia, from the bottom of my heart."

He offered to carry her bucket and walked her to her doorstep.

Early that next spring, Floti wrote his sister to say he'd met a nice girl called Maria just like she was, but whom everyone called Mariuccia because she was such a tiny thing. They were planning to be married. She was willing to care for Corrado and Ines as if they were her own. He wrote that the children were forgetting the town dialect and had started to speak with a Tuscan accent, just like that. He reminded her to tell Checco, Fonso, Savino and even Dante to be sure to give Armando a hand, since he was the one who needed it most.

At first, Maria had missed her niece and nephew terribly, but then she had a little girl of her own and she was happier. The letters she exchanged with Floti became less frequent as time passed but never stopped; for Christmas, her Tuscan sister-in-law always sent her a sack of chestnut flour and a card. The other brothers had settled into their new lives and seemed to be doing all right, except for Armando, who was finding it difficult to get work, although he was so amusing and lively that sometimes people took him on for the day mostly because he made them laugh and kept their spirits up.

Armando would pile up debts the whole winter, hoping to pay them off in the summer, but he didn't always succeed. He'd ended up living in an attic where it rained more inside than out; when the weather was bad, he covered the floor with pots and buckets that collected the dripping water. In the summertime the roof got red-hot and the heat underneath was unbearable. They had put the bed in the only corner where it didn't rain, and they all slept there: he, his wife and all the children. Three of them would come into the world, all girls, born one after another because, as they say, no one is ready to give *that* up, no matter how poor they are.

"At least," he would say, "there are no more mice, because they've figured that if there's nothing here for us, they'd better go someplace else!"

When it was time for the harvest, Fonso, who was the foreman at the estate where he worked, tried to include him among the workers who went "with the machine," that is, behind the thresher. Armando was happy to go, even if the work was hellish: days and days in the middle of the dust and chaff, with the awns of the wheat that pricked you everywhere. He liked it anyway, because it reminded him of when the family was still together, when they had threshed their own wheat. Those had been days of jubilation, with the children romping around in the hay and watching open-mouthed as the huge red machine, all full of pulleys and belts, swallowed up sheaf after sheaf at the top and spit out the chaff at the front and the shiny blond wheat at the side. And then, to their delight, pooped straw out the back, which was promptly gathered into bales by the "mule."

The other workers tried to leave the lighter jobs for Armando, like bagging up the chaff and carrying it into the shed; the sacks were big but at least they were not very heavy.

When it came time for lunch and the men found a spot under the shade of some big tree to settle down with something to eat, you could see that even among the day laborers and farmhands there were those who were better off and those who were worse off. Some had a pot of pasta with meat sauce and *parmigiano*, along with a nice chunk of cheese and some fresh bread, while others had to make do with bread and onions, or even just an apple. Armando was among the latter.

He didn't have the courage to ask for help from his brothers, because he might have been poor but he had his pride. On the other hand, he simply didn't have the strength to keep up a demanding and thus well-paid job. In the end, it was his fellow workers who took pity on Armando, and would often share whatever they had with him.

But his biggest problem wasn't in the fields or the courtyards of the farms where he went seeking work, it wasn't even in earning enough to survive. His real problem was at home, and it was his wife. As time passed, because of their increasingly difficult living conditions, she became prone to depression. Whole days would go by without a word from her, her eyes staring off at nothing. But then suddenly she would shriek and wail and become very agitated and neither her husband's attempts to calm her nor the pleading and crying of her little ones, frightened by her behavior, had any effect.

Yet Armando's love for her never wavered. She was beautiful. She had beautiful eyes and a beautiful body and nothing else mattered to him. His mother had warned him all those years ago, but it didn't make any difference, because when you're in love, you don't listen to anyone, and fate simply has to take its own course. Unfortunately Lucia was getting worse, and the neighbors, upset by the constant yelling, crying and crashing of objects against the walls, convinced her husband to call the doctor.

The town doctor was not an easy man to love. He was sharp, sometimes even brutal; he never spared his patients the raw truth because he thought that telling them the facts was his duty. Husbands were uneasy around him, for he looked at women with the greedy expression of someone who has seen death in the face an infinite number of times and has become accustomed to the thought that, when faced with dying there are only two things you can do: pray or fuck.

He didn't know any prayers, or if he did he'd forgotten

them at the front, amid the butchered bodies of twenty-year-olds that he had to cut, amputate, patch up as best he could while they were screaming under his instruments without anesthesia.

The doctor's verdict was terse: "Your wife is crazy. She needs to be taken to the lunatic asylum."

"I would never do that!" replied Armando, finding almost miraculously the courage to say no to a man who knew so much more than he did. He did not want to separate from his wife; he couldn't even think of living without her. But one day when Lucia seemed to have truly lost her mind—she had run out into the street shrieking and nearly ended up under a horse's hooves—he called the doctor again.

"I've already told you what must be done and you didn't want to listen to me. You can see for yourself that you can't leave her alone. Come by this evening at five and I'll write up a request for admitting her to the psychiatric hospital of Reggio Emilia."

The words "psychiatric hospital" sounded much better than "lunatic asylum," or so it seemed to Armando, and helped him to resign himself to the idea. He went to the doctor's house at the appointed time. The door was opened by his wife, an attractive young woman, who accompanied him right to her husband's study.

The doctor was seated at a desk and all around him were bookcases which had feet in the shape of lions' paws, full of books. One of them was open on the table and Armando could see the illustration that represented some surgical procedure. At the sides of the fireplace were two suits of Arabic armor: shields, crossed lances, conical helmets with nosepieces and scimitars, all beautifully decorated with fine wavy markings. Armando would have liked to ask the doctor if he had read them all, all those books, but he didn't want to sound stupid. Doctor Munari asked him for some general information about his wife and started filling out a form as Armando stood there at the opposite side of the desk with his hat in hand.

"Sit down," said the doctor without raising his eyes from the sheet of paper. "You're a Bruni, aren't you?"

"Yes sir. My name's Bruni."

"Are you a relative of Raffaele's?"

"Yes, he's my brother, but we call him Floti."

"I know him. We met during the war at my field hospital. He's a good man. I almost ran him over, the other night: he jumped out on the street in front of me, right after the curve."

Armando didn't seem interested in his story. "What difference is there between a psy . . . psych . . . "

"Psychiatric hospital," prompted the doctor.

"Right, between that and the insane asylum."

"They're the same thing."

"Oh no then, absolutely not. I thought that . . . "

"What did you think?"

"That it was a hospital."

"Listen to me. Your wife cannot be cured. Somehow, her brain has broken down. I'll bet it runs in her family, do you know anything about that?"

Armando lowered his head because he had always known. Even though he'd never wanted to admit it to anyone, not even himself. The doctor closed the book on the table and continued speaking.

"There's no remedy for what she has; she can only get worse. Nonetheless, there may be times, interludes, we could call them, when your wife will seem better, almost normal, but you mustn't let that get your hopes up. She's going through a very negative period right now and she needs to be hospitalized."

Armando shook his head, like a mule that refuses to follow his master. "I don't want her to. If there's no remedy, why should I take her to any kind of hospital?"

"So that she doesn't get into worse trouble. Look, Bruni, if something happens, you'll be responsible."

"I understand that," replied Armando. "But I won't sign your papers. Goodbye." He got to his feet and went out.

"Where are you going? Stop, dammit!" the doctor shouted after him, but Armando was already out in the courtyard.

It had been a difficult, curt encounter in which neither one of them had tried to understand the other. The outcome was that Armando kept his wife at home for many months after that, but there were more dark days than bright ones. Lucia was pregnant again, with their second child, and she'd taken it very badly; she had become irritable and moody. At times she was calm and her gestures had a softness about then, her eyes a gentle look. But then she became sullen and bad-tempered and would fly into fits of rage. She had the baby in the middle of January after a wretched Christmas lacking in all the atmosphere that Armando had been accustomed to at home. The only thing that wasn't missing was food, thanks to the generosity of his mother and some of his brothers, who hadn't even wanted to be thanked.

It was Clerice who sent a midwife when Lucia's labor pains started, and a little girl was born before evening. Everything seemed to go well at first. The baby was hale and hearty, and the mother, who during delivery had screamed loud enough for the whole town to hear, was now resting peacefully, exhausted.

But things worsened as the days went by. The baby cried constantly; there was no respite, by day or by night. Maybe the mother didn't have enough milk, suggested the midwife when she was consulted. Everyone knew that if a woman ate little and poorly, her milk would dry up; the baby was crying because she couldn't get her fill.

Then one evening, as Armando was just returning from work, he found Lucia at the open window, about to throw the bawling baby out. He stopped her just in time. He said nothing, he didn't scold her. He tried instead to calm her down, and in the meantime, he cradled the baby in his arms and rocked her, singing a lullaby in a mountain dialect that he'd learned once when he'd taken a job gathering chestnuts. The baby magically became quiet and Armando held her out to his wife, saying, look at what a pretty little thing she is, she looks just like you. And he called the doctor.

"Convinced now?" asked the doctor as soon as he took stock of the situation. "Do you realize that she might try that again at any moment? So what are you going to do? Stay at home and watch her all day long? And who's going to go out and earn a crust of bread?"

Armando burst into tears and surrendered. His wife was taken to the mental hospital in Reggio and remained there all that year. Every now and then he'd go to visit her if someone happened to be going out that way, or even by train or by bus, those few times when he managed to scrape together the money. He would have happily gone by bicycle, but he'd never learned how. He was always distressed at the conditions there. The doctors did take care of her but there were so many patients and so few nurses, and they were always harsh and hurried.

She was assigned to a female ward and the nurses, who were huge women with a Herculean swagger, monitored Armando's visits with arms crossed and then accompanied Lucia back to the room she shared with two or three other poor wretches. He would say to her: "Don't let this awful place get you down; as soon as you're home again, you'll feel better. It's only hurting you to stay here. The girls miss you and they really want to see you," he lied. "Do you miss them?"

Lucia looked back with big watery eyes and a confused expression that might have meant anything. Armando went to speak to the doctor, but didn't understand much because he talked too complicatedly. But he didn't give up; before taking his leave he asked a clear question, for which he wanted a clear answer: "When can you send her back home?"

"I can't say. One month, two. We'll see."

"But how will I know?"

"Your town doctor will receive a letter from hospital management specifying a date and all the rest, and you'll come here to pick up your wife and sign that you agree to assume full responsibility for her actions."

The letter arrived three months later, not because the patient had been cured, the town doctor told him, but because there wasn't enough room in the psychiatric hospital for everyone; they had to take turns. Every so often, they let out someone they considered not to be dangerous and took in someone else who was in worse condition. In any case, returning to a more or less normal life, seeing familiar faces, the house she had come to call home, and the town itself, all seemed to do Lucia some good.

But Doctor Munari wasn't tender this time around either. "You wanted her home because you couldn't do without . . . "

"So what, even if it is true?" replied Armando resentfully. "She's my wife, isn't she? And I love her."

"You go ahead and do as you like, I've already told you what I think. If you do want one piece of advice, don't get her pregnant again, you already have enough on your hands."

Wasted breath. In a few months' time, Lucia was expecting again and had become depressed and moody, with sudden fits of temper, quarreling and weeping. A tragedy, said the neighbors. But Armando laid all of his frustrations squarely on Munari's shoulders. The doctor was the cause of all this, not his wife's disease. What right did he ever have to get mixed up in Armando's personal life? He was a bastard. He was vulgar and heartless. And a hypocrite! As if he didn't like the ladies himself! He, who had a wife who could be his daughter, and where had he found her anyway? There was plenty of gossip in town about that, people were whispering on her account. So the good doctor should take care of his own backyard!

At home, however, he never ran out of patience. He was always affectionate and understanding with his daughters and his wife. Whenever he could he'd bring some little gift home: a cherry stolen from a tree, a couple of the early peaches that Fonso brought him. How he loved to see the joy that lit up his daughters' eyes!

Sometimes Fonso would go to give the doctor a hand with his grounds, because he and Maria lived very close to the house, an Art Nouveau style villa with a raised ground floor and a white cement banister on the outside stairs. In back there was a plot of land with rennet-apple, pear, plum and peach trees that had to be pruned, and a vineyard to be treated with verdigris. Fonso would usually stop by after he'd finished working for the day, to see if the doctor needed any chores done or just to say hello on his way back home.

"How's it going, sir?"

"Badly, Fonso, my arthritis is torturing me. I can't even move when it really kicks in. I've had to sell my horse because I can't ride him anymore. The only thing I can do when I have an attack is go to bed, fill up on aspirin, sweat it out and hope it'll pass."

"Is that why you always wear boots, if I may ask?"

"Yes, that's why, Fonso. They help a bit. You know, Mario Gabella was here the other day . . . do you know who he is?"

"Who doesn't? He won an entire estate one night playing tresette, and before dawn he lost another two."

"Ahh, he's a real wastrel, that one," commented the doctor. "Anyway, he suffers from arthritis as I do and he comes here to break my balls about it every day, practically. You know what I told him? I said, 'Listen, Gabella, you got arthritis going duck hunting from a blind, I got it operating on soldiers during the war, standing in water up to my knees in the trenches. You know what I say? You keep yours and I'll keep mine.'"

'That's why people aren't fond of him,' thought Fonso, 'he's too blunt and cantankerous.'

"What do people say about me?" asked the doctor as if he had read Fonso's mind.

"It depends," replied Fonso. "Many of them, most, that is, are ignorant and resentful and they look more at the form than the substance. I say the substance is that a doctor has to know what he's doing. He has to recognize an illness and cure it as well as possible. That's all that matters. Everyone has their own personality."

"You're a sensitive man, Fonso, a diplomat, even. There's meaning in what you say. For some people, talking is just running off at the mouth."

"Thank you, doctor. I'm honored."

"Have you heard anything about your brother-in-law, the one who had to leave?"

"He has settled down in Tuscany. He found a job and he's made a new life for himself. I'm only sorry that it won't be easy for us to see him again: the place he's gone to is far away, and not easy to get to. He and I have had words in the past, because he didn't want me to marry his sister, but he's an honest, intelligent person and these days, that's a rare find."

Whenever they could, Fonso and Maria went over to Dante's house to see Clerice, because she was having such problems getting around that they hardly ever met up with her coming out of church after the mass anymore. Armando was so taken up by the troubles he had at home that he thought of nothing else, and Checco refused to have anything to do with the brother his mother was living with and thus it came to be that it was Maria who kept up relations with her brothers and passed on their news. She even wrote Rosina in Florence when she could. She'd give anything to be able to go see her, or to have her come back home for a visit, but now that everyone had gone their own way, it was even harder because Rosina wouldn't have known who to stay with.

Once it was Rosina who wrote: a strange, disturbing letter that hinted at problems without saying clearly that anything was wrong. The one thing that came through was her unhappiness, a sort of dark restlessness that Maria had always connected to her sister's marriage. Before she'd left home to be married, Rosina was a joyful girl, eager to experience life, and now Maria yearned to be with her, to give her back some of that affection and warmth that Rosina had showered her with when she was staying in Florence. She even asked Fonso if it was possible to telephone her.

"It's complicated," replied Fonso, "as well as expensive. You have to find out where the telephone office closest to her is and make an appointment. Then, when it's time, we would go into town to the post office and call her. But you get no pleasure out of it, because you know how much each minute is costing you and you can't wait for the call to be over so you don't end up broke."

Four years passed in this way, with Lucia entering and leaving the mental hospital, Floti's reassuring letters that came less and less often, and Rosina's often melancholic letters from Florence. That fifth year, one day in mid-August, Clerice began to feel unwell and in the beginning of the fall she took to her bed. One afternoon in October, one of Dante's daughters arrived at Fonso's house on her bicycle, saying that her *nonna* was gravely ill.

CHAPTER TWENTY-FOUR

M aria was first to arrive, on her bicycle. She had left a note for Fonso, who wasn't back from work yet, that she'd had to run off to see her mother, who had taken a turn for the worse. Savino was there almost as soon as she was, followed, much later, by Armando who had gotten a ride on Iofa's cart, and by Fredo. The pastor had preceded them all, because Clerice had called him first: she didn't want to appear before God without having received the sacraments.

Savino had sent his farmhand to call Checco, but he didn't show up, because of the bad blood between him and Dante.

Maria found her mother in the bedroom, practically sitting up in bed with two pillows behind her back, breathing laboriously but perfectly lucid. "She hasn't been the same since the night they burned down the stables," whispered Dante's wife into Maria's ear. "She's never gotten over the fear she felt that night."

Although it was still light out, the room was deep in shadow and the priest was administering extreme unction.

"*Mamma*, how are you feeling?" asked Maria, holding her hand.

"Not well, as God would have it, daughter."

"The boys are all downstairs. Floti's not here, though. We wrote him that you weren't well, but I don't know if he can leave his work and come up . . . "

"I know. It's better he doesn't show his face here yet. It's still too soon. But you tell him that I've always remembered him in my prayers and that I'll pray for him from up there as well, if I end up with the Lord's own."

"What are you saying, *mamma*? You're going to get better!"

"I don't think so. It's time for me to give up the ghost. It's a very bad sign, my daughter, when they come to anoint your feet, a very bad sign," she repeated with tears in her eyes. Maria clasped her hand more tightly. "You're never ready to abandon life, don't think otherwise. There are so many things that hold us here: our feelings, our habits, the sacrifices we've made to earn a decent life for ourselves . . . so many things."

She didn't make it to the next morning. She died weeping because she had to go without seeing the son who was the dearest to her heart.

Checco didn't go to the funeral for the same reason he didn't run to his mother's deathbed, and that was something that, in such a small town, did not go unnoticed. People said all kinds of things, but no one ever found out the truth. The sons who did participate could not carry the coffin on their shoulders as they would have liked to, because Armando was so much smaller than the others that the coffin would not have travelled evenly. In truth, they waited until after their mother was buried to send a telegram to Floti, so that he wouldn't get it into his head to leave the safety of his shelter and show up at the funeral.

Clerice's departure was experienced as the last important event of the Bruni household since they had separated. After Clerice was gone, each one of the brothers took care of himself and raised his own children and the occasions on which the family gathered together became rarer and rarer. In the end, they met only when they happened to run into each other, except for the time when Checco set off with the intention of visiting Floti, just to see how he was doing and if he needed anything. He found that the children had grown up well and that they were very happy with their adoptive mother, who treated them just like her own in every way.

"Would you consider coming back?" Checco asked his brother the evening before he'd planned to leave, while Mariuccia was washing the dishes. "Sooner or later things will change and . . . "

"I don't think so," said Floti. "My life is here now."

"Don't you miss your friends? The family?"

"Yes, but . . . I'm managing to get used to that too. Do give everyone my regards, please."

"Yes, sure," replied Checco. "As ordered."

The next morning at dawn, Floti accompanied his brother to the bus stop. The air was slightly, almost imperceptibly, misty and the autumn foliage was starting to change color. The chestnut leaves, in particular, were a rich, intense orange and the husks were already opening to reveal the fruit inside, shiny as leather. The mountains that towered beyond the forests were already capped with snow.

"Bye, then," said Checco.

"Maybe we'll see each other again, some time or other," replied Floti. They looked into each other's eyes for a few instants, seeking something more to say, but in the meantime the bus pulled up and Checco got on. Floti stood watching until it drove out of sight.

When Savino found out about Checco's trip, it really got his back up, because he would have liked to go visit Floti as well. He promised himself he'd do so at the first possible chance, but none came up for a great number of years.

His relationship with Nello continued despite their deep differences of opinion, because friendship somehow always wins out in the end. Savino couldn't forget that, if it hadn't been for his friend, the fascists would probably have burned the house down as well. And that Nello had always warned him when Floti was in danger.

Both of them had sons. Nello's son was called Rossano and Savino's was called Fabrizio. The both attended the nursery school run by the nuns and they played happily together. Nello would often allow Rossano to go by bicycle to visit his friend at the farm where Savino worked. Rossano loved the place because there was a big soaking pond which had fallen into disuse because it wasn't profitable to plant hemp anymore. The pond had been filled with fish of every sort: catfish, tenches, carps and even goldfish, which were the ones he liked best. When they managed to catch one with a net, Fabrizio got one of the glass jars they used for canning tomatoes, filled it with clean water and put the fish in so that his friend could take it home with him.

As they grew up, the boys absorbed the attitudes and political convictions of their fathers, even if it was obligatory for both of them to sign up for the Opera Nazionale Balilla, the fascist youth organization, and wear the uniform when they did their drill exercises on Saturday afternoons.

"Do you know what *balilla* means?" Rossano asked Fabrizio one day.

"It means a fascist child," replied his friend.

"No. 'Balilla' was the nickname of a boy from Genova who was as old as us. One day a group of Austrian soldiers who had occupied the city managed to get one of their cannons stuck and they wanted to force some men to help them yank it out of the mud. Balilla threw a rock at them and all the other kids followed suit and that's how they chased the Austrians out of Genova. That's why we're called *balilla*."

Fabrizio didn't answer because his father had taught him never to repeat in public what was said at home, and that is, that the fascists had transformed all of Italy into a barracks and that sooner or later they would drag the country into war.

After they'd finished elementary school, the boys took off in different directions. Fabrizio went to work in the fields with his father. He learned to use a rake and a hoe and then, when he was a bit older and stronger, a spade and a scythe. Lastly, he learned pruning and grafting, the most difficult of a farmer's arts. And in the evening, his father sent him to take lessons from an elderly bookkeeper who taught him to keep the accounts for the farm. Savino hoped that one day his father-in-law, who didn't have any sons of his own, might entrust him with managing his properties.

Rossano, instead, was sent to a fascist party school, first in Ravenna and then in Perugia. If he studied hard and got good marks, he might go all the way to Rome.

The two boys thus had fewer and fewer occasions to see each other. Rossano did make it home during the school holidays, and they would meet up at the sports center, where they kicked around a soccer ball or even played bocce. Both tried to avoid talking about politics so as not to ruin their friendship, but it wasn't easy. The subject always came up somehow and it would be very embarrassing for both of them, especially since Rossano, after two or three years at school, took to wearing the fascist uniform, with its black shirt and silk-fringed fez.

"What do you mean by that uniform?" Fabrizio asked him one day. "Can't you wear something normal, at least when we're together?"

"This is normal for me, don't you understand? It means that I'm a volunteer for the national security militia."

"What need is there for a militia? Don't we already have the police; aren't the *carabinieri* good enough at taking care of national security?"

"We act under the direct orders of the *Duce* and we are prepared to make the ultimate sacrifice for him and for our country."

"I see you've been indoctrinated well."

"You're the one who's been indoctrinated by the reds, the defeatists and the traitors of our country!"

Fabrizio looked down without reacting: he'd learned there was no changing him and thus no point in arguing. His friend had been raised to believe in an out-and-out cult of a supreme leader to whom he owed blind obedience.

"Do we have to fight?" asked Fabrizio.

Rossano held his tongue in the face of a question that took all the fire out of the debate.

"Well?" insisted Fabrizio.

"No . . . we don't have to, but you provoked me."

"I was only trying to make you see that since you've been going to that school, you're not the same. You look for an enemy even where none exists, and it seems like you're always looking for a fistfight. Anyway, you've joined up with a group who goes around beating people up, the same ones who burned my father's stable down because our family didn't see things their way. You know what I'm talking about. Think about it, Rossano, turn back while you're still in time. An idea that splits apart two guys who have been friends since birth is certainly a bad one."

They lost touch with each other. Rossano continued to attend the party school, moving from Perugia to Rome, and on the few occasions he came back to town, there wasn't much time. If they ran into each other, after a first brief moment of delight, a certain uneasiness stepped in, reflecting their differing conditions and convictions but even more so the sensation of no longer feeling comfortable with one another. They still felt nostalgic about their childhood, when they'd spent long hours playing together or just laying on the grass watching the clouds and the birds flying by, in absorbed, silent contemplation. They would try to change the subject to girls, but even that didn't work. So in the end they'd just say goodbye.

"See you around."

"See you around."

Fabrizio got along well with Bruno Montesi, even though he was quite a bit older. Bruno had opened up a shop in the area of town that people called "Madonna della Provvidenza," since it was near the sanctuary. So everyone simply called Bruno "the Madonna's blacksmith." When some work needed doing on his father-in-law's farm, Savino would send Fabrizio to summon Bruno because he had a forge and bellows. Sometimes it would be to make the grating for a window, or a fence for the pigsty. Or a door hinge that needed replacing. He was also good at sharpening the scythes and the blades on the hoes and spades before the spring planting season. Fabrizio would sit and watch that spry, slender boy wielding a one-kilo hammer as if it were made of wood. He always had that curious smell of the forge about him.

"You smell like iron," Fabrizio would tell him.

"That's natural, it's my job. Your farmhands smell of soil."

"And the cowherd smells of manure, I can tell you that," the boy would laugh.

"Yeah, right. But did you know that your name, Fabrizio, comes from Latin and that it means blacksmith?"

"No, I never knew that. So we have something in common."

"I'm sure we have more in common than that!"

They'd always banter like that, when there was time, and you could tell that Bruno read a lot, or studied, or spent time with people who did. He knew about politics, the economy. He spoke Italian easily, although the man who leased him the shop could barely read or write.

Bruno was twenty years old when radios all over the country broadcast the voice of the supreme leader announcing the reappearance of Empire on the fated hills of Rome. Fabrizio was fifteen but he had an idea of what was going on.

Savino had a radio, a CGE with a decorated screen and three strips of Bakelite that covered the speaker. A magical iridescent eye let you know when the frequency was being picked up at its clearest. Bruno was also invited to listen, although he was there to work.

"What do you think, *papà*?" Fabrizio asked when the speech was finished.

Savino's forearms were down on his knees and his head swung between his shoulders.

"Nothing good. Big words to blow smoke in people's eyes. Anyone who doesn't go into raptures is a defeatist."

"A war that we can't afford," commented Bruno. "I can hardly believe it; the Italians, who know what it means to suffer foreign dominion, are going out to oppress other peoples? It would have been much wiser to invest all that money in Italy, to improve the conditions of the poorest classes."

But in town, and in all the surrounding towns, celebrations and parades were the order of the day. Rossano participated, marching in uniform among the *Avanguardisti*, the youth wing of the party. Fabrizio met up with his friend that very evening at the soccer field, where a game between two of the nearby towns was scheduled. Rossano, who was much taller and more muscular than most boys his age, bulging in his black uniform, looked like one of the young heroes depicted on the cover of the weekly *Domenica del Corriere* supplement. Fabrizio couldn't help but feel a pinch of admiration for his enthusiasm and glamour.

"The English and French have attacked us because we've conquered Ethiopia. Hah! They, who have the biggest colonial empires of the world, which certainly weren't conquered without destruction and slaughter."

"So why should we make the same mistakes? Wouldn't it be better to imitate the good aspects of those countries, like democracy, respect for the law, economic and civic progress, organization of trade unions?"

"They're nothing but hypocrites. Even the Americans have said so. Who told you such a crock of shit, anyway? You're repeating words that someone else put in your mouth."

Fabrizio wanted to say: "Bruno." That was the truth, but he

realized it was better not to reveal his source. He said: "I know how to reason on my own. I only wonder if you do."

Rossano put a hand on his shoulder. "I don't feel like quarrelling with you, today, buddy," he replied, obviously in a good mood. "I'm too happy. We'll no longer be a country of emigrants, a people mocked and humiliated. The whole world will have to respect us! Now we have an empire of five million square kilometers, rich with raw materials, in a strategic position for trading with the Orient. We'll build streets, airports, universities . . . there will be work for everyone!"

Fabrizio changed the subject: "Did you know that our fathers were always friends?"

"Of course, they still are. But now the socialists have to get it into their heads that the country must unite; we must become one people with a single leader."

Fabrizio cut their conversation short to avoid another argument. "So long, then."

"See you around, buddy," replied Rossano. They would not see each other again for years.

A few months later, when the League of Nations imposed economic sanctions on Italy for the invasion of Ethiopia, Mussolini proclaimed that the country would become an autarky. In this push for economic self-sufficiency, the idea was put forth that all the women in the country should donate the gold rings they'd received from their husbands on their wedding day. This collecting of the wedding bands was done in public, so that no one would dare to refuse. In reality, not all the married women in town even had gold rings to offer up, but those who did deposited them in a copper pot, which in the end was half full. Each of these women was given a steel band in exchange, free of charge.

There was a widow in town who no longer had her wedding ring because after her husband had died, she had pawned it to make ends meet, and she had never managed to redeem it. She showed up one day at the end of June, her ten-year-old son in tow, at the estate where Fonso worked, asking if she could glean the spikes that had been left behind after the harvest.

Fonso exchanged words with the steward, who happened to be passing by, then came back to tell her: "Go and gather up everything you can find, Carolina. I hope it's a lot."

With the sun already high in the sky, the woman began to go up and down the rows of stubble, an empty sack in her hand, helped by the little boy. As the hours passed, the sack filled up. She was careful to keep the contents pressed down, so that more spikes would fit, and at the end of the day, she had two big sackfuls, packed well. There was enough there to make bread for six or seven months, and both mother and son were happy. Just as she was about to load the sacks onto a wheelbarrow with Fonso's help, a truck pulled into the court-yard. At the wheel was a fellow with the pompous name of Astorre who, out of work and without a penny to his name, had begun working for the commander of the local fascist mili-tia. He made himself useful by running errands, delivering packages and carrying messages. He always wore his uniform because he had nothing else to wear anyway, and besides, he felt important and respected in that outfit. People had begun to fear him, not because of his uniform, but because they knew he was willing to spy on the villagers and report back with false and slanderous information. The very fact that they thought of him as dangerous gave him more power. But among them-selves, when no one was listening, they called him *buférla*, the name of a bird who was reputed to live on cow dung.

Having seen Carolina pushing the sacks of wheat ears onto the cart, Astorre walked up with his arms akimbo. "Well, who do I see here. If it isn't Miss Carolina!" The little boy, fright-ened, went to hide behind his mother's skirt. "I've been told that you didn't give your gold ring to your country."

"I don't have any gold. I had to pawn the ring that my late

husband gave me and I've never managed to get it back. I swear it's true, Mister *Buférla*." In her embarrassment and confusion, she had let the name slip out.

Enraged at this insult, his face as red as a pepper, he burst out: "I won't hear any excuses! If you didn't give up your gold, you know what we'll do? I'll take half of the wheat you've gathered and we'll consider your debt settled."

Fonso, who'd witnessed the scene, broke in: "You can't be serious, Astorre. She's a poor widow who can barely eke out a living for herself. We left those spikes behind just for her. She's not here asking for charity; she worked all day under the hot sun with her boy helping. There are no spikes left, and for them it means bread for the rest of the year."

"That doesn't concern me. On the contrary, I know you'll give me a hand to load this sack on the truck, Fonso, if you don't want me telling the appropriate authorities that there was a red flag flying on your thresher the other day."

Fonso bit his lip but answered back: "Do what you will do, Astorre, but I refuse to be a party to this travesty."

Buférla knew well that Fonso was too hard a nut for his teeth to crack, and he took care of loading the sack of wheat onto his truck himself. Fonso whispered in the meantime to the widow: "Don't worry, Carolina, I'll find a way to make sure you're not lacking wheat to make your bread."

But, before he could finish, the little boy threw himself at the villain, punching, kicking and biting. He shouted out: "The sack is ours! Leave it alone, it's ours!"

Buferla, infuriated, gave him a hard kick and sent him rolling into the dust. His mother ran over to help him, but he was already back up on his own, bouncing like a spring. He took a step towards his enemy and said: "When I'm bigger, I'm going to kill you."

CHAPTER TWENTY-FIVE

When Savino's father-in-law began complaining of a heart ailment, Savino was put in charge of the administration of his properties. He started out by making a number of improvements in the farm setup and in the irrigation system, and bought a couple of new vehicles, including a fifty-horsepower single-cylinder Landini tractor with a hot bulb engine and a deep-trench plow. Fabrizio went crazy when he saw them drive the tractor up, shiny and brand new, straight from the factory. When the dealer showed them how to start it up, the heavy flywheel began turning swiftly, overcoming the resistance of the big single cylinder. The only thing he wasn't crazy about was its dull gray color, he would have preferred red or orange.

All the day laborers had gathered around it, along with the two farmhands and the cowherd, to take part in this extraordinary event. In their eyes, the roaring machine was a wonder of technology, capable, they thought, of any endeavor.

"You think it could pull down that oak?" asked one of the men, pointing to a century-old tree.

"I say no," replied another.

"I say it would," shot back the first. "Why don't we try?"

Savino was obviously against it, but had he consented there was no doubt that the tractor would have been powerful enough. The men would have willingly uprooted a century-old oak tree just for the pleasure of seeing a technological force win out over a natural one. Some launched into an academic discussion as to how many pairs of oxen it would take to provide equal power, and others wondered whether it really had the strength of fifty horses, something that was a bit difficult to believe. The next day, anyway, Savino was going to plow a couple of furlongs of stubble and they'd see just what that steel horse was capable of.

Unfortunately, he wasn't able to do it himself because his father-in-law had another attack and he had to go fetch the doctor with the carriage.

When Munari reached the patient's bedside, he used his stethoscope to listen to the man's chest in several places. When he was finished he prescribed an aspirin a day and a shot of brandy when he needed it, and then walked outside with Savino.

"He won't last long," the doctor told him. "A year, two if he's very lucky. He has severe heart failure and there's no cure for it."

"Pardon my asking, doctor, but if he's so badly off, how will one aspirin and a half-glass of brandy help him?"

"Ahh, ignorance!" sighed the doctor. "Do you know why your father-in-law is so unwell? Because he's eaten too much his whole life. The time comes when the heart can't pump blood to all the parts of that huge body of his. So water begins to accumulate in the lungs and . . . " he made the sign of the cross with his middle and index fingers united, "amen. The aspirin will keep his blood fluid and the alcohol in the brandy will dilate his arteries so the heart doesn't have to work so hard. That's why it's called a 'cordial,' from the Latin word for good for your heart."

"I see."

"Good. And so he might last two years instead of one, but no more than that, I'm afraid."

Savino and his wife Linda followed all the doctor's instructions to the letter and his father-in-law lived exactly two more years; this inspired them with a faith that might have been more rightly placed in a prophet than in a town doctor.

But it wasn't the same everywhere in town. Many said that the doctor only went to examine the rich, those who could afford to pay him, and not the poor. It wasn't true, because he even treated the children of gypsies, who certainly had no money, but people believe what they want to believe and sometimes even deny what is evident.

Fonso often brought his little daughter Eliana to the doctor's house; they treated her as their own and she adored being pampered by the doctor's *signora*, as everyone called her. At home, besides her mother who was always scolding her, there were her *nonna*, her father's mother, and her spinster aunt as well, and all of them were always ordering her around. Do this and do that and learn to sew and learn to roll out the pasta. Sometimes, the *signora* would even give her a banana to eat, an exotic fruit with an intense fragrance that was totally absent from the tables of ordinary folk.

"Eat it here," the *signora* told her. "If you go out, the other little girls will see you and they'll feel badly because they can't have one."

Every now and then she took a photograph of little Eliana and this was a real luxury. The *signora* would comb her hair and put a big bow in it and have her sit on the banister on the outside staircase or on the swing, and the doctor would take her picture.

Eliana knew how privileged she was and she knew what a good heart the doctor's wife had; every year, for the Epiphany, she would play *la befana* and give little gifts to all the poor children: an orange, a tangerine, some peanuts and, for the girls, rag dolls that she bought in the city.

The doctor had the impression once that Eliana's shoulders were becoming stooped and he asked to see Maria. "I don't like the look of this," he told her, "the girl's back isn't straight;

it must be corrected immediately. You must do exactly as I say if you don't want her to turn into a hunchback."

Maria widened her eyes in terror.

"If you listen to me, everything will be fine. Now pay close attention: every morning, as soon as she wakes up, strip her down and wrap her in a sheet soaked in cold water. She'll cry and scream, she'll ask you to stop torturing her, but you pay her no mind. Just keep doing it for as long as I tell you it's necessary. She should also skip rope for at least half an hour a day and drink at least two glasses of milk, every day. Plus a spoonful of cod-liver oil."

"She hates it," replied Maria, "but I'll make sure she takes it."

"Excellent. In a couple of months' time, she'll straighten out, you'll see."

The doctor's instructions were followed to the letter and the outcome was perfect in this case as well. The consideration that Fonso and his wife had for Doctor Munari increased incommensurably.

And so Eliana approached her adolescent years fortified by cod-liver oil, freezing baths, soaking sheets glued to her young body, and shoulders as straight as those of any princess. After having brought her little sister, Tommasina, into the world, her mother Maria went back to enjoying her favorite pastimes. She hated inactivity and couldn't stand the grumbling of her mother-in-law. The old woman never spared her any criticism: dinner was either too raw or overcooked, the sheets of pasta she rolled out for tagliatelle had tears in them. They couldn't even leave the door open, the old woman complained, because just imagine if someone looked in and saw, what a disgrace!

Maria didn't let herself be annoyed by any of it. She'd been allowed to run pretty wild as a girl, in the middle of seven brothers, free to roam the fields and climb up and down trees looking for nests. The house she'd come to live in, although cozy and comfortable, was too small for her. As soon as she could, she'd slip out, get on her bicycle and take off. She especially liked going around to help the farmers' wives. Milking the cows, patching a pair of their husbands' old pants, or just sitting and chatting. She never came back empty-handed: she'd have a loaf of freshly baked bread to show for her efforts, a piece of pancetta or prosciutto, or a jar of lard for frying *crescente*.

The women knew they could confide their secrets in her; Maria was so discreet she would never breathe a word of anything they told her, not even to her husband or daughters. At times, riding her bicycle down the little country lanes in the hottest hour of the day, when the men were taking a snooze in their bedrooms facing north, she would happen to see their wives seeking another kind of distraction in the middle of the hemp or maize fields, or under the shade of a mulberry tree.

Even when her friends in town would start bringing up certain stories about so-and-so who was going to bed with such-and-such, all they would hear from Maria was: "I don't know about any of that. And even if I did, I don't talk behind anyone's back." As if to say that gossiping and slander were worse sins than the weakness of the flesh.

As the years went by and her habit of enjoying a nibble with the neighborhood ladies became more and more frequent, she began to put on weight, partly because she was letting herself go and partly because she slept so much, a lingering aftereffect of her Florentine lethargy. Fonso never made her feel badly about it, and showered her with the same attention as he had when she was a slender, shapely girl.

Her husband was the backbone of the family, but Maria did lots of seasonal work like picking cherries, showing surprising agility, despite the kilos she'd added to her figure. Her special talent was in reaching the longest, most difficult to get to branches, which produced the ripest, most unblemished fruit. The problem was that these branches were too slender to support the weight of a ladder and the person climbing it. Unwilling to leave all those delicious tidbits to the birds, the men would string up a couple of ropes from one trunk to the next, one to walk on barefoot, the other, a bit higher, to hold onto with your hands and hang the basket from.

Very few pickers managed to do this, and they were much sought after. Not only did you have to capable of walking the tightrope, you also had to have quite a lot of nerve, because you'd often be suspended at a height of ten meters from the ground. It was a piecework job, they were paid so much per basket, and the supervisor wanted to see them filled to over-flowing because that way for every three baskets he got a fourth. Maria was always careful to clip her skirt closed with a safety pin because she knew the men would be looking up from underneath. Others didn't care a whit: they didn't mind at all showing their underwear; on the contrary, they were looking for any opportunity that came their way. One in par-ticular, a buxom brunette who came from the mountains, was said to not wear any underwear at all if she was interested in one of the men below, but Maria had never bothered to find out if it was true, because it didn't concern her and anyone can show her own stuff to whoever she likes.

Although daily life still followed the rhythm of the same age-old, consolidated traditions, public life was one military review and parade after another; black uniforms were present everywhere and the radio broadcast bombastic, warmongering speeches. As time went by, the adults in town felt increasingly fearful that another war would break out. Most still had vivid memories of the last war and what it had meant for each of them, their families and their friends. Many of them had lost a son, a brother, a husband. In the square in front of the town hall there was a monument representing a soldier with a cloak and helmet, his hand on his rifle. Behind him, on a marble slab, were the names of all of those who had not returned. There were dozens of names, too many for such a small town.

They were most afraid of the man who had come to power in Germany. A small fellow, with a moustache sticking out from under his nose the size of a postage stamp, who would set himself up and shout like a maniac in front of endless formations of soldiers moving like a single man. At the town cinema, before the movie began, there would always be a short newsreel that showed how Germany was the strongest of all the European countries and Italy came right after them. Not many of the people in town believed such a thing, but were careful not to say so if they didn't want to be tagged defeatists.

Eliana was growing up and she wanted to go out dancing in the evenings, but Maria would not hear of it: "It's better for you to stay home and help *nonna* with the housework; you'll be happy one day that you did. You'll find a fiancé who will give you nice presents and marry you. Sure, men go crazy over those girls who go out dancing and let themselves be touched, if not worse, but they won't marry them. They want to marry the kind of girl that no one talks about."

"*Mamma!* All of my friends are going, why must I be the only one to stay home?"

"Let them go. Tomorrow morning you'll wake up feeling exactly the same as those who went dancing, even better. And your father doesn't want you to go out, either."

Maria had become so jealous of her daughter that whenever she saw her leaving the house, she'd ask immediately: "Where are you going?"

"*Mamma!* I'm just going to Rina's house to have a chat. It's ten feet away."

"Then the two of you can stay right here and talk," she'd reply.

Eliana couldn't take it anymore and she started to wish that she had a fiancé; he would at least take her out, to the cinema, even, or to stroll in the square on Sunday afternoon. And for Easter he'd give her a chocolate egg with a surprise inside, like the ones her friends got. But with the way her mother was, who knew when that would ever happen.

The next year, her friend Rina started seeing Eliana's cousin Vasco, who had become very handsome, and was very nice and funny besides. He must have gotten it from Zio Checco, or even Zio Armando, who always got everyone to laugh with his jokes. Vasco sometimes came by with a couple of boys a little older than himself. One was called Nino and the other one's name was Alberto, but for some reason everyone called him Pace. They were nice, but she had just turned sixteen and they seemed much too old for her.

Every evening on his way home from work, Fonso had a dip in the Samoggia if the weather was fine, or washed in the tub. Then he sat down to dinner served like a king by five women: his wife, mother, sister and two daughters. Before going downstairs to eat, he'd stop in the bedroom, lean on the chest of drawers and read a book out loud, starting from where he'd left off the evening before. And so the house rang with the words of Dumas or Tolstoy or Cervantes. He would only read softly if the book was prohibited, like those by Carolina Invernizio. When they called him down because dinner was ready, he'd take his seat and tell them how things had gone during the day. Or about what he'd read in the newspaper if he'd stopped to see Bastianino, the tailor: bad news, and always worse.

"If this keeps up, we'll soon be at war," he said. "Thank God our own family won't be at risk. I have bad eyesight so they won't be calling me up again and I don't have a son, but when I think of the others . . . those poor families. When times are bad, they're bad for everyone, even the rich. Bombs can't tell the difference. We're still paying the consequences of the Great War! How is this possible, I ask myself."

When they'd finished eating, clearing the table and putting

the kitchen in order again, they all went to bed, to save on electricity.

That following spring, Eliana was approached by Vasco's friend Nino as she was returning home on her bicycle after having done the shopping.

"Can I escort you home?" asked Nino, pulling up alongside her in the saddle of a shiny black-and-chrome motorcycle. He cut an elegant figure, in his jodhpurs, shiny leather boots, white shirt open at the neck and leather jacket. His hair was wavy and had been tousled by the wind and was going a bit white at the temples. His eyes were green.

"I can get home perfectly well on my own," replied the girl, following her mother's instructions. But he had definitely caught her eye with that devil-may-care air of his and that dazzling motorcycle that smelled of gasoline and raw leather.

"I bet you can," replied Nino, keeping the bike in first gear so he could stay at the same speed as her bicycle. "I just wanted to keep you company for a while."

"But how old are you?" she asked, struck by the salt-and-pepper hair at his temples.

"Twenty-two," he answered.

She pulled up short. "I don't believe you."

"Let's make a bet. If I can prove that I'm twenty-two, you'll let me walk you home. I'll leave the motorcycle here and we can go on foot, but I'll take you for a ride one day if you like."

"No, I believe you," she said now that she was close up to his bright eyes, his smooth, freshly-shaved skin and his muscular chest. "How fast can it go, full speed?"

"A hundred, but if I hug the gas tank and the road is asphalted, even one ten or one twenty. It depends on the road."

I did it, thought Nino. He'd managed to pique her interest and he was sure she'd accept to go out with him. What woman had ever resisted?

For Eliana it wasn't just a question of his looks and his

brand new motorcycle. It was the way he had with words. Free and easy, crackling with wit. He could carry on a whole conversation without ever getting stuck, without ever running out of things to say. And in perfect Italian.

"You do speak well," said Eliana. "Where did you learn?"

"At school, like everyone else. It's just that I didn't stop at elementary school, I went on to the *ginnasio*. Then I had to leave."

"Why?"

"Why? Oh, I'd get into trouble, I wasn't well disciplined and then, I didn't like it that my sisters were out working in the fields and I was being raised to be a some kind of a gentleman . . . But . . . won't you tell me your name?"

"You're quick to get personal, aren't you?" replied Eliana with a smile.

"I asked you nicely, didn't I?"

Eliana was getting hooked. Then her eyes fell to his hands. Working man's hands, used to laboring in the heat or frost, with wood and with iron. The hands of an honest person, one who didn't hold back and faced whatever tough job the new day had to offer him.

"I'm going to go home alone now, because if I come home with someone like you, and on that motorcycle, my mother will have a fit. I know you're friends with my cousin Vasco; his girlfriend is a friend of mine. Maybe if we all go out together, my parents will give me permission. Unless you have someone else, that is."

Nino realized that this girl deserved some serious attention and that this wouldn't be just another fling for him. "I'd like that," he said. "There's a fair on Sunday, they'll be setting up amusement park rides and all the rest. We'll have fun. Ciao!"

He turned the motorcycle around and disappeared down the end of the road at full speed. In one month's time, Fonso and Maria had given him permission to come to the house and court their daughter.

CHAPTER TWENTY-SIX

The war, as everyone had feared, caught up with them, just a year after the other countries had formalized their intentions. And so the Italians found themselves fighting against those who had been their allies in the first great world conflict, and alongside those who had been their enemies, and this created problems for a great many of them.

By then, Nino, Vasco, Alberto who everyone called Pace, and their fiancées were all fast friends; they would go out all together for a picnic on their bicycles, or a walk up on the hillside, or they'd all go dancing at Nino's house, where his three sisters were delighted to have their company. Nino was the only one of them to have a motorcycle, but for the outings with his friends he'd bought a beautiful bicycle for himself, a pale green Legnano with wooden wheel rims, a true rarity. They would often all end up at his house together. They'd cook a rabbit with potatoes, open a few bottles of Lambrusco and sing the evening away, accompanied by the accordion.

But all too soon the draft cards began to arrive: first Pace and then Vasco, a year after war had been declared. Nino invited both of his friends for dinner one evening with the girls, so they could all have one last meal together before they had to head off for the war. They did all they could to stay cheerful and not think about leaving. They tried to come up with amusing stories to tell, but there was a stone guest with them at the table: the black lady with the scythe who would rush off to the battlefield before they arrived and lie there in wait.

When dinner was over and Nino was making the coffee, he tried to convince Pace, who had a beautiful tenor voice, to sing for them, but he didn't succeed.

"I don't feel like it," replied his friend. "I'm leaving the day after tomorrow for Russia, how can I sing?" And that phrase broke up the party; there was no longer any reason to linger. The three friends embraced one another and Nino told them: "Keep your chin up; thinking about your troubles only makes them worse. I bet you that we'll all find ourselves back here in no time and we'll have one of those parties that'll go down in history."

"Let's hope," replied Pace.

"Let's hope," echoed Vasco. They walked off on foot, clinging to their girlfriends almost as if they were desperate to store that warmth for the long winters ahead, on endless fields of ice and snow. Nino went outside with them; he wanted to walk Eliana home but in truth he just couldn't stand to let them go and wanted to stay in their company for as long as he could.

Three weeks later, Nino's turn came: he was ordered to report to a clearing center in Udine, from where he would be deployed to the Balkans.

Floti's son Corrado would also be sent to the Russian front and become the second Bruni to go off to war. The only two men of fighting age, who could never have imagined that they would share a common fate.

The enthusiasm that greeted the declaration of war quickly vanished. Any news about the fighting was contradictory and difficult to decipher; the official war bulletins referred to "rectifications of the front" rather than retreats and minor progress in a single sector was a "sweeping victory." But the fact that the army corps had been sent off to Russia with scarce provisions and completely inadequate gear soon became of public dominion, because the deaths due to frostbite, and the wounded that crowded hospitals everywhere, could not go unnoticed.

The first to return was Vasco, after two years of hard combat, of nights spent without shelter, of endless marches. But the news of his arrival filled his parents with great foreboding instead of joy. Checco, Vasco's father, had learned that Nino was home for a two-week leave, and he went to show him the letter they'd received from the division commander.

"One of his feet got frozen," Checco told him, "and it doesn't look good. They're talking about a serious infection. He's near Rimini now, in one of those old holiday camps for children that have been transformed into hospitals."

Nino loved Vasco's parents as if they were his own, because the two boys had been together their whole lives, like brothers, going back and forth from one house to the other.

"Do you want me to go with you?" Nino asked. "You don't want to make the trip alone; let me come along."

"That would be a real pleasure," replied Checco. "We are a bit afraid of going alone. We might get lost . . . "

Nino hugged them, knowing full well that they were not afraid of getting lost; they were afraid of what they would find when they got there. The three of them left the next morning from the station of Bologna, after having bought a bagful of oranges from a fruit vendor's stand. They took a direct train to Rimini. It was a local, so it didn't cost much but made all the stops, and it took them a good two hours to reach their destination. There they got on a bus that took them down the coastal road. It stopped right in front of the seaside camp where Vasco had been admitted for care. Nino thought it would be best for him to enter first so he could take stock of the situation.

"You wait here, Checco, go take a walk on the beach with Esterina. I'll come and get you when I've found him," he said, and entered the building.

He found a nurse and said: "I'm looking for Vasco Bruni, I'm a friend of his." She gave him a floor and room number. As he was walking up, he stopped on the landing and saw Vasco's parents below, walking along the deserted beach, lapped by gray waves rimmed in white. He felt sorry for them.

Vasco smiled when he saw Nino, but he didn't even look like himself. When he had left for the war, he was healthy as an ox, one of the best looking boys in town. He was pale now, emaciated and gaunt, and his forehead was beaded with sweat. Nino hugged him and realized that he was feverish.

"You have a temperature."

"It's the infection, Nino. Nothing hurts, really, but this fever never goes away. If it drops during the day, it just gets higher at night."

"What do the doctors say?"

"They don't seem to attach much importance to it. There's an awful lot of young guys here, wounded, sick . . . Maybe what I have doesn't seem so serious. I've heard that they may send me to a hospital in Bologna, where they know how to cure these things."

"When?"

"I'm not sure. Tomorrow, maybe, the day after . . . I've been here for days and no one has done anything. They're not really equipped to do much here; more or less they just look at you and decide where to send you to, which hospital. But . . . where are my parents?"

"They're down walking on the beach. I made them wait; I wanted to see how you were first. Your father asked me to come here with them; they were worried about getting lost or not knowing what to do. They're afraid, Vasco, they're getting older, you know?"

"You did the right thing, Nino, thank you . . . how do I look? I don't look too bad, do I? And . . . Rina?"

"You're looking good," lied Nino, "and you'll be back to

normal before you know it. Rina is still at home, waiting for you. She was always hoping to get your letters, but I don't think many came."

"They must have gotten lost. Do you know how big Russia is? You can't even imagine how big it is. How could we have thought of attacking such an enormous country? Even if you didn't have to fight, you'd get old just trying to get from one end to the other. How absurd this whole thing is: the Russians . . . first I'd never even seen one of them and now I have to shoot at them. What are you going to do now?"

"I'm going to call your parents."

"Thanks, Nino. You're a friend."

Nino walked outside just as Checco and his wife were approaching the entrance.

"He's upstairs," said Nino. "He's waiting to give you a hug."

"How's it going, then?" asked Checco.

"Well, it could be better but I'd say there's no reason to worry. Vasco's strong as a horse, he'll kick this one."

They went back up together, but Nino waited out in the hall so that Vasco's parents could be alone with him at first. He entered a few minutes later and stayed with them for the rest of the visit. Esterina held her tears until they stepped out the door.

They went back to the station together and Nino watched Checco and his wife as they walked, stooped over as he'd never seen them before, weighed down by their worry and their pain. As they waited for the train that would bring them back to Bologna, they sat in a café and had some coffee. Nino tried to offer words of encouragement: "You'll see, at the hospital in Bologna, they'll find a way to make him better. They might have to amputate a toe, at worst it'll be his foot, but at least he'll survive, and that's the most important thing. You can get used to anything."

In reality, he had nothing to go on and no idea of what they'd be able to do in Bologna. Save him, at least. He was young, his constitution was strong, he'd make it for sure. For sure.

They transferred him to the Putti Hospital three days later and as soon as Nino found out, he went to visit with Rina, Vasco's fiancée. The hospital was located on a hill overlooking Bologna. It was a beautiful setting, with forest land all around and a lovely view of the city. Nino let Rina go ahead, and he strolled for half an hour, looking at the giant cedars and the lofty magnolias rising a good thirty meters tall. From this vantage point, he would see the villa where Cardinal Nasalli Rocca lived, a magnificent place where two gigantic nettle trees with their smooth, gray bark stood at either side of a long, stately flight of steps at the entrance.

He loitered for a while to give them some time together, then went up to see Vasco in his new room. "Cheer up!" said Nino, "they'll get you better here. There are these famous professors walking around with long strings of assistants tagging behind them; they'll know how to fix you up."

"Have you seen my parents?" asked Vasco.

"Sure, I drop by whenever I can, they say that seeing me helps keep their morale up. They've given me a package for you; there's clean underwear, cookies that your mother made, and some oranges. Your mom says be sure to eat them, they're good for you!"

Vasco thanked him again. "Come back to see me, Nino, when you can. Time stands still here, you know? Seeing someone you know is such a relief. Helps me forget about my troubles, at least for a little while. I wanted so bad to come home and look at me now."

Rina looked at him with tears in her eyes and held his hand tightly between hers.

"You're close here," replied Nino, "it takes no time at all on the bus. Now that Rina knows the way, she'll come to see you often, right, Rina? And your parents will come too. You just work on keeping your spirits up, you'll get better faster."

"Yes, I will," said Vasco, his eyes shining.

Rina kissed him and followed Nino down the stairs, drying her tears with a handkerchief. She went back the following Saturday with Vasco's parents. When they were all on the bus together, Checco said that they had to be ready to accept that the doctors might have to amputate the boy's foot, because that was what was necessary, sometimes, to stop the gangrene. It would be tough, but the important thing was for him to make it home.

"I'm just praying that he lives," said Rina. "Nothing else matters to me. I'll take him any way, without a foot, without a leg, I couldn't care less." Hot tears ran down her cheek as she spoke.

When they were finally admitted to Vasco's room, they found him in a cast from his neck to his groin. They didn't know what to think.

"What is this thing?" asked Checco.

"*Papà*, I can't understand," replied Vasco. "Yesterday two nurses came in and they put me in this cast. The doctor hasn't come by, so I haven't talked to him. I don't know why they did it."

His parents looked at each other in consternation and then lowered their eyes to the ground. Thus began the atrocious calvary of their son as his entire body was devoured by gangrene.

Nino had had to return to his unit, which was stationed in Albania. But before deploying to his next destination, he wounded himself in the hand as he was cleaning a pistol and he was discharged. A number of people maligned him, insinuating that he had shot himself so he could get out. The military authorities, however, never even opened a disciplinary procedure against him and they dismissed him without finding any fault in his performance. As soon as he returned home, Nino could sense the finger-pointing. He was angry that anyone would suspect him of desertion, and never tolerated a single insult or insinuation, always responding with his fists.

By the time he returned to see Vasco, his friend's situation had greatly worsened. Nino had to fight an impulse to retch at the smell of putrefaction that permeated the room and was shocked at the shrugs he met with when he tried to understand what had happened.

Checco managed, the following week, to stop the chief physician as he was whisked down the hall in a flurry of white smocks. "Professor, just a word, professor, for the love of God . . . "

"What is it?" asked the doctor, clearly irritated.

"I'm the father of Vasco Bruni, room 32, orthopedics. That poor boy is rotting inside that body cast that you had made for him. The smell in his room is atrocious."

The professor barely glanced his way and replied haughtily: "Who's the doctor here, you or me? You do your job and I'll do mine," and he hurried off with his assistants thronging around him.

One day that both Rina and Nino were present, Vasco asked his friend to scratch his back because he couldn't stand the itching. Nino took one of the knitting needles that Rina was using to make a sweater and poked it down between the cast and the boy's skin. When he pulled it back up it was full of worms. Vasco somehow realized and his eyes filled up with tears. "My God, the horror of this," he said. "Why does it have to be so difficult to die?" After four months of excruciating agony, Vasco Bruni, a handsome, intelligent and sensitive young man, died in the stench of his own tainted flesh, twisted and stiff as a rabid dog.

The entire town came to the boy's funeral.

His fiancée continued to bring flowers to the cemetery for

years and years, even after she finally decided to accept the proposal of a good man who had asked her to become his wife.

Vasco's father Checco, who had always been cheerful and good-natured, began to waste away. He stooped so badly that he became as bent over as a hunchback, as if some malicious demon had given him a nasty punch.

One day Nino came to visit, and asked: "How are you, Checco?"

"How could I be," he replied. "This is the kind of pain that doesn't kill you, but it tortures you every day of every month of every year, until you close your eyes."

No one could stop talking about the agony and death of Vasco Bruni in town; it was hard to believe or even explain. Why would a doctor have condemned a twenty-three-year-old boy to such a horrible death? Why force him to rot alive in a shield of plaster, without an explanation, without a reason?

Vasco was, at that time, under the power of the military authorities and there was no way to have him released from that authority, so no one blamed his family. But some people in town even voiced the terrible suspicion that the doctor had wanted to punish his patient. Could he have acted so ferociously and sadistically because he believed that Vasco somehow had tried to escape the dangers and the sacrifices demanded by the war; could he have intended to make the boy regret that, somehow, he hadn't fulfilled his duty?

Fonso asked Doctor Munari about it one day. The whole family was shaken and wounded no end by the tormented death of Vasco, a lad they had all dearly loved.

"Why did he have to die that way, doctor?" Fonso asked him as he was helping to weed the garden.

"I was an army doctor myself," Munari answered, "and even though we had to work under abominable conditions, we always tried to save the soldiers put in our care. Ask your brother-in-law Raffaele about that, if you ever run into him. He saw me at work, and I think he could tell you what kind of a doctor I was."

"I believe it, doctor, but we're talking about someone else here, not you. You know how much respect I have for you, as a man and as a doctor."

"I thank you for that. For Maria's brother and wife to see their son die that way . . . it's something you wouldn't wish on your worst enemy. There's only one explanation that I can come up with. If I'm right, the doctors should certainly have deigned to tell the boy's parents. It is probable that a latent, that is, hidden, form of bone tuberculosis developed as a consequence of the frostbitten foot and spread through his body; the doctors would have decided, in that case, to put him in a full body cast so that his bones would not crumble to pieces. Perhaps other patients had been saved using that treatment; perhaps they thought there was no other choice. Otherwise, I wouldn't know what to think."

Fonso hesitated a moment before answering, trying to understand the sense of what Munari had just explained, then he said: "One thing is certain about that professor: if it were his own son, he would never have condemned him to such a cruel death."

The sun had gone down and Fonso had nothing more to add. He leaned the spade on his shoulder and said: "I wish you a good night, doctor."

CHAPTER TWENTY-SEVEN

Alberto, who everyone knew as Pace, never came home from the war and Vasco was dead.

Corrado, Floti's son, was still too young to go to war although, just like for everyone else, it was only a matter of time. He continued to stay in touch with folks in the town where his father was born and had lived for many years. He would ride down on his bicycle from Camporgiano and stay with his Uncle Checco and Aunt Esterina. They were happy to have him; with Vasco gone, his company soothed and consoled them. He slept in their son's room. But then, before they knew it, he was back on his bicycle, pedaling the fifty kilometers back up to the Garfagnana. Not that his presence could change much; the depths of their grief were limitless, and yet, when he left, they would both embrace him with tears in their eyes: "Come back soon, Corrado, come and visit whenever you like!" He knew he was leaving a raw emptiness behind him.

He spent his days with his friends in town; they all hoped that the war would end soon and that they wouldn't be called up. Instead, the postcard arrived one day, calling Corrado to arms. He went down to the plains one last time to say goodbye to his aunts and uncles and his friends. Uncle Checco and Aunt Esterina clung to him, as if it were their Vasco, leaving again to go to war and to his death.

"Be careful! Stay out of danger's way, try to come back home, son. We'll be waiting for you," said Uncle Checco, drying his eyes with a handkerchief.

"Don't worry, *zio*, I can take care of myself," replied Corrado. "You'll see me again soon, you can be sure of it." He took the bundle that Aunt Esterina had prepared for him with the cookies that Vasco liked so much, hopped onto his bicycle and disappeared at the end of the road.

Like many of the young men who lived in mountainous areas, Corrado was assigned to an *Alpino* infantry division, the "Julia."

The Alpine soldiers were all mountain men, outfitted, armed and trained to operate on mountainous terrain, to climb wall faces and move tactically on the edge of a cliff. They were sent to Russia, to the plain along the Don River, as flat as a bread board. The reasoning was that they were more resistant to the cold.

In his misfortune, Corrado at least had the luck of finding himself in the same battalion as a friend of his from Camporgiano named Adriano Masetti, a good guy who worked as a woodcutter and was as strong as an oak tree. They travelled with their fellow soldiers for many days and many nights by train through endless, unchanging plains which filled them with a sense of infinite desolation. Sometimes the boys would sing songs for two or three voices, harmonies inspired by the majesty of the soaring peaks, the roar of the waterfalls and the bloom of mountain meadows in the springtime, but always sad. Their songs always had that nostalgic, forsaken feel because almost all of them came from little villages where everyone knew everyone else and it was like living in one big family.

After a two-week journey that they thought would never end, they arrived at their destination. It was the end of the summer, and they immediately realized what they would be up against. The Italian units already posted there, who had survived the winter of 1941-42, reported terrible operational conditions: insufficient equipment, unreliable fuel provisioning and clothing and footwear of very poor quality, totally unsuitable to the rigors of a Russian winter. They told of the friends they'd lost, of the hardships and hunger they'd suffered. They described the bodies of fellow soldiers found frozen to death, stiffened by the frost at their guard posts, in the gray dawns of January. Hard as slabs of salt cod. They were demoralized in the face of a reality that corresponded in no way to the images spread by propaganda, and humiliated by the disparaging attitude of their German allies.

"In the Great War," their officers, veterans of that conflict, would tell them, "the enemy was in front of you. Behind you, you had the Italian people, our own families, the houses in which we were born." Here, the enemy was everywhere. The only thing that kept them alive and pushed them to fight was the hope of returning.

Corrado was assigned to the drivers because he had worked as a mechanic before he was drafted and that made someone think that he must know something about means of transport. He learned to drive a truck, just like his Uncle Checco at Bligny, and was tasked to service the rear-line supply bases on increasingly dangerous missions. The vehicles on the supply routes were those which carried ammunition, spare parts, provisions and messages in both directions, and were thus the first to be targeted by the enemy artillery and aviation, but Corrado was a quick study and he always managed to get out of a fix with minimal damage. He soon became familiar with every secret of his truck, an ancient Isotta Fraschini with two hundred thousand kilometers under its belt that seemed to want to break down every time it took a jolt.

Sometimes he managed to make the supply runs with his friend Adriano at his side; they would keep each other company and talk about what they would do when they got back home. There was another great advantage to driving a truck: spending so many hours in the heated cab. Corrado had worked hard at isolating it with any scraps of material he could find: cardboard, rags, even some hay and straw pilfered from the *izbas* they found along their way. In this way, the heat remained in the cab. It seemed infinitely better, to them, to die warm with a big boom, than struggling to survive in the freezing cold with a harsh, dry, hacking cough that felt like it was splitting your chest in two.

They spent nearly a year this way, during which everyone's attention was focused on the Battle of Stalingrad, where other Italian army corps divisions were deployed. More than once it looked like the Russians were caving in and Corrado, who was an optimist at heart, began to hope that the war might be over soon.

"You're happy that the Nazis are winning?" asked Adriano with a reproachful tone.

"My father was a socialist when you were still pissing your bed. He was persecuted by the fascists, unjustly accused of attempted murder, forced to sleep in the fields like a tramp. They burned down the family's stable. What do you think, that I like these guys? I'm his son. I didn't want this war but here we are. We've made our beds, so we must lie in them, isn't that what they say? The sooner it's over the happier I'll be. Should I hope for defeat, so we can be slaughtered or be taken prisoner and sent to Siberia to die like dogs? Fighting to survive is our right, I say, no one can claim otherwise."

"Oh, calm down, I wasn't trying to offend you! Are you mad at me?"

"When you start sounding off like an idiot, I am."

Adriano let it drop, especially because deep down he knew that Corrado was right. But discussions of that sort soon became futile as the months passed. The winter turned out to be even more cruel than the one before; the Soviets drove the Axis powers from the ruins of Stalingrad and conducted a huge operation of encirclement. The Italian army corps began their retreat: a long black snake on the snow gray with the dust and smoke of the continuous explosions. Corrado drove his truck full of soldiers who had no shoes and whose feet were so frostbitten they could not walk. And yet those poor wretches were envied by the others who had to push forward on foot, one step after another, numb with cold and hunger. Most of them had been scattered from their original units and had lost touch with their comrades and officers. Many of them had abandoned their weapons once they ran out of ammunition. The only units which were still disciplined, armed and outfitted were the Alpine "Tridentina" division who marched at the head of the long string of men crossing the boundless fields of snow, some of the "Julia" units and another two or three battalions. No more than fifteen or sixteen thousand men in all, out of a total of sixty thousand in the Alpine army corps, but the distance from the head to the tail was so enormous that no one in the rear lines knew what was happening up ahead.

As the column slowly advanced it sowed the ground with the fallen. In the ranks of the walking dead, exhausted and half frozen, one after another would drop into the snow. Some were helped up by a friend or a fellow soldier and physically forced to push on, others, most of them, were abandoned to their destiny.

What happened in the end was that the "Tridentina" engaged the front lines of the Soviet army which had united in order to deny any route of escape to the retreating enemy. A furious battle broke out in the vicinity of a village called Nikolajewka. The Soviet strength was far superior, they were better armed and equipped and utterly determined to annihilate the enemy, which had already been cut off from all their supply lines. They opened a barrage of fire that blew huge holes in the Italian columns in marching order, taken completely by surprise. Corrado, who was advancing at a snail's pace, in first gear, could hear the artillery rounds and the crackle of machine guns coming from the head of the column and he imagined that the end had come.

No one could have imagined that it might mean salvation instead. Corrado could see nothing of what was happening at the head of the column but Adriano told him about it later; his friend had gone forward with a courier from the "Vestone" Alpine battalion and had seen what was happening with his own eyes. The "Tridentina" was stubbornly advancing under the crossfire of the entire Soviet front, which extended in an arc from northwest to southwest. They realized they were facing certain death, but the entire unit continued to respond to fire with all the ammunition, energy and desperation at its command. They had actually succeeded in achieving a momentary stalemate when their commander himself, General Reverberi, jumped into an abandoned German tank, started it up and drove it forward, firing with all the weapons he had on board. All the troops poured in after him, not only the Italians, but the Germans and Hungarians as well. "You should have seen these guys," described Adriano, "they were dropping like flies, mowed down by the machine guns and picked off by the snipers, but they never stopped. If it hadn't been for my buddy Bruni, stuck three kilometers back, I would have joined them myself."

"You should have," replied Corrado, as he was fussing under the hood of the Isotta Fraschini.

"No, no," shot back Adriano. "You and I left together and we'll go back together."

Corrado pulled his head out from under the hood. "Right, and how is that going to happen?" he answered back, as he rubbed his oil-covered hands on a rag which was even greasier than his hands were. He took the crank handle, fit it onto the bolthead on the engine shaft and pushed hard. The engine coughed, gave a couple of knocks, and died. Corrado tried again, cranking it up three or four times, and this time the engine started up.

He climbed into the cab: "Get in. It's warmer in here," he said.

Adriano climbed in on the other side and started up again: "Listen to me. As I was heading back, the battle was still in full swing. An inferno. But the guys from the 'Tridentina' had opened the way and they were marching behind the tank of that crazy general of theirs. Then more battalions showed up. One of their commanders was yelling like a madman: 'Forward! Forward!' and shooting with his carbine, his pistol, everything he had. He was pushing so hard I'll bet you they're still going. I'll bet you they're still passing through the lines."

"Yeah. And so . . . ?" asked Corrado.

"I know where there's a hole in the Soviet front. There's a point where there's a frozen swamp, with reeds sticking up all around; the ice is surely thick enough to support our weight. If we're smart, we can pass at that point, look for the footprints of our men, catch up with them wherever they are and that's that. When we've gotten to the other side, it's just a question of time before we're home. We're going home, old man!"

Corrado shook his head. "I can't do that, Adriano."

"What do you mean you can't? Of course you can! Come with me and tonight we'll be on the other side."

"I'm the only guy that can get this wreck to work. If they need me to transport the wounded, the men who can't walk . . . How will they do it without me?"

"They'll figure out a way, Bruni! They'll figure it out, no?"

Corrado shook his head stubbornly. "No, I can't. I really can't. You go. It'll be even easier for you if you're alone."

Adriano got out and before slamming the cab door shut, he said: "You really are a bonehead, you know that?"

"Good luck, Adriano," was the answer he got. "See you back in town. Say hello to everyone. Tell them I'll be back. I'll get back all right."

His friend couldn't listen for another moment. He bundled himself up in his worn coat, tucked a scarf under his chin and wound it around his head and, as darkness was falling, he started walking back towards Nikolajewka.

As promised, Adriano slipped through the reeds and crawled over the icy swamp. He reached the "Tridentina" camp and General Reverberi in a small city called Shebekino two nights later, starving and half frozen. From there they marched on, day in and day out, until they got to Italy. Of the sixty thousand soldiers who had left Stalingrad only ten thousand made it back.

Corrado's unit was surrounded the next day. With no ammunition, their ranks decimated by the cold and their wounds, they had no choice but to surrender.

They were taken by the Russians to their first rest stop after a four day journey in which they lost more than two hundred comrades. It was a kind of assemblage of sheds that perhaps had been used as a clearing center for provisioning the troops at the front. From there they were transported by truck to their definitive abode: a horse stable in disuse where horses had once been trained for the czar's cavalry. It consisted of broken-down stalls which offered no shelter from the biting winds coming from the north. The ground it stood on was freezing mud which sucked at your legs if you tried to get anywhere. The food was horrible, usually not even edible. Done in by the hunger, the cold, the tortures and continuous humiliations of their imprisonment, Corrado died four months later and was thrown, along with his companions in misfortune, into a common grave.

At the end of the war no one knew what had become of him, and he joined the ranks of soldiers missing in action.

CHAPTER TWENTY-EIGHT

The war dealt immense damage to the Bruni family, snatching away both Vasco and Corrado. Not even this loss, however, helped to reconcile Dante and Checco. Common wisdom has it that when a person feels offended by someone, and then trouble happens to befall this someone, the first is likely to think that chance or bad luck has punished the second sufficiently and this would normally serve to make the first feel more magnanimous or at least, nudge him into making the first step, even if he still feels wronged. But that was not the case between the two brothers; not even the death of their own mother had brought them together and they stubbornly continued to ignore each other.

Armando had no quarrel with anyone, but found himself more alone than ever in facing his misfortunes. His problems just never seemed to let up, especially because of the mental infirmity of his wife, who he continued to love with great ardor and attachment. His growing family might have been considered a burden as well but for him, it was the most important reason for living, and he gave his daughters all the affection he was capable of. He maintained an extraordinary capacity for tempering even the toughest hardships with irony and humor.

Given the situation, his conflict with Doctor Munari worsened every time the doctor had to assume the responsibility for committing Bruni's wife to the psychiatric clinic in Reggio. Armando experienced the doctor's resolution of the problem as an act of violence. He couldn't understand why, if he was content to keep Lucia as she was, someone else should go to the trouble of tearing her away from him and admitting her to a hospital where she was surely more poorly treated than at home and where the therapy didn't help her in the least.

The war was worsening every day in every way, and the fact that the United States had entered the battlefield, with all the weight of their enormous economic and military power, had already amply overturned the balance of forces. There was practically no one who had any illusions about which side would win victory in the end. Allied aircraft passed overhead more and more often, and in addition to singling out military installations, had begun to bomb civilian targets, like factories and railway stations.

Many families went hungry; only those who had enough money to pay the exorbitant prices of the black market were able to get enough food. Farmers were the exception, because the land never betrays those who work it. At least food was never lacking. There were two kinds of farmers: those who sold their products on the black market and grew rich, and the others, the majority, who gave generously to those who were suffering. Like Nino's family: not a kilo of wheat, not a piece of cheese, was sold at anything but the official price, and more often than not they were given away. Nino's mother, a minute, extremely pious woman who expressed herself in an improbable dialect which was half Emiliano and half from her native Veneto, would take care of the distribution personally. Once she was left with no more flour, not even a handful, and when a pale, spindly child stepped up to take his share, she filled his pockets with apples.

Fonso found that he had to take on jobs which were increasingly hazardous and backbreaking, just to make ends meet. In the winter he found employment in the city, cleaning snow off the roofs, risking his skin every time. It was so easy to slip on the wet or icy roof tiles, and he was often called in by people living in three or four story buildings. There was no hope if you fell from that high up.

Nino showed up at Fonso and Maria's home one night to ask for Eliana's hand in marriage. It was traditional to go to your fiancée's father accompanied by your best man, but the friend he'd chosen to carry their rings, Pace, had been swallowed up by the war; no one had heard from him for a long, long time. Rather than replace him with someone else, which felt like a betrayal, Nino went alone.

Fonso thought highly of Nino and was happy to give his consent. The wedding was held soon after. Times being what they were, there was no chance of a lavish celebration, but the newlyweds managed to take a short honeymoon, to Veneto, where Nino had relatives on his mother's side who they could stay with, without spending money on a hotel. It was there, in a tiny mountain town at the foot of the high plain of Asiago, that they learned from the radio that Mussolini had been removed from office and transported to a secret place in the mountains of Abruzzo.

"Do you think the war will end?" asked Eliana.

"I don't think so. The king will form a new government that will have to negotiate with the Americans. If those negotiations go well, which would basically mean an unconditional surrender on our part, we'd find ourselves fighting against the Germans. And the Germans are everywhere."

The facts bore out his predictions.

When they returned from their honeymoon, Eliana realized immediately that daily life in her father-in-law's house complied with Modenese customs, which were very different from the Bolognese traditions she had grown up with. Her sisters-in-law worked in the fields alongside the men. Not wanting to embarrass Nino in front of his father, she tried to fit in. After just one day of work, her hands, with their polished nails, were sore and bleeding. She soon got used to bundling herself up in coarse, ugly work clothing, formed calluses on her hands and feet, and kept up a punishing rate of work from dawn to well after nightfall.

But the darkest night of them all was on the eighth of September, when she and Nino listened to the public declaration of the armistice on the radio. Italy had surrendered to an American general with a face like a mastiff's in a small town in Sicily. The king fled to the south with his family, and his generals took off their uniforms and went to hide as well. In the following days, from one end of the peninsula to the other, the army—completely abandoned to its fate, without orders, without support of any kind, without coordination—collapsed and was overwhelmed by the Germans, almost everywhere.

A great number of Italian soldiers were imprisoned by the Germans and sent to concentration camps, among them a cousin of Fonso's who had just come back from the African front. Others went into hiding, hanging on to their weapons so they could form groups of armed resistance, often with the help of their officers, maintaining their uniforms and their flag.

Many families in town were consumed by anguish since they had no notion at all of where their sons might be. Nino was torn but he decided in the end that his place was at home because his wife was expecting a child.

In six months' time, the country had to face a calamity that was even worse, unthinkably, than the war.

Civil war.

Rescued by the Germans in a parachuting operation, Mussolini established a Republic of the North and called on all young fascists willing to fight off the Anglo-American invaders to join him. At least, this was the line of propaganda used for recruiting these youths. It soon became evident, however, that these troops would be mainly used not to fight off a foreign invader, but rather to repress the actions of the partisan brigades close to home.

In a very few months' time, every young Italian male north of the Apennines was forced into a dramatic choosing of sides: either unite with the partisan *Resistenza* groups in the mountains, or put on the uniform of the fascist Republican Army, or even its extreme wing, the paramilitary Black Brigades. Since the young are rarely moderate in any of their actions or beliefs, several thousand flocked to join the forces of Prince Junio Valerio Borghese, who commanded the seasoned, ferocious fascist assault corps known as the Tenth Legion MAS. Italy was split in two. The king, in escaping to the south instead of remaining honorably in Rome to fight alongside his soldiers, had forfeited the last chance he had to redeem what little was left of the country's pride.

"That's what a king should be for," thought Fonso, reading the paper in the tailor shop. "He should stand at the head of his people and die with his weapons in hand if need be, not run off with his own family while the sons of his people are fighting and dying in Russia or being deported to Siberia to die of cold and hunger." He thought of his nephew Vasco and his other nephew Corrado, Floti's son, and even though they weren't related to him by blood, tears came to his eyes.

Their own town mirrored the same divisions and tensions that were splitting apart Italy, that had not yet been conquered by the Allies. Many of the villagers, exhausted by hunger, poverty and the grievous loss of their sons, fiancés, brothers, had gotten to the point that they'd begun wishing that their soldiers would lose and be routed. Let them bomb our cities, sink our ships, they began to think, anything, so long as the war ends. Let us dry our tears and start to rebuild from the ashes.

One evening in September, Rossano returned from Rome and he confronted his father as Nello was coming home from work to tell him that he had decided to leave. "I'm going to enlist, father, I'm going to fight in the army of the Social Republic. I'm volunteering for the Republican National Guard."

Nello felt his blood turn to ice. "Why would you do such a thing?" he asked. "You're not being called upon to serve."

"Now is the time. We have to fight to the very last man," replied Rossano, "to restore dignity to our homeland, invaded and humiliated, to save whatever can still be saved. As far as the reds are concerned, they are the true traitors and they'll be eliminated without mercy. They are receiving weapons and supplies from the enemy!"

Nello realized then what a terrible effect the fascist education and training—which he himself had desired for his son!— had had on Rossano. His only son was likely to die, in a matter of months or weeks, or even days. Nello dropped his head, searching for the words that would convince his boy to change his mind, but he found none.

"You were the one who taught me these principles, and now that I can do something about them, you want me to back out?"

"You're only twenty years old, Rossano, it's not time for you to take up arms: you still have to study, to prepare for your future . . . "

"There's no more time for such things, father. We don't need books, we need rifles. The only thing to do is fight."

Nello's wife Elisa heard them arguing and broke in, alarmed. "What's happening?" she asked.

"Rossano wants to enlist," replied Nello. "I can't convince him to wait."

"And you're surprised?" replied his wife. "You were the one who insisted on sending him into the middle of those fanatics and this is the consequence. Remember that, if something happens to him, you are responsible. You pushed him into this. I won't speak to you or even look at you for the rest of my life."

"Cut it out, mother," said the boy. "I'm no fool; it's not like I'm letting myself be manipulated by anybody. I've chosen to do this out of my own free will. No one asked me and neither you nor father can stop me. Can't you understand that you're offending me by speaking that way? You should be proud of me!"

Elisa burst into tears. In her son's eyes and in the blood that had rushed to his face, she saw irrevocable determination. She saw that her husband had tears in his eyes as well.

"Isn't there anything we can do to make you reconsider?" asked Nello.

"Nothing, father. I don't want to cause you pain but, I swear, I'd have no respect for myself if I didn't go."

"You've never killed a man. You don't know what that means. It means you'll have to shoot, stab, take the life of other boys much like yourself. Or lose your own. You won't be yourself anymore, you'll turn into someone else, someone that would frighten you, or horrify you, if you met up with him today."

Elisa spoke up herself: "Listen to what your father's saying, for the love of God. You'll regret it if you don't!"

"I'm sorry, *mamma*. There's nothing that can stop me. But believe me, I won't be looking for death. It's life I'm looking for, for everyone, for you too. And I'll be back, I promise you."

A long silence followed, because Rossano was feeling emotional, even if he didn't want to show it.

"When are you leaving?" asked Nello.

"As soon as I can. Tomorrow or the next day. I don't want to risk changing my mind. I'm not made of iron, either."

Nello shook his head at hearing those words. They were bigger than the boy was.

They had dinner without speaking. As soon as he had finished, Rossano left the house and went to the corner Bar del Dopolavoro, where just about everyone went to meet up; they just called it the Dopo. He didn't feel like hanging around the house with his parents to watch his mother cry. He ordered a beer and sat down, pretending to read the sports newspaper that another client had left open on the table. After a while he realized that someone was standing in front of him and he looked up: Fabrizio.

"Have something to drink?" Rossano asked.

Fabrizio sat down. "Sure, a lemon soda, thanks."

"That's another difference between us," said Rossano with a half smile. "You like the sweet stuff, I like it bitter." He motioned to Gianni who was at the counter.

"That's right. I like red, and you like black. But we can still be friends, can't we?"

"These are tough times," replied Rossano, serious now. "And each one of us has to make a choice. I've made mine. I've leaving tomorrow, or the next day, at the latest."

"Where are you going?"

"I'm going to sign up for the National Republican Guard."

"You're kidding. You're enlisting with the Nazis?"

"They're not Nazis. My conscience tells me I'm doing the right thing. I'm even ready to put my life on the line. I've thought hard about this."

"I'm sorry, I can't even say good luck."

"Right, you can't. So I guess it'll have to be goodbye," said Rossano with shiny eyes.

"See you around?" said Fabrizio.

Rossano nodded. "See you around," he replied.

He left two days later with a rucksack on his shoulders headed to Cremona. By bus and then by train. At the clearing office, they gave him a uniform and assigned him to his regiment.

Three months later Fabrizio found out that Bruno Montesi, the blacksmith, had narrowly missed being captured by the Germans and had come back to town but he had decided to go into hiding, so he wouldn't be called to arms by the fascists. One evening Bruno showed up in his courtyard, skinny and scruffy-bearded, almost unrecognizable. They embraced.

"Can you believe my friend Rossano signed up with the Republican Guard?" Fabrizio told him.

"I do believe it. I'm not surprised."

"I think he did it in good faith."

"At his age that's likely. But the day he kills someone he'll be in the wrong, and worthy of suffering the same fate. I've joined the *Resistenza*. I'm studying to become a political commissar."

"Isn't that one of those guys who preach the communist ideology to combatants?"

"I don't know what you mean by that. For me it means, above all, siding against those who goaded my father into killing himself, by beating and humiliating him every way they could. It means choosing to fight for the poorest and the weakest against the strongest and richest."

"I understand. Good luck then, Bruno."

"I don't think there's luck to be had for anyone in this situation. But if you want another reason that I know I'm right, it's that after the armistice of September the eighth, the Nazis deported tens of thousands of Italian soldiers to their concentration camps, including friends of mine from my regiment. Our soldiers aren't white or red or black, or rich or poor; they're the sons of the Italian people, of all their fathers and all their mothers. Whoever collaborates with their jailers is an enemy of the nation. So we are the patriots, and they are the traitors. Goodbye, Fabrizio. Say hello to your father for me, when you see him."

"Where are you going?"

"To Bologna, for now, and then up to the mountains. There's a man up there who's organized a partisan brigade. They're fighting like lions. He's from Sant'Agata, and he's about thirty years old. They call him *Lupo*: the Wolf."

"Is that his battle name?"

"No. Apparently his friends in elementary school used to

call him that, because when he got into a fight, he'd bite like a wolf . . . He's a maverick but apparently he's one hell of a fighter."

"And he's a communist like you are?"

"Nah, not him. He's a Catholic, devoted to Saint Anthony. Sounds like he's a little mixed up—maybe I can set him straight."

"Watch out, Bruno, wolves bite."

Montesi smiled at this and went off.

CHAPTER TWENTY-NINE

Fabrizio left his home and his family three months after Rossano did. In the mountains there had been a bitter battle between a German regiment, supported by the fascists of the Black Brigades, and the partisan formation known as *Stella Rossa*, Red Star. The Germans had been put to rout and they'd left over five hundred men dead on the field. A battle in which partisan commander Musolesi, known as the Wolf, had exploited his familiarity with the terrain like a consummate strategist. The news had spread lightning fast throughout the entire area, raising incredible enthusiasm. After the founding of the Partisan Republic of Montefiorino, up there in the mountains, this was the movement's first great military success. The men were primed to fight and to give their contribution to the deliverance of the nation.

Fabrizio had been nursing the idea of joining the partisans for some time, but this cinched it for him. He'd never spoken to the Blacksmith about enlisting, for fear he'd try to dissuade him. He set off one morning before dawn, at four o'clock, one of the first young men in town to leave. His mother, in tears, had prepared his rucksack with everything he'd need, arguing with him the whole time to get him to change his mind. His father, who realized it was impossible to try to stop him, gave him a new pair of boots.

"I wanted to take you up with the truck, at least as far as Sasso, but I don't have any fuel and there's none to be found anywhere. Iofa's coming with his cart, there he is. But he can only take you to Sasso himself, then he has to turn around and come back."

Before he let him go, Savino embraced his son, weeping in silence.

Fabrizio tried to control his own emotions. "*Papà*, don't worry. I'll be back. I can take care of myself."

"That's not what I'm worried about. It's all the rest. You have no idea what combat is like. You don't know what raw violence means, killing so as not to be killed in the middle of the fray, or striking out in cold blood, having your hands, your arms, your face covered with blood, blood of other men like you. But I understand you and, if I could, so help me God, I'd leave with you, but my place is here. I have to protect your mother, defend our house."

"I know, *papà*. You were a courageous fighter and you would be today. It would be wonderful to have you at my side. But it wouldn't be right. I'll try to stay in touch. I'll find a way to get news through to you." He climbed onto the cart and Iofa called out to the horse.

Savino stood watching until Fabrizio turned for his last goodbye, waving his hand before he disappeared.

When they arrived at Sasso, Fabrizio thanked Iofa for the ride and started walking. He kept up a steady pace all day, stopping just to eat a bite or gulp down some water from his father's canteen, a relic from the first world war. The roads were in disrepair, patched up with crushed stone, and his boots, the shoddy product of a badly damaged economy, started wearing out after the first few kilometers.

Towards evening, when he'd already started his ascent through the Apennines, he met another boy who, like him, was headed for the mountains. He had a hunting rifle slung over his shoulder.

"My name's Fabrizio," he said. "You going up too?"

"Yeah."

"Do you know the way?"

"A guy who knows the way explained it to me."

"Can I come with you?"

"If you want."

They walked together for nearly an hour without speaking, then Fabrizio broke the silence:

"What's your name?"

"Sergio."

"Have you ever fought before?"

"No."

"Do you think we'll make it?"

"When you pick up a rifle, the first thing you learn is how not to get killed."

"It's getting pretty dark, what should we do?"

"There's supposed to be a hut for drying chestnuts a little further up. We can sleep there."

When they got to the shelter they'd chosen for the night, they realized that others had had the same idea: three young guys like themselves, Albino, Claudio and Filippo, the first two from Savignano, the third from Sasso, all between twenty and twenty-three. All with the intention of volunteering to fight with the partisan forces. They rested for a few hours, stretched out on the dry leaves scattered on the floor, covering up with the blankets each one of them had brought along.

In the middle of the night, they were awakened by pelting drops of rain, the rustling of the chestnut boughs and a dry crash of thunder. The rain beating down on the slate roof gave them the sensation of being safe and dry and comforted them. That should have been, for most of them, a vigil before taking up arms, but youth and fatigue got the better of them and before long they were all sleeping like babies in their cradles. Until the first light of dawn.

They started walking again up a steep and very stony trail and Fabrizio's boots, already in bad shape from the day before, started falling apart. Towards evening they reached the first roadblock that controlled access to the territory of the Wolf and his brigade.

The situation immediately appeared turbulent. Stretched out under the low roof of a sheep pen was a wounded man scream- ing, and they could hear shouting from the forest and the crackle of dry leaves being trampled. A man was standing by the trough, wearing a holster, a pistol and a cartridge belt; it could only be him: the Wolf. Had they got there too soon? Were they too close?

"Who the fuck are they?" shouted Wolf, pointing at the five boys. Fabrizio took a step forward:

"We're volunteers. We want to fight at your side."

The Wolf raised his eyes to the sky: "They want to fight, Jesus, Mary and Joseph. They want to fight and they don't even have fucking guns with them, they don't know a fucking thing, their shoes are falling apart and they want to fight. And I'm supposed to feed all these people, arm them and outfit them."

They heard more noises and a patrol burst out of the woods, using their gun barrels to shove forward a group of Black Brigade Republican Army soldiers. They were all wearing uni- forms and they were all very young, little more than adoles- cents. Wolf turned to look at them, and then turned back towards the new arrivals.

"You wanna fight, eh? All right, get over here, let's see if you've got the balls." The young volunteers stepped forward while the youths in their black uniforms were lined up against the wall with their hands tied behind their backs. "Give 'em daggers. All five of them."

Fabrizio, Filippo, Sergio and the others silently accepted the knives.

"Come forward, now," ordered Wolf. "Now, move it."

The five of them found themselves face to face with five boys their own age who were fighting on the side of the enemy. Both sides knew what was coming next.

"These are war criminals," said Wolf, "and they will be executed, immediately. I don't want to waste bullets and I don't want any shots to be heard. Use the knife you have in your hands. Now."

The five boys were a little more than a meter away from their black-shirted peers.

"Well?" shouted Wolf. "What are you waiting for?"

Fabrizio was the first to step forward with his dagger in hand until he was practically touching one of the prisoners: he could smell terror, or perhaps hate, pouring off the boy, a quiver of madness which crossed the space separating them and set off an irrepressible tremor in Fabrizio. The boy in black looked deep into his eyes with an enigmatic expression: he was trying, maybe, to control himself, not to show fear, not to fall to his knees, not to weep. Fabrizio saw Rossano in him. The same age, the same eyes. With every passing instant he looked more and more like him. The knife was just a few centimeters from the boy's throat.

"Come on," he said, "get it over with. I can't stand this. I don't want to make a fool of myself. Push it in, damn you." He was sweating profusely. Fabrizio heard a loud thud and he turned: Filippo had fainted, Sergio was struggling to stop retching. Fabrizio dropped the knife.

"I knew it," said Wolf. "You're a bunch of fucking wimps. Sugano! Su-gano!!"

A man of about thirty ran up with a tommy gun slung over his neck and a pistol in its holster.

"You take care of this. Take them to the hole."

Sugano called over a couple of his men who pushed the prisoners into the forest. Ten minutes later they heard a burst of submachinegun fire and a couple of pistol shots.

"There you go," said Wolf and then, pointing to Fabrizio and Sergio, said: "You two, go to the hole and see if their shoes are any good, you're not going to get anywhere with the ones you have on."

The two boys looked at each other in consternation.

"What the hell!" shouted Wolf. "What is it that you're not hearing? Move it, I said, or I'll kick your sorry asses all the way home."

They set off and, a few minutes later, reached the "hole": a hollow in the ground where the five black-shirted boys were laying in a pool of blood. Fabrizio saw that one of them, maybe the same one he was supposed to stab, was wearing a pair of ankle boots with treaded rubber soles that looked to be about his size. He forced himself to bend down and started unlacing them. As soon as he had pulled off the first one the boy, who was still alive, reacted: "Kill me, you coward! Kill me!"

Sugano handed him a pistol: "You might as well start now. You'll have to get used to this and anyway, you're doing him a favor at this point."

Fabrizio took the gun and shot it. The boy's eyes went dead. He pulled off the other boot. These shoes are cursed, he thought, as he walked back towards the camp.

"I know what you're thinking," said Sugano, "but there's no alternative. When the wolves are out, the sheep had better stay safe at home in their pens."

In the meantime, Bruno Montesi, who had been named political commissar for the Red Star Brigade commanded by the Wolf, was trying to find his way there. Before leaving, he had managed to make an appointment to meet one of the leaders of the *Resistenza* at an *osteria* in Casalecchio near Via Porrettana. The man's code name was Martino and he was the commander of an assault battalion of white partisans stationed near Palagano, on the Modenese side of the mountains. Montesi recognized his drooping Tartar-style mustache and the burn scar on his left hand.

"You're Martino, aren't you?" he asked.

The man nodded and replied, "And you're Montesi."

"That's right."

"Sit down and eat: stewed beans and potatoes. They're good here and the bread is fresh."

Montesi helped himself and poured out a glass of white wine.

"So you want to meet up with the Wolf."

"If I can, that's my intention."

"Then you'll need a battle name."

"The Blacksmith. That's what people call me."

"Suit yourself. Anyway, good luck because you'll need it."

"I have a letter of introduction from the National Liberation Committee."

"You know what the guy will do with your letter of introduction?"

"Don't tell me, I can imagine. But I have to see him nonetheless. I'll convince Wolf that he should join the NLC."

"Listen well, buddy: the Wolf can't stand political commissars. He says all they do is talk. What's more, he has narrowly escaped two attempts on his life and he doesn't trust anyone anymore. One of his own tried to stab him and it's a miracle he didn't succeed—it's only because his men adore him and stand guard over him all night. Then, the very guy who stayed the would-be murderer's hand, Olindo Sammarchi, a guy who grew up with Wolf, his fast friend from the absolute start, who had won Wolf's complete trust by personally saving his life, well, this is the very guy that betrays him by going over to the Nazis and organizing more attacks against him. Can you believe it? When he was found out, Wolf had him put to death on the spot. So who can the Wolf trust anymore? If he can't even trust his best friend how do you think he's going to treat an absolute stranger?"

"But why did the first man try to stab him?"

"Who, the traitor? Amedeo Arcioni, that was his name. He said he was forced to do it because the Nazis had captured his family. And Wolf forgave him. The fact is that the Wolf has defeated the Germans so many times that they now consider him their number one enemy. He even succeeded in running a train off the rails and seized all the goods it was carrying. The Nazis would give anything to see him dead. You'd be mistrustful yourself if you found yourself in his shoes, wouldn't you?"

"Is it true that there are ten thousand men in the Red Star Brigade?"

Martino shrugged. "Are you kidding me? How could he support ten thousand people? There must be seven, eight hundred at the most, but that's a good number, as much as such a miserable territory can handle. The fact is that his teams are so mobile that they manage to show up at the same time in far-flung places and act with such rapidity that it seems like there are many more of them. You've heard of what happened at Monte Sole, haven't you?"

"There was a big battle."

"You can say that again. The Germans had decided to pull out all the stops because they felt they were losing control of the situation and because a vast portion of mountain territory was already under the control of the Red Star. With the support of the Republican Army, the Germans organized a sweeping mop-up operation, pulling out all the big guns. Cannons, machine guns, the whole works. Their objective was to completely surround Monte Sole, the massif where the Wolf had set up the general headquarters of the Brigade . . . "

"Which means the Germans must have had informers."

"Obviously. The district that we control includes five or six towns as well as quite a few isolated farming settlements. It's easy for them to infiltrate someone. A farmer with a hoe, a shepherd taking his flock to pasture . . . anyone can be a spy. We've found some of them and executed them but you know more are out there. So, you know what Wolf does? He keeps all his men up at the base until the very last minute; he waits until the sentries tell him that the Germans are more or less a kilometer away and then he divides his men into a lot of small groups and takes them down to the base of the mountain. He gets them into position, hidden behind vegetation or lying low in the middle of a field of wheat, with more men posted at every trail. The Germans start to make their way up, Wolf keeps his men at the ready with their fingers on the trigger, all twenty-year-old guys. There are even some English soldiers with them, guys who had gotten cut off from their own units.

"When the sentries signal that the last German has entered the forest, Wolf unleashes hell. They're surrounded, with no way out. We took out five hundred and fifty of them. The others survived by escaping through the woods . . . Since then we've had more volunteers than we can handle, up to thirty new ones a day."

"You were there too?" asked Montesi.

"Why, wasn't that obvious?"

"It certainly was. Then you can help me get there."

"Only up to a point. You know, we have our own wrangles now and then, especially when it comes to how the air-dropped supplies should be distributed. Insults tend to fly. It's better I don't show my face in that neck of the woods for a while. I'll take you to a spot a couple of kilometers away from his headquarters and I'll point out the way from there. Then you're on your own. Are you sure you have to meet with him just now?"

"Well, those are my orders. It's not like he's going to eat me."

"I wouldn't be so sure. If you do manage to see him, you'll find that he has quite a boyish look to his face, but don't let your guard down: he can turn into a beast from one minute to the next: because he had a bad night, because he didn't sleep enough, because he didn't get screwed, because . . . "

"I'll keep it in mind. Well then, what now? We're finished here, aren't we?"

"We smoke a cigarette and then we go. My truck's outside." Martino pulled out a packet of Chesterfields and offered him one: "This is good stuff: brightleaf tobacco, from Virginia. There were about fifty cartons in the last drop."

When they got started it was after midnight. They followed the road that skirted the bottom of the valley for nearly an hour until they got to Pontecchio. They drove through Il Sasso and Fontana, Lama di Reno and Marzabotto. At about four in the morning, Martino stopped the truck at the start of a trail.

"We're in the territory of the Red Star Brigade. The Wolf's den is up there. As soon as it starts to get light, take this trail until you come to a fork in the road. Go right and continue for another kilometer through a chestnut forest. When you see the beech-wood starting, it means you're almost there."

"What do I do then?"

"Nothing. They'll find you. As soon as you hear a voice saying "Halt!", raise your hands. They shoot first and then ask 'friend or foe.' Are you armed?"

"No."

"Good. They can't stand a man with a weapon unless it's one of their own. You're heading straight into the jaws of the wolf!" he grinned. "I think it's now that I say good luck." Martino gave him the rest of the Chesterfield packet.

Montesi watched as Martino reversed and started on his way back down, until the truck disappeared around the first bend. He started walking up the path so he wouldn't be standing on the road and stopped when he found a biggish boulder he could lean on. He lit a cigarette and waited until dawn. The side of the mountain he would be climbing was still dark, but the sky above had become an aquamarine blue. He could hear the soft hoot of a horned owl that stopped as soon as the wind turned.

It took him about twenty minutes to reach the fork. He

continued his ascent up a path which became increasingly steeper, surrounded on both sides by age-old chestnuts with gigantic moss-covered trunks. There wasn't a living soul anywhere around; all he heard was the rustle of wings now and then. Through the tree branches he could see the white-streaked peak of Corno alle Scale appearing and disappearing as he walked.

"One more step and you're dead," said a voice on his left, neither soft nor loud, a statement more than an order and all the more effective for being so. Montesi raised his hands.

"I'm unarmed and I'm here on behalf of the National Liberation Committee. I have to see the Wolf."

"Wolf doesn't feel like seeing anyone. Who are you?"

"Bruno Montesi, the Blacksmith. I have a letter of credentials from the NLC."

"Take that trail on the left and walk forward without turning until I tell you to stop."

"Can I lower my hands?"

"Yes. But don't turn or make any funny moves, or . . . "

" . . . I'm dead."

"You got it."

He walked uphill for another half an hour until he found himself in a clearing surrounded by beech trees. At one end was a dilapidated shack and a shed for drying chestnuts. There was a roadblock with two partisans armed with British Sten submachine guns. The voice behind him said: "He wants to see Wolf. He has a letter from the NLC."

"That you, Spino? Where the hell did you find this guy?"

"Down at the beech-wood. So what the fuck do we do now? Tell Wolf he has a visitor, no?"

One of the two roadblock soldiers went over to the shack and shortly came out again with another couple of men.

"It's your lucky day, fucker," hissed Spino. "Wolf will see you. He's the guy on the left."

Spino was standing next to him now. Lean, bundled up in a military jacket, he looked no older than eighteen, and the other soldiers looked very young as well. Their battle names, the jargon, the arrogance of a boy trying to seem older than he is by saying "fuck" every other word: it all made them seem like kids playing at war, but instead they were damned serious.

"The one on his right is his brother Guido," said Spino, whispering now. "And the guy leaning against the door is Sugano, his right-hand man."

Wolf stepped right up to him. He looked just like Montesi had expected. A bristly beard, slightly wavy hair, black eyes that were much bigger than normal under a very wide brow, fleshy lips. His hooked nose reminded Montesi of a bird of prey. The combination was unsettling and gave him an expression of quiet ferocity. A medal hung at his neck, maybe Saint Anthony.

"Who are you and what do you want?" he asked.

"I'm the Blacksmith. The NLC has appointed me the political commissar of your brigade."

"I've never seen you and I don't like your looks. I don't need any political commissar. The last one really broke my balls."

"I'm sorry you feel that way. It's important that the combatants understand the political justification for their fight."

"I decide what's important for my brigade. Many of my men live around here. They're fighting for their families and their homes, that seems like a good enough justification to me."

"But I have precise orders from the Liberation Committee to install myself here as your political commissar. I'm sure we'll find a basis for agreement . . . "

He was still speaking when one of Wolf's men dashed over and whispered something in his ear: "They're signaling an SS unit coming up from Pian di Venola."

Wolf beckoned to Sugano: "Take him to the coal cellar."

"Wait, what's happening?" asked Montesi in alarm. "What is this business about a coal cellar? Hey. Look, I have a letter here from the NLC. Read it!"

But Sugano was already behind him and he was pushing him towards the trail with the barrel of his machine gun.

Montesi didn't know where to turn.

They walked for about ten minutes in silence, and then he blurted out: "Listen, I'm a partisan. I was sent here by the NLC. Why are you treating me like this? What is this coal cellar? What are we going to do there?"

"Die," replied Sugano. "You, that is. Wolf has ordered me to shoot you."

CHAPTER THIRTY

B runo Montesi felt his blood turn to ice, but he kept walking. "This is crazy," he said, "I'm a partisan just like you, we're on the same side. Why would you want to kill me?"

"I don't know," said Sugano. "I obey orders."

"Listen to me. The reason I came here is to convince Wolf to recognize the authority of the National Liberation Committee. You have everything to gain . . . "

"Oh yeah? What do we stand to gain?"

"First of all, the Allies negotiate directly with us and they only recognize the formations which are part of the Committee. You are useful to them right now, but if the situation changes they will not hesitate to dump you and abandon you to your fate. By joining us, the NLC, you'll become part of a regular formation, recognized by the Geneva Convention; that is, with formal recognition of the credit and prestige that you've won through your victories. If you stay out, you're nothing more than a band of armed men, no matter how much fear you inspire."

As he spoke, Montesi counted the steps and the minutes that separated him from his own summary execution, even if Sugano's silence gave him at least the impression that he might be listening. He continued.

"If you accept my proposal, the Allies will give you support through regular airdrops, in accordance with our commanders. They can actually supply you with exactly what you need . . . "

Sugano was still mute.

"Think about it. In order to provide for your men, you are forced to confiscate your means of transport and above all your food supplies from the local population, and this makes you very unpopular. There's a consistent portion of these people who are not behind you: we've had complaints, protests, claims of sacking . . . "

At this point, Montesi thought that Sugano would shoot him in the back. Nothing. So he stopped.

"With our support, you will receive provisions regularly from the sky. When you need to confiscate something from a local family, you can give them a certificate that entitles them to be reimbursed. Now, don't you think that if you kill me you'll end up losing a lot of the prestige that you've gained on the battlefield of Monte Sole?"

At that point, very slowly and with his hands raised high, Montesi turned around until the barrel of the tommy gun was pointing at his chest.

"We're here," said Sugano.

Montesi nodded. "Right. So what are you going to do? Shoot me?"

Sugano lowered the gun. "No," he said, "because you're right."

Montesi took a long breath and sat down on a tree trunk until his heartbeat returned to normal.

"What do we do now?" he asked. "What will Wolf say?"

"I don't know. But he'll have to accept it. He'll start yelling, he'll probably point his pistol at me . . . who knows. It was going to happen sooner or later."

"So we go back?"

"No, not now. We'll wait, maybe he'll calm down in the meantime," replied Sugano.

Montesi offered him one of the remaining Chesterfields and they sat and chatted. Montesi couldn't believe that in just a few minutes' time he had gone from the prospect of a summary execution to sharing a cigarette—and not the last smoke of a prisoner condemned to death!—in the company of his would-be hangman. They spoke at length, until Sugano thought that the time had come for them to go back. They did just that, walking side by side. When they arrived, the Wolf wasn't there. He had gone with a squad of about twenty men to inspect a site.

"That's good," said Sugano. "He'll get it out of his system, and when he comes back maybe he'll have changed his mind."

They entered the building they were using as their headquarters and Sugano called over Spino, the sentry, to hear what had happened in the meantime.

"We captured a fascist and Wolf ordered his execution. We were waiting for you."

"Christ, this place is a slaughterhouse," burst out Montesi.

Sugano nudged him to shut up, then asked: "Where is this fascist?"

Spino opened the door to a stable and the others followed him in. A ray of sunshine was lighting up the interior.

"He's only a kid!" said Montesi.

"He's a fascist," shot back Spino.

"You can't shoot him," continued Montesi, "he's protected by the Geneva Convention. He can't be a day over fifteen"

"Sixteen," corrected the boy.

Montesi walked up to him. "Why did you enlist?" he asked.

"To defend my country against the invaders, and traitors like you."

"Traitors? You're not thinking clearly, buddy. There's a lot to say about who the traitors are, and who the invaders are. Maybe we should talk."

"What for? Shoot me and get it over with!"

"Shut up, you idiot, are you in such a hurry to die?" said Montesi. He gave Sugano a look; the other man shrugged and they walked out together.

"Can't you do anything?" asked Montesi.

"You've got to be kidding. I've already disobeyed him by not killing you. Now we're going to spare the boy too? I wouldn't want to be around when he comes back."

"I'll talk to him," replied Montesi.

"You're crazy. But if you want to try, and you manage to survive the first ten minutes without him killing you, you've got a chance."

Sugano turned to Spino: "In the meantime, keep a close watch on the kid. If this one gets away, we'll all end up in front of the firing squad."

Spino nodded and double-locked the door.

"What happened to those five boys that just got here?" Sugano asked him.

"Wolf sent them out with Guerrino, towards Montepastore and Monte Ombraro, to patrol the zone between us and the guys from Montefiorino," replied Spino.

"When are they coming back?"

"Don't know. When they're finished."

Spino turned to Montesi: "You know? One of the five new guys comes from the same place you do."

"What's his name?"

"Fabrizio, I think," he replied. "Light brown hair, hazel eyes, sturdy build, a coffee-colored birthmark on his neck."

"Christ! That's Savino's son!"

"Who's he?" asked Sugano.

"The boy's a friend of mine, but he knows nothing about me being here. Anyway, he doesn't belong here. Can't you warn him off? The kid has no experience whatsoever, he's never fired a shot his whole life."

"Calm down," said Sugano. "It's all under control. It's like being thrown into deep water: you sink or you learn to swim fast. A lot of other guys have been through here, what makes him so special?"

"Nothing. It's just that he's a good friend and I don't want him dead."

Wolf didn't come back for three days. When they saw him, he was in a state of shock.

"The Germans have burned it all down. Homes, farms; there's nothing left standing at Monte Sole."

Montesi walked up to him: "Considering what happened, you should have expected them to take revenge."

"What the fuck is he doing here?" said Wolf, suddenly noticing the person he'd thought was a dead man, talking. "Didn't I tell you to get rid of him?"

"He convinced Sugano that you're wrong, and he also convinced him not to shoot that kid in there, in the stable," Spino broke in.

"I'm too tired to be pissed," replied Wolf. "I have to sleep, I'm falling over. But I'm not going to listen to any crap from you," he said, pointing to Montesi. "I'm in charge here. You're worth shit, you understand that?"

"You are in charge here, Wolf, but that boy doesn't deserve to die. I've talked to him and convinced him that we are the patriots. He's come over to our side and he'll be a great fighter for freedom, mark my words."

Wolf got close enough to touch him and looked him straight in the eye: "All right, I'll trust you on this one. But if you're wrong, if he runs off and tells the Nazis what he's seen here, I swear by God I will have you shot."

"That won't be necessary," said Montesi calmly. "Where do we go from here?"

"We go to Monte Sole. We have to protect our people."

"If we go back there, it'll be the end. The Germans will come back with overwhelming force and crush us. All we have are light arms; they won't get us anywhere. Let's approach it from the other direction. We'll reach the Republic of Montefiorino and unite with the Modena division. Strength lies in unity."

Wolf didn't say a word, but went inside.

"He needs to sleep," said one of the men who'd come back with him. "He hasn't closed his eyes in over forty-eight hours." Sugano picked three men from among those who were better rested and assigned them to guard the commander and watch over his sleep.

Wolf slept nine hours straight and woke up at four in the morning. He summoned Sugano and the other three battalion commanders: Corvo, Riccio and Labieno. He held council.

"Tell me straight out if you're afraid of fighting. We have never backed off. Nothing, nobody, has ever stopped us. There's no reason we can't reclaim Monte Sole."

Sugano felt cut to the quick. "What the fuck is that about, Wolf? Have you ever seen me flinch? Haven't I fought at your side for hours and hours, day and night, snow and rain? Have you ever seen me run away? Did I ever leave your ass uncovered?"

"So we'll go. Where's the problem?"

"That we have enough ammunition for one hour," replied Corvo.

"Well that settles it, doesn't it?" concluded Sugano. "Unless we want to commit mass suicide. I was talking to the Blacksmith, he says we should go towards Castello di Serravalle. There are friends there who can give us support and supplies. After that . . . "

"After that we'll discuss matters," Wolf cut him short. No one at that moment felt like contradicting him. They woke up the others one by one, each man rousing the next, without making a sound. Montesi headed one of the columns, walking next to Romolo, the boy whose life he had saved and whom he felt personally responsible for.

They walked for a couple of hours until they reached Monte Vignola, not far from Vergato. It was there that Bruno Montesi recognized Fabrizio in the middle of a group of about twenty Red Star foot soldiers. They embraced.

"You are crazy," said Montesi. "Why did you come up here? You've never fired a shot."

"Yes I have, I'm sorry to say," he replied. Fabrizio looked down at his shoes and thought of the boy that he had finished off. In his mind's eye he looked even more like Rossano, although he knew that was impossible.

"Useless asking you if you'd consider going home, right?"

"Completely," said Fabrizio. "My place is here."

"As you wish, I'm not going to insist, but be careful. This isn't a game. Dying is easy up here."

They advanced at a steady pace until that evening without particular problems. They were careful about never letting down their guard; German troop movement had been reported throughout the area. They spent the night in a hayloft near Savigno and the morning after they reached Castello di Serravalle which was at a relatively low altitude. Wolf was nervous, his eyes continuously darted around as if he sensed danger. A friend of Montesi's appeared and showed them where the provisions were: a shelter that had been used until a couple of days before by the German command.

At this point, Wolf went back to his idea of returning to Monte Sole, but he found Sugano decidedly against it. "We don't have enough ammunition and we know for certain that the Germans will be back, in strength and with heavy artillery. The Blacksmith is right: we have to go to Montefiorino and unite with the men of the Modena division."

Wolf became furious. "You are not going anywhere," he said, "I decide where we go. We've come all this way for nothing."

"I'm going with my men to Montefiorino."

"Try it and I'll kill you!" growled Wolf.

"Kill me, if you have the guts!" shouted Sugano.

Wolf was taking the safety off his submachine gun when Montesi stepped in between them. "Are you both crazy? That's all we need, you two shooting at each other. Cut this out, now, you hear me? We can talk this out, for the love of God. Stop this right now, I said," he repeated, pushing them physically apart. Fabrizio was shocked at what he was seeing: two men that he thought of as heroes were aiming their guns at each other. But his friend Bruno was getting the situation under control.

"Listen to me, let's start acting like people and not animals. Neither one of you wants to accept the point of view of the other. The only solution is to split up."

A deathly silence fell over the men. They were utterly demoralized by seeing their two top commanders fighting this way. Wolf was a mess. His authority had never been challenged before, but he had probably realized by now that it would no longer be possible to keep the brigade together. Montesi thought that the biggest obstacle to solving this dilemma was that, even if the Red Star could be persuaded to join the Modena division, Wolf would categorically refuse to submit to the decisions of another commander. Of any other commander.

Montesi looked at Wolf and Sugano, in turn, and then scanned the men, all immobile with their fingers on the triggers, trying to figure out who was on which side. At a certain point, Wolf spoke: "All right. I'm not going to force you. I've never forced you to do anything. You've always followed me out of your own free will, you've always recognized me as your commander. If you want to go, I will not hold you back, but you have to leave your weapons here. They belong to me and to my men, to the men who are loyal to me and will not abandon me."

A terrible situation had just gotten worse. The possession of their weapons was vital for both sides, and the two leaders were once again facing off with guns leveled.

"That's enough now," said Montesi, "you both know very well that no one can survive up here without a weapon. Wolf, these men have made a decision that you don't like. But is that any reason to condemn them to certain death? You know that they will never give up their weapons; the only way to disarm them is to kill them. You won't do that, Wolf, because you're their commander. Because you don't want to spill blood among these men that you've always considered your brothers, more than brothers, men who have shared everything with you: dangers, sacrifices, nights out on the field, wounds, endless marches. Let them go. Let those who think differently than you do go their own way, and they will respect you, they'll remember you and they'll tell their sons and grandsons about you. Let us leave each other as friends, in the hopes that when we meet again, it will be in a better country, in an Italy which is freer and more just."

Montesi became emotional as he spoke. His own words, the measured rhetoric he had learned at the party school, moved him. He didn't feel embarrassed, because he was the first to believe in what he was saying. Those present were simple men, who listened with their hearts, and were not difficult to influence. In the end, Wolf agreed to let Sugano's group leave with their arms and he did not try to convince anyone to remain with him. The ones who wanted to stay would be enough.

Sugano went off with about two hundred men and Wolf went back with the others. Wolf's new army were all from the Reno river valley, from places like Marzabotto, Grizzana, Vergato, Monzuno and Pian di Venola. They went back with him because they knew what was going to happen and, if they had to die, they preferred to do so fighting in front of the doors of their own homes.

There were no embraces, no tears. When they reached the ridge, Sugano turned around to watch Wolf's column as they were making their way back to Monte Sole and, from deep inside, he wished them luck, because he thought they were going towards sure death.

Although Fabrizio was a newcomer to the brigade, living through such a harrowing experience had made him as tough and seasoned as any veteran. He would exchange a few words with Montesi now and then, seeking comfort for the remorse he felt at leaving Wolf and his comrades as they headed for their destiny.

"It's not your fault, Fabrizio," Montesi replied. "Each one of us, in his own heart, made the decision he thought best. No one can know what fate has in store for us."

The next day, Sugano's brigade entered Montefiorino and reported to Mario Ricci, known as "Armando," the commander of the Modena division. He immediately assigned them to Frassinoro, not far from the border with Tuscany. Just a few days later, they received a telephone call from headquarters alerting them to the fact that two German motorized divisions had launched a massive attack against Montefiorino, at the northern edge of the territory, on the valley side. The partisans were seeking to resist in every way possible, but they were greatly outnumbered in terms of vehicles, men and arms. Sugano's group was ordered to move west of Frassinoro towards Val d'Asta on the border with Reggio, because the Germans were attempting to outflank them there in order to deny them a line of escape towards Tuscany and the Allied lines. The brigade took up position in a village on the ridge which offered a vantage point over a vast territory, allowing them to spot troop movement at a distance. At four o'clock in the morning, a courier brought the order to move further southwest, in the direction of the Forbici pass. It was a difficult, risky transfer because the Germans had already infiltrated the entire area and had destroyed several villages.

At about ten o'clock in the morning, Spino told Sugano that he had good news: "There's a shepherd who has just come through the Forbici pass; I interrogated him and he says that the route is clear."

Sugano demanded to talk with the man himself. "Well?" he asked him. "What did you see up there?"

"There's a group of your men guarding the pass. I'm sure it was them because I heard them talking."

"Are you absolutely sure?"

"As sure as I'm here talking to you now. They were men from the Modena division."

"All right, let's go see. Eyes open and fingers on your triggers."

The brigade fanned out and started the ascent. Fabrizio very soon lost contact with Bruno Montesi, who was with another couple of guys from town: Aldo Banti and Amedeo Bisi. Fabrizio felt like calling out, asking them to wait up, but he couldn't even see where they were. The unit was moving across open ground because most of the trees had been cut down, but the men had managed to camouflage themselves using the branches and vegetation from juniper bushes and oak saplings.

The silence was unreal; not even the birds were singing. Sugano was ahead of the others; every few steps, he would check that the way was clear and signal for them to proceed towards the peak. All at once, the still air was torn by the deafening din of machine guns and artillery. Sugano shouted out: "Take shelter! The Germans! Shoot that fucking shepherd, dammit! Kill him, I want him dead!" He was furious, but his men had more to think about than shooting the shepherd. Some had been hit, others were trying to find some kind of cover from the thousands of rounds that were hailing down from every direction.

Fabrizio dove into a drainage ditch, totally bewildered. In the distance, to his left, he thought he saw Montesi with Banti, Amedeo Bisi and three or four others, crawling, their bodies flattened to the ground as bullets hit the stones and rocks all around them, sending up sprays of sparks and scorching splinters. Fabrizio waited for the firing to cease and then took off at a run, bent over double, in the direction of his comrades, but the bursts started up again instantly. He felt a sudden piercing pain in his left leg as it folded under him and he crumbled to the ground.

He shouted and called out but no one heard him. He started to drag himself back to the only point of safety he knew, the ditch. Once he had rolled over the lip and into the narrow trench, he elbowed himself forward, leaving a trail of blood behind him. At least he knew that he was following the slope of the hillside in a downward direction. After a while, there was a rise in the terrain flanking the ditch that he thought would afford him some protection. He pulled himself out and crawled with great difficulty over to a big beech tree and there he stopped, propped up in a sitting position against the trunk. One of the brigade members ran by, and then another, but neither of them stopped or even listened to his pleas for help. He realized that he was bleeding to death and he closed his eyes and prepared to die. So many had died, after all, young guys like him, on one side and the other, what was so special about his fate? His had been a brief adventure; he'd done nothing worthwhile, given no real contribution to the cause. He was dying for nothing. The one thing he had done burned inside of him like a red-hot iron. The shoes . . . the shoes were still almost new. Maybe someone else would get some good out of them. Your shoes are as important as your gun, when you have to fight and to run, run, run . . .

The world had stopped and he thought his hour had come, but there was a hand on his shoulder and it was shaking him as if to wake him up. He opened his eyes: "Bruno!"

The Blacksmith was there, standing in front of him. He heaved Fabrizio onto his back and carried him to a wood of oak saplings and there they waited. Bisi and Banti showed up along with other comrades, including those who had heard him call out but hadn't stopped. "They were the ones who told me you were wounded," said Montesi. They worked together to fashion a stretcher out of ash branches, cutting them with their bayonets.

"Where's Sugano?" Fabrizio managed to say.

"I don't know. We lost him. Now we have to try to save ourselves."

They began to make their way towards the nearest town, steering clear of the German soldiers who were still patrolling. They often met up with isolated groups of partisans who were still armed and organized. There was nothing to eat and Montesi himself was bleeding from a wound in his neck caused by shrapnel. They stayed awake the whole night. There was no food, but plenty of cold, clear water, that flowed in a thousand rivulets from the mountain peaks. Fabrizio became delirious. The next day they reached a tiny village, where two doctors had set up a sort of field hospital for the wounded partisans. They were out of everything they needed, from sterile surgical instruments to medicines.

They had to amputate, without anesthesia, using a butcher's saw and a pair of pruning shears. Fabrizio's screams of pain could be heard at a great distance.

Montesi wept.

Those who could, sought shelter in Tuscany behind the Allied lines. Sugano and a small group of his most loyal soldiers returned to Bologna.

Wolf and his men reached Monte Sole and engaged the Germans in a battle to the last drop of blood with their tommy guns and pistols against the Nazi tanks, heavy machine guns and cannons. In the end, the only surviving member of the group was Wolf, pitted against a German officer. They faced each other in an old-fashioned duel, one on one, until the Italian defender ran out of ammunition.

Wounded in the shoulder, he managed nonetheless to get away and run for the woods, stemming the bleeding as best he could. Then just like a wounded wolf, he found a hidden den, tucked away in a mountain ravine, and went there to die.

His stiff, cramped body wasn't found until a year later, after the war had ended.

CHAPTER THIRTY-ONE

In the end the Germans managed to destroy the defenses of the Republic of Montefiorino, but partisan groups continued to act independently in various areas of the mountains, trying to coordinate as best they could as they waited for the Allies to launch the final offensive. Bruno Montesi took refuge with his men on the other side of the Allied lines. Fabrizio was spirited back to town using the country lanes and back roads of the region. His parents welcomed him home with all the warmth and affection they were capable of, trying as best they could to hide their dismay at the terrible toll that the war had taken on the once-perfect body of their beloved son. They did everything in their power to distract him and to help him to find ways to face this new life in which he'd never be equal to the others. But he was always sad and melancholy, and they'd often find him sitting under the big oak at the end of the courtyard with a lost expression.

Rossano seemed to have vanished into thin air. His parents' frantic efforts to locate him turned up nothing; no one had any idea of what might have happened to the boy or where he might be. Fabrizio heard he had gone missing, and in his nightmares the boy with the black shirt whose shoes he had taken became Rossano. One day when his parents were in the fields and he was home alone, he took the shoes from the closet where he'd hidden them and burned them.

Sugano managed to reach Bologna with the few comrades who had decided to stay with him, including Spino.

Disobeying his commander's orders to lay low, Spino snuck out of the safe house one night to visit his mother and let her know he was all right. He was recognized and surrounded by a group from the Black Brigades. He put up a fierce fight with his pistol, but he didn't have time to assemble the pieces of the Sten he kept in his rucksack and he was captured. He was tortured to death; for one day and one night, his enemies inflicted unimaginable abuse on him. Then they publicly exposed his scourged, lifeless body as a warning to anyone who followed his example.

Like Sugano, many other partisans had gathered in the cities, imagining that the Allied offensive was imminent, but General Alexander halted the Allied advance in November, postponing the campaign until the following spring. The outcome was that the fascists who had run off came back to trap the partisans.

Perhaps that was the blackest hour of the whole millenary history of Italy. Never had her sons been pitted so ferociously against one another.

There was no limit to the violence.

The slaughter lasted all winter and spring, when the bombing started up again on a wide scale. Alexander's armies finally succeeded in breaking through the Gothic line and occupying the vast plain, the Po river valley. The Allies entered Bologna on the morning of April 21, 1945: there were Poles, British and Americans, but also Italian soldiers from the Friuli, Legnano and Folgore brigades and a great number of partisans.

Many of the locals were finally free to return to town: Bruno Montesi, Aldo Banti, Amedeo Bisi and others. Long beards, submachine guns slung around their necks, grenades in their belts: well-brought-up people regarded them with suspicion, or with a mix of fear and scorn.

Montesi went to visit Fabrizio as soon as he could.

"How are you?"

366 · VALERIO MASSIMO MANFREDI

"You can see for yourself how I am."

"Fabrizio, what you have to consider is that you're alive. You can be with your parents, your friends, you can read and study, meet people, travel. You can see your country finally liberated and embarking on a new road, building a new future. For the dead, it's all over with."

"They're better off than me."

"That's not true. You'll get used to it. Little by little, things will change."

"Forgive me, Bruno, you did everything you could to save my life and I'm acting like a mean, ungrateful bastard."

"You would have done the same thing for me. And maybe, in your place, I would have said the same things. We still need you. I've got big plans and you can help me, right here. Work on regaining your strength, in your body but most of all, in your mind. I know you can. I'll come back to visit again soon."

When Montesi came to visit Fabrizio again, it was to lay out his projects and plans; he had founded a section of the NLC right there in town, along with Banti and Bisi. But the transition proved to be anything but smooth. In the months that followed, you could cut the tension with a knife: people figured that the day of reckoning wouldn't be far off, and they were right. A number of prominent people were justly or unjustly accused of collaborationism, of spying for the Social Republic or the fascists, and were simply dragged out of their houses in the middle of the night and put to death. For some it was a question of justice, for others ruthless revenge. In a nearly complete vacuum of rules and laws, anyone could decide, from one day to the next, to get rid of a personal enemy, to seek revenge for some perceived snub, to have the satisfaction of punishing someone who had wronged him in some way.

One day the news spread in town that Tito Ferretti, one of the most important landowners in the area, had been killed near the Samoggia as he was travelling by carriage to the stock exchange in Bologna to check on the price of pork. He had neither sons nor daughters because he was unmarried, and for this reason his workers and tenant farmers respectfully called him "*il signorino,*" the term reserved for a gentleman bachelor. His mother, an elderly noblewoman, had gone to live in the city because, she said, she didn't feel safe any longer, given the mood in town. She had often asked her son to join her, but he refused because he was much too fond of the farm, of the land and all the animals, to want to give it all up.

"And really," he would tell her, "who could have it in for me? I've given money to everyone: to the fascists, to the partisans . . . " He was throwing ears of corn to the pigs as he spoke with her.

"You just don't want to part from those pigs of yours: you care more about them than anyone or anything else. You'll end up breathing your last breath on a pig cart, Tito!" the countess continued haughtily, referring to the wagon with folding sides which her son used to take the sows and butcher hogs to market. "Anyway, you're not a child anymore and you can do as you like. Don't say I didn't warn you."

Unfortunately her prophecy was confirmed, almost to the letter.

For two days and two nights, the body of *il signorino* was left lying on the side of the dusty road, because no one dared approach the site of his murder. In the end, his niece, a twenty-five-year-old girl, went to where he lay, loaded his body onto a cart and wheeled him back home. She crossed the town from one end to another, making her way down the main road. The strain of pulling the cart soon had her dripping with sweat. There was not a soul to be seen, but closed doors and drawn shutters on either side of her. A desert of fear. The only sound to be heard in the deathly silence was the creaking of the iron rims of the cart wheels on the cobblestones. Sometimes she had to stop, when she felt she couldn't pull her load a moment longer, but then a strength born of her hate for those who had done this to her uncle gave her new energy and pushed her forward. She knew that people were watching her from behind their windows, perhaps even the murderer himself! and she wanted them all to know that she wasn't afraid and wouldn't be intimidated.

Five days later, the *carabinieri* of Verona sent a routine request to their colleagues in Castelfranco regarding a transfer of title for a horse and carriage which had been sold at the Verona horse fair. The local *carabinieri* traced the plates to Ferretti and thus the murderer's identity was discovered, although they were not able to apprehend him because, after trying to sell off the carriage, the man had fled to Belgium and was working as a miner there. He died, not long after he had arrived, crushed under the prongs of a forklift, smashed flat as a cockroach. Word had it that before he met his unfortunate end, he had decided to talk, to reveal the names of those who had organized Ferretti's murder. But if that was the case, no one would ever learn the answer.

Some in town were sure that the murderer was a partisan who had asked Ferretti for money in the name of the party, had even produced a receipt on NLC letterhead, but had then put the money in his own pocket instead; in a panic that he would be found out, he killed Ferretti to keep the story quiet. Others spoke of certain activists in the party who were plotting to install the communist party in power by forming a cooperative with Ferretti's land holdings, and had decided that the easiest way to do this was to take *il signorino* out of the picture. There was no lack of conjecture about the most plausible and implausible motives, because in that climate, anything could seem reasonable.

Each new occasion for bereavement cleared the way for more contempt and resentment. Fabrizio knew well that his friend the Blacksmith had always spoken against, and acted against, any form of violence, but he also came to realize that in such dark, uncertain, lawless times, there were others who had become accustomed to wielding power and deciding a man's life or death with impunity, and they wouldn't be easy to stop.

Astorre Roversi, known as *buférla*, craven tormentor of women and children, was found lying stiff along the road that went to Magazzino. Someone had shot him from behind the hedge.

As the months passed and the structures of the State were gradually reorganized, the worst of the emergency receded, but the tension did not let up. Many partisans had refused to surrender their arms, or had turned in defective or unserviceable weapons. But although there were many of them who believed that the time was ripe for a proletarian revolution, like the Russian revolt of 1917, very few were convinced that such nation-shattering change was really possible. Exhaustion had begun to set in, and worry over an uncertain future. They sensed that the blood which had flowed, the dead and the wounded, the terrible battles, would all be forgotten. The laws would be administered by the same bureaucrats who had served the old system; the new system couldn't get off its feet without their help.

The fire slowly turned to ash.

With the new year, as societal structures and the norms regulating everyday life settled back into place, the turbulence seemed to cease. The few remaining loose cannons of the movement were silenced. A dull, heavy calm ensued.

At the end of February, Armando Bruni found himself once again in the painful position of facing one of his wife's increasingly frequent breakdowns. As he had in the past, Doctor Munari ordered her hospitalization. It was then that Armando was heard threatening the good doctor; he supposedly said: "If you send her back to the insane asylum I'll kill you!" Or at least that was the rumor that was circulating in town.

Three months later, one Sunday in May at eleven o'clock in the morning, Doctor Munari left home to go to church, as he was accustomed to doing every Sunday. Not out of devotion, but rather because he had become fond of watching the pretty young women chatting in the square after the high mass. He hadn't walked more than a hundred meters when someone shot him three times with a pistol at close range, causing him to collapse in a pool of blood. His young wife heard the shots and, flooded by a sense of dread, rushed out into the street and found him in that state. She ran to him, screaming in despair, and reached him in time to hear his last breath. She fell onto her husband's body, sobbing.

The shots had been heard distinctly in town as well and Aldo Banti, who was sitting out in front of what had been the House of Fascism, now restored to its original role as the House of the People, took off in the direction of the noise and came back shouting "They've killed the doctor!" People would much later remember that he was the first to announce the doctor's death, as if he had somehow been waiting for it to happen.

No one else dared to approach the scene of the crime, afraid of becoming involved in some way; it was wiser to wait until the *carabinieri* came. The sergeant who showed up tried to question the people living in the vicinity, but no one had any information to offer. He wrote up a report to send to the judicial authorities, but they had no choice but to dismiss the case. The memory of how accounts had been settled in the recent past was still very fresh in everyone's mind; best to steer clear of such nasty business: no one had seen anything and no one knew anything.

Rumors abounded, however. Some even said that a woman who lived above the Osteria della Bassa had seen two individuals riding off at great speed on their bicycles towards Madonna della Provvidenza, but she never reported it, so that was the end of that. After a few months, no one even mentioned it anymore. The widow retreated into her grief. She turned the house into a museum in her husband's memory: the book on his desk was left open to the page he had been reading, his suits and shoes remained in the wardrobe, and the armor in his collection was polished every Saturday.

Fonso and Maria tried to spend time with her whenever they could, but she was inconsolable. She did nothing but speak of her husband, for whom she still had the utmost admiration. She always kept the windows closed and shunned the sunlight, she never cooked for herself and hardly ate anything. Every now and then Maria would bring her a little pot of hot soup or a piece of boiled meat with freshly baked bread. She'd say: "Eat something, *signora*! You're still young, you can't let yourself go like this." Fonso thought that only time would be able to heal such a painful wound, especially because she didn't have a guilty party to direct her hatred at.

Three years passed during which important things happened: the king was sent into exile and the Republic of Italy was proclaimed. Someone shot at the secretary of the communist party and everyone feared that a revolution, or civil war, would break out. That didn't happen, but people were still divided along political lines. Even cycling, the most popular sport after soccer, pitted right against left. The "whites" rooted for Bartali, the "reds" preferred Coppi, and the fights that broke out in bars regularly exploded into a white heat: tee-shirts soaked with sweat, neck veins bulging. Political rivalry poisoned everything; each individual saw in his adversary an enemy to be destroyed. At the same time, everyone was struggling, everyone wished that the world around them were different. There was very little work; many men had to migrate to Belgium, where they ended up working in the coal mines. In the dark, like mice, breathing in the black dust.

In order to control a situation that always seemed on the

372 · VALERIO MASSIMO MANFREDI

verge of erupting, the local *carabiniere* chief was replaced by a sergeant sent by Rome who was said to be tough as iron. With his coming, the town was once again cast into turmoil.

One day, three years after the doctor's murder, the news got out that Armando Bruni had signed a police statement in which he declared that his remorse had finally forced him to speak up and to admit that he had killed Doctor Munari. But that wasn't all: he had also fingered Bruno Montesi, Aldo Banti and Amedeo Bisi as the organizers of the crime. Political activists, all, and the founders of the local chapter of the National Association of Italian Partisans.

Fabrizio, who over those three years was slowly beginning to learn to live with his disability, was profoundly shocked. Montesi came to see him the next day, ashen faced and red-eyed, looking like he hadn't slept all night.

"I've come to say goodbye. They'll be coming to get me soon; it may be a question of days, or hours. I just wanted you to know that I've done nothing. I've always been against violence and besides that, why would I want to kill the doctor? He never bothered with politics and as far as I know, he did his job well. It makes no sense. Even as far as Aldo and Amedeo are concerned. They may be hotheads, but they're not stupid. Even if they had been planning such a thing, they would have had to run it by me and I would have said no."

"Leave here, then. Leave Italy, go to Yugoslavia—the party will help you."

"No. I'm staying here, I'll stand trial if I need to. They have nothing against me . . . except Armando's confession."

Fabrizio dropped his eyes, embarrassed.

"I didn't believe it for a moment. Your uncle is not capable of killing a fly. But the truth is that he is so hard up, in so many ways, that anyone could have convinced him to sign anything, with threats or with promises. Even just for a bowl of soup for his family."

"Bruno, they'll find other witnesses. They'll find a way to trap you, this is only the beginning. Get away while you can!"

"No, you're wasting your breath. I'm not going. This is my country and I fought to free it. Like you did. You'll see, in the end the truth will out."

Fabrizio stared straight into his eyes: "You're so sure?"

"It's what I hope," replied Montesi. "Goodbye."

Fabrizio watched him walk off with a cigarette in his mouth and his hands in his pockets, just like always. He felt tears come to his eyes.

"Good luck, Blacksmith," he said to himself.

The same evening, Maria went to the house of the doctor's wife with the excuse of bringing her the clothes she had washed and ironed, but as soon as she stepped in the door she burst into tears. "It wasn't him, *signora*," Maria sobbed, "he didn't do it! I know him well. He may be a poor wretch but he's not a murderer! He wouldn't even know how to kill someone."

The doctor's wife touched her face: "I know Maria, I know he couldn't have done such a thing. It was those other mutinous fanatics!"

Maria was confused; she hadn't meant to blame anyone else. But she left the house badly shaken: this was the second of her brothers who had been accused of murder.

The accused were transferred to Sondrio, a mountain town in the far north of Italy, so they could be tried in a court outside of their region because of presumed bias closer to home. But the trial had taken on great political significance and journalists from a number of the Emilia Romagna newspapers had been sent out on assignment. On the first day of proceedings, there was quite a crowd present in the courtroom. All eyes were on the doctor's wife, deathly pale in her black dress. Her eyes were heavily made up and her lipstick was blood red, making her look like a mythological Fury. She stared at the defendants with contempt in her eyes; the hatred that had been seething within her had finally found its target.

As the members of court filed in, the buzz of voices lowered, only to be silenced completely when the clerk said: "The accused may rise."

Armando was the lead defendant but also a witness for the prosecution; he was separated from the other three and never looked at them.

After he had had been sworn in, the judge asked him: "What pushed you to speak three years after the fact?"

"Remorse," replied Armando. "I couldn't hide the truth any longer." The Blacksmith tried in vain to meet his gaze.

Armando was not a very convincing witness: he often got mixed up and contradicted himself. The defense attorney, a clever, seasoned professional, had an easy time poking holes in his testimony. Armando was soon gasping like a fish out of water at the increasingly cogent questions the lawyer was barking out in rapid succession. The poor man was sweating, and his spit had dried up at the corners of his mouth. The day ended with the two sides more or less equally placed, and the courtroom in an uproar.

As was to be expected, the prosecution produced more witnesses. One was a twelve-year-old boy who on the day of the crime had climbed to the top of a cherry tree, from where he had seen everything. The other was a fortune-teller whose testimony was quite vague; she gave the unpleasant impression of speaking as if someone were prompting her. The defense rebutted by producing a doctor's report which certified that the boy on the cherry tree was so nearsighted that he couldn't have recognized his own mother at that distance. The entire house of cards built up by the prosecutor came tumbling down. In the end, the defendants were acquitted for lack of evidence.

The public prosecutor would not give up; he appealed the sentence in an attempt to save the face of those who had constructed the entire investigative and prosecutorial machine: the new iron-tough *carabiniere* sergeant and those who had installed him in office. The appeal ignored the fact that the sergeant, who had personally interrogated Bruni and obtained his confession, had already been accused of abuse, violence, sadism and assorted other iniquities by none other than his direct superior, Lieutenant Rizzo, in an official report. The superior officer's efforts to make the truth known were met with his transfer first, and later his dismissal from the force.

In the end, the prosecution and defense made a deal, at Armando's expense. The prosecution asked the court to take into consideration testimony from several more reliable witnesses who were present at the moment of the shooting, and came up with a more believable motive for the murder than the phrase that Armando had purportedly shouted in anger when the doctor had ordered his wife to be sent back into the psychiatric hospital.

The deal was this: the court would lighten the sentence as long as the defense agreed to pass Bruni off as the town idiot. They played their part with a vengeance: "He's a poor half-wit, as anyone can clearly see. He can't even pronounce two words in a row, the man is mentally deficient . . . "

Armando was weeping with humiliation and shame, sobbing and covering his face with his hands as those present in the courtroom snickered at the scene. But then an individual who had never been seen during the trial suddenly rose to his feet. No one had noticed him there before or knew who he was or what he was doing there.

He shouted: "That's enough!"

Floti.

He had, somehow, made his way down from his mountain haven and reached the scene of the trial in the middle of the

Alps. Before anyone could stop him, he strode towards his brother and held him close, as if to protect him from that hostile, hurtful gathering. A deep silence fell over the courtroom; the presiding judge, about to call out some stern injunction, paused with his gavel in midair. Nothing was threatening the regular proceedings of the court, nothing was endangering the safety of those present. He decided that it was best to leave room, if only for a brief moment, for the human emotions unfolding there, for the humble actors of a tragedy much bigger than they were and whose victims they had become.

"He's suffered enough," said Floti in the silence weighing so heavily in the air. His voice trembled with disdain. "Leave him in peace or I'll come looking for you, and then we'll see whose turn it is to cry!" And he walked out.

Floti went back to town, for a short time, without letting anyone know. He wandered through the fields like a stray dog. Unseen, he observed his brother Savino, the boldest and most courageous of his brothers, prematurely white-haired and haggard, marked by adversity. He watched his nephew, handsome young Fabrizio, lurching along on his crutches, making his way down to the irrigation ditch that bordered their land and sitting on its bank, grimly staring at the flowing waters.

He went to the cemetery and left his dog tags on the tomb of Captain Alberto Munari who had sawed the arm off one of his comrades in war, with the hope of saving the boy. Then he started down the road that would take him back up to his mountains. The troubles he had suffered reopened his old wounds; the unhealable grief at losing his son finished him off.

No one in town would ever see him again.

Epilogue

The trial concluded with reduced sentences, which were later completely amnestied. But Armando spent one more year in prison than the other defendants because his lawyer had neglected to sign the release papers.

The homecoming of Montesi and the others was greeted with great celebrating on the part of their supporters and comrades in the party.

No one noticed Armando's absence, no one tried to do anything about it. When he got back home he was unrecognizable.

One evening in mid-autumn, Fabrizio came to town along with his father Savino, who was driving their small methane-fuelled truck. Savino was going to the mill to load up some fodder for the pigs and Fabrizio got out to buy the newspaper. He told his father that he'd wait for him in front of the café and Savino agreed to pick him up on his way back. Every now and then he would raise his eyes from the paper to check and see whether his father's truck was coming around the bend. All at once he noticed a young man walking down the middle of the road in his direction; he was wearing a pair of fustian trousers, a gray-green high necked sweater, boots and a brown leather jacket. His long hair covered his forehead, and his beard only partially covered a scar that crossed his face from his left cheekbone to his upper lip. Greatly changed, but surely him.

Rossano.

Fabrizio was the only one to have taken notice; none of the

others sitting out in front of the café showed any signs of recognition.

He leaned into his crutches, pushed himself up and went towards Rossano. They stopped, standing face to face, at less than a meter's distance. A gust of wind carried the smell of their childhood on it and the colors of the fall.

"It's you," said Fabrizio, almost with relief.

Rossano looked at his leg. "I'm sorry."

"Yeah, well. Stuff happens . . . " Fabrizio fell quiet. "I can't even say I'm happy to see you."

"I guess not, given the circumstances. And we can't even shake hands . . . "

"No. Sorry."

"Maybe, one day or another we'll . . . talk?"

"Maybe," replied Fabrizio in a breath, "maybe, talk . . . "

"See you around," said Rossano as he started off again amidst the drifting dry leaves.

"See you around," thought Fabrizio, but he said nothing.

When the plowing season came, Iofa showed up one evening in the courtyard to talk to Savino.

"What's going on, Iofa?" he asked.

"What's going on is that Bonetti wants to level the Pra' dei Monti hills to turn them into arable land."

"So what? It's his land and he can do what he wants with it."

Iofa took him by the arm and led him a few steps away with a secretive air. "One night, many years ago, your brother Floti and I took a walk out that way after a vagabond appeared at the Osteria della Bassa, a fellow with fire in his eyes and a beard down to his waist, saying that he'd seen the golden goat there."

"So did you find what you were looking for?"

"No. But we found something else. D'you remember the umbrella mender?"

"Vaguely."

"That's who we found. He was inside a hole on the third hill, all curled up like a dog. Dead."

Savino scowled: "What the hell is this story? Floti never said a word to me about this."

"It's the pure and simple truth. We found some tools in the grass and buried him with a few shovelfuls of dirt . . . "

"So get to the point, Iofa."

"What if they find him now?"

"He's not going to mind if they find him. Where's the problem?"

"You had leased out that land until just last year. With that *carabiniere* sergeant we've got now, he's likely to think that it's one of the fellows who have gone missing over the last few years. It's you he'll come looking for, asking questions . . . Given what happened to Armando, that's all you need . . . "

"I see what you're getting at. But what can I do about it?"

"I know exactly where he is. We'll go there tonight and we'll dig him out. There won't be anything left but a few bones; it won't take us long."

Savino took a long breath and tried to sort out his thoughts.

"Let's go," Iofa pressured him. "The sooner we get this done, the better. I told you. It'll only take us ten minutes."

"All right," replied Savino. "We'll use your cart. It's less likely to attract attention."

He loaded up a basket, a sack, two shovels and a lantern and they set off, after he'd told Linda she should go to bed if she wanted to, that they would be very late.

When they got to Pra' dei Monti it was pitch black out. They began to dig at the spot which Iofa pointed out. When they were about four or five strokes down, they found the head and then all the rest. They put everything into the sack and the sack into the basket, and they didn't even bother to shovel the dirt back in, because one hole more or less, on those heaps of ground, wouldn't make any difference. They were getting ready to leave when Iofa noticed something in the middle of the freshly turned soil and shone the lantern on it.

"What is it?" asked Savino.

Iofa picked up a sort of oilcloth sack. It was smallish, and contained a leather cylinder, which he opened. Inside was a sheet of paper with about fifteen lines written in a very simple, regular hand. He passed it to Savino.

"What does it say?"

"I really can't tell . . . it must be Latin."

Iofa called out to the horse; he didn't want to stay in that place a moment longer. They headed for home through the open countryside. It was cold, but Savino barely noticed. His mind was on the words written on that piece of paper and he racked his brains trying to find an explanation. How had the umbrella mender died? Who had left that message, and why was it written in a language which had been dead for centuries?

A solution suddenly came to mind. "Amedeo!" he exclaimed. "Amedeo Bisi. He studied at the seminary with the priests and he knows Latin. He lives only a kilometer from here . . . "

"Wait, you want to wake him up now?"

"Why not? He's not going to shoot me."

"You never know these days . . . " grumbled Iofa.

Bisi, rudely awakened in the middle of the night, opened a crack in the shutters with the barrel of his rifle and peered down: "Who's there?"

"It's me, Amedeo," replied Savino in a whisper, "and Iofa's with me."

"What are you doing here at this time of night?"

"We need to talk to you. It's urgent."

Bisi's wife had become alarmed. "Who is it? What do they want from you? Don't go . . . "

"Calm down. They're friends."

Bisi went down in his pajamas, turned on the light and opened the door.

"I was about to shoot you," he muttered.

"Just what I said," commented Iofa, shaking his head, "but there was no stopping him."

Savino pulled out the leather case and told the story of the umbrella mender. "Maybe you remember him yourself."

"I do, I think I do. He was a client of Hotel Bruni, wasn't he?"

"That's the guy. Iofa told me that Bonetti is planning to level Pra' dei Monti and that maybe, given the situation, it would be best to dig up the body before someone else does. I was leasing out that land until just last year and you know, with what's been happening lately . . . "

"Do you have him with you?"

"Yeah, in a bag. But then, as we were about to leave, Iofa found this. It looks like Latin to me, and I thought that you . . . Sorry about waking you up and everything, but I started feeling I just had to know what it said."

Bisi took the paper. "It's been a while since I've read any Latin," he sighed. "Let me see . . . "

He put on his glasses and started to slowly scan the lines. Every now and then he'd scribble something using a pencil stub, on the back of the *Old Farmer's Almanac*. He got to his feet. "I must have a dictionary around here somewhere." He opened a cupboard. "As luck would have it, here it is."

He got back to work, his expression becoming more and more intent as the words took shape. His eyes, behind the thick spectacles, became wide and filled with wonder. Savino was trying to interpret every furrow in his brow, every flicker of his eyelids.

"Holy Christ!" exclaimed Bisi in the end.

"What does it say? Don't keep me hanging!"

"Do you know who the umbrella mender was?"

Savino shrugged. Iofa hobbled closer; he didn't want to miss a word of this.

"Don Massimino, the old pastor who was said to have died in a state of grace."

"That can't be!"

"His beard, his long hair, the years of living rough as a beggar, the remorse over a tragic mistake committed in his youth, the years of penance . . . made him unrecognizable."

"What are you saying? When the umbrella mender used to come to Hotel Bruni, Don Massimino had been dead for years. He's buried in the cemetery, under an oak tree."

"Don Massimino is inside a sack on Iofa's cart."

"Well then who's there in the graveyard?"

"Who knows? Sand, stones, someone else's body . . . you'd have to open the tomb to find out. Remember, it was Don Giordano who held his funeral. Maybe he knew the whole story, but he decided he would rather have the tomb of a saint in the cemetery than the memory of a disgraced priest in town."

"But why would Don Massimino have organized his own funeral?"

"So he could drop out of sight, and atone for his sins. Here it says that he had a relationship with a girl when he was a young pastor up in the mountains. The girl became pregnant and, for fear of a scandal, poisoned herself. Her mother lost her mind."

"Oh holy God," exclaimed Savino, "that's Desolina's story!"

"Right," confirmed Iofa, "right you are!"

They told Bisi they story of the poor madwoman who would come to Hotel Bruni to seek shelter and warmth in the middle of winter.

"Maybe the umbrella mender used to come back here," suggested Bisi, "to the town that considered him a saint . . . I'm not saying he wasn't fond of your family, but maybe he would come to Hotel Bruni so he could meet up with this Desolina, to ask for her forgiveness. Anyway, he never found the courage. In the end, he decided to die like the girl he loved, by poisoning himself. A horrible death, to be sure. Look at this:

"*'Venenum quod semper mecum habere consueram, sumpsi.'*

I drank the poison that I always kept with me. The Latin is quite easy to read, it's taken from an author that we did our first translations from in the seminary . . . He ends up with a phrase which begs for God's mercy. *'Miserere mei Domine.'*"

"But why did he choose to die there, on Pra' dei Monti? He always said it was possessed by a demon."

"To drive the demon away? Did he sacrifice his own life to exorcise this demon? We'll never know."

"So that's why the umbrella mender was so strange. That's why he spoke like a fortune teller, or a prophet . . . Don't tell anyone what happened tonight, Amedeo. Nor you, Iofa."

They both nodded in silence. Savino and Iofa returned home and buried the bones of Don Massimino at the foot of a century-old oak tree, on the edge of the field that bordered on the consecrated land of the cemetery.

The winter that followed was particularly harsh and, just before Christmas, there was a big snowfall. It was said that a wanderer surprised by the storm hurried down a road followed many a time in the past, sure to find refuge at the end and a bowl of warm soup. It wasn't a man, but a woman. A ragged old woman, dragging herself through the deep snow in her broken shoes, clutching a worn shawl around her shoulders. It was Desolina, who had vanished without a trace such a very long time ago.

She entered into the Bruni family courtyard, strangely plunged into darkness. She looked around in bewilderment, as if she couldn't quite recognize the place. Her eyes set on the jumble of burnt beams and crumbled walls where the enormous stable had once stood: the great Hotel Bruni. The house was still there. There was no doubt about it, that was the house. She knocked again and again, calling out with a querulous voice: "It's Desolina, poor Desolina. Open the door for Desolina . . . "

But no one could answer her from the dark, empty house. The old woman looked around, at the ancient walnut tree lifting its naked branches into the twirling white flakes and then, again, at the closed door. She curled up on the threshold to wait, unable to believe that Hotel Bruni might not welcome her. Surely Clerice would soon show up in her white apron, with the soup ladle in her hand.

Iofa, the carter, found her like that the next day, covered with snow, her head leaning against the door, the tears frozen on her ashen face, her eyes staring in pained surprise.

THE END

ABOUT THE AUTHOR

Valerio Massimo Manfredi is a professor of classical archaeology at Bocconi University in Milan. He is the author of many works of fiction, including the Alexander trilogy, *Spartan*, and *The Last Legion*, which was made into a film starring Colin Firth and Ben Kingsley, directed by Doug Lefler. His novel about the assassination of Julius Caesar, *The Ides of March*, was published by Europa Editions in 2010.

EUROPA EDITIONS BACKLIST
(alphabetical by author)

Fiction

Carmine Abate
Between Two Seas • 978-1-933372-40-2 • Territories: World
The Homecoming Party • 978-1-933372-83-9 • Territories: World

Milena Agus
From the Land of the Moon • 978-1-60945-001-4 • Ebook • Territories:
World (excl. ANZ)

Salwa Al Neimi
The Proof of the Honey • 978-1-933372-68-6 • Ebook • Territories: World
(excl UK)

Simonetta Agnello Hornby
The Nun • 978-1-60945-062-5 • Territories: World

Daniel Arsand
Lovers • 978-1-60945-071-7 • Ebook • Territories: World

Jenn Ashworth
A Kind of Intimacy • 978-1-933372-86-0 • Territories: US & Can

Beryl Bainbridge
The Girl in the Polka Dot Dress • 978-1-60945-056-4 • Ebook •
Territories: US

Muriel Barbery
The Elegance of the Hedgehog • 978-1-933372-60-0 • Ebook • Territories:
World (excl. UK & EU)
Gourmet Rhapsody • 978-1-933372-95-2 • Ebook • Territories: World
(excl. UK & EU)

Stefano Benni
Margherita Dolce Vita • 978-1-933372-20-4 • Territories: World
Timeskipper • 978-1-933372-44-0 • Territories: World

Romano Bilenchi
The Chill • 978-1-933372-90-7 • Territories: World

Kazimierz Brandys
Rondo • 978-1-60945-004-5 • Territories: World

Alina Bronsky
Broken Glass Park • 978-1-933372-96-9 • Ebook • Territories: World
The Hottest Dishes of the Tartar Cuisine • 978-1-60945-006-9 • Ebook •
Territories: World

Jesse Browner
Everything Happens Today • 978-1-60945-051-9 • Ebook • Territories:
World (excl. UK & EU)

Francisco Coloane
Tierra del Fuego • 978-1-933372-63-1 • Ebook • Territories: World

Rebecca Connell
The Art of Losing • 978-1-933372-78-5 • Territories: US

Laurence Cossé
A Novel Bookstore • 978-1-933372-82-2 • Ebook • Territories: World
An Accident in August • 978-1-60945-049-6 • Territories: World (excl. UK)

Diego De Silva
I Hadn't Understood • 978-1-60945-065-6 • Territories: World

Shashi Deshpande
The Dark Holds No Terrors • 978-1-933372-67-9 • Territories: US

Steve Erickson
Zeroville • 978-1-933372-39-6 • Territories: US & Can
These Dreams of You • 978-1-60945-063-2 • Territories: US & Can

Elena Ferrante
The Days of Abandonment • 978-1-933372-00-6 • Ebook • Territories: World
Troubling Love • 978-1-933372-16-7 • Territories: World
The Lost Daughter • 978-1-933372-42-6 • Territories: World

Linda Ferri
Cecilia • 978-1-933372-87-7 • Territories: World

Damon Galgut
In a Strange Room • 978-1-60945-011-3 • Ebook • Territories: USA

Santiago Gamboa
Necropolis • 978-1-60945-073-1 • Ebook • Territories: World

Jane Gardam
Old Filth • 978-1-933372-13-6 • Ebook • Territories: US
The Queen of the Tambourine • 978-1-933372-36-5 • Ebook • Territories: US
The People on Privilege Hill • 978-1-933372-56-3 • Ebook • Territories: US
The Man in the Wooden Hat • 978-1-933372-89-1 • Ebook • Territories: US
God on the Rocks • 978-1-933372-76-1 • Ebook • Territories: US
Crusoe's Daughter • 978-1-60945-069-4 • Ebook • Territories: US

Anna Gavalda
French Leave • 978-1-60945-005-2 • Ebook • Territories: US & Can

Seth Greenland
The Angry Buddhist • 978-1-60945-068-7 • Ebook • Territories: World

Katharina Hacker
The Have-Nots • 978-1-933372-41-9 • Territories: World (excl. India)

Patrick Hamilton
Hangover Square • 978-1-933372-06-8 • Territories: US & Can

James Hamilton-Paterson
Cooking with Fernet Branca • 978-1-933372-01-3 • Territories: US
Amazing Disgrace • 978-1-933372-19-8 • Territories: US
Rancid Pansies • 978-1-933372-62-4 • Territories: USA

Alfred Hayes
The Girl on the Via Flaminia • 978-1-933372-24-2 • Ebook •
Territories: World

Jean-Claude Izzo
The Lost Sailors • 978-1-933372-35-8 • Territories: World
A Sun for the Dying • 978-1-933372-59-4 • Territories: World

Gail Jones
Sorry • 978-1-933372-55-6 • Territories: US & Can

Ioanna Karystiani
The Jasmine Isle • 978-1-933372-10-5 • Territories: World
Swell • 978-1-933372-98-3 • Territories: World

Peter Kocan
Fresh Fields • 978-1-933372-29-7 • Territories: US, EU & Can
The Treatment and the Cure • 978-1-933372-45-7 • Territories: US, EU & Can

Helmut Krausser
Eros • 978-1-933372-58-7 • Territories: World

Amara Lakhous
Clash of Civilizations Over an Elevator in Piazza Vittorio •
978-1-933372-61-7 • Ebook • Territories: World
Divorce Islamic Style • 978-1-60945-066-3 • Ebook • Territories: World

Lia Levi
The Jewish Husband • 978-1-933372-93-8 • Territories: World

Valerio Massimo Manfredi
The Ides of March • 978-1-933372-99-0 • Territories: US

Leïla Marouane
The Sexual Life of an Islamist in Paris • 978-1-933372-85-3 •
Territories: World

Lorenzo Mediano
The Frost on His Shoulders • 978-1-60945-072-4 • Ebook •
Territories: World

Sélim Nassib
I Loved You for Your Voice • 978-1-933372-07-5 • Territories: World
The Palestinian Lover • 978-1-933372-23-5 • Territories: World

Amélie Nothomb
Tokyo Fiancée • 978-1-933372-64-8 • Territories: US & Can
Hygiene and the Assassin • 978-1-933372-77-8 • Ebook • Territories: US & Can

Valeria Parrella
For Grace Received • 978-1-933372-94-5 • Territories: World

Alessandro Piperno
The Worst Intentions • 978-1-933372-33-4 • Territories: World
Persecution • 978-1-60945-074-8 • Ebook • Territories: World

Lorcan Roche
The Companion • 978-1-933372-84-6 • Territories: World

Boualem Sansal
The German Mujahid • 978-1-933372-92-1 • Ebook • Territories: US & Can

www.europaeditions.com

Eric-Emmanuel Schmitt
The Most Beautiful Book in the World • 978-1-933372-74-7 • Ebook •
Territories: World
The Woman with the Bouquet • 978-1-933372-81-5 • Ebook • Territories:
US & Can

Angelika Schrobsdorff
You Are Not Like Other Mothers • 978-1-60945-075-5 • Ebook •
Territories: World

Audrey Schulman
Three Weeks in December • 978-1-60945-064-9 • Ebook • Territories: US
& Can

James Scudamore
Heliopolis • 978-1-933372-73-0 • Ebook • Territories: US

Luis Sepúlveda
The Shadow of What We Were • 978-1-60945-002-1 • Ebook • Territories:
World

Paolo Sorrentino
Everybody's Right • 978-1-60945-052-6 • Ebook • Territories: US & Can

Domenico Starnone
First Execution • 978-1-933372-66-2 • Territories: World

Henry Sutton
Get Me out of Here • 978-1-60945-007-6 • Ebook • Territories: US & Can

Chad Taylor
Departure Lounge • 978-1-933372-09-9 • Territories: US, EU & Can

Roma Tearne
Mosquito • 978-1-933372-57-0 • Territories: US & Can
Bone China • 978-1-933372-75-4 • Territories: US

André Carl van der Merwe
Moffie • 978-1-60945-050-2 • Ebook • Territories: World
(excl. S. Africa)

Fay Weldon
Chalcot Crescent • 978-1-933372-79-2 • Territories: US

Anne Wiazemsky
My Berlin Child • 978-1-60945-003-8 • Territories: US & Can

Jonathan Yardley
Second Reading • 978-1-60945-008-3 • Ebook • Territories: US & Can

Edwin M. Yoder Jr.
Lions at Lamb House • 978-1-933372-34-1 • Territories: World

Michele Zackheim
Broken Colors • 978-1-933372-37-2 • Territories: World

Alice Zeniter
Take This Man • 978-1-60945-053-3 • Territories: World

Tonga Books

Ian Holding
Of Beasts and Beings • 978-1-60945-054-0 • Ebook • Territories: US & Can

Sara Levine
Treasure Island!!! • 978-0-14043-768-3 • Ebook • Territories: World

Alexander Maksik
You Deserve Nothing • 978-1-60945-048-9 • Ebook • Territories: US, Can & EU (excl. UK)

Thad Ziolkowski
Wichita • 978-1-60945-070-0 • Ebook • Territories: World

Crime/Noir

Massimo Carlotto
The Goodbye Kiss • 978-1-933372-05-1 • Ebook • Territories: World
Death's Dark Abyss • 978-1-933372-18-1 • Ebook • Territories: World
The Fugitive • 978-1-933372-25-9 • Ebook • Territories: World
Bandit Love • 978-1-933372-80-8 • Ebook • Territories: World
Poisonville • 978-1-933372-91-4 • Ebook • Territories: World

Giancarlo De Cataldo
The Father and the Foreigner • 978-1-933372-72-3 • Territories: World

Caryl Férey
Zulu • 978-1-933372-88-4 • Ebook • Territories: World (excl. UK & EU)
Utu • 978-1-60945-055-7 • Ebook • Territories: World (excl. UK & EU)

Alicia Giménez-Bartlett
Dog Day • 978-1-933372-14-3 • Territories: US & Can
Prime Time Suspect • 978-1-933372-31-0 • Territories: US & Can
Death Rites • 978-1-933372-54-9 • Territories: US & Can

Jean-Claude Izzo
Total Chaos • 978-1-933372-04-4 • Territories: US & Can
Chourmo • 978-1-933372-17-4 • Territories: US & Can
Solea • 978-1-933372-30-3 • Territories: US & Can

Matthew F. Jones
Boot Tracks • 978-1-933372-11-2 • Territories: US & Can

Gene Kerrigan
The Midnight Choir • 978-1-933372-26-6 • Territories: US & Can
Little Criminals • 978-1-933372-43-3 • Territories: US & Can

Carlo Lucarelli
Carte Blanche • 978-1-933372-15-0 • Territories: World
The Damned Season • 978-1-933372-27-3 • Territories: World
Via delle Oche • 978-1-933372-53-2 • Territories: World

Edna Mazya
Love Burns • 978-1-933372-08-2 • Territories: World (excl. ANZ)

Yishai Sarid
Limassol • 978-1-60945-000-7 • Ebook • Territories: World (excl. UK,
AUS & India)

Joel Stone
The Jerusalem File • 978-1-933372-65-5 • Ebook • Territories: World

Benjamin Tammuz
Minotaur • 978-1-933372-02-0 • Ebook • Territories: World

Non-fiction

Alberto Angela
A Day in the Life of Ancient Rome • 978-1-933372-71-6 • Territories:
World • History

Helmut Dubiel
Deep In the Brain: Living with Parkinson's Disease • 978-1-933372-70-9 •
Ebook • Territories: World • Medicine/Memoir

James Hamilton-Paterson
Seven-Tenths: The Sea and Its Thresholds • 978-1-933372-69-3 • Territories:
USA • Nature/Essays

Daniele Mastrogiacomo
Days of Fear • 978-1-933372-97-6 • Ebook • Territories: World • Current
affairs/Memoir/Afghanistan/Journalism

Valery Panyushkin
Twelve Who Don't Agree • 978-1-60945-010-6 • Ebook • Territories:
World • Current affairs/Memoir/Russia/Journalism

Christa Wolf
One Day a Year: 1960-2000 • 978-1-933372-22-8 • Territories: World •
Memoir/History/20th Century

Children's Illustrated Fiction

Altan
Here Comes Timpa • 978-1-933372-28-0 • Territories: World (excl. Italy)
Timpa Goes to the Sea • 978-1-933372-32-7 • Territories: World (excl. Italy)
Fairy Tale Timpa • 978-1-933372-38-9 • Territories: World (excl. Italy)

Wolf Erlbruch
The Big Question • 978-1-933372-03-7 • Territories: US & Can
The Miracle of the Bears • 978-1-933372-21-1 • Territories: US & Can
(with **Gioconda Belli**) *The Butterfly Workshop* • 978-1-933372-12-9 •
Territories: US & Can